The Intruder

Joanna watched, with hatred, the gradual en-croachment of Mistress Captoft. She was not jeal-ous, female to female; Mistress Captoft was far too old; well over thirty, and fat. And Henry's manner toward her was never more than polite. But inch by inch she was edging Joanna out of the position that she had hoped would have been strong enough to save her from any more talk about going away. For a few days they worked together, Mistress Captoft cheerful, Joanna sullen. When baking day came round, Joanna did not take kindly to the idea that every loaf should be marked with a Cross. "They rise better," Mistress Captoft said.

The sharpest blow fell when Joanna said, in her joking way, "Henry, unless we take care, she will move in."

"I have already suggested it," said Henry.

Norah Lofts

The Lonely Furrow

A FAWCETT CREST BOOK • NEW YORK

THE LONELY FURROW

THIS BOOK CONTAINS THE COMPLETE TEXT OF THE
ORIGINAL HARDCOVER EDITION.

Published by Fawcett Crest Books, a unit of CBS Publications,
the Consumer Publishing Division of CBS Inc., by arrangement
with Doubleday and Company, Inc.

Copyright © 1976 by Norah Lofts

ISBN: 0-449-23572-6

The third volume of a trilogy; the first is *Knight's Acre,* and the
second is *The Homecoming*.

Alternate Selection of the Literary Guild

Printed in the United States of America

10   9   8   7   6   5   4   3   2   1

AT the end of the last furrow Henry Tallboys halted the plough and looked about him with grim satisfaction. Some way behind him in the field, Jem Watson, his hired man, was spreading the wheat grain—less evenly and rhythmically than Henry himself would have done, but no man could plough and sow at the same time. Behind Jem was the girl, Joanna, dragging the branch which pulled soil over the seed to protect it from weather and the ravages of winter-hungered birds.

Henry was tall. It was a family characteristic, but the name had nothing to do with stature; it was a corruption of the Norman-French Taillebois. Most men of more than average height, at the end of day at the plough's tail would have needed to straighten up; at the end of years of ploughing, would have acquired a ploughman's stoop, but Henry had adapted his plough to himself, not himself to his plough. He had fitted it with long, high handles, like a deer's antlers. So, on this October morning, with the wind from the north telling of winter's onset, he stood straight and flat-shouldered, more like the knight that his father had been—as he might have been—than the farmer he had chosen to be. Even in his homespun hose and jerkin, in heavy ankle shoes and the cloth leg wrappings of the working man, Henry Tallboys was an impressive figure; hard manual work since the age of seven, some of it, like shovelling manure, dirty work, had done nothing to impair his dignity. His looks he had inherited from his father, Sir Godfrey—in his time a knight of renown but of no great intelligence, of a curiously child-like simplicity. From his mother, the Lady Sybilla, Henry had inherited fortitude, self-will and impregnable dignity; but he owed even more to a man who was no kin at all, a sardonic, sceptical ex-archer named Walter, who had taught him the valuable lesson of ingenuity, the art of survival in a hostile world.

Unaware of all the things that had gone to his making, Henry looked around, taking stock of the situation. He could now take the seed tray from Jem's neck and say, "I'll finish. You take the horse in." If he did that the last furrows would be more evenly sown, in Walter's way, but it would leave Henry alone in the field with Joanna, the girl, the child,

5

dressed like a ploughboy, eleven and a half years old, but precocious beyond belief. So he called to Jem and to Joanna, "That's the end. I'll take the horse away. You should be finished by dinner time."

Everywhere else oxen, not horses, were plough animals, but twenty years earlier, with no ox, no money to buy one, Walter had hitched a makeshift plough to a decrepit horse, and Henry, willing pupil, had stuck to Walter's ways.

On this October, winter-threatening morning, he led the horse to the stable, unharnessed it, gave it a friendly thump and saw that the manger was full. Then, out in the wind again, he hesitated slightly. He could go to the right, enter his own kitchen door, or left, round the end of the shorter wing of his peculiar house. He chose the latter, thinking— Better get it over and done with! He hoped that Griselda was not glancing from the kitchen window. She herself did so many things from sheer perversity that she took his daily, necessary visit to two sick men, one his own brother, as a deliberately provoking action on his part. In fact the visit was a penance to him; partly because of the memories which this part of the house evoked, and partly because of the worry which the present occupants represented.

It cost him an effort to say, with some semblance of heartiness, "Well, how are you today?"

"I'm better," John Tallboys said. "I told you I ailed nothing that rest and good food couldn't cure. Not that the food has been all that good!" As he made this criticism the young man grimaced, half a smile, half something else, a sly, conniving, we're-all-in-the-same-boat look which should have taken the sting from the remark, but did not.

"You've had the best the place afforded," Henry said. It was true: milk straight from the cow, eggs, fresh meat when the pig was killed a fortnight ago, fowls which could be ill spared. Not only that, John, who was able to move about, had been provided with new clothes to replace his rags, and the one physician in Baildon had been brought out to confirm, or deny, Griselda's hasty, damning verdict of lung-rot and to offer what palliatives he could. He had confirmed it; both young men would be dead by Christmas, he said, and all that Master Tallboys could do was to see that they were as comfortable, as happy as possible during the interim. For this gloomy verdict and a few cough-relieving medicaments, the doctor had charged two nobles—the better part of a pound—and while he was tapping chests and listening as though chests were doors to be answered, his horse had claimed a guest's privilege and gobbled down what was in the manger.

That was almost a month ago and John had said at the time that the old mutton-head was wrong; he and Nick were simply suffering from colds that had settled on their chests, aggravated by exposure and near starvation. Maybe in his own case right, for here he was, chirpy as a sparrow, gathering flesh on his bones. But from the inner room, the bedroom, Henry heard the rattling, doomed cough.

"And how is he?"

"Better, too, thank you, Henry. One must remember that he is older and caught the cold before I did. I kept him in bed today because I was clearing this room up a bit and there was dust. Tomorrow he will lie on one of these divans and I shall beat about in there."

The two rooms had been furnished by a woman from a far country who had lined ceiling and walls with silk, pleated in imitation of her father's temporary pavilions, put up, taken down, well shaken at each move. Shut away, deliberately ignored for years, the two rooms had accumulated dust and cobwebs and could certainly do with a cleaning.

Henry said, "I'm glad you feel up to it. I'll go get your dinner. . . . No, I'm full early . . . John, I have something to ask of you."

"Yes?" John said, in a non-committal voice. "What is it?"

"It concerns Joanna."

"Yes?" John said. He was not being helpful; but then, Henry remembered, he never had been, even when he lived here. He'd always shirked work as much as possible and gone running off to the sheep-fold to play his lute and make songs with the young shepherd who shared his frivolous taste.

"Her mother," Henry said, avoiding as usual the use of Tana's name, "left her a small fortune—in jewels." He saw John's eyes brighten, interested at last. "The Bishop of Bywater took charge of them, and converted some, at least, into cash. At the same time he found a place for her in the household of a man with daughters of his own; a place where she would have an upbringing suitable to one of her birth and the chance of a good marriage. She absolutely refused to go."

"I always thought Tana was not quite right in the head. Her daughter takes after her."

Without knowing it Henry clenched his fist.

"You could help. You have seen the world; how people live; the comforts and pleasures people enjoy. . . . Joanna

7

dotes on stories . . . I think that if you tried, you could make another way of life sound attractive enough to make her change her mind. It's no sort of life for her here. Griselda has taken against her. She works and dresses like a plough-boy. . . . I'm worried about her."

"I could certainly spin a yarn or two," John said, recalling wistfully those glorious days when he and Nick had been in much demand with their new songs and catchy tunes; welcome in great halls, in palaces; no village green audiences, no market squares for them! They'd been on their way to Venice, by request from the Doge himself, when this cursed illness had struck, and ruined them. But the good days would come again. He himself was better, and Nick would be, given time. They'd need money at first. They'd had some on the former occasion—John's share of his father's estate.

"I'll do my best to persuade her." He said, smugly, "I'm supposed to have rather a way with women." Which was, he thought, something of an irony, since he had no liking for them. "If I do succeed, I shall expect something for my trouble."

"You shall have it." Henry had the excellent memory of the illiterate man. "His Grace sent word that some of the jewels had been sold and the money deposited with Sir Barnabas Grey, who had a use for it, and who was willing to take the child. No doubt everybody would be so glad to have the whole thing tidied up, they'd be willing to pay."

In the bedroom the man whom Henry still thought of as Young Shep, coughed again.

"I'll start this evening," John promised, "when she brings our supper across. As you say, she is interested in the outer world. She's always asking questions."

"Give her the right answers. . . . You're better, and I'm glad of it. But I think she'd better not go too near him. Griselda may be right."

"Your pardon, brother. Griselda is a bitch—and a mad bitch at that!"

"And my wife. So mind your tongue!"

Ignoring the rebuke, John said, "Speaking of supper, what's for dinner?"

"I'll go and see."

For the first time in Henry's memory—apart from the time when the plague struck and he was trying to get the harvest in, single-handed, and Sybilla, his mother, was nursing three desperately ill people, there was no sign of a meal being prepared in the kitchen. A good fire blazed on the hearth, but neither spit nor black pot were in use, and the faggot that should have been used to fire the oven—for this was bread-baking day, Henry remembered—lay there untouched. The table was clean and completely bare.

Griselda and Godfrey were by the fire playing cat's cradle. As Henry entered, Griselda said, "Godfrey, go play in the hall. Run about to keep warm. Give your hobby-horse a good gallop."

The boy was now four, with the Tallboys' precocity, tired of his restricted, mother-ruled life, and on the verge of rebellion. But Griselda had ways of dealing with even incipient rebellion. She could change in an instant, as Godfrey well knew, from fond, doting mother to something quite frightening. She did so now because he did not move quickly towards the door between kitchen and hall. She said in her nasty voice, "Get along with you. Do as I say!" and speeded him with a push and the smack on the bottom.

One day I shall hit her back!

"What about dinner?" Henry asked.

"There will be no dinner. Not today, nor any other day so long as this goes on. I've come to the end of my tether. I'm not going to work my fingers to the bone to keep a couple of vagabonds with the lung-rot! I've told you and told you. I might as well talk to the wind. You went there this morning and dared to come straight in here, with the cough in your hair; on your clothes. I told you that first time; I've said the same every day since and that's more than a month. I arranged things as well as I could, no comings and goings, I said. This is *my* home, and God knows it cost me dear enough! I'd had other offers—did you know that? If it'd only been a clod cottage, I'd have been mistress of it, not the slave I am here, working my fingers to the bone and no say in who comes or goes. That wicked, wicked girl. You sided with *her* against *me*, even when she'd nearly killed your own child! There's never any money for anything. When did I have a new gown? When did Godfrey have anything except shoes? Pinch and scrape, pinch and scrape. Then along come two rogues and the best is hardly good enough. . . ."

Henry was accustomed to her railing, skilled at turning a deaf ear, but this morning John had used the word "mad," so now he looked at her with more attention than usual. Her eyes, greenish and rather small, glittered, but with malice rather than madness, or so it seemed to him. He swung round and went towards the larder. Four pigeons, unplucked, lay on a shelf. Dinner today should have been pigeon pie! The thought reminded him that he was hungry. Jem must be fed—a good dinner was part of his wage and anything less provoked grumbling. Joanna was still growing and had done a hard morning's work, she needed food, too. And there were the two men across the courtyard. Waiting. For what? Henry seldom entered the larder but it struck him that today it was singularly bare, even for Knight's Acre in the middle of an unprosperous spell. Most of the pig killed the week before last, was now either salted down in a cask, or being smoked in the chimney, but surely, surely there had been the better half of a side of bacon from the pig before that, enough to tide them over until the new side was ready. All that was left was enough to make four or five rashers, cut very thin. Two for Jem, who would grumble even at that preferential treatment, one each for Joanna, John and Young Shep. Henry himself would make do with bread and cheese. He lifted the lid of the bread crock, which was not a crock at all, but a wooden container made by Tom Robinson, who had liked to be useful even when he couldn't work. It was a huge log, hollowed out, chip by chip, and fitted with a lid, with some air holes and a knob. It was quite empty because in any ordinary week this was the time when the fresh new bread should have come, sweet-smelling from the oven. The butter crock—which was a crock—was almost empty. And where was the cheese? He remembered it from last night, suppertime; a good new cheese which would as days passed get harder and less palatable, but still nourishing. No sign of it anywhere. Beside the poor bit of bacon the only thing the shelf offered him was yeast, of which, aware that winter was at hand, he had bought a good jugful on his last visit to Baildon. Griselda had dealt with it properly, spreading a little on a board, letting it dry, spreading another layer, and so on. The cake was now about three inches thick, nine wide, ten long. Enough to last through the bad weather, when marketing was impossible. Also there was a sack of flour.

Henry stood there, utterly defeated. He'd taken some blows in his life, faced some peculiar and puzzling situations, but the problem of how to feed five hungry people—he included himself but excluded his wife and his son for Griselda often fed Godfrey apart and ate little herself—on a few scraps of bacon, some yeast and flour, made him despair. It couldn't be done. Nobody could do it. Even Walter—and years after Walter was dead, Henry was accustomed to ask himself, in any crisis, What would Walter do? Even the Lady Sybilla, his mother, a marvel at managing and contriving, couldn't have done it.

He stood there with the North wind cutting through the slatted window of the larder and thought—How ridiculous! After all I have borne to be defeated and shamed now by a woman's refusal to cook or keep house.

The girl, Joanna, came padding in. She had remembered, as he had not, the house rule of shedding muddy footwear. She said,

"Henry. Griselda has gone moonstruck. I will make dinner."

"Out of what?"

He pointed to the remnant of bacon, the empty bread crock, the bare shelf where the cheese should have been.

"But . . ." Joanna said. "Only yesterday . . . Where can it have gone?" Determination replaced the puzzlement on her face. "I'll make pancakes. Brighten the fire, Henry."

That a girl child, eleven and half years old, should be able to cook was nothing marvellous, but ever since Joanna had offended Griselda four years earlier, she had been banished from the kitchen, from all the sheltered, domestic side of life, driven away from the hearthside into the fields or the fold.

"Can I do anything else to help, sw . . . ?" Henry chopped off the endearment, formerly in frequent use and still coming easily to his tongue, reaching back as it did to the days when he had regarded her as a child, as his ward.

"Yes. You can chop this bacon into tiny pieces while I beat the batter."

Griselda was not in the kitchen, but Jem Watson was, hungry for his food, and watchful for anything which might be related afterwards, down in the village, where what happened up at Knight's Acre was always news and he, firsthand gossip, welcome to a place by the fire, a glass of ale and a ready audience.

"Missus took ill, Master?" Not unlikely, with the lung-rot about the place. And Master Tallboys chopping some scrag ends of bacon, the little girl whipping batter.

"Not quite herself," Henry said evasively, and was immediately contradicted by a burst of laughter from the hall, where Griselda, to make up for the smack and the push, was playing with her son. He astride his hobby-horse was the hunter, she, down on all fours, the quarry.

Joanna made five pancakes.

Henry said, "I'll take theirs across."

"No. You sit down and eat yours, Henry. This is one of my jobs."

One of those which Griselda had assigned, rather more than a month ago, when the two men had arrived, ragged, coughing, dying. Griselda had refused to have them in the house, and it was Joanna who had remembered the empty rooms on the other side of the yard. Rooms which had for her as poignant memories as they held for Henry, but different.

Griselda had accepted the need to provide food for the ailing men, but she had done it grudgingly, and ordered Joanna to do the carrying. The other side of the house had a kitchen of its own; its kitchen door faced, almost exactly, that of the main house. But for good reasons of her own—which nobody knew about—Joanna's mother, Tana, who had built the new wing, had built it with a kitchen accessible to the yard, but not to the two rooms which made up the dwelling place. Even when that kitchen had been in use, anything cooked in it must have been carried out, round the end of the building, and in by the door on the garden side.

Accepting the dinner—surely the best anybody could have produced in such short time, with such little—John said, "Is this all?"

Joanna said, "For now. There will be pigeon pie for supper, I promise you." The words sounded placating, but the glance she gave him was not. Her feelings towards him and towards Young Shep were not much unlike Griselda's, though stemming from a different cause. The two men, too ill to be useful, not ill enough to die, were part of Henry's burden and loving Henry as she did, she could only resent them and regret that she had suggested housing them here, in comfort, instead of letting them go, as Griselda had shouted, to sleep in the barn. She'd acted on impulse, wishing to help Henry when Griselda turned so awkward.

"You know, Joanna, properly dressed, you'd be very pretty." John was beginning to exercise his charm. Too late. Hitherto he had taken little notice of her, answered her questions brusquely and often seemed ungrateful for what she brought.

Now she said, "I know," and hurried back to her pancake.

In the kitchen Jem Watson was displeased with his meal— a bloody pancake, like the beginning of Lent!—and displeased, also, by Henry's uncommunicativeness. He'd have liked to know what ailed a woman who was unable to make a dinner, but, to judge by the noise, was capable of romping about in the hall. It could be mere bad temper. Jem knew that the Missus was a nagger and a scold, but never before had she failed to provide, and he would have liked to know *why*.

Spearing up the last crumb of pancake on his knife, chewing thoughtfully and then speaking before he had emptied his mouth, Jem said,

"Would it suit better if I brought my bit of docky with me in future?"

"Your *what?*" That was infuriating, too. Master Tallboys wasn't Suffolk-born, but he'd lived here long enough to know the language.

"My docky, my dinner, my nose-bag. I mean, if it suited better, my owd mother could put me up a bit of dinner in a poke. Then I'd hev to ask another fivepence a week."

Henry gave a sour smile. "I'm glad you think that your usual dinner here is worth that much!" It was a third of Jem's weekly wage.

One of the reasons why a good dinner was so often part of the bargain between master and man was that in most places cash money was in short supply; even now the system of barter ruled many transactions. Between Henry and the miller who turned his wheat into flour, or the smith who shod his horse, no coin ever changed hands. The miller paid himself by withholding so much flour, the smith would accept a dozen eggs, a pint of butter, a goose ready for the oven.

Thinking of this, Henry Tallboys cast a backward look upon two things which, because they had involved him in cash transactions, had kept him poor. His brother John, seven years ago, had insisted upon taking his share of Sir Godfrey's estate out in cash, and to buy John's share of the flock, Henry had been forced to borrow and pay interest. And then there had been the question of his other, much younger brother, Robert, who had simply disappeared. Joanna insisted that he was dead, but of that there was no proof. Until there was, Henry would go on taking Robert's share of the dwindling profits from the flock, into the office of the lawyer, Master Turnbull of Baildon. Henry was well versed in the lesson that people could disappear and then, after years, turn up. Hadn't his own father, Sir Godfrey, vanished into Spain, been deemed dead, and then turned up after eight years of slavery with the Moors? His brother Robert had disappeared, a child, six years old; possibly stolen; he'd been a pretty boy . . . Roaming bands of people, half entertainers, half beggars, did recruit attractive children—or steal them. . . . Anyway, if Robert ever came home, he would find his bit of patrimony safe and ready; in cash, safely invested by Master Turnbull.

It took Henry only a second to recall these things, which with bad weather and bad luck had contributed to his present state. He also had time to think that so far, although he had taken heavy knocks, he'd never yet been floored. So he said, "Please yourself, Jem. But twopence is the limit. And mind this—if you can find another job, better paid, better fed, within walking distance, go to it. Never mind about our Michaelmas bargain."

Jem said, "I was only thinking, Master Tallboys . . ." Thinking—Jesus and Holy Mary, where would I find a job between Michaelmas and Candlemas Day? Within walking distance, at fifteenpence a week and a good dinner?

"I was only thinking," he said again. And an explanation occurred to him. The Missus had just started up another baby!

Women often went funny at such times, took against their husbands and against rounded, bulging things, like cooking pots. Not the first time so much, the first time they were in pod they were glad. . . . If they got a boy and managed to rear him out of the cradle, they reckoned their job was done. Men often felt the same.

Down in the village Jem knew of a couple—and it was odd, they'd both worked up here at Knight's Acre at one time. Bert Edgar, when he inherited Edgar's Acre had married a woman called Jill. He'd wanted *one* son, and got him; and in every following year, every time Jill came into pod again, he'd given her such a thrashing!

Had such a thing happened here? Was Mistress Tallboys away there in the hall, hiding a bruised face?

"Henry, you don't *pluck* pigeons," Joanna said in reply to his offer of help. "Is that water hot yet? Good, then I will show you." She plunged in the little bodies, heads and feet chopped off, disembowelled, but still wearing their feathers. Count a hundred and there they were, dredged out, feathers stuck together, ready, with the skin that held them, to come off like the shell of a hard-boiled egg.

"That's a trick I didn't know," Henry said. "Where'd you learn it?"

"When I was young," she said, speaking as though youth were a far distant thing, "I used to watch Griselda. There, now I have only the pastry and the bread to make. Thank you for firing the oven for me."

"Call me when you want it opened. I shall be nearby, shovelling muck."

The oven had an iron door, placed at a height in the wall suitable for a grown woman; a little too high for Joanna, though she was tall for her age; and far too heavy, hardy as she had proved herself to be at field work, ever since her banishment from the kitchen. Anxious to prove herself, anxious indeed to excel, she had often succeeded in seeming to be what she looked like—a small, but willing and capable ploughboy. Henry had always been aware that she was in the wrong place, leading a highly unsuitable life; wished he could do something about it. Had finally been able to. And to what end? He still shuddered away from the memory of that unbelievable, fantastic scene in the wood after he'd told her what plans he had made for her; but he did remember the extreme lightness, the seeming frailty of the body he'd dragged from the pool.

"Thank you, Henry. I'll call if I need you."

She was, she thought, behaving very well; giving no sign of the jubilation which shot through her—stimulating as wine— as she thought, he never offered to do that for Griselda!

Thumping the dough and setting it on the hearth to rise, turning her attention to the pastry, Joanna thought about Griselda and hoped that this latest queer mood would last forever. She knew in her bones—had known it for a long time—that she fitted Henry far better than Griselda did. They could share jokes, not only outright jokes but the unspoken things, the lift of a shoulder, the twitch of one corner of the mouth which said, Funny! He'd always stood up for her, even when, in desperation, she'd stolen Godfrey. She'd done him no harm, he was warm and snug and safe and the bargain could be struck in a minute—Promise to bring Robert home from Moyidan, where he is so unhappy, and you can have your baby back. It hadn't worked. She'd had to try other, even more desperate means—and Robert had died because of what she had done. But that was all long ago, and far away. Her attachment to Robert, motherly and protective, had transferred itself to Henry and was altogether different. Now, if only Griselda could remain moonstruck, she could prove to Henry that she was as useful inside the house, as without. That done, she could surely coax him into using some of *her* money to buy new animals, hire more help. Beyond that her view of the future was hazy, but it included fine clothes and good horses, and living in the hall which she could just remember, so splendid with candles when Godfrey was christened.

Joanna did not visualise marriage; her emotional experience was already wider than that of most adult women, but her knowledge of the world was very limited; and half her blood was Tana's, wild and free, not concerned with monogamy. Joanna was unaware of this, except in instinct, in her bone marrow. What she did know was that it would be to her advantage to manage the oven without calling Henry from his work.

The faggot which he had placed in it and fired, had burnt out now. Standing on a stool she grappled with the heavy door, felt the full blast of the heat which the bricks had absorbed and were about to give off; raked the ashes to one side, pushed the bread to the back of the hot cavity and placed the pie in the front. Slamming the heavy door, she thought of the words with which she would produce it— Henry, not the four and twenty blackbirds, baked in a pie, but the best I could do. He'd understand, and smile, at least.

Griselda had shot her bolt, made her stand. And so far nobody had taken any notice. What they'd done about dinner she didn't know. When Godfrey tired of the hunting game and turned querulous she had said, "All right then, we'll go for a walk."

"Not to church, if you please."

Quite suddenly he'd begun to grow away from her, could speak properly, watch, ask questions; soon he would be hers no longer; and he was the only person, the only thing she had ever fully possessed in all her life—except Tom Robinson's devotion, the value of which she had realised too late.

"No. We'll walk in the wood."

"And gather sticks?"

"Yes, darling. And nuts if there are any left." She sounded like herself again and her son reflected with childish complacency that she was never angry with him for long. He did not notice that she was unusually quiet or that she gathered sticks and hunted for nuts with less energy than usual.

He was never allowed to venture into the wood by himself, so he had developed no sense of direction and was displeased to find that as they emerged from the trees they were near the church and the priest's house.

"I said *not* church. Did you forget?" He spoke with the arrogance of a pampered child.

"Not to go in. Just to go past," Griselda said.

That was all right then. The little boy did not know that he led an unusually boring life every day, but he did know that he hated those long sessions alone in the church with his mother, who knelt down, covered her face with her hands, and seemed to go away. When he had studied the pictures on the walls and they were all too familiar by now, there was nothing to do; he mustn't speak, and if he moved, must go on tip-toe. By contrast he liked church on Sunday morning, with more people there, and when Father Benedict did mysterious things at the altar, and you knelt, or stood and were allowed to say things at times, even if you hadn't yet fully mastered the words.

He hoped that Mistress Captoft would come out of the house by the church and perhaps invite them in and give him a honey cake. Quite apart from her offerings, he liked her; she had a smiling face—for him, at least—her clothes were pretty and she smelt sweet.

Mistress Captoft spent a good deal of her spare time looking out of the window; not that there was anything to see, except the sheep-fold across the track, and beyond it just a glimpse of the roofs of the highest-standing village houses; but looking out of the window was a habit she had formed when she lived at Dunwich, a busy, bustling place.

Now she looked out and saw Mistress Tallboys standing stock still and staring into the graveyard, as she often did. Rather a puzzling habit, for only the dead of Intake lay under the mounds there, and Mistress Tallboys was not a native of the village. The only grave in which she might be presumed to take an interest was inside the church, where Lady Sybilla slept under a rather short slab of black marble. Lady Sybilla had employed the girl as a nursemaid. Later, after his mother's death, Master Tallboys had married her, so there was a relationship, although a posthumous one. (All this, and some other things, Mistress Captoft had learned not from village gossip—that she sedulously avoided—but from the old woman who had kept house for the former priest, and who now shuffled up to do the roughest work.)

Mistress Captoft took a honey cake, lifted her cloak from the peg inside the door and went out. She wouldn't ask them in this afternoon, for Father Benedict was in the parlour, busy with his studies, and the other little room, having no hearth, was cold.

"Good day, Mistress Tallboys," she said brightly. "And how is my godson today?"

It was true that she had sponsored the little boy at the

font, and as she placed the honey cake into the eager hand she had a piercing memory of that occasion, of all that it had seemed to promise and the nothingness that had resulted. Master Tallboys' brother, Sir Richard, had been there, one of the child's godfathers; a Cambridge man, himself ordained and a great friend of the Bishop of Bywater. Hearing him and Benedict exchanging Latin quips across the well-lighted, well-spread table, Mistress Captoft had cherished high hopes that Sir Richard would report to the Bishop that a man so learned was wasted on a place like Intake and should be offered a post. Sir Richard was then in charge of the real Tallboys estate, at Moyidan, acting as guardian to its heir; but something—nobody knew what—had happened. Sir Richard had vanished from the scene and the manor and the boy had been taken over by the Church.

All this could be remembered in the time that it took for Mistress Tallboys to come out of what seemed almost a half-trance and mumble a greeting. It struck Mistress Captoft that the woman was not quite like herself; a heavy scowl knotted her eyebrows together and her mouth was like a trap.

"Growing like a willow," Mistress Captoft said, attempting the right note, "and his hair even prettier." This was the kind of thing Godfrey liked to hear and he gave a puppy-like wriggle. It was also the kind of thing mothers like to hear, but this afternoon Mistress Tallboys made no response. *Then* Mistress Captoft remembered the situation at Knight's Acre: two men, Master Tallboys' young brother and his friend, come home to die of the lung-rot. No wonder the woman looked distraught.

In a less hearty voice Mistress Captoft asked, "And how are the invalids?"

"I don't know and I don't care," Griselda said, roughly, coarsely. Again unlike herself, for though, railing against Joanna, against Henry, against things in general, she had both in voice and manner reverted to her origins, she had so far held, with outsiders, such as Mistress Captoft, to the gentle speech and the courteous manner which she had so resolutely copied from Lady Sybilla herself.

In his clear treble, Godfrey said,

"We don't go near them. They live on the other side of the house."

Mistress Captoft knew that, for Jem Watson had carried the news to the village and by way of the old woman who came to scrub and wash, it had seeped through. Mistress Captoft had behaved as a neighbour should: she made good brews—some deliberately designed to be unpalatable—one should not encourage malingerers! But the one she had made and carried to Knight's Acre had been one of her best: the root of a plant brought from abroad—glycyrrhiza, commonly known as Liquorice, she had brought several plants of it when she was making her garden and it had flourished fairly well—then there was horehound and honey, an excellent concoction. Master Tallboys, happening to be near the door, had opened it, received her offering and thanked her most courteously—but he had not invited her in to view the sufferers; nor had he told her anything that she did not already know. A very aloof man.

"My Uncle John is better," the child gossip said. "He can walk about now. But they still have the best of *everything,* don't they, Mumma?"

He had never gone without, Griselda had seen to that, but what delicacies the impoverished household could afford were no longer strictly reserved for him. That was one of the things Griselda greatly resented. The last of a mounting list of grievances.

"You talk too much," Griselda said in a voice harsher than Mistress Captoft had ever heard her use to the child before. In fact there was about her whole manner this afternoon something different, coarser. Mistress Captoft was acutely class-conscious and knowing that Mistress Tallboys was of lowly birth, had often wondered that her speech and manner should be so very ladylike. She now thought with a touch of malice—Truth will out! Masks fall in times of strain. Then her better nature came uppermost. She was even willing to forget Master Tallboys' civil but chilly reception of her coughcure.

"You must have your hands full," she said sympathetically. "If there is anything I can do . . . I have experience; my husband ailed for several years."

Griselda, in response to this truly noble offer, turned upon Mistress Captoft a glance that was at once dull and wild.

"They can manage," she said. She took Godfrey by the upper arm and turned him away. He twisted himself free, stepped back to face Mistress Captoft and made a little bow.

"Good day, Mistress Captoft. Thank you for the cake."

"Really, her manner was most *peculiar,*" Mistress Captoft said to Father Benedict, whose aunt and housekeeper she was held to be by all but the lewd-minded who thought she was too young, too gaily dressed for the rôle. "She was quite abrupt to the child. I always thought her over-doting. And to me she was rude. Then, after hurrying away, without so much as a good-day, she stopped and stood staring. As she sometimes stares at the graveyard."

Father Benedict, born to be a scholar, had never been much interested in his parishioners, and finding the Intake people on the whole faintly hostile and curiously evasive, had lost what little interest he had ever had. But he liked supper-table talk, however trivial. Mattie had a soft dovelike voice, very soothing: and sometimes her comments were sound and shrewd. An unusual and very pleasant combination.

Half-way along the single track which led past the church and the priest's house to Knight's Acre, Griselda had stopped and stared.

There it is; the place I sold myself for. Sir Godfrey brought me here. He saved me from that horrible inn where I knew nothing but squalor, and hardship and degradation. I saved his life there, because he looked so much like the carved saint in the church and I couldn't bear to see him dragged into the barn to die. I saved him while he lay in the barn, and after-wards on the long road back from the North. He could never have managed. So I came here riding pillion on the horse I stole for him and Knight's Acre was Heaven to me, with Lady Sybilla so kind. I knew nothing about love then— I'd never met it in any form. . . . In all my life I only met it once, and that was too late. I married Henry Tallboys because I wanted to stay at Knight's Acre, the one place where I had been happy and felt secure. He married me because the place was in such a muddle that only the firm hand of an indisputable mistress could get it on the right lines again. It suited us both until the day when Henry was at market, that flipperty girl, hired to help me, out watching the hunt, and only Tom . . . Tom Robinson to help to deliver the baby. Then I knew how wrong I had been, refusing Tom's shy offer to take a walk amongst the bluebells, accepting Henry's offer of marriage which was in reality no marriage at all. Always, always, if he could side against me, he did. I was never first with him; never in all my life have I been first with anybody—except Tom, who is dead.

The extreme climax of self-pity, everybody against her, everything gone wrong, might have lifted had Griselda walked into the kitchen and found it as bare as she had left it. Earlier in the day she had hidden most of the available food, left them to starve, to come to their senses and to a realisation of how important she was. The slightest evidence that she mattered, was, however little loved, indispensable, would have steadied her tottering mind.

What faced her as she entered the kitchen was—like everything else in life—wrong. Warmth and the smell of freshly baked bread; and that little bitch, that little bastard who had once stolen Godfrey and tried to hold the family to ransom, taking a pie from the oven and saying something silly about blackbirds.

Suddenly something happened inside Griselda's head, inside her bones. She was tough, she had survived life as a beggar girl, raped in a ditch at the age of six; she had survived the austere life in a convent orphanage, and after that worse, maid of all work, unpaid prostitute, at an inn. She could bear this, though she felt weak and had to hold on to the table while she tried to explain, did to the hearing within her own mind, explain that this was her kitchen, and though she had deserted it at midday, as a protest against the various wrongs she had suffered, she had come back to cook now, that Joanna had no right to be wearing her apron.

They—Henry and Joanna—pretended not to hear, or not to understand. She spoke more loudly, forcing herself to ignore the weakness, the dizziness, the incipient nausea. Well, if they wouldn't listen or understand, they must be *shown*. Leaning heavily on her left hand she managed to move her right, pushing the new loaves to the floor. This is my kitchen! I do the baking here! How dare you take my place? Away with your rubbish! Give me my apron, you little slut. . . .

It came out as babble, the slurred words running into one another. Don't stand there staring, pretending not to understand.

They stood and stared. Only Godfrey moved, sidling away to take shelter behind Henry. Then with another wordless roar, Griselda bore down upon Joanna, meaning to snatch the apron. Henry remembered that other time when Griselda had become violent and attacked Joanna with such ferocity that she had almost killed her. He acted swiftly, seized both his wife's work-worn hands in one of his own and with the other grasped enough of her clothing to lift her from her feet. She struggled wildly and screamed. Godfrey began to scream too and Joanna turned to comfort him, saying the first thing that came into her head.

"Mummy is just being funny, Godfrey. You should laugh, not cry."

Griselda was borne away to the accompaniment of the hysterical laughter of her son.

Henry carried her to the room which she had chosen when she decided not to sleep with him any more. It happened to be the one in which many years earlier, his sister Margaret, merely dimwitted and harmless except that she was mad about men, had been confined. He pushed her inside, backed away, snatched the key from inside the door, inserted it into the lock on the outside and locked her in. He was surprised and a little ashamed to find his hands unsteady. He'd lived through many things far worse than an incoherent display of temper. Here on this very stairway he had stood, taking careful aim—taught him by Walter—with the bow and arrow—made for him by Walter—and Walter, unrecognisable in his new blue jerkin, and behaving in an incredible way, had fallen dead. The hardening process which, now completed, made him seem aloof, imperturbable, unfriendly, had begun then. But it was something imposed upon him from the outside, a suit of armour donned as defence against the world; it was not part of his true nature and in many ways he was far more vulnerable than he appeared to be.

He was not surprised to find himself very hungry—every major crisis of his life had been followed by fierce appetite. He tackled his pigeon pie with zest, admonishing Godfrey, still precariously balanced between tears and laughter, to eat up. "She'll be better in the morning," he said.

"What about her supper?" Joanna asked, without solicitude, but as though referring to the feeding of an animal. She hated Griselda, less on account of her behaviour to herself than because of the way she treated Henry, doing her best to make him miserable.

"It can wait. Give her time to calm down."

"I'll take her something presently." Again not because she cared whether Griselda ate or not, but to show Henry that she was not frightened. She'd been six when Griselda had set about her with murderous rage, and even then she'd hit back as savagely as she could. Since then she had grown a lot!

"No!" Henry said sharply. "You're not to go near her. Neither of you. Mind that. We'll see how things turn out."

How would they? In his mind he tried over various phrases: temporarily distraught; demented; possessed of the Devil.

He was an illiterate man. Sybilla, convent bred to the age of sixteen, and an apt scholar, had tried to teach him to read and write, but the business had bored him and he had been content when he could sign his name. But she had read to him, and told him stories; his vocabulary far exceeded the range of the words he used every day.

He was not sure that Griselda was merely temporarily distraught. Looking back he thought that he could see signs of a mind gone sick and getting worse, on the lines of a physical illness.

It had begun on the day of Godfrey's birth. She'd turned against Henry then, and with even more rancour, against the girl—Leonora—who had, quite unintentionally, been absent at the critical moment. It was unreasonable. So had her behaviour towards Joanna been. The poor child had done the baby Godfrey no harm; she'd simply taken him, snugly wrapped, and hidden him and made a piteous attempt at blackmail—they could have their baby back if Robert could come home from Moyidan, where everybody was so unkind and he was so wretched. There'd been some inexplicable link between Joanna, Tana's daughter, and Robert, Sybilla's son, born on the same day, but Henry had treated lightly then Joanna's claim to see, to know what was going on at Moyidan. She had been proved right. In the end Robert had run away—and never been heard of since. Back to Griselda; though Henry had gone straight to the hiding place—one he had used in his time—and brought back the baby, who had not even woken, Griselda had again been unreasonable, holding an undying grudge. Silly, too, about Godfrey as he grew and wished to explore, to share in the life of farm and yard. He must never go beyond that part of the yard well within view of the kitchen; he must never have dirty hands or clothes, or ruffled hair. Maybe, Henry thought, indulging for once in the self-examination which his busy life, the mere struggle for survival, ordinarily forbade, I have been at fault there; let her have her own way too much. But, self-consolatory, he thought that over bigger issues, like taking in his brother John and Young Shep, he had been firm. And by being firm, had perhaps turned Griselda's brain for good and all. But could a man turn from his door, his own brother, ill and fallen on evil days? Merely to humour an ill-tempered wife?

Joanna moved about, with none of the bustle or noise with which Griselda had performed such tasks. She had already lifted the scattered loaves and given them a perfunctory brush with her apron. All loaves had a smearing of the faggot ash on their undersides; these were no different; Griselda, working her fingers to the bone—dismal expression—kept a clean kitchen floor. Now, the meal over and the platters clean, she lighted one candle from another and said, "Godfrey should go to bed."

"Where?" For as long as he remembered the little boy had slept with his mother.

"You can share my bed, son," Henry said.

That was good. A possible forerunner of a new way of life. Something to be immediately exploited.

"Then tomorrow may I go out with you? To the field?"

Henry said, "Yes," well knowing that if tomorrow Griselda had recovered, there would be argument, dispute, another row.

Upstairs, in the room that darkened from dusk to night with the steady inexorable progress of the first heart beat towards the last, Griselda sat on the bed and knew that her every action, her every word had been sensible. Henry, Joanna, and even Godfrey were all in a plot against her. Pretending not to understand what she said, or why she acted as she did. Picking her up as though she were a wild cat. Locking her in as though she were mad. And she the only one in the place with a grain of sense! That thought spurred a further burst of rage: she beat on the door and screamed; took off her shoe and hammered the floor. Knowing all the time that it was useless. If they pretended not to understand they could pretend not to hear. Ah, but wait until tomorrow, she thought, cunningly. Tomorrow, dinnertime, when Jem Watson would be in for his dinner. He'd hear and ask what was amiss: he was one of the nosiest people in the world. Henry would be forced to act then; release her, make up some plausible tale—to which she would give full backing. Otherwise there'd be such a tale round the village by suppertime. Griselda knew how proud Henry was, in a quiet way, of his good name and his reputation. He wouldn't want a scandal. Come to that, nor did she. A few good thumps tomorrow, a scream or two, easily explained if she and Henry told the same tale, and she'd be out of this. She thought: I must save my strength for tomorrow. Fully dressed except for one shoe, she went to the bed, huddled the blankets around her and soon fell asleep, completely exhausted.

Downstairs, Henry said, "You'd better get to bed, Joanna. I'm going across to the other side. There are some questions I want to ask Young Shep, while he can still talk."

"He isn't going to get better, is he?"

"I'm afraid not. Good night, Joanna."

He was now as cool and aloof to her as he was to other people, and for that, she thought, as she raked the fire low and left the pot of breakfast oatmeal not to cook but to ripen in the lingering warmth, she was to blame. It was a month now, since that scene in the wood. When she thought of it she could still smell the ripe warm scent of blackberries.

Henry had explained that he had arranged for her to go to Stordford, a grand house where she would learn all that a lady needed to know and she'd said she'd sooner die, and had given proof of it by running to one of the Three Pools and throwing herself in. It had not been just a dramatic gesture; she would rather die than leave Henry and Knight's Acre. They were her life.

Henry had plunged in after her, dragged her out, revived her and when she was herself again his mouth was on hers. All in a muddle, she'd mistaken this last resort for the resuscitation of the drowned for love. She had responded, embracing him ardently, using endearments that she hardly knew that she knew. He'd been shocked, disgusted. Anyway, different, ever since then. Formerly he had called her my sweet, or sweeting, even darling, terms more properly applied to one's wife, but who could possibly use them to somebody as waspish and scolding and nagging as Griselda?

Now he didn't use such words at all. He called her Joanna; in the last month he had been to market twice, but he had not asked her to go with him. Such a pity; they'd had such fun, such a closeness on market days. Even when what Henry had to sell brought in less money than he had expected, and all that was to be bought cost more, she'd been able to cheer him, make him laugh.

And of course, Joanna thought, resolutely hopeful, time would tell. She'd counted on that before Griselda finally went so mad that even Henry was bound to take notice. In her opinion Griselda had been demented for years. Now she was locked up; would probably pine and die. And even if she lived on it wouldn't matter, so long as she was out of the way, leaving Henry and Joanna together. That was all Joanna asked at the moment; her dream of happiness did not reach to having a ring on her finger and being able to call herself Mistress Tallboys.

And one thing was certain, she thought comfortably as she climbed the stairs: Henry was now dependent upon her to cook and keep house. There'd be no more idiot talk about exiling her to Stordford to learn how to play the lute and do embroidery.

Henry went heavily and thoughtfully across the yard

towards the other part of his house. He, too, recalled that scene in the wood. The trouble was that every time he was obliged to be brusque and off-hand with the child, it was a reminder. He'd believed her dead, driven to suicide at the thought of being sent to Stordford. Desperately he'd set about restoring her in a way he had once heard described by Walter and like everything Walter had ever advised, it had worked. Under the pressure of his hands, the breathing of his mouth, Joanna had come back to life and changed from a woebegone child to an ardent woman, caressing him, using such expressions of love—heart of my heart, and similar terms—that he was shocked. The disgust was for himself, for the instant response of his body. Quickly mastered; never repeated, but a shaming memory. To a child, not yet twelve years old; a child he had always regarded and treated as a much younger sister, tried to protect from Griselda's hostility. He'd always found her company congenial, too. He was anything but a jovial man and she was far from being a gay, prattling child, but they had in common a keen sense of the ridiculous; sometimes, with no word spoken, a look, a lift of the eyebrow, shrug of the shoulder, small movement of the hand was enough.

Poor little girl; upon a few careless words, a few acts of protectiveness and many a good laugh, she'd reared a shining fantasy, spun herself a fairy tale. She was fond of tales.

Think about sheep, he told himself sternly.

It was true that ever since Young Shep had gone off, years ago, the Knight's Acre flock had not flourished: foot rot, liver rot, and scab—most injurious to the fleeces. Henry had tried to be a good shepherd, and once upon a time, he'd had the help of Tom Robinson, who was good at everything he undertook; but he was dead now. He'd survived the plague, but it had left him weak and ailing; finally he'd ended so frail that he could only give Griselda a bit of help in the kitchen; and when he was past that and took to his bed, she'd been very kind and tolerant; very different from the way she had been towards anybody else who lived at Knight's Acre and did not pull his weight.

Henry stepped into the silk-hung room and saw that John had indeed been busy. The dust and the cobwebs were gone and the room bore more resemblance to the one which Henry Tallboys had once regarded as the most beautiful room in the world.

Young Shep—but I must remember not to say that! Years and years ago, in the lost mists of youth, Henry had said

"Young Shep," and John had rebuked him, saying, "He has a name, you know."

Young Shep lay on one of the divans, propped up on pillows, purple, scarlet, rose pink, primrose yellow. He looked ghastly, skin the colour of tallow except where, just under the eyes, there was a flush. Not of health, of fever.

Aware of the falsity, Henry said, "Good evening, Nick. I am glad to see you out of bed."

John, hovering, slightly aggressive, said, "I told you he was better."

Better? A man plainly dying, but making a great effort to hide the fact from his friend.

"I hoped I could pick your brains a bit—about sheep." Again that false heartiness.

"Anything I know," Young Shep said. He produced a smile which might have emphasised the death's-head look, but strangely did not; it was a sweet and genuinely grateful smile.

It was necessary for Henry to keep his attention on sheep and refuse to remember.

On that divan where the dying shepherd lay he had known one night of love—his first and his last, but such, he was sure, as few men ever knew; the consummation of years of boyish adoration of the beautiful lady from a far land, exotic, mysterious, with whom he had fallen in love at first sight. It was Tana, who had saved his father, Sir Godfrey, from slavery in some heathen country called Zagelah, and done so at such risk to her own life that she had been obliged to flee too. She'd been pregnant when she arrived and six months later had given birth to the girl Joanna, child of a Spanish knight, now dead. Nothing, widowhood, pregnancy, motherhood, had detracted a whit from the fascination which she held for Henry. And in the end he had possessed her; with absolutely no idea that she had once been his father's lover; that Joanna was in fact his half sister. Tana was so young, and the father-come-back-from-the-dead had seemed so old.

Henry had risen from the divan where he had lost his virginity and begun to plan: immediate marriage, a lifetime of happiness. Tana, for some inexplicable reason of her own, had gone riding on her only half-broken stallion, which had thrown her, as everybody had predicted. Henry had found her, dead, just at the yard's entry.

Think about; ask about, sheep!

Willing as he was to be helpful, Young Shep was vague; what he knew about sheep had either been inherited from his shepherd father, or acquired at such an early age as to be almost incommunicable. He said, "Well, that'd depend on the weather"; or, "I'd know, just by taking a look."

His cough was not troublesome, but he sounded weak and breathless and at one point asked, "Could you prop me a bit higher?"

John forestalled Henry's move, re-arranged the pillows and settled Young Shep on them with hands as gentle as a woman's. Then he said, softly, secretly, menacingly, "Don't tire him!" And in a loud, rallying, fate-defying voice, "Do the questions matter? In a week or two Nick will be up and about, and can *show* you!"

In a week or two Young Shep would be dead. He knew it; Henry knew it. Only John refused to face the truth. But then, he never had. He'd always been, in Henry's opinion, idle, frivolous, dodging work when he could and sneaking off to consort with the shepherd boy, slightly his elder, a maker of songs and a player of pipes.

In fact even at this moment, when Henry, seemingly so stolid and insensitive, could feel the throb of conflicting emotions in the room, he was also thinking that between them John and Young Shep had been largely to blame for his present poor financial position. If John hadn't insisted upon taking the value of his share of his father's inheritance out in cash—money Henry had been obliged to borrow at an exorbitant rate of interest; if he'd settled down, and worked, as a younger brother should; if Young Shep had remained in charge of the whole flock . . .

No good thinking of that, either. What was past was past. Ask about scab!

John fidgetted about, pulled a curtain closer, added a little charcoal to the brazier. Tana had made these apartments as much like one of her father's pavilions, which had neither been in Moorish Spain nor Christian Spain, but in North Africa, as possible; she had called this part of the house her pavilion and had no hearths; just charcoal braziers. Providing the charcoal had been easy for her; she was rich. For Henry it was an extra burden, borne without grudge.

Abruptly, John interrupted.

"Did you bring the milk, Henry? We've had none today."

"No. I'm sorry. We've had a bit of an upset in the house today. I'll fetch it."

He wanted to get away from this place with its bitter-sweet memories of the past and its present sad little drama; but in the time it took him to get up from the low, soft divan, not designed for sitting upon, and to think of what he had called a bit of an upset—Griselda violent and incoherent—he saw Young Shep's eyes fixed on him in dumb appeal.

"There's more I can tell you. John can fetch the milk."

Henry thought, What now? He said in his imperturbable way, "There's a candle in the kitchen, John. And the milk is in the dairy. In a brown jug."

"You get it, Johnny," Young Shep said, and his skeletal hand made a gesture, commanding, dismissing. Something flashed through Henry's mind, a recognition of something out of order. After all, his father, and John's, had been Sir Godfrey, at one time the premier knight in England; Young Shep's father had been Old Shep. And when John and Young Shep had failed in their venture, it was to Knight's Acre that John had come home, dragging Young Shep with him.

Henry had risen to his feet, and the door had hardly closed behind John, going obediently to fetch the milk, before Young Shep moved his hand again, this time to grip Henry's wrist in a weak, yet urgent clasp of thin, burning hot fingers.

"Master," he said, reverting to the old mode of address and to the rustic way of speech. "You been here. . . . All along. Please, did you ever see or hear tell owt of Beth?"

Beth? Complete blank. The name meant nothing; conjured up no mental . . . wait a minute . . .

"She used to come with the shearers, she was their gang woman," Young Shep said, helpfully.

Then Henry remembered—not the berry-brown girl with a mouth as red as a rose hip, but the fierce, bitter, resentful woman who, after some years of absence, had appeared again, a deserted wife, sole support of her child and hating the very name of Tallboys because John Tallboys had lured her husband away.

Was this something to tell a dying man?

Henry thought not. He said, "Only indirectly. But she was well."

"I did wrong by her. Thass hard to explain. I married her and sort of settled down." His fever-bright eyes looked flinchingly towards the door by which John had gone out and at any minute might come back. "He never did understand . . . That a man could be sort of divided, neither one way nor t'other. I used to send her money. Sometimes easy. Sometimes a pinch. There was allust a row. Proper owd mess I made of things, Master. I'd've liked her to know I was sorry."

Henry was aware of something being demanded of him; aware, too, of being at a loss. Ought he to speak with false cheer, pretend as John was pretending? Tell Young Shep that he'd be up and about in no time and able to talk to his wife himself?

"If I ever see her, as I well may, I'll tell her. And now . . . Would you like the priest to come?"

"Thass a kind thought, Master. I would. But it'd upset *him*. And he've been so good to me." His voice trailed away and he loosened his clasp on Henry's wrist.

Ever since the lung sickness had come upon him he'd thought of it as a judgement on him. For being neither one thing nor the other. To die young, with all those songs unmade, unsung. He'd always been the song maker; a tune on his pipe first, then the words to go with it. John's quick ear had picked up the tune and the words and the combination of voice, lute and pipe had been just that little bit out of the ordinary that made for popularity. They'd had wonderful times, welcome wherever they went, treated like princes.

Now that the good times had gone and the end was near, Young Shep sometimes remembered that shepherds usually lived to be old, saw their children learn their craft, getting a bit stiff in the joints but able to hobble out on the first mild day of sunshine, see the lambs skipping and the primroses in flower. . . . None of that for him. And to be honest he had to admit to himself that during his spell of married life he'd been restless, discontented. It had taken very little persuasion from John to coax him away from Beth. Bad husband, and never really wholeheartedly the other thing, either. A lot of pretence. And now he must pretend absolutely, even forgo the consolation of the last rites, say each day, as he felt worse, that he felt better.

"I'm glad we got here. He'll hev you to turn to," he said.

Henry thought: And that won't be much comfort to him!

"I'll do my best, Nick," he said simply.

Going back towards his own part of the house, Henry looked up at the window of the room into which he had locked Griselda. She *might* be better tomorrow, but somehow he doubted it.

When Griselda woke she was a little confused, not instantly remembering what had happened. She came out of sleep unwillingly, as she always did, facing another hard-working, thankless day. She stirred and felt more than the usual morning heaviness, especially down her left side. Then her mind cleared and it all came back. Not merely the events of yesterday, but all that had led up to that complete loss of temper. That was all it was, just being tried beyond endurance.

Nobody knows what I have borne. Everything against me. Still, that was small excuse for throwing good bread on the floor! That was crazy! In future I must be more careful.

She went, a bit lopsidedly, to the door. As she expected, it was locked. So she couldn't get to the stool-room and must use the chamber pot. She found and replaced the shoe she had taken off, but her preparations for facing the world, for facing Henry, stopped there and she did not, as on other mornings, run the comb through her hair. Instead she sat and thought how silly she had been to hammer on the floor and scream; and to think of doing it again. Very foolish.

Presently the lock clicked and there was Henry, looking wary, edging in, carrying a tray, clumsily as all men did.

Now, be humble, placating, apologetic; the only way out of this.

She said, and it sounded just as it should: Henry, I am sorry about yesterday. Something came over me and I gave way. It will not happen again, I promise you.

Henry thought, No better! Meaningless babble. The room faced East and the merciless morning light showed him what had happened to her face, and her hair was rough and tumbling down. Her face looked as though invisible fingers were pinching it, pulling the corner of the left eye down, the mouth on that side upwards. No better; rather worse.

He felt sorry for her. He'd never loved her, but until she changed, little by little, into a nag and a scold, he had respected her, decent, amiable, industrious woman, just what he and Knight's Acre needed. But the years, the oddities of behaviour, the spurts of violence had eroded even that amount of feeling for her and now he was able to regard her dispassionately: a pitiable creature, rather like cripples and beggars with sores, seen on Baildon marketplace.

The only difference was that for her he was responsible. Because she could be violent, he must restrain her; he must feed her, keep her clean, empty the chamber pot.

Griselda said, deliberately controlling her voice: Henry *why* do you pretend not to understand? How can it serve you? What more can I say than that I am sorry? What can you gain? What harm did I ever do you that you should treat me so?

For years she had complained of having too much to do; now she had nothing. Absolutely nothing to do and that in itself was torture. And what was happening to her child?

Against her better judgement—and yet what did judgement count for in such a lunatic situation—she screamed.

Downstairs Jem Watson, all agog with curiosity, cocked his ear to the ceiling.

"Missus took bad?"

"She has some pain," Henry said. "Tomorrow, when I go to market, I shall consult with the doctor."

The doctor, who had already been once to Knight's Acre to see John and Young Shep and given the best advice possible in such hopeless cases, greeted Henry with a certain reserve but warmed to the business when told the real situation.

"How old is Mistress Tallboys?"

Who knew?

Henry could remember her arriving at Knight's Acre, a pitiable waif, who'd made a lot of growth, fed properly. She couldn't have been very old.

"Twenty-six, or thereabouts."

So it was not the menopause, that most common cause of mental disturbance in women.

"Is she pregnant?"

"No."

"Master Tallboys, forgive me. How can you be certain? Women are often secretive—in the early stages."

"I am certain. I have one son and shortly after his birth my wife said that she wanted no more children. I respected her wishes. We sleep apart."

Very odd. But then the man himself was an oddity, wearing homespun as though it were cloth of silver.

He considered the possibility of fits, the ancient, known

disease of epilepsy. And Henry, who had seen, in Baildon, men writhing, frothing at the mouth, said,

"No. She is . . . at times . . . violent." That very morning, Griselda, despairing, had sprung at Henry and tried by force to get to the door.

This stripping away of all reserve, to a man so naturally self-contained, was a painful business.

The doctor said, with the air of one propounding an original theory, "Violence must be controlled."

He was not eager to go jogging out to Intake again. On the previous occasion it had proved a longer ride than he had envisaged, and the days were shorter now, the roads more miry. And seeing the poor woman would tell him little that he had not been told already. So he said a few things about diet for the demented; nothing heating, no spices, no wine, a low diet, in fact, and said he would provide some soothing drops.

He then remembered the two young men with lung-rot and asked about them.

"My brother is making a good recovery; his friend is dying."

There was no recovery once the lungs began to fail; there were intermissions. This he did not say. He offered a little general advice. John must avoid physical exertion, exposure to the weather, any kind of coarse food. He handed over the little leather bottle of soothing drops and once again said that his fee was two nobles. Secretly Henry was appalled; so much of his scanty ready money, and so little for it; the man had made no journey, spent no time on examination. In this he underestimated the cost of the bottle's contents; its chief ingredient came, like spices, from far away.

Riding home he suffered a bout of the lowness of spirit which often attacked him on this road. He never fully realised to what extent sheer hard work had protected him from melancholy. With nothing to do—even the horse knew its way and needed no guidance—he was ready prey.

He thought of the failure of all his youthful hopes. Twenty-seven years old and if anything, worse off than ever. The last year had been calamitous.

Griselda to be controlled, cared for.

John to be coddled and fed special food.

Joanna to be by some means persuaded to go to Stordford and take her proper place in life.

Into the lane towards Intake; through the water-splash at its lowest point; onto the track which led only to the church, the priest's house and Knight's Acre. There it stood, his good solid house, with the rose trees in front, the garden to one side and the fields on the other. The newly ploughed, newly seeded furrows lay ridged, dark brown on one side and in this dying light a curious, muted purple, almost a shimmer, on the other. At the sight strength and determination flowed back into him. I have my house and my land: I shall manage. . . .

He made a mistake in the administration of the drowsy syrup. There was only one handsome drinking vessel in the house—the silver christening cup given by Sir Richard, then apparently rich and in control of the family manor at Moyidan, to his godson, young Godfrey.

With an equal amount of warm water, or milk, and well stirred, the doctor had directed.

"It's doctor's stuff," Henry said, holding out the cup. Griselda stretched out her hand as though to take it and then struck his wrist upwards, so that the dark, sticky stuff shot in an arc, soiling his best, market-going jerkin.

You can't fool me! It's some filthy brew that little slut made. I remember her doing it once before. In that same cup. Don't look at me like that! You know very well what I'm saying. I suppose you thought that locking me in here, with nothing to do, would drive me mad. But that wasn't quick enough. So now it's poison!

The noise was angry, but meaningless.

"We could try it in broth," Joanna suggested.

Griselda could resist broth; and bread and milk, well sweetened with honey; and a coddled egg, done just as she had often prepared one for Godfrey. She had learned, early in life, to stay alive on very little. She could keep alive on little sips of water, until they came to their senses and stopped the silly pretence that they couldn't understand her. That she was mad!

Mad! The word had more meaning for her than to most people, for the convent which had taken her in—a beggar child—also stretched its limited resources to offer asylum to the mad. There was no traffic between the orphanage side and the bedlam, the whole convent building and the chapel lay between, but from part of the garden where able-bodied orphans worked and regarded themselves as specially favoured, the iron grill in the far wall was visible and, behind it, sometimes faces. Some terrible faces which, if not behind bars, would have been frightening. Safely locked away, they were amusing. Sometimes there were cries from that building, too.

Griselda did not realise that her own face had slipped into a grotesque mask, or that the extremely sensible things she said emerged as nonsense. Her link with real life had not actually snapped, but it was like a frayed rope, some strands had given way. She did not ask herself *why* Henry and everybody else should be in a plot against her; she only knew that everybody was.

She still tried to reason with Henry.

Henry, I know I offended you. All those jewels which *I* found in those rooms that had been shut up for years. I thought that finding them made them mine—ours—and that we should be safe and comfortable forever. *You* said they were Joanna's because they belonged to her mother. All right. I was angry at the time, but I accept it now. Let her have them. And I offended again when John and Young Shep arrived, all in rags and nearly dead. Yes, I said then that I'd burn the house down sooner than have them in. But, Henry, I knew it was lung-rot; I knew what it could do . . . Henry, please, I must see my son, I must have something to do. Shut away here like this, I shall go mad.

He went on pretending not to hear, or not to understand. It was all babble. And apart from that, would any woman in her right mind go on rejecting food; or take a thread from a blanket and try to play cat's cradle with it—a game which after two moves needed another player?

Griselda lost count of time, but she knew that even she could not live without eating. Not forever. What she must do to save herself was to get away, find somebody who was not in the plot and explain.

The only way to do that was through the window and it would be difficult; very difficult, for it was a barred window.

Who now living remembered why that already narrow window should have been barred?

Henry had had a sister, Margaret, pretty as an angel but dim-witted beyond belief. There was this weak streak in the Tallboys family; most of the children they bred were big and strong, precocious. But now and again, as though in compensation, the family produced a simpleton.

That Knight's Acre should include a dim-wit girl was a pity, but not a tragedy. That the head of the family, Sir James Tallboys, and his formidable wife, Lady Emma, should, at Moyidan, the real centre of the family, have another dim-wit as heir was a catastrophe which neither would acknowledge. Their Richard was slow to learn, was delicate, was shy; all the usual parental excuses. Then the day came when, the Moyidan family visiting at Knight's Acre, Richard of Moyidan and his cousin Margaret of Knight's Acre had each recognised in the other the perfect mate. Found in the hay, no real harm yet done, they had been torn apart and Margaret locked in her room. This was not her first escapade, but everybody intended that it should be her last.

She'd gone out by the window, on a summer day, making for Moyidan, but easily diverted by the sight of a carter, resting himself and his horse by the water-splash in the lane. To the end of his days the carter believed that he had spent a summer afternoon with one of the Little People, the fairies who lived in Layer Wood. Margaret had been found, brought back and the window barred. At Moyidan, Richard had used one of his tried weapons—he would not eat a crumb until his parents agreed that he should marry his cousin Margaret. And at Knight's Acre, the Lady Sybilla, pious, knowing that marriage of cousins, even sound healthy ones, was against canon law and needed a special dispensation, had discovered that Margaret was pregnant; only just; a week, ten days. The marriage had been quickly and cunningly arranged, and its outcome had given everybody a delightful surprise: a lusty boy, a real Tallboys in everything but colour of hair and eyes. . . .

Of all this Griselda knew nothing; she saw the window barred and was discouraged; then hopeful. Despite the dragging lameness of her left leg she thought that if only she could squeeze through the narrow opening she would be free. Free to speak to somebody who did not pretend to be deaf, or not to understand, somebody not in this senseless plot.

It was not easy, but then nothing had ever been easy for her. Now carrying her left side as a load—but in her time she had carried heavier and more awkward ones—Griselda forced herself through and saw that the drop was negligible; just on to the roof of the new part, the other part, single-storied. From there to the ground.

The nearest house was the priest's and moving a bit crabwise, Griselda made for it. She could remember being a bit gruff to Mistress Captoft on that terrible day; but she knew how to apologise. For a long time, in fact before everything became too much for her, Griselda had copied Lady Sybilla in every way; and Lady Sybilla had once said that only a well-bred person could apologise gracefully. That piece of information Griselda had tucked away and now, dragging that side of her which seemed not to belong, she planned her apology and her appeal for help.

Mistress Captoft, as everybody knew, had money and she had spent some on the priest's house. There was now a tiny room, just to the right of the door, where parishioners needing spiritual or physical comfort, could wait; shielded from the weather, and yet not disturbing Father Benedict in the parlour. It was very difficult to get access to him; even calls to deathbeds were obstructed by Mistress Captoft, who would suggest trying a good dose first. She made very potent brews.

The day was already darkening when Griselda knocked urgently on the door of the priest's house. The light was behind her and Mistress Captoft did not notice anything strange in her appearance except that her hair was in disorder. Her errand could be guessed; one of the sick men was about to die.

Good afternoon. I have come to apologise for being brusque the other day. I need help. Mistress Captoft, you and Father Benedict must help me. I am in danger. It is a matter of life or death.

Poor woman, completely incoherent. Mistress Captoft reached back and opened the door of the little room.

"Come in, Mistress Tallboys. There, sit down. Now tell . . ."

Here the angle of light was different, revealing the distortion of Griselda's face, the wildness of her eyes.

Mistress Captoft prided herself upon being level-headed. Once when she lived in Dunwich she had been called upon to deal with a little boy, so badly bitten by a dog that one side of his nose was hanging by a mere thread of flesh. She had kept her head, clapped the loose flesh back into place, secured it—and stopped the bleeding—with a stiff plaster of flour and water, and administered a good dose of febrifuge. Later she had the pleasure of seeing the boy as good as new except for a slight lumpiness on one side of the nose; and even that, she had thought complacently, would be less noticeable when his face attained full growth.

She was calm now, though a little taken aback.

"Sit down," she said. Griselda, anxious to prove that she was not mad, sat down as bidden. The room was so small that it contained only one chair and a stool. "Take a deep breath," Mistress Captoft ordered. "Now, try to tell me, quietly."

Another burst of gibberish; not merely words mispronounced or slurred in a way for which the distortion of the mouth could account; sheer nonsense, accompanied with wild gestures.

The woman was mad; and madness was more a priest's business.

"Wait here. I will fetch Father Benedict," Mistress Captoft said. She went nimbly away, but keeping her head, remembering to pull the latch-string through so that the door could not be opened from inside the little room.

She said from pure habit, "I am sorry to disturb you. It is Mistress Tallboys. I think she has gone mad."

Father Benedict looked up from his writing and went through the process, familiar to her, of coming back to everyday life.

"In what way?"

"Talking nonsense. And looking horrible."

He thought, Poor Mattie! She made a great sacrifice in coming with me to this barbarous place where there is no one of her kind with whom to associate, no shops, nothing to see from the window except a sheep-fold. Small wonder that she tends to exaggerate! But even as he discounted something of what she said, he observed that some of her bright colour had drained away, and that she had lost some of her self-possession.

"Drink this," he said, pouring wine from the jug which invariably stood ready to refresh and strengthen him as he pursued his studies. "I will go to her."

"I think better not. In addition to the nonsense and the wild look . . . I have just remembered. There is a smell. Like a wild animal. Somebody once told me that such a smell went with madness. I will run to the house and fetch her husband. It is for him to deal with."

An indirect and unintentional reflection upon his manhood. People so often made that mistake about priests—though Mattie should have known better.

"My dear, if he could have dealt with her, why is she here? Subjected to strain, or shock, women often become incoherent."

Alone in the tiny room, seated on the stool, Griselda thought that so far she had not done badly. Mistress Captoft had listened, and seemed to understand; had said that she would fetch Father Benedict. The right thing to say, since he was the one with authority. She waited.

"I think I should come with you," Mistress Captoft said.

"She looks very frail, but the mad often have more than natural strength. She could be dangerous."

"To me?" He gave her a look, half humorous, half rebuking, No meddling!

She accepted it. But she remembered to say, "I pulled the latch-string. Put it back as you go in."

It was this adjustment of the latch-string as the priest entered which made Griselda suspicious. Here without realising it, she had also been locked in. Why? Because Mistress Captoft was in the plot, too?

Father Benedict appeared not to be. Having adjusted the string of the latch and closed the door, he stood for a second or two, a big solid man, reliable and authoritative, greeting her as a priest should greet a parishioner: "God bless you, my child."

Griselda, remembering her manners, slipped from the stool and made the bob due to his office. Then she sat again. I must remember not to raise my voice or wave my good arm about. The other, the left, was too heavy and she held it by the elbow, supporting it, somewhat in the manner of a woman with a baby.

"Now, Mistress Tallboys; take your time. Something has upset you. Tell me." He sat in the chair, folded his hands and seemed prepared to listen.

Not one intelligible word. Urgent, emphatic, fluent. Had this been his first encounter with her he would have taken it for her native tongue, one unknown to him. But he had known her for years; knew that she was as English as he was himself. Also, before he had immured himself here as parish priest at Intake, he had been clerk and general amanuensis to a merchant in Dunwich and had, of necessity, acquired not merely a smattering of various languages but also the sensitive ear which must make a bridge between people who could not allow differing languages to impede business.

But what Mistress Tallboys was now saying fitted in nowhere; not French or any of the varieties of German; not even Spanish or Italian. A language apart; the tongue of the mad. He was rather less credulous and fearful than the average man but a little shiver ran over him as he remembered that to speak in strange tongues was one sign of being possessed by devils. Such a state would be in keeping with her looks, so haggard, so distraught. Perhaps, poor creature, she knew what ailed her. He shivered again as he considered the possibility that she had come to him trusting him to act as exorcist.

In theory it was within the power of any properly ordained man to cast out devils: Christ had left such power with His Apostles, and through ordination, the touch of a Bishop's hand, the humblest parish priest was directly linked with St. Peter, the Apostle chosen to be the founder of the Church; in actuality exorcism was a dangerous, tricky business, not to be lightly undertaken. Never by one man alone. Never without consent from one's Bishop.

I am over-fanciful, he told himself. But he did move his right hand and made the sign of the Cross in the air between them. Then he said,

"Mistress Tallboys, I did not understand you. Perhaps if you spoke more slowly. . . ." It was a frail hope, but all he had.

So! Griselda thought, they are in the plot, too! He understood; she understood. Now he is keeping me here, telling me to say it all again, but more slowly, while she runs off to fetch Henry.

Father Benedict sat in the chair between her and the door. A big solid man in a chair which though not large was solid. Her glance, frenzied, sly, went to the window; not a casement, just a few panes set in the wall. No escape. Trapped again.

We'll see! Nothing to be lost by trying.

Swiftly, despite the heaviness of her left side, she jumped up, lifted the three-legged stool and drove it at him. One leg hit him in the mouth, another in the chest; the third just missed his shoulder and struck the back of the chair. The onslaught, made with all her remaining strength, inspired by desperation and fully in accord with the streak of violence which was part of her nature, toppled him. Griselda stepped over his legs and opened the door and ran straight into Mistress Captoft, who stood in the narrow entry, a freshly lighted candle in her hand.

Mistress Captoft had gone through one of those periods when a minute was an hour of anxiety. Without words he had told her not to meddle; he was priest, he had authority; he was a man of good physique, but he was not, especially when just roused from work, very alert and he was, at any time, slow at summing up a situation. And there he was, alone with a mad woman. And now she had, as the day darkened, a perfectly good excuse for going in and satisfying at once her curiosity and her protective instinct. She was taking a candle to set on the shelf which, jutting out between the chair and the stool, served as a table in a room too small to accommodate such a thing. By its light, when the door flew open, she saw Benedict on the floor, tangled with the fallen chair. She hardly noticed Griselda, pushing past, making for the outer door. She did not know, or knowing, would have cared, that the mad woman's hair had flicked across the candle and begun to blaze and sizzle.

"My dearest," Mistress Captoft said, speaking and behaving in a manner forbidden by man, but not, she was certain, by God, "she hurt you."

She helped him up and took him into the warmer room. He was bleeding from the mouth, but that, thank God, was not the deadly symptom that it sometimes could be. A bad enough injury, but superficial; both lips split. Water, ice cold from the well. Alum, the drying powder. Even as she ministered to him the broken lips swelled and when he spoke his words were blurred, too; but at least they made sense. He said, "They must be warned. She attacked me, unprovoked. There are children there."

He was showing courage, a virtue he greatly admired and had seldom been called upon to exercise. He did not even mention the other, worse hurt which the other leg of the stool had inflicted.

"You must tell Master Tallboys. She is *dangerous*."

"I can't leave you, my darling."

"Of course you can. I'm all right now. Run along, tell them to beware. Please, Mattie, do as I say."

"If you are sure . . ." But then, he had always been sure, of himself, of her. "Very well. I shall be back in no time." She put a log on the fire, lighted another candle.

Left alone, Father Benedict tried to probe his hurt and thought it curious that though from the outside it was so widespread that he could not determine whether it was in his belly or his chest, it was worse inside. A full breath was like the stab of a knife. It was nothing, and to say anything would simply worry Mattie. Leaning himself in the attitude which seemed less painful, and taking only shallow breaths, he returned to his work.

Mistress Captoft went briskly to Knight's Acre. There was no light in the front, so she went around into the yard. The kitchen window was golden and through it she saw something not unlike a scene in one of the morality plays which in Dunwich she had so much enjoyed. The girl, Joanna, dishing something out of the black pot, the little boy, already served, in the act of lifting his spoon, Master Tallboys holding a tray. Caught in a timeless moment . . . And, God be thanked, so far unharmed.

What with haste and lack of breath, she sounded slightly incoherent at first, and Henry said, "But how could she? The door . . ." Then he set down the tray, snatched up a candle, and hurried away. Across the hall in a few long strides and up the stairs, two at a time. The door was locked. The room empty, the window open, but offering so small an exit. Was it possible? Not only possible, but fact.

Downstairs again he said, "Which way did she go?"

"I do not know. My concern was with Father Benedict, injured, bleeding . . ."

"I hope not seriously," Henry said, but he was already busy with his lantern and his lack of real concern confirmed Mistress Captoft's opinion of him as an unfeeling fellow.

"A stool wielded by a maniac can be a dangerous weapon," she said, rather reprovingly, making for the door; anxious to get back.

"Wait," Henry said. "I can light you home. Joanna, bolt both doors, and on no account open until you hear my voice."

He had no idea of where to search. He'd start with the track and the lane into which it led—as far as the water-splash—in her weakened state Griselda was unlikely to have gone farther than that. He'd shout and wave the lantern on the edge of the wood. Then, and with reluctance, he would try the village. A fine lot of talk *that* would cause.

Bursting out of the priest's house, Griselda had turned left, towards the lane, towards Baildon. The mere act of running, with one side so heavy, demanded so much attention that for a little time she was not aware that her hair was blazing. (One old woman in Intake, closing her shutters for the night, saw what she thought was a ball of fire, travelling slowly along the far edge of Grabber's Green—the villagers still called it that, convinced that by turning his own land into a sheep-fold, Sir Godfrey Tallboys had cruelly wronged them. She was alone at the time and crossed herself, muttering, "Lord preserve us!" for anything unusual was a portent, usually of evil. Nobody else seemed to have seen it and she did not mention the strange sight, for since portents were uncanny, those who brought news of them were unpopular.)

Griselda, like any woman who cooked, knew the two ways

of extinguishing flames, by water, or by smothering. She tried to smother her burning hair by pulling her skirt over her head. The stuff was old and thin and since she had for a long time lost interest in her appearance, splashed with grease. It flared up like tinder. Her last conscious thought was that she must get to the water-splash.

Candles used in lanterns were thicker than ordinary ones, but through the panes of thin horn which shielded them from the wind and from movement, gave little light. Henry held his high to make it more visible from the wood's edge, and as he walked called Griselda by name. Before he reached the dip in the lane where the water ran he thought he could smell something like meat roasting. Vagrants, he thought, somewhere just inside the wood's cover, cooking a rabbit. He could see no fire though. He halted and called at the top of his voice, "Where are you? I mean you no harm. I need help." The last word seemed to hang in the silence, which otherwise remained absolute.

He almost walked into Griselda's body. Recognisable only by a piece of petticoat, charred all round, from which the flame had been extinguished when she fell. He knew it for it had been one of his mother's dresses. Griselda had taken over Lady Sybilla's scanty wardrobe and made the best use of it, both for herself and her child. When any garment was too worn for outward wear, she'd made it into shifts and petticoats. A bit of silk, the colour of a dove's neck, sorry remnant of a length which Sir Godfrey had been so pleased to find, so proud to pay for, on one of the few occasions when he had money in his pouch, now identified something half charred stick, half meat on a neglected spit.

For some reason Henry found himself unable to touch it. He'd managed to drag Walter's corpse to its secret, unhallowed grave; and Tana, with her neck broken, he had lifted up tenderly. With this he should have been able to deal, but could not; there was no sorrow or grief to mitigate the nauseating repulsion.

He must have a blanket and to go home for one would mean questions.

Questions were already there in the kitchen. In the precise, rather delicate diction which Griselda had learned from Lady Sybilla and—except when angry—had always used towards her child, Godfrey said, "What was that all about, Janna?"

"Nothing for you to bother about, my dear."

"Who hit somebody with a stool?"

"I didn't understand either," she said, untruthfully. "Your father is seeing to it. Everything will be all right. Finish your stew and have an apple. They're the last we shall see this year."

Thank God he was easily distracted. Pray God Griselda had run away from Knight's Acre, and from the priest's house and would be found dead. She'd eaten nothing for days—and Robert, whom Joanna could now remember in a dispassionate way, had eaten well—and yet died from one night's exposure. It could happen again.

"Why did father say bar the doors?"

"It is safer so."

In the priest's house Mistress Captoft said, "I blame myself for leaving you. But you sent me." He seemed rather more ill than split lips warranted. Shock, and a fall.

"You must go to bed," she said. She offered her arm, her shoulder, since he moved so slowly and so feebly.

"I can walk, my dear," he said. He could. The fall had not injured him; but every breath was a pang.

Two hot bricks, wrapped in flannel, one at his feet, one at his back. Now a wine sop; red wine, because he had lost blood. Not much, thanks to her prompt action.

She had the wine, warmed and sweetened—but no spice, no pepper to sting his hurt mouth—and was cutting the best, whitest manchet bread into tiny cubes when another knock sounded on the door. The madwoman again? Mistress Captoft snatched up the heaviest ladle she owned, went to the door and opened it just enough to enable her to strike. Tit for tat. Mistress Tallboys had attacked, unprovoked . . .

It was Master Tallboys.

"May I borrow a blanket?"

"You found her?"

"Yes. I need a blanket—if you would be so kind."

Understandable, it was a night of frost, and so far as Mistress Captoft remembered the madwoman had come out with no cloak. She hurried upstairs and snatched a blanket from the chest which held several. Then she hurried back to the kitchen and was enraged to find that during her brief absence, the red wine had boiled; which meant that it had lost all virtue. She had to start again.

In bed Father Benedict was comfortable if he did not take a full breath or shift about. Mattie put another pillow in place to raise his head and spooned in the sops-in-wine.

She talked as she did so. "Master Tallboys found his wife.

Where, I did not stop to ask. It is a curious thing; I was always against the cruel treatment of lunatics. . . . Now I hope he locks her in, gives her bread and water and beats her when she is obstropulous."

"I was to blame. For not heeding you."

He thought, Most women would elaborate upon that theme, say, Didn't I tell you? or, Serves you right. But not Mattie. She combined good sense with good nature, a sweet disposition with a talent for management. It was a pity. . . . He did not pursue that line of thought.

What had been Griselda, bundled into a blanket, made a lighter and more manageable load than many that Henry had shouldered, but it was horrible and he tried to divert his mind by thinking about the future, how decent privacy could be maintained. He wanted nobody to know the truth; it was so shocking. Some kind of stigma attached to madness, while ordinary illness and death were accepted as commonplace. What Jem Watson knew, Intake knew, and all that Jem knew was that Griselda had been ill, screaming with pain on Tuesday, and that Henry had fetched her some medicine from the doctor on Wednesday. Everything, so far, in good order; even to Griselda having grown quiet. But would Father Benedict, would Mistress Captoft talk? Would Godfrey grow up and one day hear, from some long stored-up tale, that his mother had gone mad, attacked a priest with a stool and then set herself on fire? A taint like that could cling through generations!

For a moment his thoughts veered. How had Griselda set herself on fire? A fire was not so easy to kindle. Had she carried a lighted candle, or flint and tinder? No time to bother about that; he must get this *thing* indoors, on to a bed, get it coffined, with nobody knowing. He must send Joanna to bed. What to tell *her*?

He laid his burden down, somewhat short of the kitchen door, and rapped and called. The door opened immediately and there was Joanna.

"Did you find her?"

"Yes. Dead. Where's the boy?"

"I coaxed him to bed. Where was she?"

For years, suffering under the lash of Griselda's tongue they had shared a mildly joking resignation, saying *she,* saying *her*.

"The less you know, the better," Henry said.

Joanna's ruthless spirit spiralled upwards. Griselda, Henry's wife, her enemy, dead. Her joy would have been complete, had Henry not seemed so stunned and so stricken.

"She was mad, Henry. Had been for a long time. I knew years ago. Not only by the way she behaved to me . . . Other things. Look, I have kept your supper warm. I only wish I had wine."

And why should she not have wine? She had inherited a small fortune in jewels; bright stones which she and Robert had found in one of the rooms on the other side. Pretty pebbles, playthings, a childish secret until Griselda found them and Henry had said that if they were valuable they were Joanna's, and must be used to her advantage. Some part of this fortune was already invested, with somebody called Sir Barnabas Grey, at Stordford, the place to which she had refused to go. But the rest was presumably still in the Bishop's hands and could be used to advantage *here,* if only Henry would agree.

For the first time that he could remember Henry had no appetite. Through every other extremity or exertion in his life, so long as he could remember, he had emerged hungry. But not tonight. Some of the sickening, charred meat odour clung to his jerkin. The kitchen was warm, so he removed the garment, seeing as he did so, the three-cornered tear, called for some reason a hedge tear, which Griselda had mended. Neatly, expertly, but grumbling all the time; the eye of the needle too small, or the thread too thick, the wrong colour; and why if he must do something that tore his clothes, couldn't he wear his leather coat? And how could one woman, with one pair of hands, worn to the bone, be expected to deal with everything. Only last week. It seemed a long time ago. And now she lay, silenced forever, by the house wall.

"Save it for tomorrow," he said, practically, rejecting the stew. "And go to bed. Forget all about it. Nothing to do with you."

She said, "Henry, you must not grieve. She was mad and would never have been better." It struck her that his stricken look and his refusal to eat, might indicate sorrow. Perhaps once, before Griselda turned so sour and nasty, there had been a kind of fondness. Nothing much; nothing at all like what their marriage would be, once attained. On the thought of marriage her mind halted. There might, for all she knew, be some law about the age at which one could be married. But betrothals were different; a betrothal could take place at any time; she knew that from Tom Robinson's talk. Mere babies could be betrothed, and were, especially where property was involved. And a betrothal was practically as good as a marriage.

Tom Robinson. Her mind halted again. To him Griselda had been quite different, gentle and tender. He was a sick man, towards the end bedridden; yet never once had Griselda called *him* a pauper, never once had she complained about the extra work *he* made. Enlightenment burst in upon her. Griselda had loved Tom Robinson! Then why had she married Henry? The answer was simple: Tom had nothing, no home, no money, not even health. Poor Henry, Joanna thought, how I will make it up to him? Once we are married, as we must be, will be.

She was so engrossed in her own thoughts that she did not even wonder where the dead woman was.

Henry waited, fidgetting about uneasily, until enough time elapsed for Joanna to be in bed, and asleep; then he opened the door quietly and stepped out. He was half-way towards the body when he heard crying, wild, unrestrained, on a womanish note. He went rigid and cold sweat burst from every pore in his body. Oh, God, it could not be! It was unbelievable that the faintest spark of life remained in that burnt-out body.

Then he felt rather than saw some movement across the yard, near the outjutting part of the other side of the house. It could only be John. He called and the desolate noise increased. John, weeping like a woman, stumbled towards the kitchen lights. He just managed to say, "Nick's dead!"

"He was dying when he arrived, John." The statement sounded blunt and unsympathetic, but it was true. John must have known, must have seen . . .

"I kept—hoping. And he was—better. He was taking his food. He coughed without blood. Only this evening . . . We were talking about setting out. In the spring."

You were, Henry thought; Young Shep knew he was dying. But then you always could believe what you wanted to. Did what you wanted to.

He tried to muster some sympathy, but there was something distasteful in the sight of a man weeping like a woman. Sybilla's death had broken Sir Godfrey in mind and spirit, but so far as Henry could remember, his father had never cried.

He wished he had wine; or good strong ale. He did what he could, helped John to a bench by the hearth and stirred the dying fire. Involuntarily, he remembered his own bereavements: Walter; the mother whom he had loved; and Tana. There were words of comfort, he supposed—the life everlasting, the resurrection of the body—but he had never been able to understand how that could be, and the words would sound hollowly, coming from him. They were for the priest to say.

He said, awkwardly, "You did your best for him, while he lived, John. You brought him home. Even when you were ill yourself, you nursed him."

"I owed him that," John said. Suddenly he stopped crying, wiped his wet face on his sleeve. "I took him to his death."

"That is nonsense."

"It is not! Nick didn't come with me at first. Did you know that? He got himself married, settled down. He'd have stayed, making his beautiful songs—with only sheep to hear. And I knew—I'd seen for myself—what could be done, the rewards, the favours. I loved him, Henry. I wanted him to share. So I persuaded him. And he took this cold in Padua."

"That is nonsense," Henry said again. "He didn't *have* to go with you. He wasn't a slave. He could have stayed where he was—and caught a cold tending sheep."

"Hard as stone," John said. "You always were."

Henry accepted that in silence. He waited a little, conscious of all he had still to do. Then he said, "You'd better try to get some sleep, John."

"Not there," John said with a nervous start—like a woman again. "I couldn't sleep across there! You . . . You haven't seen him."

Henry thought of what he *had* seen. But he seized the chance of getting John out of the way. He took up the candle and said, "Come along, then. You can sleep here. Come quietly, the boy sleeps lightly."

Waiting again, to give John time to settle. Then he completed his grim journey, laid the blanket-wrapped bundle on the bed, locked the door again. From the far room came the sound of John, sobbing. Henry thought, without sentimentality—No tears for Griselda! But then what purpose did tears ever serve?

Next day was Sunday and Henry was early at the priest's house. He wanted to arrange things as well as he could, before it was time for Mass.

Father Benedict was down, but not dressed yet. Wearing a voluminous woollen wrap, he sat at the table, carefully easing tiny spoonfuls of bread and milk between his broken lips. He looked very pale.

"I've come, partly, to apologise," Henry said. "I am indeed very sorry that my wife should have injured you, Father. But she was out of her mind."

"I know. Poor woman," the priest said, speaking carefully from the uninjured corner of his mouth. "I shall pray God to heal her."

"She is dead."

"God rest her in peace."

"God rest her," Mistress Captoft echoed. "But *how*, Master Tallboys? I thought when you asked for a blanket . . ."

In as few words as possible, but well chosen, as was customary with him, Henry explained.

Shocked out of being cautious, Mistress Captoft said,

"Oh! How terrible. She must have brushed against the candle as she pushed past me. But how was I to mark *that*, with Father Benedict on the floor, and bleeding?"

Cautious, as he always was about any fortunate chance, Henry said, "Nobody in his right mind would dream of blaming you, Mistress Captoft."

As he spoke he looked straight at her. He had inherited his father's singularly candid eyes, but whereas in Sir Godfrey the candid look had had nothing behind it but candour— often to his own detriment—Henry's clear look was less simple. Mistress Captoft thought—I should not have said that; *qui s'excuse, s'accuse;* for she had seen that the straight blue gaze also said—But I would! Unless . . .

"I should wish," Henry said, "that this should not be bruited abroad. I have my son to consider. People talk and exaggerate. I do not wish my son to be told one day that his mother was a madwoman who attacked a priest, before setting fire to herself. If there were an inquiry . . ."

Sudden or violent deaths were inquired into, by a coroner. And unless violence had been seen to be done, or poison suspected, the process depended upon the priest's willingness to bury. If he had doubts he was in duty bound to refuse and await the result of the inquiry.

Father Benedict deserved the high opinion, the high hopes which Mistress Captoft had once entertained for him. He had a subtle mind, which, allied to his unquestioned abilities, would have taken him far, had he been born into another class, or chanced to meet up with a powerful patron. Speaking with difficulty, not only because of his mouth, but because talk demanded breath and to take a full breath still drove a sharp knife somewhere between his ribs and his stomach, he said,

"I understand, Master Tallboys. So far as an inquiry is concerned . . . Even suicide will never be suggested. The act of self-destruction must be deliberate and a person even temporarily deranged cannot take such a decision. Of this"—he touched his mouth—"I shall say nothing. A man of my size, knocked down by so small a woman." He had his pride, too.

Henry had achieved—more easily than he had dared hope—exactly what he had come for.

"There has been another death, too. The friend of my brother. He died, last night, of the lung-rot, in his bed."

"Both shall be buried with proper rites. On Wednesday."

He named the day, not utterly at random. Time was needed, not only for the shrouding and the coffining—for those who could afford it—and the grave-digging, but to allow this inner hurt to heal. As it must. Concealing this hurt from Mattie, who would have fussed, made plasters, made him stay in bed with a bag of hot salt applied to his side, was simply to spare her. And it could only be a bruise, gone inward.

Ironically, the one person in Intake who could have helped Father Benedict at that moment was Young Shep, who lay stiff and cold with the blood of his last violent cough, stiffening on the silk.

Shepherds knew more about bones and bodies than any physician, or any surgeon. Had Father Benedict been a sheep, in Young Shep's care and met with an accident, jostled against a fence or a gateway, and then—showing no outward injury—begun to ail and take little gasping breaths, Young Shep would have taken out his knife, tripped the animal over; once on their backs sheep were helpless, and he would have slit it open, found the bit of broken rib bone which had pierced the spongy mass of the lungs and plucked it out. No such surgery was available to human beings: only amputations.

"About the laying out," Mistress Captoft said, seeing Henry to the door. "The old woman who once served Father Ambrose and now does my heavy wash and scrubs floors, does, I think, earn a few pence by such services. She will certainly be in church this morning; she is one who never misses. Shall I send her?"

"That would be kind," Henry said, thinking that if this

thing were to be secret . . . well, while the old woman busied herself with Young Shep, he must do something about Griselda.

"He shouldn't be up and about," Mistress Captoft said. "I told him. I urged that he should stay in bed. But he is very stubborn."

The old woman took her threepence and muttered, with an air of grievance, "Mistress Captoft said *two*." It mattered to her. She had always been poor, but while Father Ambrose was alive she had been sure of a roof over her head—leaky as it had been. She had been sure of food, too, scanty and plain, but willingly shared, in fact when one portion was better than another, the old priest had insisted that she had it, pointing out that she worked harder than he did. Now all was changed. Father Benedict, having Mistress Captoft to serve him, had not wanted her, and she lived on sufferance with a nephew-by-marriage, whose wife took all her meagre earnings and grudged her every bite. Sixpence would have been very welcome.

"My wife's body has already been dealt with," Henry said. "Are the coffins spoke for?"

"Not yet." It sounded mean—even to Henry himself—to think about what coffins cost; but the four nobles paid out to the doctor had left him very short of ready money. Griselda—mistress of Knight's Acre, a Tallboys by marriage —must have a coffin by right, but surely Young Shep could have gone to his grave wrapped in a shroud, as the poor generally did. But John, who never gave a thought to other people's problems and evidently regarded Henry's pocket as bottomless, had said that he wanted Nick properly buried, coffin and all.

"Shall I tell Sawyer, then, Master?" There might be a ha'penny to be gained in that way. It was a good order.

All the men of Intake were skilled at wood-work and could make spoons, bowls, buckets as well. as keeping houses and outbuildings in repair, but over the years a certain amount of specialisation had developed. Sawyer made coffins, and Gurth made most of the high-soled clogs in which people clumped about in very bad weather.

"I should be much obliged to you," Henry said.

"At the moment of the Elevation," Mistress Captoft said, "I saw you wince with pain. You must have hurt yourself when you fell. Where?"

"It is nothing," Father Benedict said, courageously. "Nothing to worry about."

But she was insistent and by now he was actually longing for the comfort of a hot salt bag to press to the hurt, or one of her willow-bark plasters to draw out the bruise. And some of her pain-killing draughts.

"It was not the fall, my dear. It was the other leg of the stool. It hit me here."

"Let me see."

"There is nothing to see. I looked myself, before I dressed."

But she must see, and he was right: there was nothing to see. Also the site of the pain was ill defined. "Here," he said, and then after a deeper breath, moved his hand slightly higher. "No, here."

An inward bruise. Worse than an outer one; but she knew exactly what to do.

He lay flat in his bed; that position was most comfortable; the warmth of the salt bag was soothing, and so were the opiate drops, with which, for once, Mistress Captoft had been generous.

"You should sleep now," she had said, taking away the cup which had contained not only the drops but a good measure of the best wine.

He drifted up to the very border of sleep and there stayed, floating somewhere high, not in the little Intake room but at a point from which he could see his whole life: the whole world, like a map, with people moving in it, unrolled before him.

A clever boy, not one of the poorest, a second son whose labour was not needed on the family holding. He'd gone to the monks' school at Norwich. The Church offered the best road—perhaps the only one—to an ambitious boy. Not that he had ever been inordinately ambitious. During his studies, and at the time he took orders, the most he had wanted and hoped for was a pleasant, quiet post, something to do with books and a chance of associating with men of like mind. He had never seen himself as a parish priest, possibly the only man in the community who could read. And he knew that he had no talent for dealing with people. An undemanding post on the staff, or in the library of some important cleric would have suited him well. It had never come his way. No particular reason except that there were more candidates than jobs of that kind, and some young men whose families had closer connections with a manorial lord than his had, often benefitted by a slight push from behind: the right word spoken at the right time into the right ear.

Still there was always a market—not highly paid, but steady—for men who could read and write and count without making notches in tally sticks. It was an anomalous position: respected as a priest, regarded as a hireling and sometimes despised—a mere clerk. He had had a variety of jobs—hours spent in cold, ill-lit rooms—by the time he had drifted to Dunwich and became general amanuensis to a prosperous man who not only shipped wool out to the Low Countries, but shipped the finished cloth. There, in the course of his work, he had met Mistress Captoft, acting in a similar capacity for her aged, ailing husband. This situation had come about because she was young, had a smattering of education and a managing way with her; a habit of saying, "I will see to it all." She could ride, she could count, she could manage.

Mutually, and violently attracted, they had been up to a point, scrupulous. Benedict had never cuckolded the old man, Mattie had never committed adultery. Then the old man died, leaving her well provided for, and she had hired a house in Dunwich and invited him to live with her. "I could at least see that you were well fed and your clothes kept in order." The outcome was inevitable.

In Dunwich there were neighbours who thought it queer that a widow, with a decent income, should take a lodger. There was also Benedict's employer, who refused to add a penny to his wage. "You had bed and board here. You made the change; you can't expect me to pay for it. I can get another man, half a dozen of them, on the old terms."

Benedict had an uncle, Father Thomas at Moyidan, and when he knew that his nephew was anxious for a living, in however poor or remote a place, he was willing to help. Intake, poor and remote indeed, fell vacant and Lady Emma Tallboys, then in complete control of Moyidan and of the Intake church and house and living, since another Tallboys lady, long ago, had built the church and endowed it, had accepted Father Thomas's plea.

There was one small falsity. By implication, rather than definite statement, Lady Emma had been given to understand that Father Benedict was recently ordained.

So they had come here; parish priest, with his aunt as housekeeper; and they had been happy. He was no longer the hired clerk, bound to given hours. Mattie had acted as a bulwark between him and the trivialities of parochial work. There were no neighbours.

From his point of view it could hardly have been better.

What about hers?

So splendid, so admirable, so lovable a woman surely deserved something better than this furtive relationship. Sinful? But sinful only because some men, dead to all human feeling, had sat at Westminster, years ago, and decreed that the clergy must be celibate. Before that clerics had had wives, and when the new rule was made, so many had threatened to resign rather than abandon them that some slight mitigation was made; those already married and determined to remain so, could continue to hold their posts and offices. Future candidates for ordination must foreswear the joys of matrimony—and of children. It was a stupid, cruel law, made by stupid men; for what had it resulted in? Every kind of squalid subterfuge, endless pretence, and the dearth of good children.

He thought of Amsterdam. He had never seen the place, though on his employer's behalf he had written letters to, and received letters from it. He had gathered—again rather by implication than by positive evidence—that learning was respected there.

Now, even nearer the verge of drugged sleep, he thought that there were ways of renouncing vows, of getting oneself defrocked; but they took time and had the inevitable concomitants of commotion and scandal. He could do better.

Mattie peeped in and saw him, asleep. Thank God. She tiptoed away, busied herself with the willow-bark plaster and another posset. When the dusk crept in she mended the fire, lighted candles, wondered whether perhaps she had overdone the drowsy drops. Heated another salt bag to place outside the plaster. Sleep, like Time, was a healer, but he needed nourishment. The night and the day had now gone their full round and he'd only taken a few sops. Far less than a full-sized body needed in good health; how much more so a body trying to heal itself from within?

Finally she ventured, carrying the wooden tray; salt bag, plaster, posset and candle.

He was awake.

He said, "My love, I have been thinking. We will go to Amsterdam and get married."

Afterwards she was ashamed of the way she had behaved, priding herself, as she did, upon being level-headed, able to deal . . .

She gave a cry and dropped everything.

"No great harm done," she said. The candle had rolled, but was still burning; the salt bag and the plaster were just as they had been, only the posset was spilled. Setting things to rights gave her time to regain her composure; time to think that perhaps this astounding proposal was due to the drops. They were known to have a curious effect upon some people. Perhaps Benny had been dreaming and was not yet fully conscious of where he was, of who he was. Marriage had never once been mentioned between them even by so little as—If only . . . He was a priest before he became her lover, and inconsistent as it might seem, she had respect for his office. Enough respect, in the early days, to make her feel guilty since she could not distinguish so clearly as he seemed to do, between the law of God and the rule made by some men at Westminster. In fact, her conscience was so uneasy in those early days that once a month, deeply hooded, she would steal out to some church where she was not known, and confess, and ask absolution. In Dunwich there were plenty to choose from, for although the sea had begun its relentless erosion, of the forty-two churches, only one or two had collapsed or been abandoned as dangerous. The sin to which she confessed was fornication. One was under no compulsion to name one's partner in sin. Now and again a conscientious confessor would ask did she mean adultery? So many people seemed to be unable to distinguish between the two. Mistress Captoft could truly say no. She was a widow. And the man? Unmarried. Usually the penance was light, almost derisory. Usually it was accompanied by the order to avoid the occasion for sin—a thing she had no intention of doing—and gradually her good sense saw that such half-confessions were worthless, and had ceased to bother. But she still thought of herself as a pious woman and was careful about most outward forms.

Father Benedict said, "Did I take too much for granted? Should I have *asked,* first?"

"I dared not answer. For fear I had not heard aright. For fear that the drops had made you—not quite yourself."

"I'm myself. And I meant it. As soon as I'm on my feet again."

He was disturbed to discover, as soon as he moved, or took a real breath, that despite everything, the pain was still there.

He could, lying very still, taking little breaths, forget it as they made their plans; all the more urgent and delicious for having been non-existent yesterday.

She would leave her property, two good farms with houses, and her sheep run, in the hands of the honest attorney who now collected her rents. But she would instruct him to sell when the time was right. She would then take passage to Amsterdam on a wool-carrying vessel. Mistress Captoft, intrepid, venturesome woman, making a visit to some relative who had settled there. Exchanges between the Low Countries and England were not confined entirely to wool and cloth, people, and language made traffic to and fro. She would find a suitable house. And she would wait. He would finish here, give up what was called a living—really no living at all—and make for London, where it was easy for a man to lose himself and change his identity. He would allow his tonsure to grow out—priests were for some reason as unwelcome aboard ship as corpses or donkeys. Then as Master Freebody, an apt name and one to which he had some tenuous claim since it had been his mother's maiden name, he would go to Amsterdam. There he and Mistress Captoft would meet and get married.

Joy would be complete. There might even be a child.

Ever since her marriage at the age of fifteen and a half, Mistress Captoft had longed for a baby, completely hers, completely dependent; but Master Captoft had been too old and in her illicit relationship with Benny pregnancy must be guarded against with little bits of lambs' wool soaked with vinegar. Now, though rather late, it was not too late.

Of this hope she did not speak, but as she busied herself, tending the sick man and beginning to sort and pack what she intended to take with her, or what Benny should bring with him, she could at last confess how dull she had found life at Intake. Imagine, she said, the joy of being within reach of shops; of being able to look out of the window and see people in the street; of having neighbours and proper servants from whom nothing need be hidden.

The only cloud on those few halcyon days was Benny's condition. If only the bruise would come out! He insisted upon getting up, kept saying that he was better, but she knew by the way he looked and moved that he was still in pain. The position of it was still uncertain, it shifted, he said, and she continued to regard that as a hopeful sign; but his breathing was still careful and shallow, and once, coming on him unawares, she saw him press his hand against his heart.

Just a pang in another place he said when she asked about it; only momentary. In fact the pain seemed to have taken possession of the whole of his rib-cage. But he would not give in. On Tuesday afternoon Mistress Captoft said, "My dearest, you are not well enough to officiate tomorrow. I will ride to Moyidan and ask your uncle to come and act for you."

"That would be absurd. Tomorrow I shall be better."

Talk reverted to Amsterdam, the golden city of their dreams.

At Knight's Acre things had gone more easily than Henry had dared to hope. The fact that there were two corpses had distracted attention from the one. What remained of Griselda, heavily shrouded, was coffined without question. John's behaviour was a distraction, too. Sawyer and his assistant agreed that if you hadn't known different you'd have thought he was the one who'd lost his wife.

Indefatigable in her efforts to earn an extra penny or so, the old woman, Ethel, cheated of one laying out, turned up again offering her services in another capacity.

"You'll need a sin-eater, Master Tallboys; the more so since they both died so sudden."

It was a very old custom, already dying out in many places, but lingering on amongst the ignorant. It was simple. A man or woman stood at the foot of the bed where the corpse lay and ate a piece of bread which had been sprinkled with salt in the form of a Cross and called upon God, and all those present to witness that by this act the sins of the dead were transferred to the sin-eater. The sin-eater then, as quickly as possible, sought absolution for all sins committed and all sins assumed.

Henry, still, after all these years, influenced by Walter, that complete sceptic, said, "No." He had three good reasons for his refusal; the ritual was barbarous and silly; it cost money, sin-eaters rated their mystical service highly, probably sixpence; and although Griselda had died suddenly and unabsolved, she had always been pious. Certainly striking Father Benedict had, even in Henry's lax view, been an act of impiety, but she was mad, and the mad were not, could not be, held responsible.

John was of another opinion; he was sodden, almost senseless from grief, remorse and sheer sentimentality. Just as he had wanted Nick properly coffined, so he wanted him to go to his grave accompanied by all the ritual, all the panoply.

"Our mother was laid to rest without such antics," Henry

said harshly. He thought of other deaths, too. Walter had not even had a shroud or a Mass; he lay in unhallowed ground, under what was now no more than a weed-covered hump which marked the one side of the entrance to the yard.

"I'd like it done," John said; and in Henry a thought of which he was instantly ashamed, took form: *Then you pay for it!* But he knew that John did not possess a penny. And if sixpence, however hardly spared, grudged, wasted because it could have been put to so much better use, did anything to stem the tears, the lugubrious self-reproaches, it would be well spent.

Old Ethel ate Young Shep's sins whatever they were, took her sixpence, and then, avoiding the path which Sir Godfrey had thoughtfully left when he made his sheep run, the shortest way between church and village, she went to the priest's house, where earlier in the day she had, as usual, done heavy, menial jobs. She wanted to rid herself at the first possible moment of the sins she had, for sixpence, assumed.

"No, you *cannot*," Mistress Captoft said in reply to Ethel's request to see Father Benedict. She had always stood, a firm, bristling barrier between him and parochial claims. "Father Benedict is unwell. As you well know! He is abed now, and I hope asleep. He must gather strength for tomorrow." Ethel went, resentful, away.

Lying flat, a wide mustard plaster covering his lower ribs and part of his stomach, a bag of hot salt cuddled against him and one of Mattie's brews soothing the pain and blurring his mind, Father Benedict did feel better; felt inclined to think that he had made altogether too much of what, after all, was a trivial accident. The fact that his split lips had healed so rapidly was a sure sign of the health of his body. The fact that the pain had shifted, upwards and inwards, towards his heart, he, like Mattie, regarded as a favourable sign. Tomorrow he would be fully restored, and his last thought, as he drifted off into a drugged doze, was of Amsterdam.

"I must tell him something," Henry said, referring to Godfrey.

The strange thing was that the little boy had never once asked about or shown any concern for Griselda, who had loved him, cosseted him, given him little secret meals, and never let him out of her sight. He was intoxicated by his sudden new freedom.

"The truth," Joanna said. "He's bound to know sooner or later and death means nothing to the young." She spoke with the authority of firsthand experience. "You remember, Henry, that day when Robert and I went to church with Griselda and found old Father Ambrose dead. We came racing to tell you, quite excited."

The death of a very old, almost totally blind priest had left no mark at all; but there had been another death which had cut her to the heart; but there again, she had been young and had survived. The fact that she could now say Robert's name in such a casual way, proved that.

She and Robert had been twins in all but fact; born on the same day but to different mothers; the Lady Sybilla's boy baby, prematurely born, frail, unlikely to survive, Tana's daughter, Joanna. They'd shared a cradle. Lady Sybilla, worn and old for child-bearing had been ill, had in fact never fully recovered. Tana had suckled them both until she grew bored with the business.

Joanna and Robert had never spent a day, had a meal apart until Henry's absurd idea of what was fitting—not for himself, but for others—had got the better of him, and he had arranged for his young brother to go and live at Moyidan and share lessons and a tutor with Young Richard; by that time in charge of Henry's brother, who, because he was a priest and also a Master of Arts at Cambridge, was known as Sir Richard.

The parting had been agonising, but what was worse was that Joanna, over a distance of five miles away, had known that Robert was bitterly unhappy. His misery flowed out and she was receptive to it. So one day, unable to bear any more —or to think of Robert bearing any more—she'd set out, dressed like a miniature ploughboy, to rescue him from Young Richard's sly persecution, from the tutor's deliberate, cruel ignoring of facts, and from Sir Richard's complete carelessness of what was going on under his nose.

It had been, in part, a very successful operation. She'd forced her way in, charmed the Bishop of Bywater, who was dining with Sir Richard that day, and got Robert away. But only for a little time. In the blizzard, which had spoiled her whole plan, which was to smuggle Robert into the empty rooms on the other side of the house, Robert, despite all her care, had died in the poor shelter she had found. She'd covered him with leaves and bracken and come home and never said a word. For quite a long time she had avoided the use of Robert's name; but there it was; she'd been young then; the wound had healed and her hungry love had fastened upon Henry. To the young death was something to be survived.

And Henry was thinking: Suppose when I was Godfrey's age, romping through the Long Gallery, the Gardens, the Maze at Beauclaire, my aunt Astallon's palatial home, somebody had come up to me and said, "Your mother is dead." Not a pleasant thought but one to be faced with honesty; it would have meant very little. It was only later when, two against the world, he and his mother had come together, bonded by common misfortune, allies in the fight against poverty and disaster.

"You may well be right," Henry said. And she was; for informed that his mother was dead, that he would never see her again, Godfrey said, "Oh!" and then, with hardly a pause, "Next time you go to market, can I come?"

"We'll see," Henry said, on the whole relieved that Godfrey had made so little fuss; for John was making fuss enough for a dozen. Crying, making self-recriminatory statements, most of which Henry did not understand, and refusing to eat.

That, at least, Henry did understand and, losing patience, he said, "Look. Starving yourself can't help Young Shep and could hurt you. It was lack of food that brought you to such a low state as you were in when you arrived here. You'll make yourself ill again."

"I only wish I could die."

Henry could only wish that John might pull himself together and be, feel, better once the funeral was over.

Mistress Captoft was also concerned about the funeral. She had suggested—sensibly, she thought—that the one committal service might serve for both. Stubborn as rock, Father Benedict said that except in times of pestilence, or war, mass committals to the grave were wrong. In ordinary times each soul must be regarded as individual, coming at birth to house in a separate body, and when the corporal frame broke down, by accident or disease, still a separate entity, to be committed, as such, into the hand of God.

Interments took place after nightfall; Mistress Captoft was glad that at this time of the year dusk came early, so that he need not spend a long evening in waiting about. He yielded to her plea that he should stay in bed until dinnertime, and afterwards he rested. He said he felt much better and well able to perform the double task that awaited him.

He had never been an assiduous parish priest; he had never,

as old Father Ambrose had done, gone visiting houses in the village, or stood after Mass by the door of the church asking about the health of the absentees—a habit which the people, mistaking the old man's motives, had resented—but he was a conscientious man, and thorough, and he missed no word or movement as he performed the two identical ceremonies.

When he came in he seemed none the worse. A heaped fire and a cup of warm, spiced wine awaited him.

"Get me the Parish Book, my love." She brought him the rudimentary parish record, sometimes called the Kin Book because the original purpose in keeping it had been the prevention of incestuous marriages. Father Ambrose's predecessor had been so careless about it that it seemed as though during his twenty years in charge there had been few marriages, fewer baptisms and no interments at all. Father Ambrose had been far more scrupulous and had recorded everything in any way to do with the parish; but as his sight had deteriorated, so had his writing; his last entries were practically illegible, sometimes written across each other.

Father Benedict wrote a clear, scholarly hand and now he entered the date, and recorded that he had buried Griselda Tallboys, wife of Henry Tallboys of Knight's Acre, and Nicholas Shepherd from the same house. He wrote firmly, allowed time for the ink to dry and then closed the book.

"This may be the last entry I shall make," he said. And smiled. After that he ate, with more appetite than he had shown lately, two coddled eggs.

He went, comfortably, to bed; bag of hot salt, mustard plaster, soothing drops. Until they took effect Father Benedict and Mistress Captoft chatted cheerfully. She would leave in two days' time. During the following week he would resign his living, which meant going not to Moyidan, but all the way to Bywater, because the Bishop of Bywater now had complete, if only temporary control of that rich family manor.

Since Father Benedict's uncle, Father Thomas, had lived through all the changes there, Father Benedict and Mistress Captoft had a rough kind of knowledge of what had happened.

Sir James Tallboys, indisputable head of the family, had died, leaving his wife, Lady Emma, in full charge of the land and of the grandson, the heir. Aware that she was carrying about within her a disease incurable, she had sent for a nephew, Sir Richard, brother to Master Tallboys at Knight's Acre. And he'd spent lavishly, lived like a lord, and come to grief. The Bishop had stepped in, settled the debts, taken charge of the manor, and of the heir—now at Eton College. So when Father Benedict resigned his living he would have to approach not a member of the Tallboys family, an ancestress of whom had founded and endowed the church, but the Bishop, who might show some curiosity as to the cause of the resignation.

"And if he does," Mistress Captoft said with some asperity, "it will be the first sign of interest he has evinced in all the time you have been here." She had fiercely resented the Bishop's negligence, having been certain all along that he had only to spend a few minutes in Benny's company to realise how wasted he was in this remote, barbarous place.

However, it was all over now. Stooping over the bed to kiss him good night she thought that one of the first things she would buy in Amsterdam would be a fine big double bed. Always, up to now, they had been careful to preserve all the outward forms of convention: separate rooms, small single beds.

He was dead in the morning. Lying just as she had left him. Afterwards she found comfort in the thought that he had died in his sleep without pain, but that was no comfort at the moment.

Aah, Intake said, when it heard the news, everything go in threes. That was so rooted a superstition that when a man or woman broke something useful, two useless things, even two twigs, would be broken to ward off the curse.

Old Ethel, first with the news and for once the centre of interest, said with spite, "Carrying on like crazy, she is. You'd think she was widowed. Take me. I was with the good old Father more years than you could reckon—and he was took sudden, too. Did I wail and weep? Though I lost my home and my job, too, and was cast on charity." She threw an ungrateful look at the relatives who had given her grudging shelter.

Old Hodgson, a village Elder, and one of those who had reason to be grateful to Mistress Captoft for one of her doses, said,

"Mark you! She *was* related to him."

A woman said, "Only nephew. Take me. My brother over at Muchanger lost three boys at a go. Smallpox. I never acted crazy."

There was much interest, but little sympathy. Mistress Captoft, with money of her own, her fine clothes, her head-dresses, her grey mule, had incurred deadly envy in women who never had a penny of their own. They earned; yes! Work like an ox in the fields, in the yard, in the house; cook, mend, spin, bear and rear children: all unpaid labour. There were good husbands and bad, sons kind or unkind, but one and all they held on to the purse strings. If you were lucky you might get a present now and again, but some man chose it and paid for it, and wanted thanks for it. And if it was stuff for a gown it was always the wrong colour. The women of Intake envied Mistress Captoft; and the men did not like her. Far too masterful, starting with the men she'd hired to add to and improve the priest's house. She'd hired them from outside, a fact which with grand inconsistency, had been resented. Asked to do a bit of building work on the little low house, or to dig enough of the long neglected glebe to make a garden, the men of Intake would have asserted their independence in a variety of ways, choosing their own time, their own pace, demanding extortionate wages. Mistress Captoft brought in hirelings, slaves, landless men who could be harried about. And the jobs had been done in no time.

Curiously, the one person in Intake who came to offer real sympathy, and, more, help, was Master Tallboys, whom Mistress Captoft had never much liked, thinking him cold and aloof and utterly unhelpful to Benny's career as she had once planned it.

But now here he was, grave, stolid, kind. For when in her agony of loss she screamed at him, "If only you had kept your mad wife under control, none of this . . .'' he showed nothing but a desire to help. He'd ride to Moyidan, he said, and tell Father Thomas and ask him to come and conduct the funeral; he'd send a message to Sawyer about the coffin; he'd see to everything.

And she needed support now. Proud and independent as she might appear to be, she had never, so far in her life, faced any serious challenge; fond parents; doting old husband; a period when, if a woman could be said to have a career, she had had one; after that Benny and all the little subterfuges, the good management, the self-control upon which she had prided herself. Always, somewhere in the background, a man. Now nobody.

A strong stone tower in collapse left more of a ruin than a wattle hut, Henry reflected. And Mistress Captoft's collapse was absolute.

There was not a place in the little house which had not a fresh blow to strike as soon as she entered: here he sat at his books; here I cooked his meals; in this room, my bedchamber, he came to me; in the other he died. And perhaps most painful of all, the little narrow room where the madwoman had struck the lethal blow and in which now lay, so carefully and hopefully packed, what she had planned to take with her to Amsterdam; the silver cups and plates, wadded with the fine linen in a leather bag. More linen and a few clothes bundled into a kind of sausage, enclosed in sailcloth. Meant for Amsterdam! Unbearable.

"And I do not know where to go," she said to Henry.

"I always understood that you owned property, Mistress Captoft."

"So I do. But leased. And I could not live . . ." The two farms with houses which her kind old husband had bequeathed her were, if anything, more isolated than Intake; and the sheep run had no proper house at all.

"Well," Henry said in his practical way, "there is no immediate hurry. If I remember rightly it takes a little time to instal a new priest. And there are houses for sale or hire in Baildon. I have to go to market next week. Would you like me to look around?"

"I don't know. I cannot decide, or plan. I just do not know." All her talent for management, her ability to organise had gone, no more substantial than the whipped cream on top of a custard pie.

Full responsibility for her Henry was prepared to shuffle off. After all, Father Thomas at Moyidan had been Father Benedict's uncle, and Mistress Captoft had been Father Benedict's aunt; so they were, if only by marriage, related, and families must hold together.

As he was holding to John, irritation weaving its way through concern. There was an expression—nursing one's grief—and that was exactly what John was doing; sitting about, hands idle, eyes vacant, taking a bite of this, a bite of that, never a whole meal, though Joanna was doing her best.

It was true that he must go to market on the Wednesday; he had two pigs ready for slaughter; one for sale; one for house use.

"Come with me, John. It'd take you out of yourself."

Nothing could do that. All very well for Henry. What had he lost? A scold; a shrew, a madwoman. Whereas I . . .

"I couldn't," John said, tears welling up again. "Just the sight of people, alive while Nick is . . ." He went, choking and stumbling out of the kitchen.

Godfrey said, "You promised, Father, that next time you went to market, you'd take me."

Rasped by his failure with John, Henry said, "I made no such promise. You're old enough now to get things straight." That was the way Walter had talked to him; and what was wrong with it? Yet he felt compunction, looking at his son's wide blue eyes, hurt.

I must not take out on this poor little boy, this motherless little boy, my exasperation with these two people who cry so easily.

"Of course you can come," he said.

Baildon market was really three: the big general market, a wide space dominated by the church and the inn; the beast market with the shambles adjoining it; and, at a little distance, the horse market. In the big market Henry halted to let Godfrey out of the waggon. As he did so he had a sharp memory of the days when his nephew, Richard of Moyidan, had come to market with him. There'd been a time, just after the Church took possession of Moyidan, when the boy had been sadly neglected; his loving grandmother dead, his idiot parents dead, his unofficial guardian, Sir Richard, gone back to London. Henry had taken him in, against Griselda's loud protests and much against Joanna's wishes. And he'd been badly rewarded! So now, presenting his son with a farthing, he said solemnly,

"This is for you to spend. You can buy yourself a cake or pie. You can *look* at things, but you are not to touch. Do you understand me? You can have whatever your farthing will buy, and nothing else." Young Richard had gone around pilfering for quite a long time before he was caught, thus disgracing the family name. "I'll pick you up by the church," Henry said, and drove on to sell his pig.

On his way he passed what he and Joanna always referred to as the rubbish stall, kept by a man with so glib a tongue that Joanna once said, "He'd sell you Knight's Acre, Henry, if you stood there long enough." Amongst the jumble of broken or inadequately mended things there was sometimes an article of which a handy man like Henry could make use, and Henry decided that on his way back from the beast market, he'd see what was on offer.

"Is that a lute?" His mother had had one and played it beautifully; she'd tried to teach all her children, only John had taken to it, and Sybilla's lute had gone with him when he left home.

"Right you are, sir! Beautiful thing and in splendid condition. Not a broken string. Un-tuned of course. I have no ear. Try it, sir." The battle was half won if a customer could be persuaded to handle any article. He pushed the lute into Henry's hand and turned to persuade a woman that a cooking pot, properly tinkered, was as good as, even better than, a new one. "Where it's mended it's thicker, you see. Last a lifetime."

To Henry, never enamoured of any lute, this one was anything but beautiful; shabby, chipped and dirty. But with a clumsy stroke of his thumb he assured himself that some sound could be produced and he thought of John, who had been obliged to sell his own beloved instrument somewhere on that long hungry journey home. A lute might cheer him a bit, rouse a spark of interest.

"How much?"

"Well, to anybody else, it'd be seven shillings, sir. But I can see you've taken a fancy to it, and I like to see a thing like that go where it'll be appreciated. Say three, and at that I'm robbing myself."

Most customers enjoyed a haggle. Henry, despite his perpetual lack of money and need to exercise the utmost thrift, thought haggling undignified. The price was extortionate, but he paid.

Godfrey was waiting. As he clambered into the waggon, Henry asked, "Did you enjoy yourself?"

"Oh yes. Except for the dog. It danced, but the man was *rough* to it. I didn't like that. So when he came round with his cap I didn't put my farthing—you did say it was a farthing?—in."

Rough was about the most derogatory word in Godfrey's vocabulary. Drilled into him by Griselda, who, so far as her son was concerned, had only two standards of behaviour, rough and otherwise.

"So what did you spend it on?"

"I bought something for you, Father. I don't know what it is, but the woman said it was nice. And more than a farthing, but I was a pretty little boy and could have it."

Shyly he produced an orange.

Such a luxury that Henry had not been within arm's reach of one since, at about the age his own son was now, he had left Beauclaire, that rich place where luxury was commonplace. Oranges came from Spain. Henry could remember his father saying that there they were common as apples in England and grew on peculiar trees which bore sweet-scented flowers and golden fruit at the same time. In England oranges were rare and very costly because picked when unripe and hard they shrivelled; picked ripe and luscious, unless the ship that carried them had a favourable passage, the wind behind her all the way, they rotted. Not a cargo to appeal to the ordinary ship's captain who preferred to carry the oranges in preserved form. Rendered incorruptible, because saturated with sugar, this concoction was an even more costly luxury. But Henry had known it, and short of a miracle, his son never would.

Henry's thought teetered. Beauclaire, so rich and splendid, had, despite all his uncle's endeavours to be neutral in the war between York and Lancaster, been utterly destroyed; whereas Knight's Acre, bare, humble, poor, had survived.

One could think a lot in almost no time at all and Godfrey had not been aware of any lapse.

"The woman said it was nice to eat."

"No doubt about that. We'll share it with Joanna." Then a rush of feeling came over him. That his son should have spent his poor farthing . . .

"You're my boy," he said.

Godfrey said, in exactly the manner with which he had accepted the news of his mother's death,

"I always was. Wasn't I?"

John recoiled from the lute.

"As though I could . . ." Another proof of Henry's complete lack of understanding.

Disappointed, but now skilled in concealing any emotion, Henry said, "It'll serve as firewood!" Inside him something cried—Three shillings for what could be gathered, for nothing, at the wood's edge.

But though John had repudiated it, he kept looking at the lute. Poor thing; derelict, like me! It had once been beautiful; not unlike the one he had been obliged to sell. It had been inlaid, either with silver or mother-of-pearl; ill used, exposed to the damp, it had lost most of its decoration; but it still had its strings. Finally he put out a hand, reluctantly, tentatively, and retrieved the poor thing.

Wrecks, both of us, he thought, but still . . .

The time between supper and bed-time he spent in cleaning and retuning it. Under the dirt even some bits of the decorative inlay came up shining. A good lute, full bodied. He thought of all those songs that Nick had made; the words conveyed by word of mouth, the tunes translated from the rather thin, though pleasing sound that a hazelwood pipe could produce, into lute music.

Nick would never make another song; but those he had made were all there, stored away in John's memory.

And while John remembered, played and sang them, passed them on, so that even grooms whistled them as they tended to horses, and young gallants who could sing or strum a little, used them for serenading—then something of Nick would remain. All suddenly his shattered life began to mend, acquired aim and purpose.

For a similar restoration, Mistress Captoft had to wait a little, suffering meanwhile another blow. Master Tallboys had been mistaken in saying that there was no hurry, that it took some time to instal a new priest. Father Thomas could see very plainly that while this living remained vacant he would be expected to be at least partly responsible for it; and since Moyidan was his parish and hardly a day passed without some servant of the Bishop coming to see that all was in order there, he was in a good position to expedite matters. A word in the right ear . . .

Henry was in his sheep-fold, gloomily unloading the hay which would soon be needed to keep this wretched flock alive through the winter. His father's decision, taken years ago, to rear sheep at all had been a mistake—Walter, never yet proved wrong, had said Intake was no place for sheep; and his own decision to be his own shepherd had been an even worse mistake.

And there, at the door of the priest's house, was Mistress Captoft, lying in wait for him. Oh, God give me patience! I've only just got John on the mend. And she is none of mine. But in the time that it took for him to make the hay enclosure safe against greedy sheep who would have gobbled it down in a day and all swollen up as though they were pregnant, and to lead the horse and waggon on to the trail and close the gate of the fold, he had been given, if not patience, an inspiration. John had stopped mourning as soon as he had something to do—something acceptable—and plainly what this poor grieving woman needed was employment.

"I was coming to see you, Mistress Captoft. To ask a favour. Very shortly I must kill a pig and I am ignorant of how to preserve and cure pig meat. I wondered whether you would be so kind as to come and give advice. There would be no heaving and hauling. I could do all that. Joanna and I simply need guidance."

Something within Mistress Captoft sprang to life. She knew all that there was to know about casking and curing and smoking, though she had never actually seen a pig killed. In her father's house, and in her husband's when it was pig-killing time she'd always shut herself away or taken a walk. Pigs did squeal so, with an almost human sound. Once it was dead it was meat and though she had never been obliged to dabble her hands in brine or expose herself to the smoke in the chimney where hams and sides of bacon were cured, she knew all about the processes.

"Have you salt, Master Tallboys? Saltpetre? Honey?"

"Salt, yes. For the other things I cannot answer."

Helpless man, with nobody in charge of his kitchen but a mere child.

"I think," Mistress Captoft said, "that I had better come, straightway and take stock."

She was needed again; active again.

Joanna watched, with hatred, the gradual encroachment. She was not jealous, female to female; Mistress Captoft was far too old; well over thirty and fat. And Henry's manner towards her was never more than polite. But inch by inch she was edging Joanna out of the position which she had hoped would have been strong enough to save her from any more talk about going to Stordford. For a few days they worked together, Mistress Captoft cheerful, Joanna sullen. A newly killed pig meant some meat, at least, fresh roasted on the spit; naturally Mistress Captoft must be asked to share it. And baking day came round. Joanna did not take kindly to the idea that every loaf should be marked with a Cross. "They rise better," Mistress Captoft said. And she'd brought from her home a little packet of spice and dried fruit, and gently suggested that *one* loaf, given this stuff, and some melted butter would make a cake loaf. Much enjoyed.

The sharpest blow fell when Joanna said, in her joking way, "Henry, unless we take care, she will move in."

"I have already suggested it. The new priest will be here any day now, and she has as yet made no arrangements."

Rage almost choked the girl. But she must not, would not behave like Griselda. Lest her face should betray her she turned quickly to the hearth and prodded the sausages in the pan. She did so with exaggerated gentleness, again not to resemble Griselda, who when angered banged things about.

Unaware of the feeling he had roused, Henry said, "The rooms on the other side will hardly accommodate all her furniture, but it is only a stop-gap arrangement. Some of her things can stand in our hall."

But those rooms are mine! I only lent them to John and Young Shep because Griselda said she'd burn this house down sooner than take in two vagabonds with the lung-rot. You had no right!

It was a slight shock to discover that it was possible to be so angry with the person you loved. And that simply because he was doing a kindness. Instantly penitent, she said, "Or, if Mistress Captoft preferred, we could move some of those divans into the hall."

"No! I wouldn't want . . . I mean they would be quite unsuitable there."

Planning for Amsterdam, Mistress Captoft had been ready to abandon her furniture since the cost of transport and shipping would be so vast. She'd thought, quite happily, how comfortable and well furnished the in-coming priest would find the little house. But she had had Benny then and material things had mattered less. Now they mattered a great deal, so when Henry's waggon made its last creaking journey between the two houses all that remained in the empty one was what Mistress Captoft had found there, old Father Ambrose's poor stuff, which she had banished to a shed. However, taking a last look round, she made a kindly resolution. If the new priest—Father Matthew—proved to be a pleasant person, she would bring back, as gifts, certain things to make the place more habitable. Then he would be grateful. And he would be grateful, too, when she requested a Mass every day for a year for the benefit of Benny's soul. She knew how totally inadequate the stipend was. She would be generous in other ways later on.

Her court cupboard, though not so beautifully carved as the one Walter had managed to find for Sybilla, looked well in the Knight's Acre hall, and her well-padded settle made the one already there look small and shabby. She unpacked her silver and distributed it between both cupboards. For the first time in its life the hall lost its half-empty, ill-furnished look.

Joanna had half hoped that since the rooms across the yard had their own kitchen, inconveniently as it was placed, Mistress Captoft would busy herself there and cease to meddle. It was a vain hope. Mistress Captoft was a born meddler, and had a convivial nature, long denied outlet. She was in and out all day, every day, generally with an excuse to which no reasonable person could take objection. Her own furniture must be dusted regularly, and polished occasionally; her silver must be kept bright. She included Henry's furniture in her ministrations. She came bearing gifts; she'd made some of the honey cakes of which she knew Godfrey was so fond; she'd just opened a barrel of pickled herrings which, though small, was more than she could possibly eat by herself; she had some wine, better than average, which she thought she must share.

As the weather grew colder the question of fires arose. The only hearth across the yard was in the kitchen; and a brazier though it gave a good steady heat wasn't the same as a fire, was it? And for the sake of the furniture and the fabric of the hall itself, it was advisable to have a fire there at least once a week.

If Henry ever thought her intrusive or meddlesome, he gave no sign; he was always courteous. Poor woman, she was lonely. Godfrey was always pleased to see her, and John was almost effusively welcoming. He said how pleasant it was to try a tune with a listener who could tell a lyric from a dirge. Actually he was employing his winning ways with women with a sharp eye to self-interest. He intended to make his second assault on the wider world the moment the weather improved with the coming of Spring, and he needed money to start off with. If Henry couldn't, or wouldn't help, Mistress Captoft might. She was obviously well-to-do and open-handed.

Only Joanna remained unfriendly, sullen—though she was glad enough, Mistress Captoft noticed, to hand over the making and mending. And Mistress Captoft was glad to do it, for she had received another little shock from which her mind must be diverted.

Father Matthew had arrived and she had disliked him at first sight. She had not, of course, ever imagined that Benny's successor should be even half worthy; but this man was an oaf. Ill-spoken, mannerless.

Mistress Captoft had suddenly remembered that a mild day in early November was the ideal time for moving plants. Accompanied by Godfrey, who claimed that he could push the flat, two-wheeled, long-handled barrow and that he could also dig, she'd gone up to the empty house to fetch away the best of the things which she had cherished over the years. She had four rose trees which because they had been pruned and fed on the grey mule's dung, were in far better condition than the six at Knight's Acre, lately sadly neglected. She had the usual garden bushes, rosemary, lavender, southernwood, barberry; and also, because she had lived in Dunwich, a port in close contact with the Continent, a number of imported, rather rare bulbous plants.

They must all be lifted and transplanted, because, though Henry regarded the present arrangement as a stop-gap measure, Mistress Captoft did not. She had been so eager to get away from Intake, but now it was different; the place where Benny had spent his last, happy days, and, though he was not an outdoor man, had often lifted his eyes from his books to comment on the beauty of Layer Wood as the changing seasons touched it; and the place where he lay buried. Lifting the rosemary bush she thought of breaking off a piece and placing it on his grave. Because rosemary remained not only green but fragrant even in winter it had come to be regarded as the symbol of remembrance.

A coarse voice said, "Who're you? And what d'you think you're doing?"

Mistress Captoft straightened up. She was a woman who had always been, and would always be, acutely conscious of her appearance; at the same time sensible enough to match clothes to the occasion. This, being a workaday occasion, she wore, not a head-dress, but a plain linen hood and her skirts were hitched up a good six inches above the stout shoes needed for digging.

"I am Mistress Captoft. I am removing a few plants. My own. And you are Father Matthew." She managed to poise those words between question and statement, while her glance reminded him that he had not shaved for two days.

He had no tact at all. "If they're yours"—he indicated the plants, and somehow managed to sound as though he doubted her word—"then you lived here. Was it always the way it is now?"

"In what way?"

"So bare." And that he managed to make sound as an accusation; as though she had stripped it.

"I had my own furniture," she said crisply. "And indeed you find the place in far better fettle than I did on my arrival. There was not even an oven, then."

She was angry with him because his unmannerliness had made her unmannerly. Naturally she had a high standard of what behaviour to priests should be. But then such an oaf had no right to be a priest at all.

This hasty decision was justified by the way he said Mass, mispronouncing several words. The thought of him in Benny's place was so hurtful that she decided to attend Nettleton church in future, and it was to the priest there that she entrusted the duty of saying a Mass each day for a year.

With her plants transferred, she was ready to throw herself into preparations for Christmas. It could not be merry this year with bereavements so recent, but Joanna learned with some surprise, that Christmas must not go unmarked; there must be a bag-pudding, and something called mincemeat, things she had never seen and knew nothing about. No matter, Mistress Captoft would see to it all. And just as she had suggested the lighting of the fire in the hall now and then, so she now suggested that Henry should coop and fatten a goose. She knew—and possessed—just the wine that went best with goose. The modest feast, it was tacitly assumed, would be communal.

It was difficult for Joanna to have a word with Henry alone these days. But the chance came. Godfrey in bed, Mistress Captoft gone to her own place, escorted by John, who had taken his lute, which meant that he would be away for a while.

Joanna went straight to the point.

"Henry, this is something I have been wanting to say. That day in the wood . . ." Never before referred to, and now hastily skirted around. Cool; quick. "You said that *some* of my money had been placed with Sir Barnabas Grey at Stordford, but that there was more to come. I said I wanted it used *here*. You refused. Please, Henry, think again."

"I said what I meant, Joanna. I hold to it."

"Then you would rather be beholden to *her* than to *me?*"

"It has always been my wish, my intention, to be beholden to nobody."

"You drink her wine."

"Very little. John is the one with the ready mouth. Set against it, I stable and feed her mule."

"You will eat her pudding and her mincemeat."

"And she will eat our goose."

"But, Henry, surely you see . . ." She changed, gave one of those closely observed, rather cruel imitations. "Oh, Master Tallboys, you must just *taste* this wine. Master Tallboys, my saffron cakes turned out *exceptionally* well. Master Tallboys, I have a self-winding spit, too wide for my one hearth, but it would just fit . . ." She dropped the mimicry, which had

73

not been exaggerated, and said in her own voice, and almost fiercely,

"Is that how it is to be forever? When your jerkin is past mending, she'll buy cloth and make you a new one. Godfrey will outgrow his clothes, she will provide. Can your pride bear it? Even if her mule had five meals a day?"

That was what she hated, even more virulently than the meddling, the subtle reduction of Henry.

"It will not come to that, dar—— Joanna. It just happens that we are at low ebb now. The tide must turn."

"But why wait? With my money there to be used? Why is it all right for Sir Barnabas Grey to use some of my money and not for you to use the rest?"

"There is a world of difference. You see, it is a question of *how* the money is used; what return it will bring. I might take your money, buy stock that'd sicken, clear a field that took three years to come to fertility. Then where should we be? As I understand it, Sir Barnabas is a man of business. He would not put the money entrusted to him into a farm, only just holding its own. And nor will I."

"Not just *a* farm, Henry. It is my *home*."

A true, perfectly natural thing to say, but that was not the way he wished her to think. His desire to get her away, into a different life, was genuine and of long standing.

"It is your home, in that you were born here. And of course you will always be sure of a welcome." For some reason that sounded pompous. He hurried on: "But it isn't suitable. First, working like a farmhand, now like a servant. I want you at least to see, to try, something different."

"Like Stordford?"

"Yes."

The matter had never been long absent from his mind, and now that Mistress Captoft seemed to have settled in and certainly seemed prepared to stay until after Christmas, he had given his own circumstances some thought. He could manage, he thought, with the cheapest possible kind of kitchen labour, possibly an orphan girl, just glad of a home. To her Mistress Captoft would gladly give such elementary instruction as was necessary and all would be well. Henry had never done any cooking, had only seen it done and was inclined to underestimate the skill required.

Joanna closed her eyes for a second; the lashes, some shades darker than her hair, lay in crescents against the warm pallor of her cheeks. Pretty, pretty little thing, Henry thought; she must not be wasted here!

She was trying to visualise what her next remark would mean in terms of homesickness and misery. She was deliberately inviting the kind of seeing forward, or seeing into the distance which had afflicted her sometimes in the past. Now nothing came; she'd lost that kind of eye. All she could see was the immediate situation; Mistress Captoft encroaching, inch by inch; Henry's pride and independence being worn away; and herself reduced to servant status. There was a world of difference between doing hard, even rough and dirty work, in your own place, of your own choice, and being ordered about, even when the orderer was punctilious about saying, "my dear."

Her eyes, which could change so rapidly through many shades of blue and blue-green, were bright aquamarine when she opened them and said,

"Very well then, Henry. I will go. On certain conditions."

"Well?" He was eager. Willing to comply.

"First, three years, not the four you mentioned."

He was certain that six months would suffice. Six months of the kind of life he could remember his aunt Astallon's ladies living at Beauclaire, and she'd forget all about Knight's Acre.

"I agree."

"And what remains of my money to come here and be used."

"Joanna, I have tried to explain. It would not be right. No, to that I cannot agree."

Stubbornness was a recognised Tallboys characteristic. Sir Godfrey amiable—some said stupid—had had his full share; the Lady Sybilla and Tana had both been resolute characters.

Deadlock across the kitchen table.

Joanna said, "Then I must get John to marry me and use my money. He would, you know!"

With a jolt everything inside Henry, heart, breath, came to a standstill; and then with another jolt went on again. John would!

Ever since the shabby old lute had restored him to life John had been talking about setting out again in the Spring, and the absolute necessity of having some money to start out with. Unless a musician, however good, had something to fall back upon, so that he could pick and choose, he ended on market squares or village greens, singing, literally, for his supper. He knew, he'd seen it happen. He'd aimed such remarks about equally between his brother and Mistress Captoft and neither had responded immediately. Henry had thought that he would do what he could, when the time came and Mistress Captoft had realised that to make any promise prematurely would be unwise. While he was still unsure John would continue to be attentive, escort her across the yard and stay for a while, mitigating the loneliness.

"Yes; he *would*," Henry said almost viciously. "He'd take whatever was yours that he could get his hands on and then leave you—like Young Shep left his wife; shamed and deserted. You don't know what you're talking about."

"I know enough to know that that would suit me splendidly! He's not a person I should wish to live with."

She spoke lightly but she was watching Henry with narrowed, hard eyes. Behind them some compunction stirred; poor Henry, to be so forced! But it was for his own good.

Henry thought: She's capable of it! There had always been a wild, reckless streak in Tana. And John, of course, wouldn't hesitate for an instant.

A feeling of helplessness added itself to his anger. He could do nothing; she was not his ward; she was not a member of the family of which he was the head. If she put this preposterous suggestion to John . . . Henry was not accustomed to feeling helpless. Within the limits imposed by lack of money he'd always been master in his small world. True, Griselda had nagged and scolded, but he'd soon learned to ignore what was a mere fretful noise. Nothing vital; nothing like this.

"God damn it all! You leave me no choice! All right. Sooner than see you ruin your life, I'll take what money the Bishop still holds for you, and use it here. Putting what is due to you away, as I put Robert's."

"There is one other thing," she said.

Somebody had spilt a little water on the table and she dabbled her finger in it, making a pattern. Watching, Henry thought how strange it was that neither work out of doors nor indoors had affected her hands at all: slim, smooth, cream-coloured. Beautiful hands. Her mother's hands.

Stop that!

"Well?"

"Nothing difficult. Just a promise. *If* I go to Stordford, for three years and learn *all* there is to be learned, and behave like a *saint;* and if you haven't found someone you prefer—and I haven't either—you'll marry me. At least, *think* about it. Seriously."

Nothing to be lost by promising that. The bargain with Sir Barnabas and his lady—made through the Bishop of

Bywater—included the arrangement for a *suitable* marriage. And just as Henry visualised Joanna being one of the gay, butterfly ladies of Beauclaire, so he imagined suitors, very much like the young knight who, during Sir Godfrey's absence, had visited Knight's Acre from time to time. Young, handsome, rich. Once installed at Stordford, she'd forget Knight's Acre and presently, wooed by somebody young, handsome, rich . . . Nevertheless, something about that wild threat to marry John had rung a warning bell.

"In return for that," he said, "I must exact a promise, too. Nobody expects you to behave like a saint, but you are not to do anything secret, try no madcap scheme or trick."

"How could I? You have my promise, Henry, and I have yours. I regard it as betrothal. Tom Robinson once told me about betrothals. As near as nothing to marriages, he said, unless one or the other didn't agree when the time came."

Three years of exile; but she'd got what she wanted. Her mother had borne a longer servitude; but nobody knew that.

Mistress Captoft, asked to help and advise in this new direction, was in her element; sensible enough to know that she was herself out of date in the matter of fashion. Of course the girl must have some new clothes, but the minimum; Lady Grey would know and decide what was needed apart from two decent dresses, one of woollen cloth, one of velvet; and, of course, a hooded cloak.

Mistress Captoft was, secretly, so delighted to know that the unfriendly girl was about to depart that if required she would have stitched sailcloth.

Joanna's going would not only remove something hostile, it would leave a bedchamber vacant. Mistress Captoft would not admit it, even to herself, but she never felt comfortable, really comfortable in the beautiful silk-hung rooms which, only so short a time ago, had seemed like a haven of refuge. She knew and John constantly reminded her that Young Shep had died in the bedchamber; that meant nothing to her; it would indeed be very difficult to find a house, or part of a house in which somebody had not died. It was just she felt out of place, uneasy, as though—this was the way she expressed it to herself—as though her skin didn't fit. Once— and it was a moment she remembered with self-shame, she'd heard something, a kind of tap and a fumbling at one of the windows . . . Just a spray of ivy, moved by the wind, she realised, but not before she had cried out, sharply, "Who's there?" She looked forward to moving into the main house, and to being in full control.

Stitching away, she said, "I really think, my dear, that you should master *plain* sewing. Far more exacting forms of needlework will be expected of you at Stordford."

"Embroidery!" Joanna said with supreme contempt: hurtful to a woman who prided herself on her skill in that art.

"It is one of the things that a lady needs to know," Mistress Captoft said tartly.

"I have no need to learn how to be a lady. My mother was a lady of Spain."

A plain statement of fact, innocent of malice, yet it hurt, too. Annoyance deepened the colour in Mistress Captoft's cheeks. She was herself a member of the emergent middle class, daughter of a prosperous merchant, wife to another. In manners and style of living they were as good as any in the land, in learning and in morals superior to those who regarded themselves as more well bred. To have such a remark made to her by an unlettered girl who could not even sew a seam! And yet, and yet . . . It was something, Mistress Captoft reflected, about the way the girl held her head.

"Unfortunately, she did not live long enough for you to benefit either by her precept or her example." That should even the score.

His Grace of Bywater had a liking for Henry Tallboys, with whom he had come in contact over the business of Moyidan's young heir, who, by some extraordinary oversight, a failure in communications, had, in the winter after the Church had assumed control of the estate, suffered a little privation; grossly exaggerated by the boy himself. He'd gone running to his Uncle Henry and Henry had offered to be responsible for him, with no profit to himself. The fact that the boy was a born liar was proved later, when he'd been caught stealing in the market and given as his excuse that he was hungry. A boy born to make trouble, born discontented; as he had vilified the Bishop when he lived at Moyidan, and his Uncle Henry when he lived at Knight's Acre, now he was vilifying Eton, where—at some little trouble to himself—the Bishop had secured him a place.

As proof of his approval, the Bishop had Henry admitted immediately and greeted him affably.

"This is most timely, Master Tallboys. I was about to ask you to call upon me. I have been away for a while, and a letter from Lady Grey awaited me here. She and her husband are anxious about the child."

"Naturally, my lord." Henry had no intention of explaining the delay. It would sound absurd to say that Joanna had defied him. "I have been unable to give my full attention to the business." He could have listed the distractions, spoken of Griselda's death; but he wanted no formal expressions of sympathy for a grief that was no grief. "She is ready to go now and I think it would be well if she could be there by Christmas."

"An excellent time. She will enjoy the merry-making."

Henry had thought of that, too.

It was twenty years since he with his mother, with Richard and Margaret, and John, a baby in arms, and, of course, Walter, had set out from Beauclaire, just missing the Christmas festivities; but he remembered the Christmas before that. Everything topsy-turvy, the Lord of Misrule in control for the Twelve Days, enormous feasts and open house for all. At such a time, he thought, a stranger would not feel strange, and by the time the season was over, Joanna would have settled.

Now, he thought, in order to keep his bargain—and he'd never failed yet in that respect—he must raise the question of the rest of Joanna's dowry. Hateful. Not begging exactly, since he intended to make the money work, but something that went against the grain. His father, Sir Godfrey, had always had a curious, almost ambivalent attitude towards money; it was necessary, something to be pursued at the risk of life and limb, once obtained—by honourable means—to be spent, given away, lent. As a result he had stumbled from crisis to crisis and died poor. Henry had, of sheer necessity, taken a more practical view of money, but he never haggled even on the market. (Unknown to him, that attitude—take it or leave it—had on occasions served him well.)

Now he was spared. The Bishop's hands moved amongst his papers. On one smooth plump finger he wore the amethyst of his office; on the other, the great glowing red ruby which, out of all Tana's hoard, his covetous and knowledgeable eye had fixed upon. Now he had it; fair commission for his efforts.

"Then that is settled," he said. "But I needed to talk to you, Master Tallboys, about the child's inheritance. You entrusted me with her jewel hoard and of some I disposed easily. As you were informed, wealth enough to secure her a place in Sir Barnabas Grey's family and a modest, but adequate dowry. Some of the stones I held in reserve. As you know, these are troublous times, everything in a state of flux. But the market will recover and my agent in London will be the first to take advantage of it."

"Nothing here and now?"

"I am afraid not."

"That's all right, then," Henry said. He looked, the Bishop observed, as though he had just received good, not bad, news. Very odd.

The jewelled fingers moved again amongst the heaped, but orderly papers.

"I have here another letter which may interest you. The boy, your nephew. He has written before, always the same strain. He is ill housed, ill fed, ill treated." His Grace listed Young Richard's grievances in a light, mocking voice, inviting Henry's amusement. Not instantly forthcoming. Inside Henry the sense of family responsibility moved a little. He'd never really liked Young Richard, knew him to be dishonest and a liar; but there were excuses, he'd been so spoiled from the first, and then suddenly no longer spoiled.

"Is there any truth in it?"

"None at all," His Grace said with conviction. "The demand for places in Eton College is now so high that the one schoolroom will presently no longer serve. Men of substance—and rank—Master Tallboys, are not over-anxious to have their sons starved! And certainly, I perceive a great improvement in his writing."

Never once had Joanna had cause to doubt Henry's word; but now suddenly she did. He'd been from the first so averse to using her money, except for what he so wrongly thought was to her advantage, that she believed that, forced to it, he had concocted this tale about the rest of her mother's jewels being unsaleable. She could not hold that against him; he was fiercely independent, he was pig-headed, he was Henry, altogether admirable in all his works and ways. But he was wrong to think she could be so easily fooled.

Between himself and unwanted visitors the Bishop had the great man's usual defences: servants, secretaries, chaplains, all skilled in the art of diversion, and not a few of them open to bribery.

Joanna had seen only one building—except for the church at Baildon—more imposing than Knight's Acre, and that was Moyidan; years ago. There she had not accepted a rebuff; nor did she here.

"Tell His Grace that I am Joanna Serriff. He will understand. He will see me." Told to wait, she said, "No, I cannot wait. The days are short now." As though in contradiction of this statement she sat down and seemed prepared to wait forever. There was some scurrying about and then she was admitted into the presence.

The Bishop had seen her once before, at Moyidan, where he had been dining with Sir Richard, when dressed like a little ploughboy, she'd burst in, demanding to see Robert. Her curtsey, and when she flung back her hood, her hair and face, had revealed her sex and His Grace of Bywater had thought then—Give her ten years and she'll be a beauty.

It had taken a shorter time. To her, flowering had come early. Vaguely, His Grace remembered some mention of her foreign origin. Spanish? Yes. Spanish. And he remembered his pilgrimage to Rome. In the South girls ripened early; nubile at eleven, married, often mothers at twelve. He had always conducted his secret affairs with the utmost discretion, but he had great knowledge of, was a specialist in the subject of women, and as he greeted her with great cordiality two saddening thoughts flashed through his mind. He, alas, was growing old; and early ripening of beauty all too often meant early decline.

Joanna gave her best curtsey, combining it with a down-sweep of long lashes. Her eyelids, her lips, were luminous with youth. An attraction older women strove—sometimes without success—to recover by the use of salves. When she lifted the lashes, her eyes, blue as cornflowers, were fixed on him in a look of appeal.

"My lord, I was obliged to come to you. Only you can help me."

"You did rightly. Rest assured that I shall do all that is possible. Sit here. Loosen your cloak. This room is warm."

His mind worked quickly. She had come about the rest of the jewels; and he must explain again about the sluggish market. With the Yorkist cause completely triumphant most of those who had supported the Lancastrian side had lost their lands. Lancastrian ladies had sold their ornaments in order to buy necessities; and though there still was, and would always be, a demand for stones of exceptional quality, such as Lady Serriff's diamonds and emeralds, there was a glut of more mediocre jewels.

And yes, he had been right. That well-shaped head, so elegantly well poised on the slender neck; the way the hair grew from the forehead. The hair itself, such a warm brown as to be almost russet, lending warmth to what might have been a rather cold and austere beauty. Nose, perhaps a trifle high at the bridge. As she aged she would probably become sharp-featured. In the meantime, delectable.

"It is about my mother's jewels—the rest of them. Henry said they couldn't be sold."

By accident or intent her glance shifted to the great ruby. She recognised it. She and Robert, finding the hoard in the long-empty rooms had pried the pretty pebbles loose and used them in their childish games. They had agreed that the big red one was best of all. It had been the prize pebble.

Once more the Bishop explained.

Joanna said, "Oh. Then I wronged Henry. In my mind." The thought that she had suspected Henry—Henry!—of deceiving her was horrible. And the truth made her errand here seem foolish.

Mistaking her look of dejection, His Grace said, kindly,

"It will not affect you, my dear. Enough of the best stones were sold to ensure your future. And the others will be sold, at the right moment."

"That," she said, making a gesture with one beautiful hand, "doesn't matter. It is Henry, and Knight's Acre. Henry needs money *now*. And all mine is with Sir Barnabas. . . . Can it be recovered?"

"Not without much inconvenience—and possibly some offence to Sir Barnabas."

"I did so want to help Henry. He has been so *kind* to me. I was an orphan, you know; and until Griselda found those jewels, I was a pauper, too. Henry was always kind and once or twice, when I did silly things, he stood up for me."

Who wouldn't?

She looked down at her hands; and then up again. Her eyes had changed, grown paler, harder.

"Master Turnbull might help."

The name of that meddlesome, anti-clerical lawyer jabbed His Grace like a knife. Joanna regarded Master Turnbull with great respect.

Ordinarily when she and Henry went to market together they'd gone their separate ways, to meet at the pie stall. But one day Henry had taken her along with him to Master Turnbull's office and there Master Turnbull had made one more attempt to persuade Henry that saving money for Robert was not very sensible. Joanna had thought: I could prove that. I could tell you something about Robert. He's dead! She did not speak, of course, because to have done so would have been to reveal herself as a cunning and stubborn liar and disgust Henry. So she sat silent while Master Turnbull talked about money, what could be done with it; what he was doing with it; and she had thought him very clever, and a friend to Henry.

So she thought of him now.

"Master Turnbull?"

"Yes. At Baildon. He's very clever about money, Henry says. Perhaps he could think of a way of getting some of mine back. Some would do. Henry doesn't need much; but some he must have."

His Grace looked at her with close attention and decided that she was innocent of all malice. Had she been less appealing to the eye he would not have reached this decision so readily.

Over the matter of the jewels, the arrangement with Sir Barnabas Grey, there was nothing to be feared from Master Turnbull. All open and above-board, except perhaps a slight overestimation of the value of his negotiations in assigning himself the ruby. Moyidan was another matter. The meddling, near heretic lawyer was the one who had first drawn attention to Sir Richard Tallboys' mal-administration of that estate, and was doubtless enraged by the outcome, the taking over by the Church; the use of the Castle as a summer residence by the Bishop. No legal questions had been asked, but they could have been. Still could be. Set a really good hound on a hare's trail and he might start bigger game.

"I do not think that Master Turnbull need be involved. Or Sir Barnabas put to inconvenience. There must be some simpler solution . . ."

It flashed upon him. Neat. Obvious. But he pretended to be thinking deeply.

"Suppose I bought what remains of your legacy. I can afford to wait until the market improves."

"Would you? Oh, that would be wonderful." Every line of her vivid little face expressed gratitude, and then, abruptly, dismay. "I have just thought, my lord, Henry might think it his duty to put most of it away for me. He is such a stubborn man. And what he really needs is stock. A little money perhaps, but mostly animals. He couldn't go hurrying them off to Master Turnbull, could he?" She gave him a dancing look of amusement.

"It is difficult to tell what a really stubborn man may do. We can but try. What, in your opinion, does he need?"

The question was only half serious. Newly clad through Mistress Captoft's efforts, and of such ethereal appearance, she looked unlikely to know much about stock animals.

"Sheep," she said with assurance. "Two hundred. And the long-legged, black-faced kind. They do better on our land." And with a larger flock, Henry would need a shepherd. Talk about that later. "Store cattle . . ." It was her turn to doubt. Would this kindly old man know anything about them? "Young bullocks. They have to be fed through the winter, but we did save our hay crop. Then in the Spring they can eat grass and fatten up before going to the shambles. Oh, and pigs. A few young and an in-pig sow. And . . ."

They watched one another across the polished table. Was she asking too much? She had no idea what the remaining jewels were worth, or of the cost of what she listed. Her experience of money was limited to meagre shopping with coins of the smallest denominations; had she gone too far? Apparently not.

He was watching her, completely fascinated by the combination of delicate beauty—look at those hands—and downright earthy commonsense. How fortunate some unknown fellow was to be! And if circumstances had been a little different, if the Tallboys-Grey connection had not been made, he would, God forgive him, have risked just one more amorous venture.

He did not flinch when she spoke of two cows. A bull.

"Henry," she said, "would welcome a bull of his own. There is one in the village, but nobody there likes Henry and we do not like them."

Still no protest, so she said, "And a horse. It must be young. Heavy enough to pull the waggon, light enough to ride. Then, just a small sum of money. Because I shall not be there to help, with the flock, in the field."

The house, she judged rightly, could be left in Mistress Captoft's busy-body hands.

Then she remembered her manners. Handed on to her through Griselda, who had learned from the Lady Sybilla, who had been in fact an unlikely pipeline, conveying courtesy from one generation to another.

"It is much to ask of you, my lord, but I shall be grateful forever."

Tears rose and stood in her eyes. The aging man, with experience, knew how those tears would fall. To this girl had been granted one of the rarest assets that a woman could possess, the ability to weep without disfiguring herself. The tears would spill, dewdrops on a rosebud. He waited, but she blinked rapidly and banished the tears.

Another doubt had assailed her. He had noted down Henry's needs, but who would do the buying? Somebody ignorant, or careless.

"I should like Henry to have the best beasts, my lord."

"He shall. I have experienced men on my staff. They will understand that they are buying for *me*."

"Thank you." She was thoughtful for a moment, and then appealed again. "I know it is a *great* favour to ask, but would it be possible to allow Henry to understand that this arrangement came from you, not from me. That might not be quite . . . straightforward, but it would make it easier for him to accept."

Here she was not quite sure of her ground; the kind old man was a churchman and she was asking him, practically, to act a lie. It did not trouble her at all, although she knew the rules that supposedly governed Christian behaviour. She could not know that half her blood stemmed from a pagan, Sun-worshipping race who had moved from Persia to North Africa long before the birth of Christ. They'd carried their own religion with them, and even when overtaken by the wave of Islamic invasion, they had conformed only in minor ways. Tana, captured and enslaved, had lived in Moorish Spain for years, in Christian Spain for as long as it took to ride across it; and then for a longer time in Christian England, but she had never been converted. To her, Christianity had been the ridiculous rule that allowed a man only one wife. She had held to her tribe's code, very simple, the Sun the giver of all, master of all; and a rough kind of ethic: one never forgave an enemy, never betrayed a friend.

Joanna only knew that the cold little church, the three-in-one God, and the Virgin Mother in her niche were for her meaningless.

"I have no doubt it could be managed," His Grace of Bywater said.

And he wondered what she could possibly learn at Stordford, or anywhere else. She'd been born, knowing it all.

"I must get back, before, I hope, Mistress Captoft misses her mule."

"Borrowed? Without permission?"

"It was necessary," she said, and gathered her cloak about her, hiding the long slim arms in the tight sleeves and the small but fully shaped breasts, and with the pulling into place of the hood, careless, charming gesture, covering her beautiful hair.

All he could do was to say that he hoped she would be happy at Stordford. After all, he had found the place for her; another swimming glance of gratitude was no more than his due.

"I think I shall be very unhappy. But three years is not long."

No. Not to the young. When he was young what had three years been? Mere steps on the ladder, aims, ambitions, achievements. And now? In a way even less, as time counted, the days filled with business, speeding by, the nights—he slept rather badly—seemingly endless. "I chose the place with an eye to your happiness," he said, a slight reproach in his voice. "Sir Barnabas has daughters of about your age." Even as he said it he thought: How ridiculous! She is older than Eve!

She was on her feet now, and he rose, too, intending to pay her the courtesy of seeing her out himself.

She said, "My lord, I am most grateful for *all* that you have done. Most of all for this." Then something flashed into her eyes and she said, in a different voice, "I am even thankful to you for finding an *unhappy* place for Richard of Moyidan."

He thought that a strange thing to say. Certainly he had no liking for the boy himself, and Master Tallboys had not pursued the subject of the complaints.

"Why do you say that? Did he ever . . . affront you in any way?"

If he had, Heaven help him! His last complaining letter would go to the Provost of Eton with a little admonitory note suggesting that the writer of it needed another flogging.

"Me? No! He would not have dared. But he was very cruel, in a horrible, sly way to a gentle little boy who could not stand up for himself. For that I wished him ill—and always shall."

Now His Grace saw another flaw in her beauty; her eye-teeth were too prominent, wolfish. And her eyes were as green as her mother's readily saleable emeralds.

Into the over-heated, well-furnished room something alien crept. Something cold, old, evil. The Bishop entertained a thought inconsistent both with his calling and his sophistication—I would rather she wished me well than ill.

Absolute nonsense!

And yet, was there not, in the Bible, as well as in heathen mythology, some hint of god-like creatures consorting with the daughters of men and breeding, begetting, something out of the common rut? "There were giants in the earth in those days." Size, naturally, the masculine ideal; what of the feminine? Discount the looks, extraordinary as they were. How, isolated out there at Knight's Acre, just a farm with a better-than-average house, had she acquired such manners? Such style?

A puzzle to anyone who knew nothing of Griselda, faithfully aping the Lady Sybilla to a point where even Henry had once been deceived. A pipe which, before it broke, had conveyed courtesy, airs and graces between two generations.

A puzzle. Nonsense. Rubbish, His Grace of Bywater thought, and sharply rang his silver bell; sternly began to dictate—"Item: two hundred black-faced sheep of the best quality."

"But you told me . . . I was prepared for . . . a child of between eleven and twelve. She is fourteen at least. She makes Maude look like a dwarf!"

Lady Grey's protest came from the heart and her husband made haste to soothe her.

"My dear, Maude still has growth to make. This girl has probably completed hers and in a year's time Maude will overtop her."

Just the kind of remark that Barnabas, with his resolute over-optimism *would* make!

"Had you ever *seen* her?"

"No. How could I? This was all arranged in London. I told you at the time. My good friend, Shefton, told me that the Bishop of Bywater was anxious to place a girl of good family and moderate fortune in a respectable household, with other children of her age, and with a view to a suitable marriage. I owed Shefton money at the time; he was doing himself an immediate service, and me a long-term one. I volunteered immediately. It isn't every day that three thousand marks, free of interest for five years, drops into one's lap."

Lady Grey took a long look at the two men, inside the same skin, to whom she had been married for fifteen years. Perhaps she should think herself fortunate that his double personality operated only in the financial field; he'd never taken a mistress that she knew of, never caused even the merest whisper of scandal in *that* way. Remembering what other women suffered—she'd seen them sitting frozen-faced in the stands around a tiltyard, while in the dust and clash of the mêlée, their men wore favours given to them by other women: a sleeve, a glove, a flower even. It was, in a way, a kind of secret language, not words, signs; and she, thanks be to God, had never been compelled to endure that humiliation. But what she had borne was Barnabas's attitude towards money. One Barnabas was shrewd, hard-headed, businesslike; the other was a gambler of the utmost recklessness. What one Barnabas could *make* in a week by diligence and attention to business and no small physical effort, riding hither and thither, the other could lose in an evening, over a card game, or throwing dice. She was resigned to it now, knowing that he was capable of making a sharp good deal with the Hanseatic League at the Steelyard in the morning, and then making some senseless bet upon which fly could clamber up a window pane faster than the other.

He had a good reputation, for he had never dodged a debt; what one Barnabas lost, the other would repay. And living in style was a help. So perhaps was this tenuous relationship to the Queen. There had been ups and downs, but Stordford had never gone short of anything, partly because Lady Grey was so excellent a manager. When money was available, the estate came first; more acres, more stock. All under her immediate, personal supervision. She went to London very seldom, preferring country life and country activities, and preferring to entertain in her own home, where as hostess and lady of the manor she could not be overlooked, as had so often happened when she had ventured into wider and more glittering circles. Even as a girl she had not been pretty, and then only with the bloom of healthy youth, and she had not been born with nor bothered to acquire the vivacious manner, the witty tongue, the avid attention to fashion and cosmetics with which many plain women compensated for their lack of looks. In addition to this, as the youngest of a large family, three boys and five girls, her dowry was small. She was twenty before any man showed any interest in her. Yet of all the Tetlow girls she had made the best marriage. Everybody was astounded when Sir Barnabas Grey, gay, handsome and popular and experienced, chose to marry plain, dull Gertrude Tetlow. What could he possibly see in her? He was twenty-seven, and much sought after. What he saw and recognised almost instantly, was the balance, the ballast that he lacked himself.

It had been a successful marriage. Within a year she had presented him with a son, Roger, now serving his time as page—soon to be squire—in the household of Lord Bowdegrave at Abhurst. A second son had died in infancy. Then had come Maude, and after three years, Beatrice.

It was a common belief that sons resembled their mothers in looks, daughters, their fathers. In this case, regrettably, the rule was reversed; Roger was handsome and the girls even plainer than their mother. Maude *was* squat, in or out of Joanna Serriff's company; she had sallow skin, hair and eyes the colour of mud; Beatrice was fairer, in fact, too fair, almost bleached-looking.

Lady Grey, who had borne her own lack of beauty with a kind of defiant fortitude, and then made mock of the whole thing by marrying well, was truly concerned by her daughters' lack of comeliness. Baffled, too—at least in her youth she had carried a good colour! Still had it, in fact, the one agreeable thing about a face too heavy featured, too square. And even to her loving maternal eye, other flaws were visible. Maude was lethargic, Beatrice frivolous. What would their future hold? Such sheer good fortune as she had met, with Barnabas, was unlikely ever to come their way. They would, of course, have dowries far more substantial than hers had been, but curiously, inside this solid, stolid woman, a romantic streak lurked, assuring her that marriages made entirely for money were not, on the whole, happy. That was what accounted for those signs of infidelity on the tourney ground —and for the number of children, the results of secret intrigues, whom men accepted as their own, rather than wear the horns of a cuckold. (The dull, plain girl, always overlooked, had been sharply observant.) She was working and scheming so that her daughters should have good dowries, but she did not wish them to make what she called money marriages.

So the régime into which Joanna now stepped was rigorous. Exercise in the open air—good for the complexion. A spell in the covered tennis court—good for the figure. A dinner, meagre, when Sir Barnabas was away, as he often was, but luxurious by Knight's Acre standards. Immediately after, the day being fine, a spell at the butts. Archery was not regarded as a feminine pastime, but Lady Grey believed that it straightened shoulders. After that, lessons. Reading, writing and reckoning. Lady Grey knew that her learning, acquired in lonely moments, when the mainstream of life had appeared to pass her by, had stood her in good stead.

After the lessons came supper; a very different meal from that at Knight's Acre, where people ate because they were hungry and needed sustenance, and went briskly to bed in order to sleep and be ready for another day's work. Supper-time at Stordford was a long, leisurely meal, taken in what seemed to Joanna circumstances of confusion. Almost invari-ably there were guests, for the house stood near the point where the road to London, the road to the East and the road to the North met, and it was known for its hospitality. Any-one with even a nodding acquaintance with Sir Barnabas was welcome to break his journey there. Minstrels, mummers, men with performing dogs or bears would appear, uninvited, but welcome. Sir Barnabas thought nothing of coming back from London with a riotous company of five or six other men. Neighbours came to supper and stayed overnight; members of the Grey or Tetlow families came and stayed for a week, a month; one indeed, an aged woman known as Aunt Agnes, had come to stay, taken a fall and remained ever since. In the midst of all this noise and bustle and apparent disorder, Lady Grey ruled, unruffled; the spider in the centre of a web of her own weaving, its strands reaching out from kitchen to attic, by way of delegated authority, rigid rules and con-stant watchfulness. Hospitality might appear to be prodigal, but the lady of the manor knew exactly how much of the best manchet bread should be served and to whom; how much was left of the great joints, brought hissing from the spit into the hall; to whom the best wine should be offered or not.

On the rare quiet evenings, or when the company in the hall became too riotous, the ladies retired to the solar, and even there Lady Grey continued to be indefatigable. Out with the embroidery; try a tune on the lute; practice some steps of a dance, so that next time that there was dancing in the hall, there should be no clumsiness.

Joanna was, from the first, aware that this was exactly the life, the education and training which Henry had desired for her, and that, in order to keep her part of the bargain, she must endure it for three years. But she hated it, all of it, and would continue to hate it. She missed Knight's Acre, the brooding quiet of the woods. Here there was no quiet, no privacy at all; she shared a sleeping chamber, half a stair-case above the hall, with Maude and Beatrice, who prattled. She had never been idle, but at Knight's Acre even the most laborious jobs had proceeded at an even pace. Here all was hurly-burly, with Lady Grey, rather like a well-trained sheep-dog, making no obvious fuss or noise, constantly rounding up a flock. Do this; do that; go here, go there.

Joanna had never before been ordered about. Banned by

Griselda from the house, she had gone into the fields, the yard, the market, and worked hard—but always because she wanted to, not because she must.

She had immediately sensed that Lady Grey disliked her, though, so far as she knew, she had done nothing to offend. And even, disliked, she was more fortunate than Maude and Beatrice, who often suffered chastisement, slaps on the hands or face, cuffs on the ear. Nothing unusual, Joanna learned. Some ladies behaved very violently to their daughters and dealt blows that broke their heads. Lady Grey never so much as laid a finger on Joanna, perhaps because she was not her daughter, or because she did not entirely lack sensibility and knew that, struck, the girl would strike back. Her disfavour showed itself in other ways. Cutting little speeches: "Of course, coming so late to learning . . ." "Any child who has not mastered a needle by the age of six . . ."

There was also the question of clothes. Mistress Captoft had very sensibly said that Lady Grey would know what was needed beyond the one good woollen gown and the velvet. Winter ebbed away and the warmer weather came. Maude and Beatrice had pretty new dresses, two or three of them; Joanna had one of indeterminate colour and hideous shape.

Never mind! Six months of the three-year sentence already served, and at the end of it Knight's Acre and Henry.

The Knight's Acre about which Joanna dreamed—and was to continue to dream—was being changed, both within and without.

Soon after Christmas one of the Bishop's officials arrived with a message. After all, His Grace had succeeded in disposing of the rest of Joanna Serriff's property, but not for cash money, for stock, of which his lordship assumed that Master Tallboys would wish to take charge.

Henry was first astonished and then angry.

"What do you mean by stock?"

"Animals, Master Tallboys. Sheep, pigs, cows, steers. Oh yes, and a young horse."

Of all the stupid, clumsy arrangements, this was surely the worst! Mid-winter, after a disastrous summer, with both hay and corn harvests well below standard.

"And what am I supposed to feed them on?"

"May I continue? A proportion of the property was sold for money. I have it here."

He was plainly accustomed to dealing with vast sums, for he shot, out of a leather bag, more coined money than Henry had ever seen at one time before as though offering a sample of beans. Enough to buy fodder for many animals for a long time. But *what* animals? Surely to God, if he had to take charge of them, regard them as part of Joanna's heritage, keep them, rear them, breed them, he should have had some say in their choosing. He could just imagine what he would get; the wrong kind of sheep; cows with only two working teats, steers which somebody had hoped to keep alive through the winter and then found an unprofitable business. And a horse, young, but already ruined by ill handling.

Oh, if only he had learned to write! Left with nothing but the spoken words, which might be garbled, Henry said,

"You may tell His Grace that I regard this as a most *unsatisfactory* arrangement. Say that. Word for word. That is an order."

From time to time, without intention, and without knowing it, Henry could pluck a word, or a phrase out of the past. Nothing to do with what he appeared to be, a farmer, clad in homespun, illiterate, so that messages must be carried by word of mouth. Walter, long ago, had noted this oddity in Henry, who, trained by him to disregard chivalry as an outworn thing, sometimes came up with phrases like Upon my honour. I pledge my troth. It was another language, almost.

"They are all good beasts," the Bishop's messenger said placatingly.

Unplacated Henry said, "That remains to be seen."

Astonishingly they were good. The first to arrive was a flock of sheep, all of the right kind. Henry could not have chosen better himself. Black-faced, long-legged. And with them came what Henry knew he needed, a shepherd, knowledgeable, single-minded; a gnarled-looking old man, but spry, accompanied by a shaggy, sly-eyed, slinking dog, called, very rightly, Nip. But for the old shepherd's gruff, incomprehensible order the dog would have nipped Henry.

"I'd like to stay with them," the man said. "I don't hold with flocks you can't count. I know all these and if agreeable to you, Master, I'll stop with them. I can build a shack for myself . . ." He had already looked about and seen what Intake offered; down by the river, willows in plenty, and willow boughs, being supple, made the best foundations for a shack. "I'd like my dinner regular, and say . . . shilling a week . . ."

He could have earned more, but on uplands, vast wide places from which people had been driven to make room for sheep. He thought that Knight's Acre looked cosy, enclosed, more what sheep-folds had been before everybody went mad and began to look on sheep as so much wool, so much mutton. He knew it must be so; they were wool and mutton, or breeding ewes and rams, that was the way it went. But somehow, for no reason at all, this place seemed to offer a chance of something a little more human. He did not crave the company of his fellows, his sheep and his dog sufficed, but he liked to be within sight of dwellings. Here only the width of the track separated the fold from the church and the adjoining house; Knight's Acre was in full view, and some of the roofs of Intake were visible. He had a feeling of having come home.

Other animals arrived and Henry realised that the Bishop had done him a singular service. Months of searching markets at Baildon or Bywater, or of visiting farms and manors could not have produced so many first-class beasts. Faintly below the surface imposed by repeated disillusionments, some of the old ambition woke and stirred. He might yet attain a moderate prosperity.

Withindoors it looked as though prosperity had already arrived. Mistress Captoft moved into the main house as soon as Joanna left, and proceeded to reorganize everything, and to spread comfort, even a certain elegance around her.

She could have servants, now! Throughout her association with Benny it had been wise to manage with casual help—like Old Ethel, who came, did the roughest work and departed. Servants pried and listened, were prone to gossip, inclined to invent what they did not know.

She decided against seeking servants from Intake—not because it would be useless; she was unaware of the enmity that existed between the village and the house; but because she knew from experience that servants within walking, or even running distance of their homes were forever wanting to visit; my mother is ill, madam; my sister is having a baby, I must go. And if it wasn't going it was coming, relatives of every degree dropping in for a chat, a good warm-up by the fire, and a bite of whatever was going. And there were smugglings out from the larder. All this Mistress Captoft knew from ruling her husband's comfortable house. She would seek servants in Bywater, a good muleride away.

She handed over her mule to a stableboy in the yard of The Welcome To Mariners, and then went into the inn. The morning, though sunny, was cold and a glass of mulled wine would be welcome. Also inns were centres of information.

In this inn something quite extraordinary had happened, a fortnight ago but not forgotten—never to be forgotten, because of the gross ingratitude. And the shock. And the giving a well-conducted house a bad name . . .

Katharine Dowley, age uncertain, neither young nor old, entered service at The Welcome To Mariners, in the most humble capacity; worked herself up, became cook, very good.

Dozens of customers, all expecting the best, and each to be served as though he were the one person in the world. Offer a perfectly spitted roast and what about the fresh fish for which Bywater was so famous? Have the fish ready and the brutes had already had fish earlier in the day, or yesterday; what about a change, grilled lamb?

And no limit to the hours. Travellers on land in the ordinary way timed their journeys more or less; but a ship depended on the wind, could come in at almost any time.

Subject a woman, conscientious by nature and very slightly hysterical at times, to this kind of régime, year after year, and something was bound to go, to give way.

It had given way very late on an evening when a customer asked for roast duckling and Katharine Dowley, whimpering and howling—"like a dog locked out, or locked in," the landlady said—had brought the duckling in, not on a dish, on the practically red-hot spit and flung the whole thing in the customer's face.

Fortunately no great damage had been done; but naturally Katharine Dowley had been summarily dismissed. She had gone back to the Lanes, from which she had come.

The Lanes were a feature of Bywater about which little was known. Towards the sea the little port showed a pleasant face. The inn, some solid, respectable houses, occupied by solid, respectable citizens. And there were the shops, in streets running off at right angles, shops which offered, in more plenty, and at cheaper prices, some goods from abroad. The Lanes, as Mistress Captoft realised with a flashback of memory towards Dunwich, were a different thing altogether. Hovels, crowded together, upheld by one another, in which lived the poor, not poor as country people were, with a cabbage patch, and onions, often a pig, sometimes a goat. Here no such palliatives to poverty were available. Young men, or tough older men could go down to the harbour and offer their arms, shoulders, legs to the business of bringing a weighty cargo ashore. And women, ages ranging from the too young to the too old, offered the services of *their* bodies in a different way.

It was a sinister district and malodorous, but Mistress Captoft entered it without shrinking and without trepidation. She found Katharine Dowley still, after a fortnight in such a filthy place, looking clean, and though miserable, calm.

"Suddenly, it was all too much. That's the long and short of it, Mistress. Never a proper night's sleep. And now . . . Twenty years," she said, "twenty years' hard work, all wiped out and forgotten. That one time remembered and handed about, so's nobody'll ever want me again."

Except in one way, which she didn't fancy, the thing she had tried to avoid, preferring work at the inn, kitchen slut, cook's assistant, cook. And no chance to save; always on her heels the clamorous, growing family, which, when she was chucked out had not been welcoming, but had indicated, in the most deadly way, how she could, and must earn enough to make a contribution—if she wanted to stay here. To Katharine Dowley Mistress Captoft appeared like a shining angel; a deliverer.

Thus fortuitously provided with a woman who could cook, Mistress Captoft thought wistfully of a serving boy, neat and nimble like the ones her own family and Master Captoft had employed. She visualised him in tawny hose and jerkin; a well-scrubbed boy between eleven and fourteen years old, waiting upon her and Master Tallboys in the hall and making himself generally useful. There were, no doubt, boys of that age in the Lanes who would have been glad of a good bed and two meals a day but she was wise enough to know that in such a district any boy by the time he was eleven would have acquired bad habits. She decided to wait a bit, until she chanced upon a boy, poor but of decent family, whom she could train in her own ways.

She walked back to the inn, where she intended to dine upon fresh fish, a luxury now unknown at Intake, though Master Tallboys said he could remember the time when an old woman, with a donkey, had occasionally brought fresh fish as well as the salted or dried kind. Apparently she had brought the plague, too; and died of it herself, just in the lane. Nobody had replaced her.

Mistress Captoft would dine upon fish straight from the sea—probably herring with a smear of mustard sauce; then she would go out on to the quay and buy fresh fish, hurry the mule home and give Master Tallboys and the child a delicious supper.

Somebody at the corner of the inn's forecourt said,

"Mistress, of your charity . . ."

She turned about and confronted a beggar who did not look like a beggar. Young; not a day over thirty, poorly clad, but clean and tidy, and with no obvious disability. Thin, certainly, her rapid assessing look informed her, all the face bones prominent under the taut skin, sea-blue eyes rather sunken.

She was not an indiscriminate giver of alms. She had lived in Dunwich, which was infested by beggars, and she had learned to harden her heart, except where children were concerned, and even that kindly attitude had shifted a little when she learned that beggars often borrowed, hired, bought or actually stole children in order to appeal to the softhearted.

She knew that there were genuine cases of men unemployed because sheep runs were proliferating and that acres where many men had once ploughed and sown and reaped were now in the charge of one man and a dog. There were the partially blind, cripples, people who had fits, but alongside them were those who were merely idle. Face to face with this man, who did look hungry, she said, briskly,

"Surely an able-bodied man like you could find some better way of making a living."

One of her beliefs, oddly at variance with her sheltered upbringing and her inherited income, was that, cast out upon the world, with nothing, she would not have been reduced to beggary. She would have made brews, baked bread, checked tallies, done miles of stitching, dug and hawked cockles, scrubbed floors . . . Anything.

The man reacted to her astringent remark. He said, "Tell me one, lady. Tell me where a lame man is wanted—and I'll be there. Ready and willing."

"In what way are you lamed?"

She was prepared for some horrible sight; a self-inflicted sore; some trivial cut or blister kept open by diligent irritation with sand or wood-ash. And sometimes the so-called "sturdy beggars" would stop by a shambles where animals were butchered and daub themselves with blood or stick bits of completely inedible offal onto their arms, legs, faces.

None of that trickery here. As the man bared his leg Mistress Captoft immediately saw how lame he was, and why. The bone of his left leg, mid-way between knee and ankle, had been broken and not set even by some unskilled but sensible woman like herself. Nobody had known enough, or cared enough, to lash the broken leg to a broomstick! As a result it had knit in its own way, at a slight angle, and his left leg was some two inches shorter than his right. The man had done his poor best to remedy the fault by tacking a wedge of wood to his left shoe.

She saw instantly what was wrong with that. Not flexible and not graduated. In any shoe there should be a difference between heel and toe.

"What happened?"

"A cask broke loose. In a storm."

"You are a sailor?"

"I was. Since I was about seven. I know no other trade."

"Could you learn?"

"Learn what?" It was all too plain that he was not going to get anything from *her,* though she'd looked likely, good for a farthing, so he allowed his anger with life to sound in his voice. "Who'd take a man of my age as an apprentice? Who'd lay down the premium for me? Everything's tied up, either with the damned Guilds, or some family."

For a second his eyes showed some animation, then reverted to their expression of dull despair. "Once you're beached, you might as well be dead," he said.

Keeping her dignity and her calm—unusual as it was for a beggar to swear until finally turned away—Mistress Captoft said,

"Walk ahead of me to the inn door."

"Even *that* I can't do," he said angrily. "The landlady warned me off. She didn't like her customers being accosted."

"You are about to *be* one," Mistress Captoft said. She was a woman of impulse and had decided that having seen him walk, whether or not she considered him likely to be useful, she would buy him a good dinner.

He was lame, would always be lame, but a properly made shoe would mitigate his disability.

He ate hungrily, but not grossly, and refused a second helping.

"Mustn't overdo it after a long fast," he said.

She then told him of the job she had to offer. A boy's job really but there was no reason why it should not be done by a man; waiting at table, mending fires, keeping silver bright, that kind of thing. A good home and a shilling a week.

Somewhat to her consternation—for this was, after all, a public place—his face twisted, his jaw began to tremble and his eyes filled with tears, two of which escaped and ran slowly down his hollow cheeks.

"There, there!" she said kindly. "Don't upset yourself, David. If you perform your duties—none of them heavy—to my satisfaction, I shall have done myself a service, too."

Knuckling the tears away, he said in a broken voice, "I'll serve you to the death, madam."

She began to issue instructions. He was to find a cobbler and have his shoe built up with leather. Two and a half inches on the heel, one and a half on the sole.

It would no more have occurred to her to provide transport for a maid-servant within walking distance, than it would have done to anyone else. But it was a long walk for a lame man. So, as soon as his shoe was improved, David was to go round to Tanner's Lane, to the cottage next the tanyard, and tell Katharine Dowley not to start walking first thing tomorrow morning, but to come to the inn yard and join him. He was to hire a carter to bring them to Intake. She explained where that was; on the road to Baildon. There was a turn-off to the left, avoid it, it led to Moyidan only. Eventually there was a turn-off to the right; avoid that, too. It was the Baildon road; keep straight on, along a narrow lane with trees on each side and there was Intake. The house itself could not be missed.

She handed over money for the cobbler, but not for the carter. That she would pay, she said, at the end of the journey. It was the general rule, for carters were notoriously tricky; paid in advance they got drunk and either did not turn up at all, or were days late, with some excuse that the horse had fallen down, or a wheel had come off the waggon.

Riding home, with enough fresh fish for two days in a rush basket, Mistress Captoft thought with some complacency about her hirings. Neither quite ideal: a woman of uncertain temper, a man with a lame leg. But both so *grateful*.

"I never take that road," said the first carter whom David approached.

David misinterpreted this as an admission of ignorance of the way.

"I can direct you," he said, and oblivious to the change which had come over the carter's hard, weathered face at the mention of Intake, he repeated what Mistress Captoft had told him. And surely it was a journey any carter would gladly undertake; such a light load. One woman with a small bundle, a man with nothing at all. No strain on the horse, no weight on the waggon.

"I never travel that road."

"Why not?"

"Thass my business. Find somebody else." The carter had never told anybody what had happened to him on a midsummer day, ten, eleven years ago. He'd never forgotten it either; it had profoundly affected his life.

Taking his ease, lolling on the sun-bathed bank of a little stream, with a dock-leaf full of wild strawberries as an end to his dinner, he'd been visited by one of the Little People, wreathed with flowers, and so loving that no mortal woman had ever since been of any use to him. To this day the sight of the big white daisies which she had worn, a crown on her head, a garland about her neck, or the smell of strawberries could take him straight back to that enchanted afternoon, the delight, then the fright, he had trodden on forbidden ground; and then the way she had run after him, crying: "Take me with you."

He did not know that his son was now at Eton, being flogged into shape.

What he did know was that never again would he travel that road. So he said, "Find somebody else." Which David did without difficulty.

Now Mistress Captoft wallowed in gratitude, a thing she needed as a plant needed water. It was a weakness in a competent, self-assured woman—the desire to serve and to have her service recognised. One of the things which had alienated her from the people of Intake had been their marked ingratitude. She was clear-headed enough to admit that many of her doses had been provided for a double purpose—to protect Benny from going out to administer the last rites to somebody with a belly ache. Try this first. Very often it worked, but what thanks did she get? Yes, the patient was better. The dose was all right. It did the job. One of the most poignant stories in the New Testament—something with which Mistress Captoft was more familiar than most because Benny's life work had been an attempt to dovetail the four Gospels—was the one about Christ healing ten lepers; one came back to thank Him; and He had said, "Where are the nine?" If the Son of God could ask such a question, be so sensible of man's lack of gratitude, why not mere Mattie Captoft?

However, now in the kitchen were two intensely grateful

people; both wrecks, both saved. By her. She was reasonably sure that Katharine, waked in the dead of the night, would rise and without so much as a secret feeling of resentment, do whatever was asked of her. As for David, his devotion was dog-like.

About Master Tallboys she was not so sure. She'd come back, hot-foot from Bywater with fresh fish for supper and the news that she had found two servants. He'd seemed a bit dubious.

"I fully realise that you could not be expected . . . I intended to look around, ask around Baildon, next time I went in."

"Well, now you will have no need to do that."

Personally he thought the engagement of two fully adult people, one of them an experienced cook, was somewhat in excess of their needs, but to say so would sound mean.

"What wage did you agree upon?"

"Now, now, Master Tallboys, you must not give that a thought! Both Katharine and David are *my* servants—not more than I should have had had I set up house on my own. Any small service they do you, is paid for by your providing bed and board."

"We'll see," Henry said. He had money now, but not to squander. He had fodder to buy until sheep-fold and pasture sprang green in mid-April. And when John left, as he fully intended to do at winter's end, he must be provided for. And when the day came for Joanna's dowry to be handed over, he was determined that the money invested in Knight's Acre should be seen to have been as well invested as that entrusted to Sir Barnabas.

No friendliness had ever existed between Knight's Acre and Intake, but interest in Knight's Acre was keen in the village, where most people were inter-related and anybody's business was known to everybody. Anything to do with the big house was news; and Jem Watson was the one who carried it.

Lacking more accurate information he attributed all the signs of new prosperity to Mistress Captoft.

"Ah, she proper rule the roost there and no mistake. And they don't eat alongside us now. No! Fire in the big room now and the table set—you'd think the King was coming. Silver all over the place. Him at one end of the table, her at the other, Master John and the little boy in between. Still, give the new woman her due, the grub is better nowadays."

"And what do the new man do?"

What didn't he do? With a few good meals behind him, every mouthful a strengthener, the adjusted shoe on his foot and burning desire to serve in his heart, there was practically nothing that David couldn't do. He had told Mistress Captoft that he knew no trade but the sea, and that was true in a way, but sailors knew almost everything. Many ships carried livestock, to be cherished and coddled until the death blow came; so he could feed bullocks and pigs; he could milk a cow. Given space and the right tools he could make butter, and cheese. Any sailor worth his salt knew how to deal with wood and in no time at all David had built a proper bullock yard. With every bit of outside work he did, something of his manhood, so sadly humiliated, sprang to life again; and his gratitude to Mistress Captoft, who had made this rehabilitation possible, deepened.

"Hop about like a flea, he do," Jem said, with the lazy man's disapproval of one less sparing of himself.

There was time to gossip, the winter days so short, and now around the shared firesides was a new listener, an encouragement to the dragging out of old tales. The new priest, Father Matthew, had done what Father Ambrose, trying hard, and Father Benedict, not trying at all, had failed to do: he had become one with his parishioners. He came of the same stock, knew about animals, especially pigs, he had a hearty manner and an earthy sense of humour. And although he never actually said so, they sensed that he was no fonder of Knight's Acre than they were themselves; his lack of fondness showed itself in the avidity with which he listened to the hostility-tinged talk. His dislike, if so strong a word could apply to a feeling so shadowy, was based on the fact he hadn't taken to Henry, cold, aloof, superior, and that, thick-hided as he could be in certain areas, he had sensed Mistress Captoft's scornful disapproval.

The Intake people's hostility was older, deeper rooted. It went back to the time when Sir Godfrey, taking only what was indisputably his own, had come and built his house there. On a site which had once been a farm but long left derelict, ever since an outbreak of the Sweating Sickness, so long ago that no one had even a memory of it. What most did remember was that the untilled ground and especially the great oak tree around which the house was built, had provided space, and food for pigs and a few goats. Pigs thrived on acorns, goats liked the self-sown saplings.

The building of Knight's Acre had put an end to that. The

grievance had begun there and presently found other things to feed upon.

Take the common land. Sir Godfrey had pastured his great horse there—as was his right, common land was common land—but a thing of that size ate a lot, and was in addition very dangerous. Once when Gurth went to fetch in his donkey, the warhorse had as good as attacked him. Great yellow teeth, up-lifted iron-shod hooves.

Then Sir Godfrey, and his dangerous horse, had took off to some war somewhere and stayed away for years and years.

The whole place had been ruled and run by a man called Walter, a horrible fellow.

Aah. Hadn't he one time tried to rape Bessie Wade—then a servant in the house—and hadn't the Lady Sybilla stood up for him, when the Elders went to complain. Lady Sybilla had said nonsense, she had been there all the time; she didn't believe a word.

And what happened to Walter?

To that there was no answer. Nobody knew anything more about Walter, dead, than of Walter alive. He'd just gone off, they said.

What they did all know and remembered with hatred was that after all those years Sir Godfrey had come home and taken three quarters of their common land to make his sheepfold.

No credit was given him for the fact that he had left them a quarter of it.

Then he'd died, got killed fighting up in the North somewhere and one of his boys—no, not Master Tallboys up at Knight's Acre, his brother, Sir Richard, had swooped down and upset everything. A priest—Father Matthew was aware of some sidelong glances—yes, a priest, but a lawyer too, and he'd found flaws in the parchment which his great-grandfather—or his great-great-grandfather—had given theirs.

Ah, that had been a proper old confluffle; you had to trace your family back and then either buy or get out. The fact that their status had gone up a notch, that they now owned the land they tilled and were entitled to call themselves yeomen, affected the Intake people very little.

Now and again, during these most interesting talks, Father Matthew tried to bring up the question of his glebe. Glebe was the ten acres of land which was, by custom, attached to every church.

His was wilderness, neglected for many years, and since he

could see that serving a church so poorly endowed, he and the ugly, rather dim-witted boy whom he had brought with him as his servant, would be largely dependent on the produce of the glebe, he was anxious to get it ploughed. It was when he mentioned the glebe that the Intake men tended to remember that it was time for bed, or that some job awaited them elsewhere. An ox was lame, a plough needed repair.

Father Matthew did not press the matter; he had a peasant's patience. One day, when they knew and liked him better, they would volunteer. Meanwhile he managed to buy a pig, and on the bit of the glebe which Mistress Captoft had made into a garden, though she had taken away as many of the roots as she could, the ugly boy was growing onions, cabbages, peas, beans. They'd survive. Anything rather than widen the gulf between priest and people which had plainly existed in former times. More people attended Mass, and observed their other religious duties than ever before.

"I can't pretend to favour this," Henry said. "You'd be better off here, with a warm bed and sound food—and doing light work about the place."

"And going mad?" John asked. Light jobs about the place, and Nick's songs lost forever. He knew, with a knowledge not of the head but of the heart, the lungs or the bowels, that restored as he might seem to be, he had no time to waste.

"Mind this," Henry said, "wherever you are, if that cough comes on again, make for home. Don't wait till you're on your last legs."

When that time came, John thought, he would simply creep into a corner and die; it was only his determination to get Nick back to England, back to some kind of comfort, that had kept him going all the way from Padua to Knight's Acre.

He thought Henry's parting present—ten nobles—miserly. Henry felt that he was stretching generosity and brotherly responsibility to the extreme limit. When the Bishop's man had tipped out all that shining money on the table one of his first thoughts had been that now he could clear another field, hiring the labour; now he would do it himself, so every penny he gave John represented an incalculable outlay in toil and sweat.

He felt the need for more land because he had a belief, inculcated by Walter, that arable ground was more reliable than livestock, so subject to disease. A dead animal was a dead loss whereas even the worst harvest left the fields waiting for next year's, which might be better.

At Stordford Lady Agnes had finally and reluctantly taken to her bed. So long as she could hobble, with the assistance of a sturdy servant, down the stairs, she had done so, eager for the life and bustle in the great hall, or the spiteful talk in the solar, but now she needed assistance on both sides, and the stairs, originally built with the idea of defence, were too narrow. Lady Grey could have made room for her on the ground floor but had no intention of doing so; old, ailing—and often irritable—relatives were best at a distance.

On the other hand, Aunt Agnes must not be allowed to feel neglected; for she was wealthy and had no children of her own. There was always the possibility that she might will her money to the Church. So each morning and each evening Maude and Beatrice were required to make a short routine visit, with a curtsey and a greeting and a little conversation. Their great-aunt considered Maude very dull and Beatrice insipid—partly due, no doubt, to their being over-rigidly disciplined by their mother. Lady Agnes was one of the many who could never see why her gay, pleasure-loving nephew should have married such a dour, charmless woman.

Joanna was under no obligation to make these visits, but, at first urged by Maude, who liked and admired, almost *loved* her, she had gone and somehow, just by being there, had lightened the whole atmosphere. She had a way of saying things, of seeing the comic side, nothing much that you could put a finger on, or a name to, just different and refreshing. Also, she was lovely to look at, and like many old women who had once been pretty, and then with age grown wrinkled and grey, Lady Agnes liked girls to be comely— myself when young! Presently, if Joanna failed to appear on one of these bi-daily occasions, Lady Agnes would ask why; what was she doing; where was she? Be sure to bring her next time.

She regarded the summer-weight dress which Lady Grey had provided for Joanna with a mixture of disapproval and bewilderment. What exactly was wrong with it? In her day the old lady had been devoted to clothes, had cut and stitched many of her own dresses. The answer she gave herself was: Everything, but in a subtle way. Granted the stuff, though of no quality, had not been skimped, there was plenty of it, but in all the wrong places; where it should have clung close it bulged and sagged, where it should have taken on a smooth, flowing line it looked—constricted. A dress deliberately designed . . .

"It looks like a sack," Lady Agnes said.

"So I thought, at first sight. It made me feel that at any moment I might be put on the scales and weighed and my quality tested between a miller's teeth."

"About the colour nothing can be done; but the shape could be altered to great advantage. Bring me my basket." Every lady of quality had such a basket, a pair of scissors, a fat cushion stuffed with sawdust and a little pounded beeswax to save needles and pins from rusting even in the dampest weather; skeins of wool, spun very fine, and silks.

I am old; I am lame; but I still have my eyesight and the use of my hands. I can make something of this sack!

And after this another. No girl could manage with only one dress. What was Gertrude thinking of?

The girl was useless with a needle—she'd have been handier with a hay fork, Lady Agnes concluded, little guessing how near she was to the truth. But when the no-colour dress was re-shaped and made gay with embroidery, she remembered that she had many dresses—never to be worn again. But before she parted with one of them she must know that it was necessary, that the object of such charity *was* an object of charity.

"Are you so poor?"

"I am not at all poor, Lady Agnes. My mother, a lady of Spain, left me a considerable fortune, part of which Sir Barnabas is handling; and part—in another place."

Oh, and the green grass springing on the pasture and the sheep-fold at Knight's Acre; Layer Wood, a haze of green and a flood of bluebells. In the fields the young corn, stroked by the young wind. The violent homesickness which she thought she had mastered, surged up. She had overcome it before, and could again, could now. Obediently, but without much enthusiasm, she opened the chest where the old woman's dresses lay, smelling of lavender and rosemary and thyme—and age. Sad.

"Red," said Lady Agnes, "is for the very young—or married women. Yellow? No. You would look as sallow as Maude. Tawny would suit you well, but that is a winter colour. Ah, that is what I had in mind. Hold it against you." It was mid-way between the young green and the bluebells.

Lady Grey was not particularly pleased that her intention to make Joanna more ordinary-looking should have been frustrated by an old woman's whim. On the other hand she was not displeased that Joanna, wearing the sea-green silk and looking far from ordinary, should catch Lord Shefton's eye. *He* was not what she wanted for either of her daughters, rich though he was. She still cherished the hope that both her girls, plain, but well-trained and well-dowered, would make happy marriages. Lord Shefton was far too old. There was something to be said, in some cases, for marrying a rich old man who would die and leave you a widow, wealthy, and still young enough to re-marry. But this particular old man had a son, by his first marriage, which had been to a very young girl; too young perhaps; she'd died in childbed. His second wife, again young, but slightly older than the first, had borne a son and a daughter before she met with an accident, strange enough to warrant an inquest. Left, unaccountably, alone in one of his more remote houses, she'd fallen downstairs and cracked her skull; without disarranging her headdress or her skirt. Death by misadventure. . . . But there were rumours that the second Lady Shefton had been on the point of running away. One story said back to her own family; another said with a lover. Un-named; possibly Scottish. Gertrude Tetlow, sitting neglected in corners, Lady Grey, ruling in her own house, had not missed much, and though she was prepared to entertain Lord Shefton, one of Barnabas' *business* associates, she certainly did not wish him to take a fancy to either of *her* girls, whom she loved in her own fashion. Far too much to hand them over to old men with rotten teeth and stinking breath . . . Really so bad that when, as was his due, he sat on her right at the upper table, and with courtesy—his manners could not be faulted—helped her first to the dish proffered by a page down on one knee, she felt slightly nauseated. She told herself, as sternly as she would have told a child or servant—Tainted breath cannot affect food. But the feeling was there, a repulsion, and she was glad that the rheumy old eyes focussed on Joanna.

Time plodded on. Or raced—

"A bit near the river, and all shut in," Joseph, the old shepherd, said. "What we need is a bit of drainage." A lifetime ago, Walter had said almost the same thing. Intake not the place for sheep.

"Then we'll drain." And that was hard work, too. But it fitted in with the clearing of the other field; an abundance of twigs and small branches. Dig the trench, and another and another, across the sheep-fold, lay in the bundles of twigs and small branches, end to end so that they carried off surplus water towards the river.

"There'll be less foot rot now," Joseph said.

With the house running so smoothly, Mistress Captoft could turn her attention to the garden, to giving some elementary lessons to Godfrey, and to the completion of a remarkable piece of embroidery which had occupied two generations of Captoft women. In the early days of her marriage, before she became so busy with Master Captoft's affairs, she had worked on it herself. Then it had been rolled up and forgotten, though she had taken it with her to Dunwich and then to Intake. Whoever had planned it had been artistic and ambitious—and no prude. It had been designed to hang on a sizable wall, and even had Mistress Captoft, in Dunwich or Intake, made time to work upon it—servantless as she was—it would have been difficult in such small rooms, with Benny's books always on the table. It depicted the Garden of Eden, with Adam and Eve, almost life-size, standing under the Tree of Knowledge—every apple and every leaf in place. There were other trees, too, and every known flower, every known animal.

Possibly some Captoft long ago, had gone on a pilgrimage to the Holy Land and remembered what he had seen, come back and given descriptions which had been handed down and fired some woman's lively imagination. Some of the beasts were very strange indeed.

Adam and Eve were naked, except for, in his case, the fig-leaf, and in hers—symbolic touch—one coil of the Snake, which she appeared to be fondling.

When Master Captoft's household was broken up, nobody wanted this article. Two of his daughters said they had spent so many tedious hours on it in childhood that they never wanted to see it again—in fact just to look at the tiny forget-me-nots and pansies made their eyes ache; the third had an aversion to snakes. One of his sons thought so much naked flesh indecent, and the other said he had hangings enough. Their stepmother was more than welcome to it.

Very little work remained to be done on it and now Mistress Captoft realised how useful a seemingly useless thing could be. It would look splendid on the unbroken stretch of wall over the hearth. And it fitted as though made for it. Jem Watson was called in to help Henry and David with the hanging of it, for it was so long that it needed two men to hold it level and taut while a third drove in the nails. Everybody then stood back to study the effect.

Since when not being worked upon it had been kept rolled,

the colours were as bright and clear as ever, and the glowing, crowded panorama altered not only that one wall, but the whole hall.

Mistress Captoft was enchanted with it—so beautiful in itself and another contribution to Knight's Acre. David was under the misapprehension that she had stitched it unaided and was dumbstruck with admiration. Henry said, practically, that they must never in future put a smoky log on the fire for fear of dimming it. Jem reserved his opinion, until he was back in the village.

"You never seen such a thing in all your born days."

"Tell us about it."

"You wouldn't believe me if I towd you." But he proceeded to tell. A man and a woman, stark naked, not so much as a clout between them, standing together under a tree. Close together? Yes, hand in hand. And all around such beasts as never went on four legs. Things with stripes, with spots, with humps; one with a single horn in the middle of its head, and one like a dog, but with a face like . . . "not unlike your Timmy, Father." That was a most accurate piece of observation.

It could be, thought Father Matthew, who was one of the gathering in Bert Edgar's kitchen that evening, a picture of the Garden of Eden.

"Is there a snake?" he asked.

"Is there a snake? Thundering great thing as thick as my arm. And the woman a-nursing it, like it was a baby."

That brought a gasp of horror from all the women in his audience. All women had an inborn horror of snakes. And was not a snake as much the representative of the Devil as a dove was of the Holy Ghost?

"Suckling Old Scrat, eh? And she stitched that into a picture! Well, you don't surprise *me*." That was Old Ethel, still venomous against Mistress Captoft, who had, she felt, usurped her place as priest's housekeeper, then employed her in a very menial capacity, and seen to it strictly that the humble jobs were properly done—and then, crowning injury, not employed her at all after the move to Knight's Acre. A born gossip, Ethel could always give the impression that she knew more than she chose to say. In fact she knew nothing of the relationship that had existed between Father Benedict and Mistress Captoft, for until the shutters were closed and the door barred they had acted their parts to perfection. Father Benedict, priest of this parish, and Mistress Captoft, his housekeeper and his aunt.

Jill Edgar, hostess for this evening—in winter the people of Intake saved firewood by taking it in turns; letting the fire die on three or four hearths, gathering around another—had no specific grudge against Mistress Captoft but she hated Knight's Acre and Master Tallboys because she'd once had an easy job there. Then Master Tallboys had chosen to marry Griselda, a fellow servant of Jill's; jumped up, pernickety, unbearable. So Jill had married Bert Edgar. A plain case of out of the frying pan into the fire; with Bert such a *beast*. Worse. Beasts at least knew whether a female wanted it or not; Bert took no notice of her wishes, and then when what couldn't be helped happened, beat her. As though a woman deliberately made a baby; on her own. Out of her own deep misery Jill Edgar was prepared to take some slight comfort by criticising another woman, apparently more fortunate. So she said,

"You mean to tell, Jem Watson, that him and her sit there together and take food with naked people looking down from the wall?"

"Ain't that what I been saying? Anyway, they're as good as married. Leastways they oughta be."

Many of these evening gatherings ended up with a bit of bawdy talk. It was the thing everybody understood and found amusing. Father Matthew—except for a little learning—was one of them, earthy and coarse-humoured. He was capable of understanding why nine out of ten brides coming up to the altar to ask God's blessing on their marriage, were pregnant. He understood that any working man needed to know that a woman was capable of bearing a child before he committed himself for life—till death do us part. Jokes about children born seven, six, five or even four months after their begetters had been united in Holy Matrimony did not bother him at all. But, plodding home, Father Matthew recognised that he was a priest and responsible for what went on in his parish—not in the ditches and hedgerows, or under the shelter of hay-stacks, but openly, in the only big house, occupied by the very people who should be setting a good example.

He was unaware—or unwilling to face the fact—that he liked neither Master Tallboys nor Mistress Captoft. He considered the master of Knight's Acre to be mean; he never proffered the invitation to share a meal or a mug of ale, leave alone a glass of wine, as the better-off parishioners should do; and his manner, through invariably civil, struck the priest as cold and unfriendly; Mistress Captoft he had sensed, criticised and despised him: she'd taken herself—and her order for Masses—to Nettleton.

These personal feelings combined with a sense of duty which was not lacking in him, to assure him that a rebuke, a warning would be in order.

Mistress Captoft opened the heavy front door herself. Of two servants only so much could be expected; Katharine was in the kitchen and David busy with one of the many jobs he had taken on.

"Oh! Good morning, Father," she said, her tone betraying the surprise she felt. She was no longer of his congregation and Master Tallboys was not a man who needed to be rounded up and reminded of his religious obligations. Although he never gave any other sign of piety, he never missed a Sunday Mass, or a Holy Day.

Now that he was in her presence, Father Matthew realised the awkwardness of his mission.

Mistress Captoft knew how a priest should be received. She indicated a seat on the more comfortable settle, near the bright fire, and bustled about, producing wine, and silver cups, and small saffron buns from one of the cupboards. She made an affable remark or two about the seasonal weather, and how the leaves were falling.

Father Matthew seated himself, clumsily, perching on the edge of his seat, spreading his knees wide and placing his coarse hands upon them. A peasant's stance. For a second the contrast with Benny sprang to mind again, but it no longer pained her. Pouring the wine she thought, in a way unusual to her, that some people had quick-healing flesh, and in the same way some people had quick-healing spirits. While he was alive she had given Benny all she had to give; when he died she had given him deep grief, misery that had driven her almost distraught—and Masses for a year to shorten his time in Purgatory. So the wound had healed, not festered.

She seated herself on the other, less comfortable settle, the one that Walter had somehow procured for the Lady Sybilla, and waited for Father Matthew to state his business—if he had any.

She thought it might concern the glebe. For, despite his hobnobbing with the people of Intake, his—in her view—lowering attempt to be one of them, he hadn't got his glebe ploughed. And never would at this rate. Though she had held herself aloof from the village, she knew the people of Intake. With one exception, ingrates.

And if, having failed with them and their oxen, he'd now come to ask aid from Master Tallboys and his horse-drawn plough, she had her answer ready: Master Tallboys had all he could deal with; offer the men of Intake elevenpence and the job would be done. She was willing to give the money; for she, of all people, knew how utterly inadequate the living was.

Since she was thinking such fundamentally kind and charitable thoughts, it was all the more shock to her when the clumsy man, after some false starts, some mumbling, managed to say what he had come about.

Unpleasant talk about her and Master Tallboys down there in the village!

She always carried good colour in her face; now it darkened until it matched the crimson velvet of her new winter gown, brought into use only two days earlier, when the wind changed and the leaves began to blow about.

Unless I control myself, master this rage, I shall be taken with a fit.

And she was schooled in self-control. No protest, or sullenness when she was informed that the husband her parents had chosen for her was an old man, with children older than she was. And after that, when she was running the old husband's business for him, patience and calm had been demanded of her; and after that the years of secretive, rigidly controlled life with Benny, every word to be watched, and the little vinegar-soaked tuft between her and what she most wanted—a child.

Draw in, hold, count to twenty before releasing the breath. It worked. She felt the hot flush subside; knew that she was again in command of herself, and of the situation.

"I wonder at you, Father Matthew, giving an ear to village gossip."

The contempt in her voice was a spur to him and he said, "You live close."

"Certainly we eat together, at this table. Would the people of Intake prefer that I ate with servants in the kitchen? As for sleeping . . . Between my bedchamber and Master Tallboys' are two others; one occupied by a maid-servant; the other by a child—except when he chooses to sleep in his father's room." And she thought: The irony of it! All those years with Benny, being careful, dreading this very thing, and now to be accused of it with Master Tallboys! Good night, Mistress Captoft. Good night, Master Tallboys. And each to a lonely bed. "I daresay," she said, keeping her temper, but feeling the worse for it, "your village cronies may find it difficult to believe that a man and a woman can share board but not bed. If so, you have my permission to question my cook-woman about any comings and goings in the night." Suppressed anger made her vicious, willing to wound and knowing exactly where to strike. "When tongues cease to wag about Master Tallboys and I living close as you call it, they may turn on *you* and accuse you of sodomy with that ugly boy."

It was a word that most people understood but seldom used, except in its shortened form, silly sod, poor sod, terms of derision or pity. Never, never used by decent women.

Father Matthew did not know—and had he known, would have discounted—the fact that Mistress Captoft had for years lived close with a scholar who had used words as words. He was therefore shocked and appalled. He stood up, clumsily, and said,

"That is an insult, to me; to my office; to Christ Himself."

"It was not so meant. A mere warning." Mistress Captoft rose, too, and faced him. "Who started this scurrilous talk? It is someone to beware of."

Being ushered in he had caught only a glancing look at the picture; sitting below it, he had had no view of it at all. Now, backing away, he saw that it was all and worse than Jem Watson had said. Though the serpent was not actually being suckled; its head lay on the woman's arm, its lidless eyes staring with defiant malevolence.

Confused; shocked; an evil woman and an evil picture, Father Matthew said, "I do not know. The kitchen at Edgar's Acre was crowded."

With that he made for the door.

The ugly word rang in his mind all day, the more clangingly when he looked at Tim, so like the strange beast in the evil picture. An object for charity if ever there was one. And the priest had been charitable. It was so unjust. Such a terrible insult. Grown man as he was, Father Matthew could have wept from sheer mortification. At one point he seriously considered finding a lodging for the boy in the village—for what that evil woman had *said*, others might be *thinking*. He rejected the idea; nobody would lodge the boy for nothing, and he simply could not afford to pay even the smallest charge. Besides, it would expose the poor creature to the harsh cruel world from which he had been rescued.

In addition to that most repulsive word the wicked woman had used others. Village gossip. Your village cronies. In a lonely parish like this, with whom could a priest consort except with the villagers? With whom had Christ consorted during His earthly sojourn? Humble men! It was all very well for her to be so scornful; when her nephew occupied this living he'd had a mule and could ride around making visits to his own kind. Moyidan was five miles away; Nettleton as far if not farther. Besides, hadn't friendliness with the villagers borne good results? More people came to Mass now than ever before. A nasty voice—not unlike Mistress Captoft's—spoke in his mind, stating the fact that the ultimate sign of friendship had not yet shown itself. His glebe was still unploughed. Father Matthew spent a miserable day. He was an earnest, conscientious, practicing Christian; but he lacked the mysticism that had kept old Father Ambrose going; nor could he, like Father Benedict, seek consolation in books.

Mistress Captoft, finishing off the wine, was thoughtful, too. If such things were being *said* . . . Why not? But this time no subterfuge. Marriage—and perhaps, after all, a child.

She was not skilled in the art of cajolery. Her marriage had been arranged by her parents, and the attraction between her and Benny had been mutual, both in a way fighting against it but caught in a net. Now she faced the task of attracting a man somewhat her junior, a grave, courteous, reserved man and one with whom, as Father Matthew had said, she had lived close for over a year without the slightest sign of familiarity.

Her glass—just large enough to show her her face—assured her that though youth had gone, the years had treated her kindly, fresh complexion, firm flesh, bright eyes, hair fading a little but still plentiful. Her figure had lasted well, too, though thickening slightly around the waist. Something could and should be done about that.

She had other assets. She was capable, level-headed. She had money of her own.

She had the affection of her godson, who had taken to calling her Mamma-Captoft. At first he had resented being taught, but a little bribery—a cake or a sweetmeat or a ride on the mule—worked wonders and Henry had used his influence. "When I was your age, son, I had the chance to learn and didn't take it. I've often been sorry."

"It is never too late," Mistress Captoft remarked. "I could teach you at the same time."

There was something not quite acceptable to his pride in

that suggestion; to attempt to remedy a defect was to admit its existence.

"That is a kind offer. I'm too old a dog to learn new tricks."

"What nonsense, Master Tallboys. You are in the prime of life."

"For doing things that I know, maybe. Not for learning."

That was before Father Matthew's visit. Now she could see that this lack of learning might be to her advantage. She began to make frequent references to the great service she had been to her first husband.

"He was old and infirm, you see, when we were married—his children were all older than I was myself. Quite soon he became house-bound and relied upon me absolutely. I assure you, Master Tallboys, that if at any time I can be of assistance to you, in any way, you have only to ask."

"Thank you; but I do little business in that sense of the word. And I have a fair head for figures."

She spoke of the child. "I have come to look upon him as my own. I have always felt that a child does better with *two* parents."

"Most of my youth we made do with one. Our father was so often absent."

"Ah! I see that you are looking at my new gown, Master Tallboys. Do you think the colour too garish? I hesitated myself between this and crimson."

"Poppy colour is cheerful on a dull day, Mistress Captoft."

"One of the *sad* things about growing older—away from the place where one was young—is that there is nobody to use one's given name any more. Mine is Martha, but I was always known as Mattie."

"It has occurred to me, from time to time," Henry said, "that you live rather a lonely life, Mistress Captoft. But I thought you would know that any friend of yours would have a welcome here."

A snub direct? Inside herself she reacted with spirit. And why not indeed? Who provides the wine, the silver, the spices, the servants, everything which lifts this house above the level of an ordinary farm?

Impervious, that was the word to describe him. Deaf to all hints; blind to new bright dresses and a waist rendered more shapely by the cruel clench of iron-braced stays.

She tried other approaches; an appeal to self-interest. Under pretence of consulting him as to whether this was or was not a good time to sell, she let him know exactly what she owned. Henry listened, pondered, asked a few cogent questions about lease terms and rents and then said that so far as he could see land was the one thing that had real value. It didn't go sick; it couldn't get up and run away.

There was one trick left. Withdrawal. And that she tried. She had, she said, sometimes considered buying or hiring a house in Baildon or in Bywater. Which did he advise?

Again that careful consideration.

"Bywater is livelier, all the year round. When my Uncle William was Bishop there, we used to look forward to our stay with him, though he supported so many charities that his guests were half starved. And there is the East wind to bear in mind. It is tempered a bit by the time it reaches Baildon, but having lived in Dunwich you know about the East wind."

He was impervious. He'd lost his heart and, presently, his virginity to such a different woman: a cloud of black hair, great black eyes, and bones like a bird's—and as easily broken. He had then married; sensibly, prosaically, as most men did, and that—except for Godfrey—had been a disaster. He had finished with that side of life. He'd known a moment of weakness—and not a pleasant memory at all. Anyway, Joanna was safe at Stordford, and by degrees he was paying off his debt to her. He'd never sold a calf or a fattened steer without going along to Master Turnbull's office and putting half of the money into trust; he paid in all that came from the sale of her wool or any sheep marketed. His obligations to his brother Robert—so mysteriously vanished—and his obligations to Joanna, kept him poor. And though everybody thought he was stupid to go on saving up for a lost child, Henry could always fall back upon his own experience. His father had vanished, been deemed dead, and come back.

Lady Grey said, "I never *quite* believed that she was short of twelve when she came here. So very mature. And with such assurance. Well, that means that she will be at *least* fourteen in the June of next year. I see nothing against a betrothal."

She wanted Joanna out of the house, or at least firmly spoken for. Maude, who had developed tardily, was now marriageable—and who would look at Maude, except to make unfavourable comparisons?

Sir Barnabas' usually cheerful face had a troubled look and she attributed this to his feeling about the discrepancy in the ages. Men could be very sentimental—where a pretty face was concerned.

"Not perhaps an ideal match," she said with the air of one conceding a point. "Not what I should wish for Maude or Beatrice. But compare their families! You were told that she was a girl of good family; she says that her mother was a lady and her father a knight, of Spain. There has never been the slightest evidence of the truth of such a claim."

"I'm concerned about the dowry, my dear."

"What about it?"

"I'd counted on it until she became sixteen. Shefton has an eye to money, for all his wealth. And to hand it over now would put me in a muddle."

"Oh," Lady Grey said, and became thoughtful. She understood the running of a household, the management of the estate, but of higher finance, dealings in London and such like she knew nothing. For some reason they never seemed real to her. "Leave this to me," she said. "Tell Lord Shefton that I do not favour the match."

"But you just said you did."

"Tell him otherwise—but that I am willing to discuss it with him."

Well, Sir Barnabas thought, he'd never known Gertrude to make a muddle yet, while he seemed to blunder from one to another, and to a man of his nature the words Leave it to me, were welcome, particularly when they concerned a matter which threatened to be troublesome.

Resolutely, Lady Grey raised every possible objection. Far too young, she said; not fourteen until next June and as yet quite unfitted to occupy the position that she would hold as Countess of Shefton. In another two years, perhaps. She flattered his failing virility by a discreet reference to the inadvisability of girls bearing children too young. There were other aspects of the matter. In the course of Nature, barring some catastrophe, the expectation of life in a girl of fourteen exceeded that of a man in his sixties. "You have other children, my lord, with prior claims. The poor girl might find herself a widow in straitened circumstances." And after all she had been consigned to the Greys' care with a view to her making a *suitable* marriage. She hoped his lordship would not take offence at her plain-spokenness, but she had never been one to take responsibility lightly.

It was an impressive performance, but the mention of the girl's prospects as a widow, seemed to offer a shred of hope that if a satisfactory financial settlement could be reached Lady Grey might be less obdurate over the matter of age. He was a mean man, but he was also enormously wealthy, cost meant nothing and he was infatuated by the girl, not only with her looks, which were remarkable enough, but by something else quite undefinable; the nearest he could get to it was a hidden promise; and the thought that even with a sack over her head she'd still be attractive. He proceeded to make promises so lavish—including asking no dowry—that Lady Grey had a wistful thought about Maude; if only he weren't quite so old; if only his teeth were better . . .

Outwardly she kept up a pretence at reluctance. All these promises must be set down in proper legal form. And the nearest thing Joanna had in the way of a guardian was the Bishop of Bywater, who must, of course, be consulted. It would all take a little time. Perhaps if his lordship cared to keep Christmas at Stordford, and came prepared . . . She herself would do her best to prepare the girl for the high destiny that awaited her.

At Intake, though at a ploughman's pace, things went forward inexorably.

Father Matthew could not forgive—never would forgive the dreadful insult. He knew that he should; it was a Christian's duty to forgive, "seventy times seven." And in every Pater Noster one prayed that God should forgive as man forgave man. It was impossible. Every time he looked at Tim, so ugly. No bridge to his nose, wide, almost lipless mouth, eyes with red rims and no lashes, he was reminded of that shocking word. That anybody could possibly *think* . . . And since the boy cooked, served, cleaned, tended the pig and the bit of garden, he was constantly within view, keeping the wound open like a beggar's sore. And since one of any man's needs is self-justification, Father Matthew moved from the effort to forgive the unforgiveable to a question: Should one forgive evil?

Christ on the Cross had said, "Father, forgive them, they know not what they do." A plea for forgiveness for the ignorant. But Mistress Captoft was far from ignorant—the very use of the word proved that. Christ on the Cross had promised the dying thief, "This day thou shalt be with Me in Paradise." But that man was simply a thief, paying for his crime by dying a dreadful death. There was a difference.

"As you said, Jem Watson, it is an evil picture. One no

decent woman would have stitched upon, no decent man hung upon his wall. And she is an evil woman." Having made this statement he felt better, more justified.

Now some idle thoughts—less than that, mere speculations—came drifting up. Put into words for the first time because nobody in Intake was prepared to risk being thought fanciful. A bit of embroidery on an old, accepted tale, a bit of exaggeration here and there was perfectly in order. Any kind of fancy was likely to be dismissed with laughter. But now . . . What about?

Aah! What about Mistress Tallboys: a young woman, in the best of health one day, in screaming agony the next, and dead in a week?

What about Father Benedict: standing up there one day, burying two, and dead the next day?

What about the brews Mistress Captoft made? Bitter and horrible. Bitter as gall, sour as a crab-apple.

One dissident voice. Old Hodgson, really so old that he should be dead now, but alive and hearty—apart from a bit of stiffness in the joints, a common affliction with all over forty.

"She make a good brew," he said. "But for her I'd be dead now. Five days I hadn't been to the privy and I'd got a lump the size of a millstone, just here." He struck the lower part of his belly. "I reckoned my time had come and I said to Ted, 'Go fetch the priest; my last hour is come.' So off went Ted, at the trot, and Mistress Captoft she sent a dose and said try that first. So I did and it shifted. Afore morning light. In the dead dark I got myself to the privy and was there till dawn. Give them all a surprise when I walked into the kitchen, cleared out and as good as new."

It had given them a surprise, and not a welcome one. His son Ted and his wife, Bet, would have been only too glad to have him out of the way; he knew that. Ted wanted Hodgacre for his own and Bet wanted the extra room. Mistress Captoft's dose had saved his life, for which he was thankful; it had also thwarted their little schemes; almost as important and decidedly more amusing.

Old Ethel said, "Them that make good brews can make bad ones too."

The talk swung round again to the suddenness with which Mistress Tallboys and Father Benedict had died, and the haste with which Mistress Captoft had moved in and begun to rule Knight's Acre. This time Father Matthew asked his question aloud. What then prevented them from marrying?

"Could be the money," somebody said. "Left to her so long as she didn't marry agin. Lotta men put that in their wills."

It fitted, the priest thought. Living in sin for the sake of money. What one would expect of a woman who had stitched that picture and used such language. One day he'd borrow Johnson's horse and ride to Moyidan and ask Father Thomas what he knew about Mistress Captoft's circumstances. That errand was delayed; it was almost as difficult to borrow Johnson's horse as it was to get the glebe ploughed.

Father Thomas said, "I really know very little about Mistress Captoft. In fact I never heard of her, or saw her, until my nephew—your predecessor—came to Intake. She called herself his aunt, but I could never trace a direct kinship. Relationship by marriage possibly. I never bothered. Why do you ask?" Why come to Moyidan on a borrowed horse and disturb an afternoon's rest? Father Thomas felt rather peevish.

"I wondered about her money. Whether it is hers or only hers on conditions?"

Father Thomas blinked the sleepiness from his eyes. Widows with money were the Church's best friends and maybe Mistress Captoft was making a will in favour of the church at Intake, which, God knew, needed such an endowment.

"That I can tell you—at least what Benedict—God rest his soul!—once told me. And I have no reason to doubt his word. He said . . . Yes, I remember almost his exact words. I ventured to say that I thought she was frivolous and worldly, and he said, on the contrary, she was a near saint, burying herself in so remote a place and keeping his house, when she was well-to-do, in her own right. What her first husband left to her, he left absolutely, without conditions. Had she stayed in Dunwich she could doubtless have married again."

(Even then, years ago, while Father Benedict was grateful to his uncle for having procured him a living—though a poor one—he had not been able to accept even the most glancing criticism of Mattie, his love.)

Jogging home on his borrowed horse, Father Matthew thought—Then there is no impediment; except the will of a wicked woman.

There was one bull in Intake—apart from the one at Knight's Acre, newcomer—and it belonged to Bert Edgar, who, because his father died and his elder brother met with an accident, had inherited all. This bull, a black and very savage beast, served the cows of Intake, Clevely, Nettleton and Muchanger, and occasionally those from further afield, since he was known as a good sire. Every year in autumn—cows varied in their seasons, it could be September or October—men would come, leading the meek yet suddenly frisky cows. While the bull was taking the only exercise in his cruelly restricted life, the cow's owner and Bert Edgar struck the bargain. So much down now, either in cash or kind, and so much more when the cow was visibly in calf. After that Bert had no responsibility; the cow could slip her calf or the calf could be born rump first. None of his business.

This year, instead of bringing the second payments, man after man came with complaints. The Edgar's Acre bull had failed.

At first Bert was truculent: "You gotta a barren cow, you gotta a barren cow, no good coming here whining to me."

At the best of times Bert was as ill-tempered as his bull. He'd married Jill, knowing her to be lazy, but convinced that given enough stick, she'd improve. He'd wanted *one* child—a boy to inherit—and he'd got him; but he'd got more. Every year, regular as the changing seasons, pregnant again, growing heavy and useless. Every time, after the first, he'd given her a thorough good thrashing, but she wouldn't learn. Five gaping mouths to feed now. And no second fees to come. And the whole thing a bit of a mystery. Everybody knew that bulls, like all other animals, like people, grew old, grew tame, went unresisting to the butcher, or to the bull-ring.

But the black bull was not all that old. Eight years at most, but useless.

Like a witch's strike!

Everybody in Intake *knew* about witches and what they could do. Some long-remembered, handed-down stories, some less remote. All but the very young could remember Granny Robinson, who had lived in their midst and been tolerated, partly because she was one of them, partly because in the main her activities had been harmless. She made love potions, brews that got rid of an unwanted pregnancy, and she could charm away warts. People had been very careful how they behaved or spoke to her, however, because she could turn very nasty if provoked. Aah! What about her granddaughter who'd married against the old woman's wishes, or advice, and remembering some sharp words, did not invite her grandmother to the wedding.

"No. I ain't going," Granny Robinson said. "And *he* might as well not go hisself!" People remembered that remark when the marriage proved to be childless, and the girl confided to her mother, in the strictest secrecy, that her husband was useless in bed. In strict confidence meant telling somebody else, after swearing her to secrecy; soon all the village knew. And naturally pleas, even bribes failed to persuade the old woman to lift the spell, for to do so would have been to admit that she had put it on in the first place. "Nothing to do with *me*," she said.

Impotent was not a word used in the village; Bert's bull was useless; past it; not up to his job.

There was a perfectly good bull, young and of surprisingly mild temper, so Jem Watson said, up at Knight's Acre, but to use him would mean doing business with Master Tallboys and that would go against the grain. Added to the tradition of unfriendliness between village and house, there was a dislike for Henry personally. He worked just as they did; he wore much the same clothes, but he was different. Even in the market. Did he ever greet a man who'd made a specially good bargain, with a hearty slap on the shoulders? Did he ever drink a mug of ale in The Hawk In Hand?

The Elders of the village held a meeting to discuss the question of the bull, and after much talk decided upon a practical arrangement. Every landowner in Intake, whether he kept a cow or not, would subscribe to the cost of a new animal, which would be kept at Edgar's Acre because Bert had the experience. Any Intake cow would be served free of charge; those brought from outside would pay fees as usual— the charge to be slightly higher than in the past, and to be paid in money. One fifth of this money was to go to Bert Edgar for feeding and managing the bull, the rest was to be divided between the men who kept no cow. A just and sensible arrangement and one which would not be questioned, for in village affairs the Elders' word was law. Intake had never had a lord of the manor to rule from above, but since some order must be maintained, the men who had hacked their acres out of the forest, had reverted, unwittingly, to the fashion of a far older day, of the free settlements of Danish origin. They had chosen seven of their oldest, presumably wisest men to settle domestic matters. When one died, or grew senile, the six remaining chose someone to take his place. Such choice, never openly disputed, had on occasion led to ill feeling between families; but on the whole it worked.

Old Hodgson, a good hand with a tally stick, was chosen to keep the accounts.

The new bull was bought and installed, but a season had been lost; next year there'd be no calves in April or May to romp on the common or in the meadows; and cheese and butter would have to be bought. Still, the future was provided for.

Then a new disaster struck, beginning at Edgar's Acre, but threatening the whole community. Jill Edgar, pregnant again, and with another black eye, went to feed the pigs: a sow and six young, one destined for home consumption, five for market just before Christmas, when young porkers were in great demand. Ordinarily the sow came pushing and grunting at the sight of the swill-bucket, but this morning she lay in the corner and did not stir. Jill thought bitterly that there were mornings when she felt like that herself! She took a stick and prodded the animal, alive though listless, with measured ferocity. The sow did not move, and emptying the bucket into the trough, at which the young began to guzzle, Jill went back to the house. She said nothing to Bert; he was not a man who would take a bit of bad news without venting his wrath on the bringer of it; so let him see for himself.

He saw, later in the day, and recognised, in the reddened eyes, the dripping nose, the quick, panting breaths, that curse of all who reared pigs: the dreaded swine fever, as deadly as the plague or the sweating fever was to human beings. And as catching. The last outbreak had occurred before Bert inherited, when, second son, he had no expectations but was working as a hired man, up at Knight's Acre. Then every pig in Intake had died and the year was still remembered—the year we had to buy bacon. Bert remembered it well and presently saw that this disease was different. The sow did not develop the rash of spots around the ears or on the belly; instead she coughed, more like a cow or a steer with the husk than any pig suffering from swine fever. And instead of her innards—and those of the young, who promptly sickened—turning to water, this went the other way. Stopped up, blocked up. No mess at all.

He asked advice and his neighbours came, looked, standing well away, and said they had never seen anything like it.

No other pig was afflicted.

Once again the all-stand-together spirit triumphed over old feuds and personal disagreements and the village combined to provide Bert with the start of a new styeful. Jem Watson's father sold an in-pig sow for a trifle less than market price. Father Matthew contributed a halfpenny and gave the procedure a decorative touch—in helping an unfortunate neighbour, he said, they were offering thanks to God for sparing their own animals. Most of the men felt sorry for Bert—no bull fees this autumn, no porkers ready for Christmas; five children at table and another on the way! A few women thought it was a judgement on him for ill-treating his wife. Though when you came to think of it, it was a queer kind of judgement, for she was being punished, too. It had long been the custom at Intake to share when a pig was killed; you have a piece of mine now, and I'll have the same from you, when you kill yours. Jill's new sow wouldn't farrow until after Christmas, and she'd have nothing to share until well after Easter, but you couldn't stand by the rules at a time like this. They'd share, and wait.

But the Watson sow lay down in the Edgar's Acre stye and died in the same mysterious manner as the others had done.

Three blows, coming as fast and furious as those Bert dealt out to his wife and the unwanted children.

"Somebody put the evil eye on me, no doubt about that," Bert said.

But who? But why? The only person with an obvious grudge against him was his wife, and even *she,* senseless as she was, must know that his ruin was hers.

Father Matthew was present at many of these fireside talks, and suddenly, one evening, inside his mind, something flared, like a dry old log on a dying fire. Mistress Captoft!

He remembered exactly what she had said, after dealing him the wound that never healed. Who started this scurrilous talk about me? And he had mentioned Edgar's Acre.

Apart from a bit of desultory schooling, aimed at a single end, he was exactly like the Intake people, which was why he had become part of the village in a way that Father Ambrose, ascetic, near saint, and Father Benedict, remote and scholarly, had never been. He was just as superstitious, and with a smear of learning to prop up beliefs not openly accepted by educated men nowadays; but lurking in the background. Our Lord had admitted the existence of evil; during His forty days in the wilderness He had actually talked to the Devil: "Get thee hence, Satan." He had also said, "Go!" to two evil spirits which possessed two men, and so banished them into a herd of swine. The Gadarene swine.

And he, humble parish priest, had recognised evil; in the picture, in the woman, in the word she had used.

Just about a year ago.

Yes; October had come round again, and last year's October ale was ripe for drinking. The brown jug went round and tongues loosened. Bert Edgar's mention of the evil eye seemed to have unlatched a door. Somebody recalled and recounted the spell Granny Robinson had put upon that poor man. Somebody else raked up an older tale. But that had happened at Nettleton.

The October wind rattled the shutters, howled at the door. Make up the fire, draw closer, pass the jug . . .

Well, there was this old woman at Nettleton who was a witch and could turn herself into a wolf. As a wolf, at night, she went round robbing hen roosts and lambing pens. Everybody knew, but nothing could be proved until a man, three times robbed, set a trap. It didn't go off quite as it should, and in the morning all he found was a bit of a paw, and some hair, all bloody. But that was enough; taking some neighbours with him he'd gone to the old woman's cottage and there she was, with her left hand wrapped in a cloth. The top joint of the first finger chopped off. *She* said she'd done it chopping wood, meaning to spit a fowl. Aah, but what fowl? One of her own, she said; but hers were all speckled, and the feathers of the one she was about to cook, were white—just like the ones which the man had set the trap to protect.

Old Sawyer, father to the coffin maker, and Old Hodgson's senior by just eighteen months, could vouch for the truth of this story.

"She went afore the Justices, all fair and square, and she was burnt for a witch on Baildon marketplace. My grandfather journeyed in to see it done. And he towd me hisself. Time she roasted, he said, the smell wasn't like meat cooking. More like burnt hair, same's you'd get burning a wolf."

Except as the eldest of the Elders, Old Sawyer no longer counted for much; his son had taken over his trade and his holding, and his memory for anything recent was so faulty that, as his daughter-in-law complained, you couldn't even trust him with a message; send him to borrow a little salt and as like as not he'd come back with a spoon. But for by-gone things his memory was as good as ever. Most of his tales—including this one—had been told and re-told so many times that nobody listened any more. Tonight they did, and he enjoyed being the centre of attention for a change.

"She confessed, in the end. It was done by brews."

Father Matthew thought—Mistress Captoft wouldn't turn herself into a wolf; no, it'd be a snake. The snake in the picture was marked green and red and he now remembered that the woman had worn a gown which in some way combined those two colours.

The October ale was potent, and he could see, in his mind, a snake slithering through the night, striking a bull with impotence, bringing disease to the pigs. And leaving no trace.

They were talking about brews now; about Granny Robinson, who had carried the secret of hers to the grave with her, so that nobody in Intake could make such things nowadays.

"Except Mistress Captoft," Ethel said. Still relentless.

Well, suppose then, just suppose that Mistress Captoft could cast a spell, as well as make brews, *why Bert Edgar?* What had *he* ever done to offend her?

"I never even spoke to the woman. Never even seen her, except across the church, two-three times."

"I may be to blame," Father Matthew said, hatred and ale combining to make him incautious. "I went"—he gave a loud hiccup—"to speak to her about her way of life. She insulted me. And she asked who started the gossip. I couldn't say who. I did tell her where."

"My place?"

"Yes. I'm sorry. Very sorry, if I brought all this on you."

(So you should be, damn you! I'll get even with you, you blabber-mouthed bastard!)

When Bert Edgar was angry with Jill or the younger children, he struck them with his belt, or anything that was handy. On men he used his fists and his feet. But he couldn't very well set about a priest, especially one so popular. And at this moment Father Matthew, by proving how thoroughly he was one with them, sharing their belief in magic, was very popular indeed. But just let him wait! This year the men of Intake were actually on the verge of ploughing up his glebe. It wouldn't be done if Bert Edgar had any say in the matter. He wasn't an Elder; he was no longer even one of the prosperous, but he still had his fists, and most men were a bit scared of him.

This was the time of year, mid-days still warm, chill coming with sunset, when foggy nights were known at Intake. The people believed that it came in from the sea, blowing up along the river and trapped by the encircling woods. Carrying his lantern—almost worse than useless on such a night— Father Matthew blundered his way home.

So far as he could tell no snake crossed his path, but in the morning he woke with no voice. A croaking, a hoarseness could follow, he knew, upon an ordinary cold—but he had had no cold. He'd simply lost his voice. And that confirmed—had confirmation been needed—that Mistress Captoft could cast spells. Because he had joined in the talk against her, she'd struck him dumb. And what good was a dumb priest? Intake was a poor living, but it sufficed; once his glebe was under cultivation—and some of the Intake men had practically promised that this year, their own ploughing done, they'd spare a little time for *his,* things would be better. But dumb-struck, what future awaited him? He hadn't learning enough to be a clerk, or a professional scribe. He had no powerful friends, no family. And the shocking fact was that if you couldn't speak, you were regarded as idiotic.

He faced this dismal prospect for three days and then, as suddenly as it had gone, his voice came back and he was able to tell Timmy that he had been a good boy. As indeed he had. Timmy knew all about bodily afflictions; his face for a start, and as though that weren't bad enough, a fit now and then, everything lost, a whirling darkness and then the long, slow climb back to life. Timmy owed Father Matthew more than any amount of faithful service could ever repay.

Speech restored, conviction hardened, Father Matthew borrowed Johnson's horse again and this time rode down to Bywater and with peasant patience, under which lay peasant doggedness, waited, this room, another room, men who had done better in life, flitting in and out, telling him that His Grace was busy, but would see him presently. And presently he was admitted to the presence, knelt, kissed the amethyst ring, sat when invited to do so, on the very edge of the chair. Ungainly, as Mistress Captoft had judged; knees apart, coarse hands planted on the knees. But His Grace was a realist and knew that it was upon just such men as this one that the Church depended. The complicated, glittering structure had, like all others, to have foundations, roots. St. Peter, the humble fisherman—*"Upon this rock I will build my church."* He was prepared to listen patiently to what he sensed would be a rambling, trivial story, to advise if he could, reprimand if he must. What he was not prepared to do, and that appeared to be what Father Matthew was asking of him, was to take action against a so-called witch.

Enlightened men no longer believed in such things. That French girl, Joan of Arc, had been burned as a witch and by the very manner of her death—she had asked for a cross and an English soldier had hastily made one, two sticks tied together—she had brought the whole business of witchcraft and magic-making under fresh examination, in which intelligence over-rode prejudice. Most reasonable, modern-minded men—and the Bishop of Bywater was one—were now of the opinion that she had been the victim of political strife, condemned by judges who were biassed—or bribed. Simply by dying as she did she had brought witch-hunting into disrepute. So although His Grace listened with some semblance of patience, he listened sceptically to this tale of bulls rendered impotent, pigs dead of swine fever that was not swine fever, pictures of nude people and snakes that struck men dumb, the whole thing protracted, in true rustic style by what he said, what she said, what I said. At the end of the jumbled tale, Father Matthew said, "So I thought, Your Grace, I'd best come and ask your advice. What should I do?"

"Nothing."

"Nothing? But, Your Grace . . . What I have been saying . . ."

"A hotch-potch of out-worn superstition, some coincidence, and, I suspect, even more spite. I think that you will find, Father Matthew, that when you look into the matter more dispassionately, you will find that somebody—possibly more than one person—has a real or an imagined grievance against this poor woman, and, failing other means of redress, concocted this charge against her. Such an easy charge to bring; so difficult to refute." He saw it all, he thought. Intake, that remote place, backward, and Father Matthew, lonely, consorting with peasants, his own kind, except for a little, a very little education. But even so, a priest was an ordained man; he should maintain a certain dignity and not get himself so entangled with bulls and pigs and gossip.

He gave Father Matthew a little homily on the subject; gentle, because he was not an ill-natured man, and because he could, in a vague way, see the man's predicament. At the end of it, sensing something stubborn and resentful in the man, to whom he had—look at the measured glass where the sand dropping, marked the hours, and their halves and quarters—already devoted more time than he could really spare, he said,

"You came for advice and I have given it. Do nothing. Above all do not go running to the secular authority. Take this tale to the Sheriff and you will bring not only yourself but the Church into ridicule."

Father Matthew rode home in a curious state of mind. Angered, yes. He was furiously angered; he'd gone to seek support which had not been forthcoming. He'd been given a lecture; told to be friendly but not familiar, to lead rather than follow. All very well, but hadn't he, by being familiar as well as friendly, got far more people to Mass? However, there was another side to it. Spite had been mentioned and in all honesty he was bound to admit that he had not only felt spite against Mistress Captoft himself, but encouraged it in others.

Johnson, at Johnsacre was waiting for his horse. There were a few men; waiting. No women, they were busy with the last meal of the day.

So, what had the Bishop to say?

Do nothing.

Just the sort of bloody silly thing somebody sitting down there in Bywater *would* say! But they'd always been independent, acting on their own, sticking together when the occasion demanded it. This was a job for the Elders.

Now Old Hodgson faced a predicament. To speak up for Mistress Captoft, as gratitude demanded he should do, would be useless. It'd do her no good; one voice carried no weight against six; and it would do him harm. Sticking up for a witch. Who wanted that to be said about him? Especially just at a time like this, when Old Sawyer was failing, mumbling about, making no sense of what was happening around him. Any day now he'd be asked to stand down, and Old Hodgson would be eldest of the Elders. So he sat quietly, making no suggestions of his own, but with nods and sounds of agreement going along with it all.

Having dismissed Father Matthew, the Bishop turned to correspondence, writing two letters in his own hand. One to Lady Grey, expressing his hearty approval of the proposed match and conveying his congratulations on the splendid management which had produced such a satisfactory result. The second letter was to Lord Shefton, slightly sycophantic and deftly calling to his lordship's attention the fact that to some degree he had himself been instrumental . . . The Earl was not only very rich, but very powerful, too.

"He's off to market tomorrow," Jem reported.

"You sure?"

"Certain. He was altering the waggon this afternoon."

Most fattened bullocks walked to market, spending two

days on the journey if necessary, and being beaten all the way, not only by their drover but by any casual person who cared to take a whack—the blows were supposed to make the meat more tender. Henry, though not unduly sentimental about animals—no farmer could afford to be—thought it a barbarous custom as well as quite useless. So he conveyed his in the waggon, and since a well-fed beast was too much of a load for one horse, he had made a contraption consisting of one shaft, so that the two horses could pull side by side. Even so, with one horse getting old it was a slow journey and he left home early, and disregarded Godfrey's pleas to be taken, too. "You'd add to the weight. You shall come next time." It didn't do to let boys have their own way all the time.

"Perhaps even on my mule," Mistress Captoft said. "That is if you try really hard with your sums."

The lesson was going on in the hall, on the side of the table nearest the fire, for it was a cold day; Katharine was making bread and David was busy in the dairy when the iron ring on the main door—serving both as handle and knocker—banged. Mistress Captoft went to the door herself. Opening it upon two Intake men in their working clothes, she thought it insolent of them to have come to this door and was about to send them round to the back, when she became aware of a kind of urgency in their manner.

"What is it?"

"Can you come, mistress?"

"What is wrong?" Her thoughts went at once to her store of curatives. The people of Intake had done nothing to endear themselves to her, had indeed grossly offended her, but she was not the woman to deny help to an individual in order to punish a whole community. Also she half recognised one of the men—he had come for the priest and been sent off with a dose, which had worked, and the father, restored to health, had actually thanked her.

"Thass what we don't know. Thass why we come for you."

Possibly an accident, requiring prompt attention.

"I'll just get my cloak," she said. She left the door open and in the half minute that it took her to run upstairs and down again, Ted Hodgson and Bert Edgar made the most of their chance to study the picture stretched across the wall, over the blazing hearth. The only other pictures they had ever seen were those painted on the walls of the church; once so faded and peeling from damp as to be almost meaningless, then restored by Sir Godfrey. And those pictures had been painted in the then contemporary fashion, so that Mary, and the other Mary at the foot of the Cross wore nun's garb; and even the figure on the Cross wore a decent breech clout. The almost life-size nude figures were quite shocking, and the snake was horrible.

"Can I come, Mamma-Captoft?" Godfrey asked as she ran down the stairs. Anything to avoid sums, which he could do, but hated.

Expecting blood, or somebody in a fit, choking on his own tongue, or a breech-birth, Mistress Captoft said, "No," in a voice sharper than that she usually used to him.

They took the shortest way to the village, Sir Godfrey, remembered only as a grabber and a tyrant, had had a sharp eye for terrain, and had realised that unless he planned well the people of Intake would have to trudge around the perimeter of an irregular oblong in order to get to church; so he had left them, in addition to a good part of the common, a path which skirted his sheep-fold on its shorter side, emerged practically in front of his house and so to the church.

It was not a wide path. People used it when they came to church; Jem Watson used it every day, coming and going to work; it was well trodden, but not very wide. Was there, however, the need to jostle? As they were doing, almost as though . . . as though she were a wrong-doer being hustled along to the lock-up.

Put them into place, she thought. After all, they had sought her aid, they could at least be respectful.

"What is it? An accident?"

The man she did not recognise—Bert Edgar had said himself that he had never spoken to her, only seen her across the church a few times; he was not much of a church-goer, just Christmas and Easter; he'd never ailed himself, and nor had his first boy; for Jill, and the other unwanted children he would certainly never have gone plodding along asking aid—said, "You'll see when you get there."

And then she sensed something wrong. Sinister.

She was not a timid woman; she said, in the face of something wrong, wrong in a way she could not account for, "I refuse to take another step until you have explained your errand."

"You'll see," Bert Edgar said, speaking as roughly as he did to his downtrodden wife. The most tricky part of the business was over now. He put out a big, work-hardened hand and took Mistress Captoft by the upper arm.

Godfrey Tallboys, curious as all children were, wanted to know what was happening. If he opened the door Mamma-Captoft might look back, see that he had left his task and hold it against him when it came to lending of the mule. But he could look out of the window. He was tall for his age, all Tallboys were, but not yet quite tall enough to have much of a view from a window which Master Hobson, who had built the house, had deliberately set high and narrow. But Godfrey dragged up a stool and attained a wider, longer view and saw Mamma-Captoft being manhandled. One man on each side.

There was no thought about it. He came of fighting stock—belligerence could be diverted, as it had been with Henry, fighting the weather, fighting circumstance, fighting himself. But in the boy, softly reared, pampered, spoilt, the old tough spirit sprang up. He took the poker from the hearth and ran out.

Something warned him not to shout, not to give any warning. Take the enemy by surprise! Hit where you can hit hardest. Both hands!

He hit Ted Hodgson on the side of the knee; a really crippling blow. The man let go of Mamma-Captoft and clasped his leg in both hands, yelping. Mamma-Captoft, thus released on one side, twisted around, but still held by the left hand of the other man, who also swung round, still grabbing Mamma-Captoft with one hand, his other ready to snatch the poker. Which he did. The boy's strength and fury were no match for a full-grown man's. Bert Edgar's left hand, hurt, but not much weakened, thrust the poker back, straight into the face of the fierce little cub, who fell backwards into the brambles that edged the path, and lay still.

Mistress Captoft, truly alarmed now, struggled frenziedly and flailed about with her free hand. Bert Edgar said,

"Lay ahold of the bitch on the other side, Ted. Never mind your knee." He had little sensitivity to pain himself and no sympathy for it in others. "If you must hobble, lean on her," he said.

Once, in Dunwich, Mistress Captoft had seen a woman of known bad character, dragged out of town on a hurdle. Every seaport had women who lived—and often supported families—on their immoral earnings. Now and again some almost symbolic action was taken against them, and that woman had been the victim of one of the brief purges. Banned forever from the town itself, and from the "hundred" of which the town was the centre. Mistress Captoft knew that the term hundred dated from long ago, when each hundred families was regarded as a responsible unit, answerable in law for the behaviour of its members and thus eager to expel anyone really recalcitrant.

Much the same thing, she imagined, was about to happen to her. The way she had been treated; the bigger man's use of the word *bitch:* all pointed that way. As she was hustled roughly across a yard and into a kitchen, she prayed urgently if incoherently: God, save me, Jesus, help me, Holy Mother of God, let them leave me my skirt . . . And all in a muddle her mind was still capable of thinking: How ironic; I lived in sin as they would call it, with Benny; and no stone cast; now, after two years with Master Tallboys and not even a fond word . . .

But it was not that.

Six Elders sat around the kitchen table. Old Hodgson was suffering one of his fairly frequent bouts of stiffness of the joints and was confined to his bed. The unwritten rules demanded an odd number, seven or five, so that on any vital question there should be a casting vote, but this morning that rule could be ignored, for Old Sawyer no longer counted, babbling away about things long ago. Ignore him and that left five, all good men and true—and all violently prejudiced.

They used curiously formal terms, brought out of some remote past. They said: "You are accused . . ." They said: "You are charged . . ." They asked: "How do you plead; guilty or not guilty?" All was in order. She was invited, given the opportunity, to defend herself. But against something that she had never, even in nightmare, imagined.

Witchcraft.

The Bishop had described it exactly, a charge easy to bring, difficult to refute. Had the charge been of immorality she could have demanded that they send for Katharine Dowley to swear on the Bible that though her room lay between she had never seen or heard any comings or goings, that she made both beds and had never seen any evidence. David Fuller, who waited at table and mended the fire, could have sworn that no fond word or even glance, had ever passed between Master Tallboys and Mistress Captoft. Also, distasteful as it would be to drag in a child, Godfrey could have been asked: Where do you sleep? And the answer would have been: Often in the little bed in my father's room. Oh, that would have been easy.

Also—and this was a thought to chill the heart—even had such defence failed, she would still be alive; publicly whipped perhaps, and wearing nothing but her petticoat, run out of Intake on a hurdle. But alive. A so-called witch had no chance at all. Procedures varied. Sometimes she was stripped and searched for any unusual mark, a mole or a wart by which she was supposed to suckle her familiar; or she was pricked with pins to discover an insensitive part—held to serve the same purpose. She could be starved, denied sleep, forced to walk up and down until her feet were bloody rags and she made a confession simply to escape further torments. Death was certain. Burn the witch! There was another way, ironically called a test. Throw a witch into water; if she floated, she was a witch and could be taken out and burned; if she sank, she drowned and was regarded as innocent. Then everybody said what a pity and gave her Christian burial.

Oh, God, I have sinned, grievously, but grant me, of Thy mercy, death by drowning.

Except for prayer there was nothing she could do except deny all charges, which she did stoutly, though without hope. She said that she knew nothing of Bert Edgar, had never spoken to him; did not even know that he had a bull. She asked why should she wish to harm him?

Aah, they knew the answer to that. From the mouth of the priest himself. They could have called him in and confronted her with him, but Father Matthew, though informed of what was planned, had excused himself from taking any part in it. A priest, they must understand, could not disobey a direct order from his Bishop. His Grace had told him to do nothing; therefore he must do nothing.

What was planned was a swimming; it was the showiest way and provided most entertainment for the ordinary people.

Outside Bert Edgar said to Ted Hodgson, "Come on, walk about, else it'll stiffen on you." That was, in Intake, the rough-and-ready method of dealing with most injuries, short of a broken bone. Bert had a suspicion that his thumb was broken—and for that Ted Hodgson was to blame. Hit on the knee by a brat no older or bigger than Bert's own firstborn, and dancing about as though his feet were on fire. If Ted hadn't let go the woman's arm so that he'd been left to deal with her *and* with the young rascal, he'd have given him something to remember.

Hobbling, forced to walk about the yard, each step more painful, Ted Hodgson said, "Wait a bit, Bert," and propped himself against the rails of the empty pig-stye. "You ever known a young 'un behave that way?"

"No, I never. It'd be leather'd out of them, afore they was that size." Even his own wanted, eldest son, always privileged in the matter of food and general treatment, knew the limits of paternal indulgence and never over-stepped the limit.

"Come up without a sound," Ted Hodgson said, anxious to explain why he had been taken unawares. "And struck with the strength of ten. And then, when I looked round, he wasn't there. I'm beginning to wonder. . . . Bert, some of *them* have cats and toads and such things."

"Never mind about that. She's as good as done for. Come on, walk. Don't you 'o'n't get down to see her swum."

"I reckon my leg's broke."

"Don't talk so daft. Broke bones grate. Listen to this!"

He gave audible evidence of his own broken bone, and was too ignorant to know that a knee-cap, without being broken, could shift.

Godfrey Tallboys disentangled himself from the brambles. He couldn't breathe through his nose, which hurt when he put up an experimental finger, and seemed to be lop-sided. There was nobody on the path now. And, his blow struck, he knew that he was no match for two grown men. He thought of David and dismissed the thought, lame. But there was Father. And there was the mule which now he did not need permission to use. He began to run, breathing heavily through his mouth.

Many people had hung about Bert Edgar's yard while the trial went on in the kitchen—his premises were used because he was the injured party and the Elders had no settled meeting place—but some had already gone down to the riverside, to get a good place for the show.

There was one main dipping place from which most women fetched water. There were only two wells in Intake, one at the priest's house, the other at Knight's Acre. When the river ran high, anybody could dip a bucket from anywhere along the bank, thus saving a bit of a trudge, but when the water lowered, women—always the water carriers—went to the Steps, cut into the clay bank and reinforced by lengths of sawn timber. Awaiting the winter rains now, the river ran slow, but steadily, level with the fourth step from the bottom.

To this place, Mistress Captoft, her thumbs already tied

together, was brought. A few people crossed themselves to ward off the evil eye, most hissed and jeered. Women held up their small children, so that they might see and remember.

The bound thumbs held her hands in the attitude of prayer and though she was shaken by fear and deathly pale, she was still thankful. Not to be burnt. And still to be clothed. And in a way she was resigned; she *had* sinned, in loving Benny; had confessed and been absolved too seldom. Now, if only she could drown quickly . . . Some time in Purgatory—for who would buy a Mass for her?—and then Heaven; a reunion of disembodied spirits all within the aura of the glory of God. Her parents, the brother she had loved and who had died before he was four; kind old Master Captoft. In Heaven, where there was neither marriage nor giving in marriage.

As somebody tied her skirts about her ankles with a cord, she prayed again. God, let me die quickly. Lord, into Thy hands I commend my spirit . . .

She fell with a splash and went down like a stone. Was under long enough for some people to have doubts. The innocent drowned, didn't they? More people crossed themselves. Then, some way down river but well within view, she rose to the surface and seemed to be riding on the water, bobbing a little, as though taking leave of Intake with a curtsey this way and that. A witch, all right.

They were prepared for that. Plough ropes with nooses all ready, young men, swift of foot and practised in catching one wanted animal out of a number, all set to run along the bank and take her, alive, to the fire, also ready in Bert Edgar's yard.

And then the impossible happened, just where the river made a slight curve, but still in the sight of all, Mistress Captoft was literally taken up, seemed for a breath-space to walk the water and vanished into the forest on the further bank.

Nobody lived, or had ever lived, so far as anyone knew, on that side of the river. Along the bank where the curve of the river deposited silt at certain seasons, there were trees, and there were trees too on some islands of higher ground so that looking across the river, the far side gave the appearance of being wooded. There were, however, stretches of dangerous swamp. Nobody at Intake had first- or even fourth-hand experience of the place, but some old tales had survived. Once upon a time . . . Stories of men stepping on to what looked like green pasture and sinking to the knees, the thighs, the chest. The swamp began a few miles south of Baildon and extended, growing less and less wooded, to the coast. There it changed into sand dunes. Because of its reputation as a dangerous place it was avoided even by charcoal burners or refugees from justice. No wolf howled there, no fox barked, no deer flitted. Waste Wood belonged to birds, squirrels and snakes.

It was plain that Mistress Captoft had not been saved by any human intervention.

"Sick it up," Old Hodgson said, thumping her back. He loosened and lifted the noose from about her body, and with his knife cut the cords. She was sick, dizzy and bewildered, drenched and terribly cold, but in her right mind. Blue-lipped and with teeth chattering she tried to thank him, but he cut her short.

"Never mind that now. We gotta get on the move." He removed the outer one of the two rough coats he was wearing and pushed her arms into it. "Soon warm up," he said. "Drink this." He removed the plug from a small leather bottle and she gulped down a dose of what felt like liquid fire. He unhitched and wound the rope which he had fastened to a tree-trunk. He had had faith in his eye, and in his judgement but had not trusted his strength to haul her in unaided; she was a well-fleshed woman and wet clothes weighed heavy. "I gotta be back in my bed by sun-down and the ford's a way up. You all right, now?" Telling her to keep exactly behind him, he set off at a good pace. The path which he had trodden down and hacked out earlier in the day lay clear ahead; it'd have been different in summer, when vegetation could spring back into place within an hour. Once he paused and said, "Careful now. That ain't grass. Jump!" He did so himself, surprisingly spry for an old man whose stiffness of joints had for years prevented him from doing any heavy or unpleasant task. His daughter-in-law had once said, very sourly, "The only thing about him that ain't stiff is his jaw. He can allust eat." Ted Hodgson had added, "And his tongue!" He was a carping old man.

Now he jumped over a space where the swamp was encroaching and waited to see how she managed. "Well done!" he said, and set off again. Here, because the swamp was creeping in, the screen of trees grew thinner, and Intake, on the other bank was visible.

"There's the village," he said. "The ford ain't so far now."

It was not a ford in the proper sense of the word—a place

where a river is shallow enough to be crossed by foot. Long centuries earlier some indefatigable Roman engineer had planned a straight road, and a bridge which would shorten by twenty miles the distance between Baildon and Colchester. The fact that on the other side of the river the land was swampy had not deterred him: he planned a causeway. With thousands of others he had been recalled when the barbarians threatened the Empire and his work had never been even half completed. His length of straight road—though its solid foundations and its paving stones remained almost intact—had been forgotten, neglected, overgrown; and of his planned bridge only some piers remained, worn smooth by the river. Old Hodgson—Young Hodgson then—and another boy had discovered the stones one day, a day between hay-making and harvest, when even hard-worked little boys had a few leisure days. They'd spent a happy afternoon, jumping from one stone, only just awash, to another, and then gone home and forgotten all about it.

The other boy was dead, and Old Hodgson had only remembered when he had to.

They crossed, and were in Layer Wood.

"Now, mind what I say," Old Hodgson said. "I take this short cut, straight back to the village and get myself to bed. *You* have a longer road. You can't go near the village. So walk straight on and you'll come to a pool; bear to your right then and you should come out not far from the back of Knight's Acre." It was dusk already under the trees and he'd never known a woman who had any sense of direction or who wasn't scared of the dark, so despite his own urgent need for haste he spared her another minute, telling her the way again and adding, "And there's nowt to be scared of; there ain't the wolves about there used to be."

"I can never, never thank you sufficiently; but I shall remember you in my prayers."

"If *they* ever guess what I been up to, it'll take more'n prayers," he said, and trudged away.

The steer sold well. Henry went along to Master Turnbull's office and deposited half of the price. Master Turnbull could see more sense in putting money aside for a living girl than for a boy who had vanished—eight?—yes, eight years ago; he was only sorry that the whole of the young lady's fortune had not been entrusted to him, with no consultation with the Bishop of Bywater. He could have done better for her. He would have repudiated hotly the term money-lender—the

Jews had been money-lenders, usurers, until they were banished, nearly two hundred years earlier; Master Turnbull was a manager of money, his own and that of sensible people, like Master Tallboys, who entrusted him with sums, great and small. He was scrupulously honest; knew that small sum added to small sum mounted up; believed that money, properly handled, could breed money and that a man should be flexible. He was fiercely anti-clerical. But when he had once mentioned the pity that it was that a Bishop should ever have been involved, Master Tallboys had given him one of those candid blue looks and said in a way that robbed his words of any offence, "No doubt you could have done better. But you could not have obtained a place for her in Sir Barnabas Grey's household." And that was true. A law man who was not also a churchman was still regarded as a man of inferior breed; but Time would see to that. Master Turnbull, always alert to the drift of things, was pretty certain that the day of the middle-class man would come. Maybe not in his time, but in his son's.

Henry bought—since he had the waggon—some household things which Mistress Captoft had asked for—and thank God he could now pay—even for small luxuries. Even for a cask of wine. Reared for the most part in great poverty, he always felt slightly guilty when he spent anything on what was not absolute necessity. Mistress Captoft had, in a way, imposed standards on him for which he was not yet ready. Admirable standards; it was true that Godfrey needed new clothes; that Katharine deserved the good servant's Christmas dole of stuff for a working dress. He didn't grudge, but even spending what he could afford *now* reminded him of the past, when he could afford so little, and made him think of the future, always uncertain. When he felt like this he was always disgusted with himself, and gave a thought to his father, who once, for the first time in his life, with a hundred pounds in hand, had built Knight's Acre, sparing nothing, even the pargetting. Sir Godfrey had spent his last penny on the house—and then could not afford to live in it. It was Walter who had made the farm, the thing which had sustained the house for more than twenty years, and must continue to do so.

The lightened waggon rattled along; even the older horse was now headed for his stable, his manger, and the paces matched better. And Henry knew why this stretch of road depressed him. With no need to urge or guide a horse he had nothing to do but think. Ordinarily he could avoid much thought by flinging himself into work, or sleep. Too much to remember; it didn't do to remember.

The road curved slightly and he saw, coming towards him at a smart trot, very different from its usual sedate movement, Mistress Captoft's mule. No mistaking that unusual silvery grey. And astride it, Godfrey, his hair all aflutter, and some rags too. And what in God's name had happened to his face?

He'd taken a fall. Naughty, over-venturesome boy! Yet he was not riding like a boy who had been thrown. He wheeled the mule expertly so that he was level with the seat of the waggon, which Henry had brought to a halt. His nose looked crooked, there was blood. And when he spoke it sounded as though he had a heavy cold in his head.

"Change with me, Father. Go and save Mamma-Captoft from those horrid, rough men."

"What men?"

"They were rough with her. You go. I'll take the waggon." He was already scrambling out of the mule's saddle onto the waggon seat.

Henry was capable of thinking quickly when he had to. Abductions were not uncommon. In fact when Robert was lost everybody's first thought was that he had been stolen. Violent and lawless men did take people, and hold them to ransom, sending messages—such and such a sum, in a hollow tree; under a stone. It had never yet happened at Intake; but there was a first time for everything.

"Which way did they go, son?"

If into Layer Wood a difficult search and perhaps futile.

"Into the village."

That sounded strange. Local people didn't abduct local people in broad daylight. Still, they could have set off in the direction of the village, then veered off into the woods.

He was now on the mule; saddle too narrow, stirrups too short.

"Father, hurry!" Godfrey said. Henry set the mule to a gallop.

The boy with many knights among his ancestors, shouted, "Take a *pitchfork!*" But by that time he had set the horses in motion and his snuffly voice did not carry above the clatter of twelve hooves and the creaking of wheels.

The people of Intake, like all people faced with the unknown and the awesome, sought comfort and courage in human company. Clustering and murmuring like a swarm of bees, they moved from the river bank into the village, into Bert Edgar's yard, where the firewood was stacked and ready. Somebody brought a brand from the kitchen and set it alight. The warmth and the brightness dispelled some of the dread. A spirit of hysterical hilarity began to grow. They had all seen an amazing, a terrible thing; they were all acutely conscious of the Devil only just across the river, but here they all were, untouched so far. Survivors. Johnson, a man prosperous enough to own a horse, took his son and another man to his place, next door to Edgar's Acre and came back with a cask of October ale—last year's and very potent. That struck the right note. *Make a feast of it;* fetch mugs, fetch food. Everybody bring what was available. Unrecognised, a feeling of competition sprang up. The bee-swarm scattered—but nobody went alone through the deepening dusk. You come with me to my place, then I'll go with you to yours. Even men felt that way tonight.

At Hodgacre, Bet Hodge said to Jill Edgar, who had accompanied her, "I'd better just look in on the old man."

Holding a lighted candle she opened the door of the room she so coveted. Selfish old pig, he refused to share even with his eldest grandson, a quiet boy who did not snore.

"And about time too," the old querulous voice said. "Here I laid, stiff as a plank, and nobody to bring me so much as drink of water."

"Thass wrong, Granfer. I looked in time after time. You was allus asleep."

He gave an inner chuckle. She could be lying. She could be telling the truth. If she *had* looked in, that was proof that he'd made a good mommet, mounding up, under the bedclothes, what from the door could well be mistaken for a sleeping man.

"Is there anything you want now?"

"Is there anything I want?" he echoed sardonically. "Yes. My dinner. Four rashers, cut thin and well frizzled, and two eggs, turned in the pan. You should know by now."

She had been undecided which little cask of home-made wine to take to the feast; the pale, flowery cowslip or the rich dark blackberry which she had been saving for the old man's funeral feast. Now she knew that it was safe to take the blackberry; the old man was tough as hickory wood; he'd live for years; she'd have time to make more and see it well ripened.

On some of the farms the pigs were feeling as neglected as

Old Hodgson had pretended to be. They squealed and were fed.

The young nimble men who had run, with ropes, to dredge the witch dead or alive out of the water, said that they'd seen nothing. One minute she'd been there, bobbing on the surface of the water, the next she'd been in the thicket. Later this story was to be embellished, and passed down through two generations, included a vivid picture of the Devil, cloven hooves, horns, tail and all, leering out of the thicket.

One thing was certain, even at the end of this confusing day. Mistress Captoft was being punished, wherever she was. Satan, Old Scrat, might have saved her from the water, from the fire, but everybody knew that those who sold themselves into his service, were in the end abandoned. He was the Father of Lies, the past master of deception.

The impromptu feast was well under way when Henry arrived. The grey mule was over-fed and under-exercised; urged on by a kick or a slap, it would gallop a bit, then begin to blow, a warning sign to anyone who knew anything about four-legged things. Breath must be recovered, then the easy, ambling pace resumed, more urging, a short gallop and blowing again. The younger of his two horses, despite the miles it had already done, would have been a better mount, Henry reflected, blaming himself for not thinking of that before. But at last he was at Intake, the lane going on towards the village, the track diverting to the right, towards the church, the priest's house and Knight's Acre itself. And there the mule, who for years had turned here, gave proof of its breed's proverbial stubbornness. Nothing would budge it. Angrily, Henry dismounted and continued his journey—about a quarter of a mile—on foot. He intended to go from house to house asking whether anyone had seen, or knew anything of Mistress Captoft. He was spared that tedious business by the light and the noise coming from Bert Edgar's yard.

It was, he thought, like a scene from Hell. Faces reddened and distorted by the glare; drunken laughter; the smell of meat being toasted at the end of pitchforks, or sharpened stakes. Amidst so much noise one voice, however loud, would be lost. He walked to the fringe of the crowd and brought his work-hardened hands together in a clap. Those near enough to hear, jumped and fell silent, and the quietude ran, like panic through the rest. Suddenly everyone, except a wailing baby, was silent and staring towards Henry. At any time he was a good head taller than any one of them, and now that most were sitting or squatting, he loomed enormous, and with his face lit from below, not unlike the Devil they were dreading. And it was only Master Tallboys! There were gasps, even sniggers of relief.

"Does anybody here know anything of Mistress Captoft?"

The Intake dumbness clamped down; what you didn't say couldn't be held against you.

"She was taken from my house," Henry said, "and roughly handled."

He was not accusing them. He still couldn't believe that any Intake men would do such a thing. He'd come here for information, possibly help, if Layer Wood had to be searched. And a fine lot of help he'd find here, he thought, looking at the blank faces, the drunken faces.

"Did anybody see strangers?"

Somebody hushed the baby and for a moment the silence was not just merely an absence of sound but a positive thing. Then Jill Edgar, downtrodden for years, but now borne up because she had been first at Bet Hodgson's good blackberry, said,

"She was took for a witch and swum."

That broke a barrier. Varying voices intermingled to tell the astounding tale; the fair trial, the test, and the Devil himself snatching the witch away into Waste Wood.

Henry listened to the babble sceptically. When he was young and impressionable Walter had derided anything that could not be seen and handled as nonsense. Even Sybilla herself could never get him to Mass. Hell, he said, had been invented to make people behave, and Heaven to cheer up their miserable lives. As for witches and warlocks and ghosts, for them Walter had only one word: Rubbish.

So now Henry thought only in practical terms. That poor woman somehow struggling out of the water and finding herself in Waste Wood, where she would find no shelter, no succour. She'd be drenched and half drowned; she'd die of exposure in this bitter wind.

He had no knowledge of the ford. He knew that there was no bridge and that the only way for someone who could not swim was to go down to Bywater, hire a boat and cross the mouth of the river, land among the sand dunes and work upstream through the swamps and the trees. It could take days. There must be a quicker way. There was. Hire a boat, with men who would row in relays, and come upstream that way and land near the spot where she had disappeared. That meant getting down to Bywater this evening and setting out at first light tomorrow morning.

He stayed just long enough to ask two questions.

"Where was she last seen?"

They could all answer that. Just by the first curve after the Steps.

"Who fetched her from my house?"

Dead silence.

"God damn you all," Henry said, and set off for home, now running, now walking with his long loping strides which were almost as fast. He had actually reached his own ground when he saw a faint, bobbing light, heard his son's treble voice call, "Father," and David's deeper one shout, "Master! Master Tallboys!" Henry shouted back and the hero of the day burst into tears.

"We thought . . . something had happened . . . to you. The mule . . . came home alone."

"Thank God you're safe, sir," David said. "Mistress Captoft, too."

"She mended my nose," Godfrey said, gripping Henry about the thighs.

"You *have* had a day," Henry said. "Come on, up you get. I'll give you a ride home."

"How *is* Mistress Captoft?" Henry asked.

"All right," David said. "Very quiet."

They'd all had a day. Katharine had made a mutton and apple pie, ready to serve at mid-day. Joseph came punctually. Jem had not stayed for dinner; he said he'd come early to help load the steer and there was something he had to see to down in the village. So the three of them had waited, expecting Mistress Captoft and Godfrey—assumed to have gone for a walk—to arrive at any minute. It was utterly unlike Mistress Captoft to absent herself from a meal without warning. Joseph had become impatient and finally, unwillingly, Katharine had cut the pie. Then it was discovered that the mule had gone and Katharine and David had assumed that Mistress Captoft had taken Godfrey, riding pillion, to Nettleton. The observance of Saints' days varied from place to place; she had probably been asked to stay to dinner there. Dusk began to threaten, worry to mount. Then, almost simultaneously, two things happened. Mistress Captoft soaked through, and unusually silent, had come in, demanding a bath.

She was a fastidious woman; she took at least six baths a year, using a cut-down cask. While the water was being

heated and carried up, Godfrey arrived with the waggon—
and a flattened nose and one of his last milk teeth hanging by
a thread. Mistress Captoft, cutting her bath short, had dealt
expertly with his nose, tweaking it back into shape and fixing
it with a plaster of linen, heavily smeared with flour and
water paste. She had also plucked out the loose tooth, saying
that it was no loss; it would have fallen out soon, anyway.
After that the mule, empty-saddled, had come clattering into
the yard; and then Godfrey had begun to talk about his father,
who had gone to Intake . . . about the two bad men whom
he had hit with the poker, and the one who, with that same
poker, had broken his nose and practically knocked a tooth
out.

Now, all safe again under one roof, everything would have
been made plain, except for Mistress Captoft's unusual reti-
cence and curious attitude. She gave Godfrey his due: "He
behaved like a hero. You may be proud of your son, Master
Tallboys." But she repudiated, absolutely, the idea of vengeance.

"Godfrey said there were two men," Henry said. "Both
from the village. Did you recognise either?"

She said, "No." Adding hastily in her mind: God forgive
that lie; told in a good cause; to tell the truth would be to
start a feud. *Blessed are the peacemakers; for they shall be
called the children of God.* Struggling home, soaked, muddy,
her teeth chattering, Mistress Captoft had undergone a spiritual experience. God had, though the instrumentality of one
grateful old man, saved her from the water and from the fire.
In future she would belong to God and to Him only.

She said, with unctuous piety, new to her, and to Henry
infuriating, "We must forgive; as we hope to be forgiven."

"A fine sentiment! My boy's face was smashed in. Am I to
forgive that?"

"Yes. *Vengeance is mine,* saith the Lord."

She was equally secretive about the identity of her rescuer.
Someone who had reason to be grateful to her, she said; and
to name *him* might lead to trouble, the people of Intake being
so ignorant and misguided. And while praising Godfrey's
courage in going to her defence, she tended to make light of
his hurt. His nose was as yet hardly more than gristle, and,
attended to so promptly, would show no sign of injury. To
make a fuss, to put thoughts of malice and vengeance into his
mind, would be infinitely more harmful.

Whoever, long ago, had devised the Tallboys badge—the
hare defending its young, and the motto *I Defend What Is*

Mine—had not chosen haphazardly. Henry felt that the whole affair was an affront to him. No doubt everything the silly woman said was true; in a way saintly, but he could not feel so. Somebody had come to his house and taken away a woman who, though no kin to him, was living under his roof and therefore under his protection; and when a boy, little more than a child, had gone to her aid, somebody had jabbed him brutally in the face. Henry, who would have described himself as a peaceable man, knew that he would never rest easy until the insult was avenged.

There was another aspect, too. The people of Intake being so ignorant and—Henry rejected Mistress Captoft's tolerant word, *misguided*—so bloody barbarous, they might try again. He couldn't be on guard all the time, and David was a lame man, easily thrown off balance. Therefore they must be shown, made to understand, taught a lesson.

Of his intention he said nothing to Mistress Captoft, suddenly so sickeningly pious. The thought did flash through his mind that one person who would understand completely was Joanna—but she was far away.

In the morning he questioned Godfrey again. The white plaster stood out like a little white snout. On either side of it dark bruises showed. That anybody should have *dared!* Godfrey had nothing to add to his former account. Two men, one bigger than the other; he'd hit the smaller. "I lamed him, Father. I hope I hurt the other one too, before he jabbed me." He might, Godfrey said, have seen the men before, in church, but he did not know their names.

Henry waited for Jem Watson to come to work; get him talking and he might let slip something useful; but Jem did not come.

The whole village, except for Old Hodgson and the children, who had been given only a sip of this, a sip of that, slept late that Thursday morning. Children got up and foraged for themselves on what was left after the orgy: Old Hodgson would have done the same, but thought it wiser to maintain his pretence for at least another day. Lying wakeful, and hungry, he wondered about Mistress Captoft; had she found her way home?

One early morning sound was not heard in Intake, and when, thick-headed, bleary-eyed, men eventually lurched out into their yards, they saw why. No healthy, hungry squealing pigs. Some dead, more lying down, waiting to die.

They all knew, by the rule of thumb, taught by experience,

that swine fever was catching, and called to inspect Bert Edgar's pigs which were suffering from swine fever that wasn't quite swine fever, they had kept their distance while uttering sympathetic or exclamatory words. But that the disease could lurk in a place where no pig was had not occurred to them and on the previous day, intent upon the trial, then upon the feast, they had given no thought to the matter; they'd leant against, brushed against the empty stye; some had even stood in it to get a bit of shelter from the wind. Then, after the swimming, or after the feasting, they'd seen to their pigs . . . Now the incredible disaster had struck. This would be another year when bacon must be bought. Stunned, made apathetic, they stood about in groups, asking how? asking why? Because they'd made a mistake and fixed on the wrong woman— whom God, not the Devil had reached out and saved? Curiously no suspicion now attached itself to Mistress Captoft. Superstition could swing like a weathercock.

Into one of these miserable little groups Henry came. He was looking for a lame man. The other, the real culprit, the one who had jabbed Godfrey might not be so easy to find, but Henry was reasonably sure that a little pressure, or a little bribery would persuade the lame man to give a name to his confederate. And *he* would be smashed into pulp.

There was a lame man, leaning on Nature's own crutch, a forked bough. And there too, was a man—recognisable— Bert Edgar, who'd once worked at Knight's Acre, with his left hand roughly bandaged.

"You hit my boy," Henry said. Not quite a statement or quite a question.

"What if I did? He lamed Ted. He'd hev lamed me. Bruk my thumb for me."

"All right," Henry said, and began to loosen his belt.

His belt was the weapon that Bert Edgar used most often upon his wife and his unwanted children and he saw meaning in Henry's action.

"You hit me and I'll strike back. I still got one good hand."

Henry pushed his own left hand behind him, into the back of the belt, loosened to admit it, then tightened to control it. He was being fair, chivalrous, though long ago he had turned his back on all that chivalry meant.

Ah. Then began a fight that was long to be remembered, together with the witch-swimming, the baconless year.

Instinctively everybody moved back, even Ted Hodgson on his crutch, to form a ring, an amphitheatre with no seats.

There never had been; there never would be again, such a fight.

Actually Henry was doubly handicapped; he'd immobilised his left arm; Bert, while not wishing to engage his injured hand, had an elbow free; and Henry had never given or received a blow in anger since he and Richard had fought with the miniature spades which Walter had made for them, and Walter had said that the two of them were too much to control; one must go. Richard went and Henry had lived peaceably, whereas Bert Edgar had been in many fights, both as boy and man. Village squabbles easily erupted into blows, and since he was usually the victor he was always ready to carry a quarrel to the limit. He was sturdier than many of his kind because, having only one brother, he'd fed better in his childhood than members of larger families. He had indeed the build of a bull and although Master Tallboys was superior in height, possibly in reach, too, Bert did not doubt his ability to floor him.

That was what made the fight so memorable. Most people knocked flat by Bert Edgar, stayed down, either because they were knocked silly or thought it prudent not to get up. Master Tallboys went down no fewer than four times, but he kept getting up and rushing in again. He was savage enough but quite unskilled. Bert had learned the art of dodging and some of Master Tallboys' blows never found their mark at all, or simply glanced off; almost all of Bert's landed and the final outcome was all too easy to foresee, especially when one of Bert's punches split Master Tallboys' eyebrow and blood poured down, blinding one eye.

It was time for the Elders to exercise their authority, as was their right and their duty when it looked as though a man might be killed. Death in a fight was always the subject of an inquiry and nobody wanted that. The Elders had the power to stop a fight that had gone far enough by calling upon all good men and true to intervene, an order traditionally obeyed. It was occasionally obeyed in a way that led to more damage, for most bystanders took sides and in intervening dealt pretty roughly with the man thought to be in the wrong. Amongst these watchers opinion was rather divided. Bert Edgar was one of them, but in the crowd that had rapidly gathered there were those who had, in the past, suffered from Bert Edgar's fists and would not have been sorry to see him floored, just once. There were a few others who, while not completely on Master Tallboys' side gave a grudging admiration to a man who, put down four times, and clearly out-matched, wouldn't stay down. It showed pluck.

Before the Elders could act, Bert Edgar made the most dreaded move of all. He was getting tired of the fight, which had lasted longer than any he could remember; knock a man flat four times when once was usually enough. In this kind of fight there were no rules—you could punch, make painful hacks at shins, even bite if chance offered. So he played one of the oldest tricks; took a step back, seeming to invite a blow, and then brought his knee up sharply into Henry's crotch. It should have been over then, but it was not. Seemingly Master Tallboys did not feel, or heed the dreadful pain—about the worst anybody could inflict. Instead he seemed to rally, came forward and aimed a blow which did reach its mark. Smack on the point of the chin. Bert Edgar reeled and fell and stayed prone. Breaths that had been withheld during that last minute were let loose audibly.

Henry said, short of breath, "Anybody who touches any-thing of mine will get the same." Then, wiping the blood out of his eye with the back of his hand, he turned and walked away. *Walked*.

It took some doing, for a blow *there* was the most agonising of all. But pride demanded that he should walk away, and not until he was out of their sight, try to discover what damage had been done—nothing so far as he could make out—and limp a little.

Mistress Captoft dealt expertly with his other injuries, but at the same time admonished him with trite pious phrases about violence simply leading to more violence and the only way being to forgive and forget.

Regarding his swollen knuckles with some pleasure, Henry said, "Well, I can forgive him now. I think I broke his jaw."

"Retaliation might come in a way you could not so easily avenge. If you found your horses hamstrung or a cow's udder mutilated in the night . . . You could not fight the whole village."

That was worth thinking over.

"I shall buy a truly savage hound," he said. But not today. The thought of riding just now was something to shrink from.

Sitting opposite her at dinner, it occurred to him that Mis-tress Captoft looked different; washed-out seemed an apt term; some of the brightness had gone from her hair, much of the colour from her face. And she was wearing, not one of her usual fanciful head-dresses but a cap of white linen, very plain and unbecoming; as was the charcoal-coloured dress, devoid of all ornament. Her ordinarily hearty appetite seemed to be impaired and she took no wine.

Jem Watson turned up in time for dinner and for half a day's wages. The orgy of the previous evening had made food in the village short; the loss of the pigs would mean tightened belts for all for some time to come; and that made a paid job, with a mid-day dinner, a thing to be valued.

Mistress Captoft, in her forgive-and-forget mood had said the least possible to Katharine and David, but she had spoken fairly freely to Henry, who in any case knew what had happened. She had named no names, but what she had said had been in the presence of Godfrey, to whom the whole affair was a drama in which he had played an admirable part. It was he who supplied the vital bit of information which Jem carried back to the village that evening.

"You coulda knocked me down with a feather, when *she* come walking into the kitchen, perky as a robin. And then I heard, from the boy. *Somebody chucked her a rope and pulled her out.*"

The Devil, they decided, would not have used such an ordinary thing as a rope. Why should he, with all the forces of evil magic at his command?

And all Intake had been here, on this side of the river, barring Old Hodgson, stiff in bed, and a woman even more crippled.

Barring Father Matthew and his ugly boy.

Joseph, the Knight's Acre shepherd, could be entirely discounted. He'd been seen going about his work just as people turned away from the river bank. Besides, he knew nothing.

But the priest had not been seen. And he *knew* what was planned. Had seemed to approve. His excuse for not being present—that the Bishop had ordered him to do nothing—had seemed all right at the time. Now it sounded very flimsy indeed.

They were all extremely vulnerable. So much had happened in so short a time; the peasant stolidity had cracked and must be melded together again by some communal belief and purpose.

Abruptly the mind of the mindless mob thought it saw everything. Father Matthew wasn't one of *them*, he had only pretended to be so. With equal suddenness everybody decided that actually they hadn't liked him very much. He was *greedy*, always looking in at about suppertime and eating as much as a man who had been ploughing all day. The popularity which

Father Matthew had gained by seeming unlike a priest, rebounded with horrible force. He wasn't like a priest because he wasn't one.

"Even to the words," Old Ethel said. "I've noticed." And she should know, for the habit formed when she was Father Ambrose's housekeeper had never been broken. She never missed a Mass.

"I don't *know* the words," she admitted. "I ain't no scholar. What I *do* know and *can* say is that there's things he don't say like the good old man did. Nor the new one, neither—I mean the new one *before* him."

That remark struck a note in some minds. Weren't there some shocking tales about Church ritual being garbled, Pater Nosters said backwards, the Host itself being used for evil purposes?

One thing linked with another. What about that boy he kept? So ugly—except for the fur, the living spit of the thing in the picture—and talking as though his tongue was too big for his mouth. Could be his familiar. And if Father Matthew was a witch it would account for his being able to cross the river; witches could fly, couldn't they? Well, then, say he was a witch—or should it be wizard?—what had they ever done to *him* that he should kill their beasts? Plain as the nose on your face; they hadn't ploughed his glebe.

Then where did Mistress Captoft come in? They were two for a pair; in league with each other. Then why had he called her an evil woman and gone down to ask the Bishop what to do? He'd done it to draw attention from hisself and who knew that he'd ever been near the Bishop? He'd *said* so; but the Devil was the Father of Lies, so naturally them in his service would tell lies. Or it could be they'd fallen out—rogues were said to fall out—and he wanted to teach her a lesson, let her nearly drown and then save her, just to show who was master.

Another thing, too. What about his own pig?

A lot hinged on the well-being of that one animal; if that was ailing or dead it'd prove . . . No, it wouldn't; he'd be cunning enough to strike his own pig, just to fool them.

The talk went on and on, and round and round. It served to take their minds off the dismal prospect of a winter when bacon must be bought.

One thing emerged fairly clearly, to Old Hodgson's great delight: there was no talk of further action against Mistress Captoft. Once suspicion had fastened upon a man, this almost entirely male-dominated society could regard her as women were generally regarded, helpless tools, willing or unwilling. Irresponsible creatures.

Henry, whose notice and solicitude would have meant so much only a week earlier, said,

"But you have eaten almost nothing. And you look poorly. At least take a cup of wine."

"Thank you, no. To speak frankly, Master Tallboys, I am weaning myself from the lusts of the flesh. On Monday I intend to go to Clevely and ask for admission there."

"Clevely! You mean the nunnery?"

"Where else?"

"That is impossible," he said. "Years ago, when my father was looking for a place for my sister, he went there and came away without even stating his errand. I remember it well. He said the place was a ruin, and the few nuns left, either deaf or blind or senile. Time will not have improved it." Henry knew he was right there. The time of lavish gifts to religious houses was over. Shrines at which miracles were said to be performed, like St. Egbert's at Baildon, and maybe St. Edmund's in the town that bore his name, were still patronised and prospering, but places like Clevely . . . Who'd leave money to restore and support a place where the most that could be hoped for was a few prayers, mumbled by old women who couldn't tell Sunday from Monday?

"But that, Master Tallboys, is just what I need. In such a place what money I have will be welcome and useful. And by living in discomfort—as I doubtless shall do—I shall give proof of my gratitude to God. For sparing my life."

Something in Henry's mind asked: To what purpose? Alive just in order to be miserable? And something else asked: What about *you*? What is *your* life, Henry Tallboys? Work like a horse; eat; sleep; get up to work again. To what purpose?

He knew the answer to that. He had Knight's Acre; he had his son. What more could a man ask?

He said, in that deceptively stolid manner, "I'd sleep on it, if I were you. And I'd think about Lamarsh, a different place altogether. Water-tight at least."

Saying that he gave her one of his rare, singularly sweet smiles; a joke, come on, share it!

He didn't care where she went; or when—just this little, typical male interest in whether a roof was water-tight or not. And to think that she had dyed her hair, painted her face, latched herself in an iron corset in order to attract him!

The thought shamed her to the core. God be thanked, he'd never noticed her antics!

Maude Grey cried very easily and was inclined to take advantage of this ability. Free-flowing tears could often cut short a scolding or forestall another blow. So she cried as she obeyed her mother's injunction to use her utmost power of persuasion upon Joanna. Joanna, being tactfully prepared for betrothal to Lord Shefton, had simply said, "He is too old." After that she had listened unmoved to Lady Grey's earnest and reasonable arguments, and to Sir Barnabas' more jocular, light-handed attempts at persuasion. So Maude had been entrusted with the task. The young who wouldn't listen to their elders, might take note of a near contemporary. Maude had been told exactly what to say and she said it.

"It could be such a happy occasion, Joanna. Christmas *and* a betrothal. We shall all be so deeply disappointed." Tears gathered and spilled.

"Why *disappointed*, Maude? Disappointment can only come from a failed expectation. The only ones I can see in this case, are Lord Shefton's, and he deserves disappointment. Old enough to be my grandfather! And those teeth! They stink."

Diligently, obediently, Maude mentioned all the advantages to be set against age and ill-smelling breath; a castle, four other abodes, one in London, access to the Court; the fact that it could only be a short servitude; an old man could not live forever; and with his death Joanna would be free, and rich; even her own dowry untouched and much added.

Like everything else about this place, this way of life to which Henry had condemned her, false and mercenary. Hateful.

"I won't do it."

Maude cried harder. "The lady, my mother will be angered with me. She will say that I did not try hard enough to persuade you."

"Why should she expect you to succeed when she has failed?"

"She thought that as we are much of an age, and friends . . ."

"Surely even *she* could not expect me to enter into such a marriage simply to save you a beating, Maude."

"No, but I could say—and I do say it with all my heart—*I wish he had chosen me.*"

"So do I, with all *my* heart." I should have been spared all this; and Maude would not have minded; poor downtrodden girl, knowing nothing of love; thinking only of the castle and four other abodes—and being a Countess, taking precedence of her mother!

Maude said, using the disrespectful *she*, "She has her mind set on it, Joanna. And when her mind is set . . . She has ways of enforcing her will."

"Not on me! She could order me to keep to this room and live on bread and water for a year. And I still wouldn't do it." She had intended to keep her secret, something hidden and private and precious in this alien world, but now, to save further argument, to save poor Maude from rebuke, she revealed it, harsh, abrupt, conclusive. "I couldn't. I was betrothed before ever I came here."

In the only sure privacy that their way of life afforded them, in their bedchamber, Lady Grey said to her husband,

"I do not believe it. It is an invented story. Why, it is only a few days ago since I had a letter from her guardian, His Grace of Bywater, fully approving and congratulating me—us—on such good management; on attaining such a match. Would he have written thus, knowing her to be already betrothed? When he consigned her to our care, was not the ultimate aim to see her suitably married?"

"So I understood."

"The whole thing," Lady Grey said, dealing with pins and lacings as though they were the offenders, "has been a mystery. And a burden. For one thing, she now denies that the Bishop is her guardian, or that she has one at all. Grand talk about her lineage—but all Spanish. Such airs and graces, with no backing at all. And now, just when I thought the whole thing settled, and the way made clear for Maude, this happens. I shall write to His Grace of Bywater again, first thing tomorrow, and send a fast rider."

Riding, but at the mule's pace, Mistress Captoft went along the track which led to Clevely. It went downhill and there were no trees, and a curve, so that one saw the place suddenly. Henry had prepared her to some extent—a decayed, ruinous house, full of old women, but she had not envisaged such complete decay, something resembling a broken-down haystack. Still her spirit did not falter. She dismounted and rang the bell, which was briskly answered by a nun who in no way fitted Henry's description: a brisk, able-bodied woman, little, if any, older than Mistress Captoft herself. They exchanged greetings and each recognised in the other a mirror image.

"I wish to speak to the Head of this House," Mistress Captoft said.

"That, I regret to say, is impossible. Our Prioress is unwell; keeping to her bed."

A kindly way of describing that state of senility which much resembled a vegetable existence.

"I am Dame Isabel. At such times, I am in charge. If you would be seated and tell me the business that brought you here . . ."

It was both invitation and challenge. Those about to dedicate their lives—and their fortune—to God, should not be easily deterred. So Mistress Captoft seated herself on a bare and not very stable bench, in a room, presumably the convent's parlour, which not only smelt of damp and decay but gave visible evidence of it; a frond or two of fern in a crack in the wall, another growth, small, woolly-surfaced mushrooms along the skirting where rotten wall joined rotten floor. Most deplorable, but such things could be remedied. Mistress Captoft was fully prepared to bring her money, her energy—all that she had—to the remedying. So, under the steady and unsympathetic stare of Dame Isabel's eyes—one always thought of bluish, greenish, greyish eyes as being cold, but brown ones could look like pebbles at the tide's edge— Mistress Captoft explained her situation and her intention. And having offered her all, she was repelled.

Dame Isabel said, "Decisions taken upon impulse—as this sounds to me to be—are often regretted. I feel that you would be wise to think again. And even then, this is hardly the place. Clevely has not taken a novice for at least twenty years, so far as I can ascertain. We have no Mistress of Novices; no facilities for instruction. I am sorry."

She said the last words with finality. She did not want the woman here. Even in her present subdued mood, the very contours of Mistress Captoft's face betrayed her as a masterful, managing creature who, once admitted, in whatever capacity, would be a threat to the absolute authority which Dame Isabel exercised over the other inmates by right of being young and active and in full possession of all her senses and all her wits. She was also a woman of good family and had brought a little money with her. The decayed house was not quite so near the brink of starvation as it had been when Sir Godfrey visited it.

"You are rejecting me?"

"Not I. Circumstances."

Since Henry had proved so unsympathetic to her plan, she had confided in David, telling him that she could doubtless arrange to take him since Clevely sounded the kind of place where a handy man would be welcome and useful. He'd looked glum, but made no protest. She had hastened to explain that it would make little difference to him; he would not be bound by the convent's rules, he would simply be doing much the same work in a different place.

He was cleaning out the stable when she arrived home and he limped forward to take the mule. He still looked glum, but there was a question in his glance. She could not bring herself to tell him that she had been rejected; nor, in her present mood, could she tell a downright lie. So she said,

"My plans are somewhat changed."

On the way home she had thought of Lamarsh, and might have ridden there, but it lay in the other direction and the days were short now. Tomorrow!

She had also thought that perhaps in the very rejection God had given fresh evidence of His will, and power. The poverty of the place had not dismayed her, but she had not cared for Dame Isabel. Something in her manner, her voice, her glance. And a good nun must consider herself utterly subject to her superiors.

The glum look vanished from the man's face and was replaced by an expression not easy to name.

"There're other ways of serving God, madam," he said across the mule's neck.

"I wish I knew one," she said rather bitterly, for on the last stage of her journey it had occurred to her that at Lamarsh—or any other religious house—there might be a Dame Isabel, or even worse. In fact the impulse was already weakening, as two such different people as Henry Tallboys and Dame Isabel had foreseen.

"I could tell you one," David said, half shy, half eager.

"It is too cold to stand and talk here," she said. "When you are finished here, come into the hall."

It was a cold day, and ordinarily, on such a day, after such a ride she would have taken a glass of mulled wine; but since her miraculous rescue she had abjured such luxuries, had even eaten sparingly, denying herself, preparing herself for further privations.

Now she was tempted, but she resisted the temptation,

for although her nature was not all of one piece, soft volatile layers as it were alternating with more solid ones, on the whole she did not lack determination.

Warming herself by the fire, she was still determined to leave Intake, partly because of what had happened—though she had forgiven the people concerned—and partly because *now*, she was uncomfortable in Henry's presence. Those deliberately planned attempts at enticement she now saw for what they were, shaming and shabby. Thank God he had been so blind!

David came in, washed and changed into the clothes he wore when waiting at table. From the time when he had first begun the outdoor work which had restored his manhood and his self-esteem, he had been meticulous about not bringing the odours of stable, byre and stye into this part of the house. Master Tallboys was not so particular; he'd wash his hands and if his boots were very muddied or muckied, drop them at the kitchen door. For other fripperies he had no time—which was understandable.

Aware of his lameness, Mistress Captoft said, "Sit down, David. I don't know what you have to say, but I warn you. Little acts of charity, bread and broth for beggars and washing pilgrims' feet—that was not what I had in mind."

"Nor I, madam. What I had in mind was a great enterprise."

"Oh," she said. "What?"

"Something new. So far as I know nobody ever gave a thought to poor sea-faring men. And I don't mean cripples like me. I mean . . ." he began humbly, diffidently, fumbling for words, but he warmed to his subject and began to speak with passionate emphasis.

"Say a ship, out of Lowestoft or Yarmouth or any other place further north, is forced to put in at Bywater, and glad to be. Maybe a short time—just a wait on the weather—or a long, while she's being tacked together again. There's no pay till they're back in the home port. There's only pay when she puts in where she started from. Waiting men are in poor case. Take the others, out from Bywater, back in Bywater and paid off. Where do *they* go meantime? Oh, I know the inn sign, Welcome To Mariners, but the ordinary chap ain't welcome there. So it's the Lanes, low-down ale houses and bad houses for him! In my time I've seen some good men ruined that way. And there's some like me, not so crippled and not so lucky. As I was, thanks to you, madam. Ones with smaller injuries, or sick; chucked out to live or die.

Beggars get broth, pilgrims get their feet washed, but I never knew anything done for the poor ordinary sailor."

"Nor did I. Though I lived for a time in Dunwich." She brooded. Dunwich seemed a long way, and a lifetime, away.

"Sometimes," David said, "there's prize money. And I always thought that if I was lucky *that* way, I'd get hold of a house somehow and throw it open to all. I mean sailors. But I never had a stroke of luck till that day I fell in with you, madam. So I never could. But *you* could. And it wouldn't be all out-go. There's them that could pay, and glad to, for a decent meal and a clean bed. And I'd work like a galley slave."

The seed fell upon fertile ground, rooted, sprouted, grew tall and branched out, like the grain of mustard seed in the parable. Far, far more useful, she thought, than immuring herself in a convent where her gift for management would be lost, subject to somebody else's managing will, and her money absorbed into some general fund over which she would have no control at all.

"It is worth thinking about," she said. David knew the tone of dismissal, got up and went away, and Mistress Captoft went straight to the cupboard and poured herself a glass of wine. And very heartening, after four days' self-imposed abstinence.

Sipping the wine with relish, she thought of the other rules which she could now relax. She could wear her gay dresses, her trinkets, her becoming head-dresses. And *still* be doing God's work by providing a service to mankind, a thing no one else had ever thought of. Behind it all she could see clearly the hand of God at work. That drastic purge which inspired such gratitude in Old Hodgson; the terrible experience which had brought her to her senses and made her anxious to serve God in a positive way; her rejection at Clevely, and now the moment of true illumination brought about by a serving man whom she had saved from starvation. It all wove together, making a neat and pleasing pattern.

And think of the gratitude those poor men would feel. Consider David, so grateful that he had been willing to go with her to Clevely, little as the idea had appealed to him. Her volatile, impulsive mind looked into the future and she saw herself busy, managing, competent, imposing a firm but gentle rule on dozens of men, all like David, all deeply grateful, all calling her madam. And, as she had once thought of Amsterdam, she now thought of Bywater, and tasted in anticipation the joy of living in a town again; of being able to look out of a window and see something going on; of being able to shop every day. She thought of the house she would need, a big house, in one of the larger streets, or better still on the quay itself. She had no doubt, in her secret heart, that it was there, just waiting for her.

Henry had also taken a ride that morning, and as he expected, sitting in the saddle was extremely painful. Fortunately he had only to go to Muchanger, where a man named Walker had much the same name for breeding dogs as Tom Thoroughgood had for horses.

Ordinary dogs were, of course, obtainable anywhere, especially in the market—but there you might get a stolen dog, a stray dog, a dog spoiled by pampering, or by ill usage. Henry wanted a properly trained guard dog, for what Mistress Captoft had said about sly retaliation by the maiming of animals, had been sound good sense. The Walker guard dogs were well known, a careful cross, stabilised over the years, between hunting hound and mastiff, with the virtues of both breeds. It was said that Dick Walker was so knowledgeable that one glance at a litter of puppies could tell him which were worth rearing and which not, and his training was so painstaking and patient that by the time he had finished with it, any dog of his could tell friend from foe, and both from neutral, simply by scent.

"You caught me at a bad moment, Master Tallboys," Walker said when Henry had given his name and stated his errand. "I got puppies of course, useless at the moment. And one, nearly a year old. . . . Should be just right, but I ain't sure whether I oughta sell him. He's *slow*. Not on his feet, I don't mean. Slow to learn. I allus reckon about eight months. But this 'un fared a bit slow. I don't really know why I bothered with him except that he's a handsome dog and got the makings—given time."

"May I see him?"

The dog produced was handsome; physically the perfect cross between the litheness of the hunting hound and the solidity of the mastiff; coat neither rough nor smooth, just ruffled and brindled in colour, grey, dark and almost russet hairs blending happily. Eyes of clear amber which took on a greenish hue at the sight of Henry, the stranger.

" 'S'all right. *Friend*," Walker said. "Well, if you like, sir, I'll show you how far he's got, then you can decide for yourself." He began to remove his own sheepskin jacket, thought better of it. "No, that wouldn't be a fair test. He knows my scent. If you'd put yours down, just there. Now we'll see. . . . You! Guard." The dog obeyed, sniffing the coat cautiously and then standing by it.

"Now," Walker said, "try to take it." Henry attempted to do so and was confronted by a mask of sheer hatred; eyes green as grass, muzzle wrinkled back showing sharp fangs.

Walker said in the rather worn voice of one who has said the same things many times, and must say it again,

" 'S'all right. Give over!" The dog again obeyed and Henry retrieved and thankfully donned his coat. The wind was even colder today.

"I reckon," Walker said, "I was right about him, after all. He got the makings. You want him? Mind, no pampering. And best that *one* person do the feeding. Then show him what you want guarded; beat your bounds as they say, and I reckon he'll do. I'll get a collar for him." He always sent his dogs out into the world equipped with collars; for dog often fought with dog and they always went for the throat. He produced a band of leather, three inches wide and set all over with sharp steel spikes. Naturally there was a charge for collars too. And for the bit of rope to be attached to the ring of the collar in order to lead the dog home. All in all, Henry reflected, he had been a bit extravagant.

Godfrey was waiting in the yard.

"For me, Father?" The perfect reward for having been brave, even when his nose was pulled back into shape and the loose tooth tweaked away.

Dismounting painfully, Henry said, "Yes. If you feed him. But remember, he's not a pet. He's a guard dog."

"I'll call him Guard," Godfrey said. The attraction between the boy and the young dog was mutual, immediate, irrevocable.

Mistress Captoft did not really approve of dogs in the house. Her husband had had six, all of careless habit, but about Guard she was lenient. No concern of hers; after all, she would soon be gone. And Henry, seeing that the purpose of that painful ride was about to be defeated, was lenient, too. Poor little boy, no brothers or sisters, no friends; his mother dead, Joanna, of whom he had been fond, gone away, and Mistress Captoft about to go. Only Father would be left—and Father was a busy man. So, if the boy wanted to share his supper with the dog—giving him, Henry noticed, all the choicest pieces—did it matter so much?

"I have changed my plans, Master Tallboys," Mistress Captoft said. Once again she could not bring herself to say that she had been rejected at Clevely. Instead she spoke enthusiastically about what she intended to do.

"So tomorrow," she said, "I must go down to Bywater and find a house." Then suddenly she clapped her plump white hand, now with all the rings back in place, to her mouth.

"Dear me," she said. "What with this and that, I *forgot*. While you were away, Master Tallboys, a messenger from the Bishop arrived. His Grace wishes to consult with you and hopes you will go to see him as soon as is possible and convenient. I gathered that the matter is urgent."

Another and a longer ride tomorrow, Henry thought, pain stabbing at the thought, though he sat comfortable now, a cushion under him. Well, it must be faced. And he should be better tomorrow. The fight had taken place on Thursday; tomorrow would be Tuesday. All his other hurts were practically forgotten, even the deep split in his eyebrow healing fast. Only the invisible wound ached on. It was not better on Tuesday and he was quite glad that, riding to Bywater in Mistress Captoft's company, he was obliged to match the pace of his horse to that of her mule.

In the yard of the inn, with its deceptive name, Henry said, "I hope you find a house to suit you, Mistress Captoft."

"I am sure I shall," she said, and went off as confident and light-footed as a girl keeping tryst with a sweetheart. Moving less easily, Henry went up the slight incline towards the building which was beginning to justify the name of palace.

The Bishop liked Henry: an honest man if ever there was one; a man with dignity, too.

"It was good of you to come so soon," he said. "You have had an accident?"

"Oh, this?" Henry said, touching the half-healed wound over his eye. "A mere nothing, Your Grace."

"I only hope that the matter upon which we must consult is a mere nothing too."

"It concerns the girl? Joanna?"

"Yes. I thought it unnecessary to trouble you when Lady Grey first wrote to me. From the first a *suitable* marriage was the objective, was it not? And when I heard what Lady Grey had achieved, I thought she had done admirably—for a demoiselle of only moderate fortune and no family. A chance in a thousand. Or so I thought. I wrote to congratulate Lady

Grey upon her good management; and Lord Shefton upon his good fortune. Now"—His Grace's voice became acidulous—"I receive *this!*" He tapped his long, oval, cleric's nails on the last communication, a slightly frantic one, which Lady Grey had sent him.

"Give me the gist of it, my lord."

It was difficult, in Henry Tallboys' presence, to remember that he fell, as the saying was, between two stools. He was completely illiterate, like a peasant; yet he had the manner and speech of a nobleman, or a knight—and there were many of them still who, illiterate themselves, always had a clerk at their heels.

"The gist of it is that the girl refuses, pleading a previous betrothal. If true, a valid plea. But I knew nothing of it. Did you?"

Henry thought of that makeshift, haphazard, unwitnessed promise, made over the kitchen table.

"Lord Shefton, you say? Is he known to you, my lord?"

Claiming rather more than he should—for the truth was that Lord Shefton had no friends; he had sycophants, political and business associates, a vast circle of acquaintances, but no friend—His Grace said,

"Yes, Master Tallboys; Lord Shefton is a friend of mine. Indeed it was through him that I secured a place for the girl in Sir Barnabas Grey's household. . . ."

And now, if what she says is true, made a fool of myself.

Henry sat, looking stolid while his mind spun. It was exactly what he had always wanted for Joanna: another, more comfortable way of life, and a suitable marriage. She'd been gone for two years. She must, by this time, have outgrown that silly, childish infatuation for him . . . Living in a wider world, she must realise that a few hasty words across a kitchen table did not constitute a betrothal and if she had fallen back upon it as an excuse for avoiding marriage to another man, it must have been in desperation.

"Be so good, my lord, as to tell me something of this Lord . . . Shefton."

Quite unconsciously, Henry, who had come here to be questioned, had taken control. He had, from both his parents, inherited a dominant streak. Most of Sir Godfrey's friends in the past had thought him feckless, improvident, practically simple-minded, but when he spoke they had listened: Sybilla's friends had pitied her, poor, for years without a roof of her own, and four children; not a penny to spend; but when she gave an old head-dress a new twist or altered an old gown, others had instantly, anxiously copied.

"He is immensely rich," the Bishop said. He elaborated on that. "Extremely powerful too. He has the King's ear—or rather the ear of those to whom the King gives heed. And as regards this marriage—that is when it was promulgated—generous beyond belief."

"Of what age?" Henry asked, brushing wealth, power and generosity aside.

"Not young," the Bishop said.

"That tells me nothing. How old?"

The irritation which His Grace had felt ever since he had read Lady Grey's letter—which made such mockery of the two he had written—rose to the surface.

"Really, Master Tallboys! One cannot go about among friends, looking at teeth, as with horses!"

"I know," Henry said. "But with friends you can gauge within a year or two, surely. Is he about your age? Older? Younger?"

His Grace could have chosen any answer since Master Tallboys and Lord Shefton were unlikely ever to meet, but there was something about the directness of the question and the straight blue stare, and about his own feeling of suppressed irritation that made him tell the truth.

"Older," he said shortly.

"By how much?"

"Really, Master Tallboys," His Grace said again. "How could I know? Five years, possibly six."

"I see."

To Henry the Bishop had always seemed old, and now, looking across the table, seeing the jowls under the jaw, the folds below the eyes, the brown blotches on the plump hands, the paunch, he thought: Add five years to *that* and it's easy to see why the poor child was desperate; they must all be out of their minds!

In fact the Bishop had aged in a way which only he knew about, in the last couple of years: it was no longer hard to be celibate; it was difficult, impossible, to be anything else. Joanna had been the last female to rouse the least response in him; and his fulsome letter to Lord Shefton, dictated by self-interest, had been written with a feeling of envy, and some cynicism; what the fellow was getting was something pretty to look at and something to warm his old bones in bed. No more. His letter to Lady Grey had been far more sincere. To have extracted such terms from a man with a reputation for miserliness was indeed an achievement.

"We seem to have wandered from the point," he said, taking charge of the interview again. "I asked you if you had knowledge of a previous betrothal?"

Henry seldom acted on impulse; most of his behaviour was governed by good sense, or, as when he took Moyidan Richard, and later John and Young Shep into his home, by a recognition of responsibility. He felt responsible now. He must save Joanna, and could see only one way of doing it.

"Yes. I knew of it."

Colour that almost matched that of the ruby on his finger began at His Grace's jowls and ran upwards.

"And you did not see fit to inform me? By such deception, Master Tallboys, you have placed Lord Shefton, Lady Grey and myself in a ludicrous situation. When I was exerting myself to find a home for the girl, an attempt to find her a suitable husband was part of the bargain; Lord Shefton's proposal was made in good faith and Lady Grey had done her utmost to arrange a marriage settlement of exceptional generosity. Now this!" In anger he rose and began to walk up and down behind the table, the silk of his gown rustling. "Why the secrecy? Tell me that."

Henry, trained by Sybilla—one did not sit while one's elders or superiors stood—rose too with the now familiar twinge.

"She was so young at the time," he said. "Too young to know her own mind. Ignorant, too. I thought it likely that she might change."

"Which she has not."

"So it seems."

His Grace saw a glimmer of a possibility of doing Lord Shefton a singular service. He dropped back into his chair and Henry reseated himself.

"A betrothal, as you know, is a solemn ceremony. But it may be annulled—by mutual consent. The girl may be unaware of this; but if the man concerned would withdraw, it is possible that she could be persuaded to do so. As you say, she was, still is, very young. Then this most desirable marriage could be brought about."

Desirable? A man nearing seventy at least. And how would she feel, poor child, having made that last, desperate stand, only to be deserted and betrayed?

"He will not withdraw, my lord."

"How can you be so certain? A little money often works

wonders. And money would be available. As I say, Lord Shefton is very rich."

"He's not a man to be bought," Henry said.

"How do you know? Most men have their price. Who is he?"

"Myself, my lord." There; now I am definitely committed.

His Grace of Bywater sat silent for a moment, fighting his rage. In the Bible there was a very cogent question: *Doest thou well to be angry?* The answer was: No! *You did ill to be angry,* especially as age crept on. And quite apart from the physical risk which men past their prime ran by indulging in anger, there was the fact that rage made one splutter, choose the wrong words. Choosing his very carefully and speaking in the cold, distant way in which he would have rebuked a clerk who had made an error, he said,

"I perceive that I was mistaken in thinking you different from your brother, that rogue and thief whom I most misguidedly protected. Deceit and deviousness are plainly characteristic of the Tallboys family."

Henry stood up—that twinge again—and said, with more edge to his voice than even the experienced, sophisticated man on the other side of the table could produce,

"I cannot sit here and listen to insults levelled at my family. Richard was plainly in the wrong. But your protection of him was well rewarded, I think. You now have Moyidan, have you not? As for my deceit. What was it except that I kept silent over a betrothal I thought premature? All right, I said a *suitable* marriage. That was what I wanted for her. And had one been proposed—and she agreeable—I should have welcomed it, and withdrawn, wishing her happiness . . ." He could have said much more, challenging the Bishop to go to Baildon, or anywhere else where the name of Henry Tallboys was known and ask if on a single occasion, he had ever acted deceitfully or deviously. But he knew that if he stopped to say this, he would be dismissed, ordered out of the place which had once been one of his childhood's homes.

"I have answered Your Grace's questions, and ask leave to withdraw," Henry said, and bowed—that hurt too—and made for the door, leaving His Grace more annoyed than ever. He controlled himself and sat brooding. He must, of course, write to Lady Grey and say that the girl was right and that nothing could be done. But he must also think of a way in which to get even with that insolent, arrogant, homespun-clad fellow who had flung Moyidan into his teeth.

He rang his bell sharply and of the clerk who came, hasty and willing, demanded that every paper and parchment concerning Moyidan and Intake should be brought to him immediately. What had once been a single, rather faded document, a deed of gift—with conditions—granted to a few serfs, giving them leave to go and hack themselves holdings out of the forest, and to call themselves freemen, had now, over the years gathered accretions as a ship's bottom gathered barnacles. All in order. Even the one thing His Grace had hoped not to find. For as Henry withdrew, the Bishop had thought of the venery laws—who might or might not shoot a deer in Layer Wood. It should have been possible to catch Henry Tallboys there. But it was not; for written sideways along the margin of the oldest parchment, was an addition. Henry's Uncle James had been a meticulous man, and he had made a note of the fact that he had granted his brother, Sir Godfrey, his heirs and assignees, permission to take a certain number of animals, at the right season. Even in his wrath the Bishop realised that it would be unwise to question that clause now when ostensibly Moyidan was being held in trust for the young heir, and he was merely a custodian.

Later, when his rage had subsided a little he puzzled over Henry's motive for behaving as he had done. It certainly was not money, for he had had the girl's person, and her fortune completely in his own control. To enter into a betrothal, then send the girl, with the better half of her dowry, away, never mentioning the betrothal, practically *inviting* other marriage offers . . . turn it which way you would, it made no sense at all. In the end His Grace found himself forced to accept the man's own explanation; he was betrothed to the girl, but felt it to be premature, had sent her away so that she might learn more of the world, meet other people, and would have been prepared to withdraw, to release her should occasion arise. In fact, Henry Tallboys of Knight's Acre was what the Bishop had, until today, judged him to be: a man of exceptional integrity. The honest man whom he had accused of deceit and deviousness! Regretting the words now, but almost immediately justifying himself; chagrin speaking, the flash of anger provoked by the thought of those congratulatory letters, His Grace of Bywater, who was far from stupid, reflected that honest people were so rare that there were no well-tried rules for dealing with them.

Perversely, now that he had regained calm, it pleased him

to think of the dignity with which the honest man had taken leave. Neither hurt nor humbled.

Henry was neither hurt nor humbled. Plain, downright, damned angry. He'd stipulated a *suitable* marriage and the fools had tried to rig up a match between a girl who wouldn't be fourteen until June of next year and some old man doddering on the verge of the grave. Disgusting! Disgusting too that suggestion that another man could have been bought off; that every man had his price. It simply was not true. He thought of Walter. Of his own father, whose story had to be patched together since he was a man so unhandy with words; but Henry knew that his father, offered riches and honours as a reward for betraying his own kind, had chosen slavery instead. For the first time in his life, Henry felt a fleeting wish that he could have known his father better, admired him more, been less critical. Too late now.

Mistress Captoft did not observe that Master Tallboys was even more silent than usual on the ride home. She was so happy, ebullient, and talkative. She did not even bother to ask him what his errand had been or what had been urgent about it.

"I found *exactly* what I wanted. It was there, waiting for me, as I knew it would be. A big house, and old, at the upper end of the harbour."

Pulling himself out of his brooding Henry said, "The Knights' House? A vaulted hall, like a church?"

"The very one. How did you know?"

"I went there, once or twice with my father. Long ago when I was young and the war was at its height. Invasion from France was expected and knights were stationed there. My father was in command."

He hadn't given the place a thought for many years, but he remembered it vividly now. The atmosphere, men young and not so young, all, Sir Godfrey included, merry. Eat, drink and be merry for tomorrow you die. Shining suits of armour, swords, lances ready against the wall. Vast amounts of food and wine on the table and no sparing of candles. Perhaps even then his father, taking him there, had hoped to woo him into knighthood, away from the farm. And if he had been thus cajoled, joined that boisterous, glittering company, where would he be now?

Dead. And Knight's Acre gone to ruin; fallow for a year with grass and pretty little flowers, sappy, expendable; and then, longer neglected, developing the tougher growths, going back to the wild.

"Yes," Mistress Captoft said. "It still has that name. The Knights' House. So similar to Knight's Acre that I was immediately aware of the significance and of the several vacant places on offer, decided to see it first. Of course I was *guided*." She smiled happily and then ran on. "Of course it is in a state of sad disrepair, but the fabric is sound enough. Nothing wrong which a little money and labour cannot restore."

It was in fact a stone building, built—though nobody now remembered this—to house a new Order of nuns who had come to England just after the Conquest. The Order had been short-lived and the design of the building had made it unsuitable as a family dwelling: the huge hall, intended for refectory and living place, the one sizable parlour, briefly occupied by the Abbess, the many small rooms which that particular Order preferred to the communal dorter. During most of its long lifetime it had been used for non-domestic purposes, fish-curing, wool-storage, flax-retting, the making and mending of sails.

"It could have been built for my purpose," Mistress Captoft said, "and I have hired it on very favourable terms. The owner is an old man and said he favoured short tenancies. I could see why; with each change of tenant he can raise the rent. A short lease would not have suited me at all; I should just have got things ship-shape. So I offered him five years' rent in advance—with an option of buying at the end of that period."

She did not feel it necessary to add that she had callously reminded the old man that at his age money in the hand was better than expectations in the future, and that the final disposition of the property was, to put it mildly, unlikely to concern him very much. She had done so, however, and that reminder of mortality, added to the unfamiliar business of dealing with a woman, a woman who used words like *tenure*, had unmanned him.

"Finding the house took no time at all; but I thought it wise to go along to a lawyer. Then I had to find a carpenter, and a plasterer. That is why I am a trifle late. I should like to open the doors on Christmas Eve. It would be apt, would it not?" More than apt, she thought happily; the anniversary of the day when at Bethlehem there was no room at the inn.

"Most apt," Henry said, politely breaking away from his

own preoccupation. "And I hope that everything concerning the house will go as easily as the finding of it."

Not a word about missing her. He was one of the ungrateful.

"I shall leave you in good hands, Master Tallboys. I shall take David with me, and leave Katharine with you. She was an able cook when I found her and now she is trained to my ways. She will keep you comfortable."

The decision to leave Katharine at Knight's Acre had been taken, as usual, on impulse, but for two excellent reasons. It would have worried Mistress Captoft to ride away and leave a man and a boy with no woman to care for them; the other reason was more worldly. Men straight from the sea or from destitution were hungry for other things besides food, and Katharine, though no longer' in the full flush of youth, had a certain comeliness which might lead to trouble. Most sailors could turn their hands to practically anything, as David had proved, and some cooking was done aboard ship. Mistress Captoft did not doubt that she would find two men, like David, slightly disabled, capable of manning the huge kitchen, which had two hearths and one oven. They, she had decided, would be permanent, so that they could learn her ways. Fully able-bodied men could stay only for a limited time, dependent upon circumstances; that was a thing which she must discuss with David—as also she must discuss the name the house would bear. Knights' House was completely wrong.

The idea that she herself, one female amongst many men, might constitute a disruptive element in the happy family that she planned, never once occurred to her; she would walk among them, benefactress, nurse, hostess, Madam. Invisibly armoured.

The news that she was to be left behind dealt Katharine Dowley a shattering blow; for nothing but gratitude to Mistress Captoft, and dread of being thrown out into the world again, had kept her in this—to her—sinister house.

At first, being basically a woman of good sense, she had tried to explain herself to herself by saying that it was the *quiet*. She had gone from the Lanes—six to a room—to the inn, again six or seven to a room, an attic with a rough canvas screen between men and maids. As cook, eventually she had been given a little room of her own, but not isolated; seven steps up, the other servants, six down, the guests. Never before had she known silence, or that it could in itself be menacing.

She was often alone in the house and at such times the feeling became so acute that she'd drop what she was doing and run out into the yard, with some made-up excuse to talk to David, and if possible get him to come back inside with her; she wanted him to taste something, or help her to lift something. She hated being in the hall alone; she dreaded the stairs. She went to enormous pains to time her comings and goings so as to be within the range of another human being. Her bed-time was never of her own choosing.

Mistress Captoft, always considerate, would sometimes say "It is a beautiful day, Katharine. You should take the air. Go for a walk in the woods; the bluebells are in flower." After just one such walk Katharine never ventured into the woods again—if anything, they were worse than the house. Quiet and dim, and full of this nameless threat. After that she never went further than the garden, where some job could always be found, or made, and even there she was aware of the wood, as though some hidden watcher had an eye on her. Not a friendly eye.

So when talk began about the move to Bywater, Katharine was filled with joy; and correspondingly downcast when she learned that the move was not to include her. She wept and implored. She had never mentioned her fears to anyone— they would have sounded so ridiculous, put into words—so Mistress Captoft interpreted the tears, the near hysteria, to devotion to herself.

"I cannot possibly take you with me. What would Master Tallboys do?"

"He could get another woman."

"Doubtless he could. But not one trained by me, capable of running this house so smoothly that I shall hardly be missed."

Missed! Katharine thought of the days, no David clattering about in the dairy, or whistling in the yard, sitting by the dying fire in the evening. Joseph, the shepherd, came to eat his dinner and then went away; Jem left at sunset; earlier on market days. Imagine a market day with Master Tallboys and the boy just a little late, dusk falling and she alone here with whatever it was that watched and waited, still watching, still waiting, ready to close in. She'd be alone with the dog and although a big fierce dog should be a comfort to a woman alone, Guard had proved otherwise to her. She did not doubt that he would tackle a robber, or a wolf, but with fear-sharpened sensibility, Katharine had seen that he, dumb, four-legged beast that he was, *knew*. In the hall, on the stairs, and at one place in the yard, down went his tail, up went his hackles.

"I implore you, mistress. Take me with you."

The chastisement of servants was common practice but Mistress Captoft, even in her husband's house, had never agreed with it. A man or a woman who must be struck in order to be made to work, or to behave properly, was not worth employing. So now the hand she laid upon Katharine's shoulder was kindly though, because impatient, gripping.

"Stop it," she said. "Bywater is not the end of the earth! When I have things in order there—and the days lengthen—I will come to see you. To see how well you are managing. And perhaps Master Tallboys, when he has business in Bywater, will ride you down, so that you can see me. We are not parting forever."

This well-meant but mistaken remark merely produced more sobs, more hiccuping pleas.

"If you can't do with me in your new place, mistress, just let me come along with you and stay, till I find another job."

Exasperated, Mistress Captoft gave Katharine a little shake.

"Be sensible, woman! Who would employ you? Without a good word. The landlady at the inn would not give it. And how could I? If you leave, without reason, any easy place; a comfortable home and an undemanding master. Mop your eyes and nose and let's to work. There is the mincemeat to make. What with this and that, I am so busy as to be almost distraught."

No sympathy, no understanding.

Glorying in her busyness, which, so far from driving her distraught, was a stimulant, Mistress Captoft jogged down to Bywater, harassed the workmen, complained and wrung her hands over the delays. Sometimes she lodged at the inn—for days were short now. There was a time when one step forward looked like two steps backward; boards which looked sound proving rotten as pears, old leprous-looking plaster which broke away as soon as new was applied. The well in the courtyard behind the house took two men a day and a half to clear of the rubbish which various transient tenants had flung into it, and another two days for the sullied water to be wound out. She had furniture to buy. All but the sick, she decided, must lie on straw-stuffed mattresses on the floor; the sick must lie higher to save stooping when they were being attended. For them beds were needed. She must have a long solid table and some benches for the big room;

she must have mugs and platters and cooking pots, and blankets, and stores of such things which—experienced housewife as she was—she knew might be obtainable now, just before Christmas, and then, later in dead winter, either not for sale at all or costly beyond belief.

She had money. Throughout her widowhood her income had exceeded what she spent. She could have gone to Amsterdam and set up house at a moment's notice. This was a more expensive enterprise—but rents were due to her at Christmas.

Presently it was evident to her sensible eye that, despite harassment and lavish expenditure, the old house would not be fit for occupation before Christmas. The next date worth noticing was Twelfth Night. The eve of the Epiphany. Again an apt date, for it marked the end of another journey—that of the three wise men from the East, with their gifts of gold, frankincense and myrrh.

"Your room and mine, David, should be ready before then," Mistress Captoft said. "And by that time we should have found a name."

They had decided against *Hostel*—a bit on the religious side. *Refuge* smacked of charity; *Infirmary* sounded as though only the sick were welcome; and *Home* indicated a permanence impossible to provide.

"I have thought about it, madam. *Sailors' Rest*. If you like it I could do a bit of a board to hang over the door, for the sake of them, like me, who can't read. Not that it'll be needed. The word'll spread like wildfire."

"If we are to open by Twelfth Night, David, you and I must move in well before. There is still work to be done and men must be harried—or bribed—to lift a finger over Christmas."

Twelve Days of riotous idleness celebrated a winter festival which was far older than Christmas and which could still be observed by those who lived in great houses, and by those who lived close to the land. The winter ploughing completed, the pig killed, there was little to do in that dead season. In towns and among people who worked for wages, the custom was dying out, but a pretence was kept up and any man who did so much as drive in a nail between mid-day on Christmas Eve and Twelfth Night was conferring a favour which must be returned in the form of extra wages, or a gift.

Mistress Captoft began to pack again, watched by Katharine's gloomy, increasingly wild eye. David painted his gay and eloquent sign-board.

Stordford was one of the great houses where Christmas was kept in traditional fashion. The holly, the ivy and the mistletoe brought in and hung on the walls. The Yule Log, a great tree trunk, dragged to the hearth, there to be kindled from a piece carefully saved from last year's; it would smoulder throughout the night, be prodded and encouraged by the application of thinner, more easily combustible wood into a blaze. It would last through the Twelve Days and would leave a charred fragment from which next year's Yule Log would be kindled. At Stordford everything was ready, even to the boar's head, stripped down, cooked, reconstructed, with burnt sugar whiskers, blanched almonds for teeth and preserved cherries for eyes. But although Lady Grey's preparations were as thorough as usual, her mood was far from festive; she had Lord Shefton to face, with only the feeble excuse that she had known nothing, that she and her husband had been grossly deceived.

Immediately upon the receipt of the Bishop's letter, confirming the truth of Joanna's story, she had proposed sending the wretched girl away, but Sir Barnabas said that would not be honourable; they had engaged themselves to keep her until she was fifteen, or married, and although the girl had been secretive and the Bishop negligent, they must stick to the word of their bond. On any matter concerning codes of behaviour she deferred to him. She then visualised the horrible embarrassment of breaking the news to Lord Shefton when he arrived, with the marriage contract and the ring. He must be forewarned. "I shall write at once," she said; adding hopefully, "It may be that in the circumstances, his lordship may wish to cancel his visit altogether."

"My dear, that would be unwise. There is no need to ruin Christmas." He named two of his other guests—both valued business associates—who were very anxious to meet Lord Shefton.

"But imagine how he will feel! The very sight of the wretched girl makes me sick."

"He should have a stronger stomach, at his age," Sir Barnabas said, easy-going, as always. She knew for a certainty that she would have the distasteful task of breaking the news, and facing the first brunt of his lordship's displeasure. Once that was spent, Barnabas would appear, probably with a joke: Well, who can now say that no female can keep a secret? That kind of thing.

An Intake the hostility towards Father Matthew continued. He could understand the withdrawal of hospitality; the loss of their pigs, the necessity to buy fresh stock, had hit them hard. But a seat by the fire cost nothing; nor did civility. He still made visits, but he was never invited into any house and nobody showed a disposition to chat with him. Possibly they blamed him for encouraging the idea that Mistress Captoft was a witch—and he still believed that he had been right. Nobody had told him that she had been saved by a rope, so he regarded her survival as supernatural. Innocent women drowned, witches swam. Certainly they blamed him for not being present; perhaps they thought that by merely being there he could have frustrated the Devil.

Maybe they were resentful because his pig was alive and well.

Some of them had already replaced their stock, at fearful cost, winter prices, pre-Christmas prices. (Some nights and days of iron frost had killed the disease, though nobody knew that.) Father Matthew knew that there were pigs in the styes again—he could hear them—but even when he tried to take a friendly interest in new pigs, he was rebuffed. Never once asked to come and look them over.

The witch-swimming had had two indirect results. Young Hodgson was still lame and Bert Edgar's jaw had—and always would have—a lump about the size of a pigeon's egg. Did they blame him for these things?

Attendance at Mass, once so much improved, dwindled, was reduced on one Sunday morning to Master Tallboys, his son, his shepherd and the old woman called Ethel.

And then, suddenly, everything changed. Led by Ethel, getting lame, poor old woman, almost the whole of the village came trooping in.

It was understandable, the priest thought as he went through the ritual, that a woman, weakened by age—and possibly some privation, for in hard times the old and the young were the first to suffer—should need a stick to lean upon. But need she strike the floor with it from time to time?

Ethel had said, "You all listen. Every time he say a word different, I'll bang with my stick and you count."

Quiet and stealthy as bloodhounds, they were now on *his* trail. On the way home there was a bit of an argument about numbers. Six times? No, five. You went to sleep and missed one. How could I go to sleep standing up? I ain't a horse! Old Hodgson, that recognised good hand with a tally stick, said seven. And with that, in itself a magic number, most people were inclined to agree. Seven times Father Matthew had said words wrongly. All their suspicions were confirmed.

They had no intention of swimming him. No story, however far back-reaching told of a man being swum as a test. It only applied to women. The test they intended to apply was very old.

And no need in this case to send two men. One little girl would do.

The little girl—the first of Bert Edgar's unwanted daughters, knocked on the door of the priest's house—once so stoutly guarded by Mistress Captoft—and said to the ugly boy who opened it,

"Father's wanted. Down in the village."

She had been told what to say and she had learned to be obedient.

It was another bitterly cold evening. Streaks of red sunset —no warmth in it, merely the promise of frost again—were just visible beyond the stark black trees.

"Who is it?" Father Matthew asked, already reaching for his cloak. It was good and warm, lined with coney fur.

"I don't know. I was sent to say, Father's wanted."

"Somebody took ill?" he asked, thinking about the stole, emblem of unworldly authority, and of the Host to be brought from the church.

"I don't know," the little girl said again. "I was sent to say, Father's wanted. And I said it, didn't I?"

He thought it as well to be prepared.

Old Father Ambrose had carried all that was necessary for the administration of the last rites in an ancient, broken-down basket; Father Benedict, on those errands from which even Mattie's vigilance and doses had not protected him, had gone out armed with a stout leather satchel. Father Matthew had a container even more suitable, a bag, beautifully embroidered. For before he was appointed to the living at Intake he had held subservient offices and some kindly women had felt sorry for him, so rustic, ill provided and temporary. One of them had given him his cloak, another had embroidered the bag.

Out in the cold, holding his bag in his left hand, Father Matthew lifted the right-hand side of his cloak and enclosed the little girl in it.

"Walk close to me, child," he said. She was clumsily wrapped against the biting wind, but he could feel the sharp bones of her shoulder.

"Where are you taking me?" he asked.

"To home," she said, her voice very small. It was not a question to which "I don't know" would suffice as an answer, and yet in replying properly she felt she was disobeying her orders. Father Matthew was rather fond of children. So he asked her name, trying to overcome her shyness. Her name was Emma and she felt obliged to say it; asked how old she was she could rightly say, "I don't know."

Innocent decoy, she led the way into Bert Edgar's yard, and recognising it, he thought: No wonder she is so thin! In a time of shortage, as this was, Bert Edgar was not the man to deny himself in order to see that his children were fed. It took little time to cross the yard, but Father Matthew had time to think that when he last saw Jill Edgar she was pregnant and might now have miscarried and be at death's door. All those poor little children, he thought.

His guide opened the door and said, with curious formality, "He's here."

He stepped into the kitchen and found himself confronted, as Mistress Captoft had been, by the village Elders.

There were more candles than usual in a farmhouse kitchen. And a fire heaped high and bright enough to make the candles unnecessary. Seven men, stern-faced, at the table.

He knew, from the friendly days, about the Elders. How they had decided to buy a new bull; how they had decided to swim Mistress Captoft. He had never seen them in session before, had not even known who, exactly, composed this body of authority. Now he recognised them all; ordinary peasant farmers, so like his own father, brothers, cousins that he had instantly felt akin to them, and they, he thought, with him. Now something had happened to them—not unlike what happened to *him* when he officiated at the altar. It was something there was no word for. It was the thing, not of this world, which had been conferred upon him at his ordination, the thing which Mistress Captoft had with one word—ill chosen? well chosen? Yes, well, since the intention was to insult, insulted.

Old Hodgson was now active again, and was the Eldest Elder. Sawyer, now so daft as not to know Christmas from Easter, as the saying went, had been asked to stand down.

No difficulty there; he had not even realised that he was being thrust aside.

The word for which Father Matthew fumbled, narrowing his eyes against the light so sudden and so brilliant, was *power*. These seven simple men were invested with it; not as he had been, when ordained, but power none the less. Seven men, of one mind, that mind governed by the most resolute character.

In this case Old Hodgson. In *his* opinion the priest had been largely to blame for the ordeal inflicted upon Mistress Captoft, and so deserved all that was about to happen to him. And more.

The charge—again delivered in that curiously legal and formal way—startled and dismayed Father Matthew as much as a similar one had dismayed and startled Mistress Captoft. The Elders had held preliminary meetings and decided to use the word wizard. There had been some argument about what form of accusation should be brought against him regarding Mistress Captoft; should he be charged with working with her and saving her from her rightful fate, or with using an innocent woman as a cover for his own activities and thus almost bringing about her death? Old Hodgson was for leaving her out of it altogether. "Surely there's enough agin him without dragging *that* in," he said. But his was a lone voice. Old Gurth said, "But she was saved, by a rope. Who chucked it if he didn't? And why should he chuck it if he weren't hand in glove with her?" It looked to Old Hodgson as though the trial of the priest—for which he was as eager as anyone—might lead to more trouble for Mistress Captoft. "We got no proof that there was a rope. Only something the youngster said, or made up." "Then how did she get out?" "Willow root," Old Hodgson said. "I seen 'em, so hev you, this side of the water. Long and thin and grey. Woman that'd been dowsed like she'd been wouldn't be in much state to judge. Got herself tangled in a willow root and took it for a rope." Old Watson said, "Well, if so. How did she get back to this side? Our Jem saw her, the very next day." "Same way the priest got over there in the first place. Flew through the air." Old Hodgson saw that he must come to her rescue again. "I dunno," he said. "If you remember, I was laid aside just then. Had a bit of time to think. And I fare to remember, when I was a tiddler, my father, or maybe it was my granfer, saying something about a place, upstream a bit, where there was stones in the water, stepping stones, like. I recall my mother telling me not to go near 'em. And I never did." If he must tell a lie it might as well be a good one.

There remained a difference of opinion. Out with the beans!

Each Elder came to the meetings armed with a few beans, some black, some white. With these, if an agreement could not be reached, votes were taken. The Eldest Elder carried, symbol of his office, a worn leather bag, into which each closed fist dropped a bean in such a way that secrecy was maintained. White meant yes, black meant no, and the matter upon which the vote was taken had to be framed in such a way that yes or no could be the answer. Old Hodgson unwillingly produced the bag; it looked as though Mistress Captoft's innocence must be questioned, after all; unless he could twist the words about a bit.

"Now," he said, "we ain't met together to try Mistress Captoft a second time. It's him. So I'll put to you this way— Did he fool her as well as us?" It was the best he could do.

They all wanted the case against the priest to be made as black as possible, so when the bag had gone round and come back to Old Hodgson and he tipped the beans onto the table, all seven were white.

He thought smugly: I not only make a good mommet. I got a way with words, too.

So now Father Matthew stood charged with being a wizard; with having overlooked one bull and forty-one pigs; with garbling church ritual; with harbouring a familiar; with trying to shield himself by accusing an innocent woman.

Like Mistress Captoft, he was given the chance to defend himself and he took it. He was particularly vehement about the boy, Tim.

"I had temporary charge of a parish. A backward place." That should flatter these hard-eyed men, implying as it did that Intake was not backward. "The poor boy was living like a stray dog. Hunted about by other boys. Jeered at, stoned. One day he came to me for shelter and I discovered that he was not the idiot they had taken him for. I could understand what he said and he could understand me. I took him in and he has been my servant ever since."

Talking of Tim brought back to his mind the time when the village was friendly, and Jem Watson, the first to see that evil picture, had remarked upon the resemblance between the strange animal and the boy.

"I never accused an innocent woman," he said with some vehemence. "You—or your neighbours—did that. Poisonous brews, you said. And I agreed that she was an evil woman, that the picture was an evil picture."

So far he had been dealing with them on their own level. But when he came to refute the charge that he garbled church ritual, he remembered that he was a priest, a member, however humble, of the vast, powerful Church. A King, Henry II, and St. Thomas of Canterbury had fought out a bitter battle about clerics being subject to secular law. St. Thomas, simply by being martyred and becoming a saint, had won. So now Father Matthew could say, with confidence, "If you have any complaint against me, you should take it to my Bishop."

The wrong thing to say at Intake, that curious community, born of freed serfs, told by Henry Tallboys' great-great-grandfather to go and hack little fields—if they could—out of the forest.

"We don't need outside interference," Old Hodgson said. "We hev our way of doing things. And we decided to put you to the test." And it was—in a way—a fairer test than that to which Mistress Captoft had been subjected. She could sink, innocent and drowned, or swim and be burned. No middle way. Whereas trial by ordeal offered a chance. Merely by submitting to it he proved his faith in his own innocence; and if that failed and his guilt was proved, he would be regarded as sufficiently punished; the real test was the willingness to take the test; the real punishment, crippled feet or hands, for the rest of his life.

"Red hot," Old Hodgson said. "To be carried nine paces." He indicated the iron bar heating in the fire.

Father Matthew broke into an icy sweat, feeling already the searing pain across his left palm—it must be the left, less useful hand. His bowels stirred and a slight fear added itself to the greater; was he going to disgrace himself before them all?

Speaking, so dry-mouthed that he sounded rather like poor Tim, he said, "I refuse."

"Then you're guilty and know it," Old Hodgson said.

Old Gurth said, "Look outa the winder."

Father Matthew looked. Someone had lighted a huge fire.

"Refuse and you burn altogether. Self-confessed wizard."

A terrible tremor began in the marrow of his bones and worked outwards; his knees gave way. God. Mary, Mother of God. Christ. His trembling hand went to the crucifix upon his breast. A gift from his mother; made specially for him; made by a carpenter and crudely carved. Perhaps by its very crudity more expressive than most of sheer physical agony.

"I swear," he just managed to say, "on the Holy Cross of Christ, I am innocent."

And what was that worth from one who even at the altar said the wrong words?

"Prove it," they said.

Suddenly a most extraordinary thing happened. As his hand clenched upon the crucifix—one village carpenter's representation of another village carpenter's dreadful death—calm took the place of terror. He knew he was innocent; God knew he was innocent.

In a different voice, firm and clear, Father Matthew said, "I will." He knew he could do it—with the help of God.

Somebody said, "Is it ready?" And somebody else said, "Yes. White hot."

Old Hodgson took Father Matthew to the door and flung it open.

"From here to that wand. Nine paces; I measured 'em myself."

The wand of peeled willow gleamed white in the firelit yard; and all the assembled faces were red on one side, black on the other.

There was a sound, like wind rustling through corn.

One of the Elders, holding the cooler end of the iron in a cloth-protected hand, thrust the glowing, white-hot end towards Father Matthew, who took it in his *right* hand. The surest proof of faith in God that he could produce; faith must be all or nothing.

His hands had been hard as horn before he ever left his father's poor holding, and nothing in the following years had done anything to soften them. Even at school, where those with a gift for penmanship, or for advanced learning had been indoors, he'd been out, using a spade, a scythe, a hay-fork. Even at Intake—well, poor Tim couldn't do everything—Father Matthew had handled the broom, the bucket, kept the church speckless. He'd used a spade, too. The only reason why he had not ploughed his glebe himself was that he had no plough, no draught animal—and no money to hire them.

He took the glowing, white-hot end of the bar without hesitation. Set out on the nine paces.

They had been measured by Old Hodgson, who was old, and who, despite his daughter-in-law's assertions that he was an old fraud, just wanting to sit about and watch other people work, *did* suffer from rheumatism. Nine of his paces could be covered by a man in the prime of life, as Father Matthew was, in about five. But the priest did not hurry. Faith must be all or nothing.

He reached the wand, and there laid down the still glowing bar. Then he held up his hand, unscathed. When they had all had time to look and understand, he acted as though he were in church, not in a farm yard crammed with his parishioners come to watch him being burned, or hurt.

He held up his crucifix and spoke the first words of the salutation they all knew: "Ave Maria."

Mistress Captoft, frivolous, worldly woman, had found it easy to forgive. Father Matthew could no more forgive the people of Intake than he had been able to forgive Mistress Captoft for her insult. All the arguments he had used then went through his mind again, and were argued down. This time with the added assurance that he was right, they were wrong, and must be shown to be wrong. They would be shown, for they were now clay in his hands.

Now his glebe was ploughed and cross ploughed as was the custom with land long neglected. No nonsense now about ploughs needing repair, oxen needing a rest, or being lame. Converted at last, awed, penitent, admiring, they came willingly and when the ploughing was done, offered seeds. A handful of this, of that. Ill-spared, he knew, for he had been reared on a holding where even the best harvest must be cut three ways: how much to sell for cash money in order to buy such essentials as salt; how much to eat, to keep alive through the winter; how much to plant. He knew all about that.

And always, under his right hand, so miraculously saved from the white-hot iron, he could feel that little sharp shoulder blade.

Something must be done for the children.

There were some, he knew, who were still fed well. There were families where, before the pigs died, hams and bacon had been preserved and pork laid in casks of brine. But every housewife was not foresighted, or had, until disaster struck, needed to be. With other pigs coming along in the stye such hoarding was not necessary. They were the ones who now suffered most; and as Father Matthew knew, the time-honoured custom of sharing a fresh carcase now proved to be an added hardship for some. There was a lot of meat on a pig, killed at the right time, so one man would bargain with another—You have so much of my pork now and pay me back when you kill your pig. It was practical and sensible, but now there were many such debts which would never be paid, or at least not for a long time. The new pigs had, of necessity, been bought for breeding, not for eating.

It was the children with whom Father Matthew was concerned. The adult people could go hungry for all he cared. And he was so wretchedly poor himself. Some ancestress of Master Tallboys had built the church and endowed it, as she thought, generously. But the value of money had declined steadily since her day and his stipend hardly served to keep him and the boy on the most meagre fare. When he had eaten so heartily in the farmhouse kitchens it had been less from greed than from genuine hunger. So how could he feed others?

Well, he had one apparently prosperous parishioner and he must appeal to him. It went against the grain; Master Tallboys had always seemed to him—as to so many others—a cold, remote man. Certainly he attended Sunday Mass, and brought his son, but the priest sensed something perfunctory about this performance of duty. And he was not a giver. Never once in two years had he pressed a coin into Father Matthew's hand with the almost ritual remark: For the use of the poor, Father. And lately, of course, Knight's Acre had simply meant Mistress Captoft. Still, he must go there and ask. First thing tomorrow morning.

He was surprised to see preparations for a move going on. A waggon, bigger and sturdier than Master Tallboys' stood in the yard; the carter, the lame man, Jem Watson and Master Tallboys himself were loading it. The boy stood watching, holding a great dog by the collar. As Dick Walker had said, Guard was not yet fully trained and despite assurances that the carter had a legitimate errand, was a friend, seemed to distrust him. Carter and waggon had arrived overnight, ready for an early start.

Mistress Captoft was carrying out various small parcels and wedging them into crevices between larger articles; she was also supervising and admonishing: Mind this. Mind that, it would balance better if placed on this side. Her greeting was preoccupied but quite without animosity. He had been included in the general forgiveness.

Henry said, "Good morning, Father." Civilly, but with a question in it.

"I should like a word with you, Master Tallboys."

"I think the heavy things are out now," Henry said with a glance at the waggon. "Come in and sit down."

Henry was glad of an excuse to sit for a while. His injury was far less painful than it had been; he could ride now with only mild discomfort, but lifting still sent sharp pangs.

"I have come to ask your help. For the poor."

Something like humour, but not quite, crossed Henry's face. "What poor?"

Father Matthew hastened to explain; and Henry listened, with some scepticism. He had never regarded the villagers as poor. Not as he had been, and still was, in a way. For generations they had been singularly favoured, their rents fixed, for perpetuity, at some ridiculous figure by some old document. Henry's father, Sir Godfrey, the best knight in England, had always depended upon what he could win, and had been married for eight years before he had a house of his own. However, when he died, Richard, second son, trained lawyer, ordained priest, had found a flaw in that old parchment, and most of the tenant farmers had been told to buy their holdings or get out. They'd all found the money from somewhere; Henry, wanting to keep the flock together, had been obliged to borrow in order to give Richard, and John, their share of it in money. Paying interest on the loan, paying back the loan had kept him very poor. Also the holdings in Intake could all be run by families, he had to hire labour.

And even now, when the place looked so prosperous, what with putting money aside for Robert and for Joanna, he was as short of cash money as ever.

"You have so much, Master Tallboys; your swine did not sicken. And it is the Christmas season. A children's festival. I would like to give the little children of Intake a meal, now and again. So I ask your charity."

"It would have to be in kind, not in money, Father." He was not the man to go into detail, to say that most of his so much was really held in trust. He thought of the sheep-fold, where his depleted flock, and Robert's—separately marked— had been joined by Joanna's, unmarked. And Joseph had recently mentioned an old tup or two, rams growing old, fit only for butchering. Joseph loved his flock, lived with them, talked to them, would sit up all night during the lambing season, or when a sheep ailed; but he was completely unsentimental about them. He or she had had a good life and must go. "We all come to it, Master," Joseph said.

"I can let you have a sheep. And a sack of flour."

Better than nothing, Father Matthew thought. Not what he had hoped for, but better than nothing.

He had been so intent on his errand that the only thing he

had noticed about the Knight's Acre hall was that it looked a bit bare, and the horrible picture was still there. Over the hearth. Hearth. Abruptly he was reminded of the tax called Peter's Pence because presumably it ended up in Rome, in the revenues of St. Peter's direct inheritor of office, of authority, of everything—the Pope.

A penny a year on every hearth.

Father Matthew suddenly realised that he had not been strict enough. Peter's Pence had never increased during his time—nor, judging by the records, during Father Benedict's, or Father Ambrose's. And yet the number of hearths must surely have increased over the years; some young couples built a dwelling apart, some were content by adding an extra room to the family house.

Anxious to ingratiate himself in a parish he had sensed to be hostile—and now knew to be so—he had never questioned the number of hearths. Nor had the tax collector questioned his returns. But in future he would be less lenient. He might even . . .

It was a shocking thought, but he toyed with it. Why not? Extract the last possible penny from the men he could not forgive, and spend the difference between last year's returns and this upon the children.

Henry thought about the sack of flour. If he acted quickly enough the carter, a sturdy fellow, with a little help from David, could heave it into the waiting waggon, and drop it off at the priest's house. He was about to rise and go to arrange this when Mistress Captoft rustled in, cloaked, hooded, gloved.

"I apologise for interrupting you," she said, "but the man is ready to go. I could not leave without a word. Master Tallboys, I thank you for your kindness when I was in such distress; and for your hospitality. I hope that whenever you are in Bywater you will look in upon me."

"I will indeed—though I seldom go that way. I wish you all happiness in your new life . . ." Then even at this moment of leave-taking, practicality took over and he mentioned the sack of flour.

"Certainly," she said. "No trouble at all. But a whole sack! That will leave you short."

"No matter," Henry said, "I have wheat I can take to the miller."

Even Father Matthew, ignorant as he was of such things, saw that this was no parting of people who had ever conspired together, or been intimate. There again he had been completely deceived by those false village people.

As he watched the sack being tucked under the sailcloth covering which protected Mistress Captoft's possessions, another thought occurred to him. Every village priest could claim as his right the cloth—blanket or quilt—in which a dead person, awaiting interment, had been wrapped. That was another rule which he had never enforced. But he would in future.

"Tell my shepherd," Henry said, "when you want the sheep. He'll know which one to kill."

Katharine watched the waggon leave and then ran upstairs. She, too, was ready, immediate essentials in a bundle. She was taking only what could be easily carried on a long walk. Leave the two light-weight summer dresses, leave the old soiled working one. Leave the worn down-at-heel shoes and also the new ones, not yet broken in; wear the middle pair. Some faint echo of the fury which had made her fling the spit, stirred in her as she stole out the house, as though she were a thief, making off with what was not her own. No justice in this world! All those years, working conscientiously and indeed very skillfully at The Welcome To Mariners, one moment of madness to which she had been driven, and out on her ear. Then this place, so seemingly ideal except for that something, no name for it, no explanation, which brought the goose-pimples out even on the warmest day. She'd prayed: God, give me strength to face it, whatever it is. God, let Mistress Captoft change her mind about taking me. No answer. So now she must steal away and go back to the house by the tanyard, where she'd be welcome, just so long as her meagre savings lasted. After that . . . No time to think, now. It was a bright day for the time of year and she felt that she could just brace herself to the necessity of skirting through the fringe of the wood, thus avoiding observation. Being careful of direction, she should come out in the lane, somewhere near the watersplash. After that she should be able to keep up, preserving a cautious distance, with the heavily laden waggon. Mistress Captoft and David were unlikely to look back; the carter certainly wouldn't. In their wake she could creep into Bywater, to Tanner's Lane—a place where at least nobody was alone, with the silence and the watching bearing down.

Once again, in this seemingly fated kitchen, no fire on the hearth, no pot boiling, no woman in charge. Henry said, "I must have misunderstood. I thought Mistress Captoft was leaving Katharine. She must have changed her mind."

Bread and cheese again. Only as a stop-gap, of course; the larder was well stocked, and Henry, who had never attempted it, believed that cooking was largely a matter of common sense. And time. Which he could spare just now.

Lady Grey had thought of the perfect way of saving Lord Shefton the embarrassment of meeting that wretched girl again; of punishing the girl for her deceit; and of solving the problem presented by Lady Agnes during the Twelve Days, when service was slovenly or resentful.

"You will absent yourself from the hall and the company entirely and spend the Christmas season in attendance upon the Lady Agnes. By night as well as by day. You will sleep on the truckle bed in her room."

Maude or Beatrice, sentenced to such a dreadful fate, would have wept, implored, grovelled. Joanna made a faultless curtsey and said,

"As your ladyship commands."

There were dungeons below the castle keep, and condemned to one of them, bread and water once a day, she would have gone happily. The fact that Henry had confirmed the betrothal had produced such a state of euphoria—the more so because it had been preceded by a period of uncertainty. She knew more of the world now, knew that a betrothal to be binding must be witnessed and that even then there were ways of rendering it void. So in the days between her desperate statement to Maude and the arrival of the Bishop's letter, she had lived on a knife edge of trepidation. For after all, in two years Henry had shown no sign of acknowledging her existence. She knew that he could not write—but Mistress Captoft could—and he must have realised that within six months of her arrival at Stordford, she would have learned to read. That was one of the things she had been sent into exile to learn, and nobody knew better than Henry how quickly she could learn anything she gave her mind to.

No message, either verbal or written, had ever come and presently she had ceased to expect one. But nothing, no power on earth—even Henry's repudiation of her—would make her marry that old man with his rotten teeth and bald head and spindly shanks. So she had taken the risk, and back the answer had come. The right answer. All the other desperate things she had planned—including going to London and forcing her way into the presence of the King, who, though aging himself and said to be completely under the thumb of his latest mistress, was still the fount of all justice—these could be put away. Henry had stood by her.

She went cheerfully to wait upon Lady Agnes, upon whom the final humiliation of old age and its infirmities had come. Completely bedridden now, with all that that implied. . . . Even servants sometimes wrinkled their noses. And the dutiful visits had become shorter and shorter. The old woman's spirit had flagged; why bother to stay alive? Why not make the will—the thing they were all waiting for—turn your face to the wall and give up?

"I have come to spend Christmas with you, Lady Agnes," Joanna said, radiating not resentment or reluctance, but happiness of such strength that it communicated itself even to an old bedridden woman whose joints had failed her and whose only hope of happiness lay in Heaven. And in her more desolate moments Lady Agnes knew that between now and then there lay the moment of death which—though she sometimes accepted it, angrily; have done with it all—she dreaded; and after that Purgatory. Not that she'd been a great sinner, and when she could bring herself to make her will, she intended to leave something to the poor, and another sum for Masses for her soul, which should shorten her time in Purgatory. When she thought about it—as lately she had been inclined to do—she thought it curious that though the joys of Heaven and the pains of Hell had merited exact descriptions, Purgatory had never been clearly defined; it was left as vague, as unimaginable as the Limbo to which unbaptised infants were consigned.

Upon such morbid meditations the presence of the girl—whom she had always liked, rather better than her grand-nieces—broke like a ray of sunshine at the end of a dismal day. Like a breath of fresh air, which became actuality, for Joanna, realising that she must live, eat, sleep in this room, made up the fire, wrapped an extra blanket over the old body, and flung open the window. The pure clean air—mild for the time of year, and not a good omen—streamed in and the room freshened. Then, because she was so happy herself—happy even to have escaped the noise and bustle of the hall—Joanna set herself to make Lady Agnes comfortable if not happy.

"If you could hold on to me . . . Put your arms round my neck . . . I could get you on to this stool and fluff up your bed."

Somewhat cautiously Lady Agnes embarked upon this operation. Over the last two years she had observed, idly, how differently girls developed. Maude had put on flesh, become curved but remained short of stature. Beatrice would probably go the same way; this girl, mature-looking when she arrived, two years ago, had grown upwards, a full two inches, and thinned out in the process, taking on a look of frailty which was, Lady Agnes learned, completely deceptive. Strong as steel.

"Just let yourself go. I've lifted heavier weights than you."

"Where?"

"At the farm."

"I understood that you came from Spain."

"My mother did." With those words began the story, the series of stories, which afforded the invalid more entertainment than she had had for a long time. The manner of life depicted was outside her experience, almost beyond the reach of her imagination, but the girl had the knack of description, and a gift for mimicry. The place, the people all came to life. Except Henry, though it was of him that Joanna spoke most often. He remained an enigma.

"Why did he not give you a ring when you became betrothed? It would have saved a deal of bother."

"It would have been an expense. And he thought me too young. I don't suppose the idea that somebody else might not think me too young ever once occurred to him. Henry is very . . . single-minded." It was not an adequate word but she could think of no other.

Sir Godfrey's name had inevitably been mentioned, and Lady Agnes could remember him: very handsome, extremely brave, but so single-minded as to be almost simple. So devoted to his wife—when at last he had decided upon marriage—that he'd missed some good opportunities of pleasing ladies who could by influence have advanced his career; so no sinecures had come his way, and he'd died poor; his son ploughed his own acres!

It was all fascinating and Lady Agnes was insatiable. Tell me more about . . . What happened after that?

They were well fed, well supplied with firewood. That will was still to be made! Much of the service was provided by young squires because Christmas turned everything topsy-turvy. Maude and Beatrice made their morning visits as usual. Nothing to say for themselves, anxious only to get away. Lady Agnes' keen eye did, however, presently perceive a slight change, an improvement in Maude. She looked less sallow. Possibly applied colour, or a reflection of the hue of her latest new dress, which was rose pink.

One day, two, three days after Christmas, when Joanna had finished the dramatic story of how Griselda had found that hoard of jewels, the old woman said,

"You must see mine, my dear. Not that I can show you a ruby an inch wide." She had a feeling that upon this subject the girl had tended to exaggerate, but what matter? There was drama in the tale of gems lying hidden, being used as playthings, and then being discovered and tumbled on a kitchen table.

She handed Joanna a key. "It opens the small compartment in my clothes chest," she said. "Inside there is a box, bring it to me."

Lady Agnes' jewels were well enough, but set in the English style, flat into the gold, so that some light and sparkle was lost. Now it was her turn to reminisce: wedding gifts, birthday gifts; the pendant her husband had given her when her first and only child had been born; a boy, dead of the whoop before he was two. There was something sad about this recountal of glad days, grievous days, the visible evidence of things outlasting their owners. It was difficult to look so far ahead, and see herself old and ailing. Henry too . . . No, such an unthinkable thought must be put away.

Lady Agnes, out of the less important items at the bottom of the box, selected a ring. It had no sentimental associations for her for she had won it from another lady at a tournament—each had wagered an ornament upon the outcome and her knight had won. It was a ring, a plain gold band with a cluster of small garnets set together, rather like a squashed raspberry. If she remembered rightly, she'd worn it only once; at the banquet which followed the tournament, just to show that she had won it, being a better judge of a man and a horse.

"I want you to have this," she said, holding the ring towards Joanna, who made no move to take it, who backed away and said, "No. It is kind of you. But I could never wear it."

"Why not?"

"Am I not in disgrace enough already? If Lady Grey thought that I had taken advantage; turned a penance to pleasure, the very worst might happen. She could send me back and then the bargain . . . the agreement between Henry and me would fall to the ground. I must stay here, another year and a half. Until I am fifteen. Henry honoured his part, I must honour mine."

Still fingering the ring, Lady Agnes said, "It would be a guard against unwanted suitors."

Joanna said, with a touch of savagery in her voice, "There will be no need. I know now. Lady Grey flung at me the charge of being deceitful, of having encouraged Lord Shefton. That is untrue. *She* placed me by him at table; *she* told me that it was discourteous to refuse a choice tit-bit, offered by one's neighbour; or to refuse to stand up and dance when invited. It was at her bidding that I behaved in a manner she now chooses to denounce. I am wiser now, and need no ring as guard. But it was a kind thought."

"Put them back, then," Lady Agnes said. She retained the squashed raspberry ring, pushing it, with some difficulty, on to her little finger—the only one it now fitted. Strange to think that on an evening, long ago, she had shown it off, not only as a win from a wager, but as a ring far too big, her fingers being more slender that those of its former owner. A double triumph.

Lord Shefton was a self-indulgent old hedonist but he had been properly reared. Never, never lick a wound in public. As Lady Grey had expected, the task of breaking the unpleasant news had been left to her and she, fearing some display of displeasure, was relieved by his apparently calm acceptance of it.

"You are in no way to blame, Lady Grey," he said gallantly. "The fault, if any, lies with His Grace of Bywater, who was, to say the least, negligent."

Under the surface venom seethed. By withholding a vital piece of information, the negligent fellow had made Lord Shelton look a fool, and nobody did that with impunity. Let this Christmas season get over and the official wheels turning again and the Bishop of Bywater's affairs would be looked at by an eye eager to find a fault. It would be found. For just as all men had a price, all men had a vulnerable point.

Lady Grey was much impressed by his lordship's manner, and also by the fact that the rotten teeth had been removed. His breath was no longer offensive, and when he smiled, some new teeth, somewhat irregular, but clean and white and sound, could be seen.

It had been a painful, tedious, expensive and rather hit-or-miss operation, but Lord Shefton had faced it bravely. There was a tooth-puller in the Strand who specialised in the extraction and replacement of teeth—mainly for vain, aging women. Well fortified by wine and some pain-killing potion, Lord Shefton had submitted to the crude, but swift surgery, while a number of boys, each willing to sacrifice a tooth, or even two, for sixpence each, sat waiting. Pluck out the old rotten one, dab the socket well with salt; take the young tooth and press it in firmly. If it took root, well and good; if not it was simply unfortunate. It was not an operation that could be repeated. Lord Shefton with six seemingly well rooted had had above average good luck.

Nothing, of course, could restore his youth, but as she observed the new teeth and was grateful for his courtesy in not blaming her, there hung at the back of Lady Grey's mind the details of that marriage settlement.

She still wished her daughters to make good and happy marriages. And with Joanna safely out of the way, she had dared to hope that perhaps Sir Gervase Orford, another guest for Christmas, might look at Maude with a favourable eye. He was personable, well connected, and from the point of money, just right; not rich enough to despise Maude's dowry, not poor enough to covet it.

She was forestalled. Lord Shefton's pride recovered, like an angry snake, from the blow which had been painful, but not mortal. He could still make it seem as though the quarry he hunted and which had escaped him, was not indeed what he wanted, and the easiest way to do that was to pay attention to Maude. Meek and submissive, she was not to his taste, not even pretty, but she was *young*. And of late there had been a dearth of young virgins—either girls were growing more wilful, or parents more indulgent. He had, before settling on Joanna Serriff, had a set-back or two. Now, with the marriage settlement properly drawn up in his baggage, and the ring in his pouch, he had, he realised, not too much time to spare. Time enough, however, to make a defeat look like a victory. Let everybody, except Sir Barnabas and his lady, think that *he* changed his mind; it only meant the scribbling out of the name *Joanna Serriff*, and the substitution of *Maude Grey*.

True to her principles Lady Grey said, "Maude should be consulted." And Maude, crushed down, rebuked, scolded, smacked, even beaten on occasion, gave the correct answer—

"As you wish, Mother."

"No, Maude, this is the decision of a lifetime. You must take it."

Free! Away from here. Countess of Shefton; taking—if

they ever met after the wedding—precedence over her mother.

"Then I agree," Maude said. "When it was Joanna, I wished myself in her shoes."

"Forget that," Lady Grey said, commanding her daughter for almost the last time. "You are *sure?*"

"Yes. I am sure."

The ring, Lord Shefton admitted to himself, was not quite right. Out of his hoard he had chosen a ring for another finger, the finger of a girl whose eyes varied: emerald, sapphire, crystal. So he had brought an aquamarine. Had he foreseen what would happen he would have chosen something of warmer shade: a topaz, or one of the rare flawed yellow stones rightly called Cat's Eye. He had, of course, jewels of greater worth—the Shefton diamonds were quite famous—but a betrothal ring should not be ostentatious.

Maude displayed her aquamarine and told her news with a blush and a show of animation which transformed her into something approaching prettiness. Lady Agnes wished her happiness with a heartiness which concealed some doubts. However, she reflected, there would be compensations: escape from her mother's domination, a grand title—and it could not be for long.

Joanna embraced the girl whom she had always thought of as poor Maude and of whom she was mildly fond, and said, "If you are happy, Maude, I am pleased for you."

Maude said, "I could jump over the moon for joy."

Beatrice, simpering, said, "It will be my turn next. These things always go in threes."

"And when is the wedding to be?" Lady Agnes asked.

"They are discussing it now. Sometime before Lent."

It was possible to celebrate a wedding in Lent, but it was not regarded as an auspicious choice.

Impatient now, Lord Shefton said, "Would Candlemas Day be too soon?"

Lady Grey could understand his impatience. He was old. And now that the decision had been taken—by Maude herself; *no* pressure brought to bear—had she not practically invited the girl to refuse?—it would be a thousand pities if death intervened between Maude and that title, that marriage settlement. Certain observations of rites were supposed to precede a wedding, but when one had a household chaplain . . . There would be no difficulty there! Aloud she began to muse about the weather. These few exceptionally mild days—including Christmas Day itself—spoke of a hard winter still to come. Roads impassable . . . snow probably, and then as it melted, the slush and mire. And if Lord Shelton had welcomed the idea of a short betrothal, how much more would he—and everybody—welcome Twelfth Night? Without actually seeming to do so—and there lay the secret of her power—she had it all arranged. A *little* less food for a few days, and she had enough provisions for a splendid wedding feast. And Maude had another gown, as yet unworn. Guests were already here—neighbours within easy distance could be invited. Family ties were frail. Stordford had never been a family place; Lady Grey's relatives were too modest and Sir Barnabas' too grand.

Twelfth Night it would be.

Above stairs, Lady Agnes had fallen into a strange, unusually quiet mood. It had come upon her with the reflection that Maude's marriage, happy or otherwise, could not last long. She and Lord Shefton were near contemporaries, and that thought struck home. For the last few days, her bed made so comfortable, her mind distracted by Joanna's tales, she had felt better, lively. Now melancholy set in. It was strengthened by the thought that she must give Maude a wedding present. And how to decide about that? It must be something, out of that locked box, good enough to pass muster, and yet not good enough to be wasted, because ignored amongst those which Maude, Countess of Shefton, would for a short time own and wear. A short time . . .

"I want Father Gilbert—the chaplain," she said suddenly, just as Joanna was beginning to light the candles. Aware that the chaplain had come to the sick-room on Christmas morning, Joanna said,

"Are you feeling worse?"

"I'm as well as I shall ever be! *And* in my right mind." There was a touch of tetchiness. "This is business. Tell him to bring pen and parchment and two copying clerks. Then stay out of the room, but within call."

On her withered yet knuckly fingers Lady Agnes checked over the details of the will, about which she had been brooding all day. First, a generous bequest, fifty pounds, to the chaplain himself—that would ensure that the document was not mislaid or overlooked. One had to be wily about such things. Fifty pounds for a hundred Masses to be said for her soul; fifty for the poor—to be administered at Father Gilbert's discretion. Maude would want for nothing and in any case would have received a wedding present; possibly the pearls. To Beatrice, a hundred pounds to be paid when she married, or reached the age of eighteen. Over Barnabas and Gertude she hesitated. Certainly they had housed and fed her, but they could not be said to have been very *attentive* since she had been stuck away here; hurried little visits. Fifty pounds apiece. Oh, and Roger, of course, must not be forgotten though she remembered him only somewhat dimly, he'd been from home for so long. Still men needed property and property needed a man to see to it, as she had learned, employing middlemen. So, to Roger—my nephew—my manor of Foxborough. . . . And *that* also would ensure that this will was executed correctly. But she owned another, bigger manor, nearer London and now almost entirely devoted to supplying the rapidly growing city with fresh, immediately consumable food. She had not seen it since her fall had disabled her, but to judge from the returns it was prosperous, though the house—actually the house to which she had gone as a bride, which she and her husband had occupied whenever business or pleasure had drawn them towards London—was now, according to her agent, all chopped about and let out to working people who toiled on the land, or trudged into the city to earn a wage. "My manor of Finchley," Lady Agnes said, "and everything else of which I die possessed . . ."

Joanna had spent the time sitting at the head of the stairs, hugging her secret happiness and oblivious to the sound of voices and laughter coming up from the hall below. She felt the wind change. Real winter on the way, and if the old beliefs were anything to go by, it would be a severe one. She remembered one of Tom Robinson's rhymes.

If the ice in November'll bear a duck,
There's nothing to come but mud and muck.
Warm weather at the year's back end
Snow drifts later on do send.

The chaplain and the clerks eventually emerged, all looked pleased. He had his legacy, and for witnessing the signature the clerks would each receive two shillings. Joanna went back into the room and made up the fire.

"Now tell me a story," Lady Agnes demanded. "A merry one if possible."

Well, if not actually merry, there was a comic side to the

story of Young Richard stealing from market stalls and being thoroughly beaten by everybody who could get in a blow.

"But he was Henry's nephew, you see, and was a Tallboys; so Henry thought he was responsible, and offered to pay. *Everybody* on the market claimed to have been robbed, if not that day, last week, a month ago. And that was most unfair; Richard certainly hadn't stolen pots or pans. Henry hadn't enough money, so he sold Richard's pony and cleared the family name. That *was* fair, but it started some talk about Henry being unkind and the poor boy stealing because he was hungry. That was a black lie. Much good it did him though!" Her eyes flashed green malice and she laughed, showing those sharp teeth. "He was sent to school at Eton, where he says he is half starved and frequently flogged. He may be lying again, but I hope with all my heart it is true!"

Now that the will was made, the old woman felt better; it had been the prospect of parting with her belongings which had depressed her. Once more she was easily entertained.

"You bear him a grudge. Did he steal from you?"

"That would have puzzled him! No, he tried to be friends. Once he tried to give me a string of blue beads. I told him to go and hang himself with it!"

"You *are* pretty, my dear, but when you are spiteful your face changes. You look like a wolf."

Joanna laughed again.

"Once I tried to *be* one." She began on the story of her futile attempts to make magic brews so that she could turn herself into a wolf—like the old woman at Nettleton in Tom's story—and go to Moyidan in the night and scare Young Richard into behaving better to poor little Robert.

"I could *see* how unhappy Robert was, though Moyidan is five miles from Knight's Acre. Henry didn't believe me. But I had seen right."

That kind of seeing, she decided, was something she had outgrown. Homesick as she had been and still was for Knight's Acre, much as she had thought about it, and during the last days talked about it, calling it so vividly to mind and describing it, it had been just the ordinary eye of memory that she had used.

Supper came and Lady Agnes was sufficiently restored to complain both of the quantity and the quality.

"Very meagre," she said, surveying the food—enough by Knight's Acre standards to keep two people for four days. "I can see what is happening. Everything will be saved towards the wedding feast. We are all to go hungry until

Maude is married. And this venison is green! It needed two days in the ground to sweeten it. Eaten like this it is very bad for the bowels." Nevertheless she ate her share and a good portion of Joanna's, slipped unostentatiously on to her plate. Lady Agnes noticed, but did not protest. The girl would have her reward. But not yet! The melancholy mood had lifted and the old woman thought that if she could survive starvation until after the wedding, and if Joanna could continue to be in disgrace, she was good for a long time yet.

Next morning they learned that the time of threatened scarcity would be short. Maude was to be married on Twelfth Night.

"Indecent haste," Lady Agnes said when the girls had gone giggling away. "I suppose my lady was afraid the bridegroom might take a fit from excitement! It would be scandalous were it not well known that Maude has never done a thing, or thought a thought, without her mother's permission. She is a virgin—and likely to remain so." She sniggered.

For some reason which she did not understand, Joanna disliked that kind of talk. It was part of the falsity which pervaded this kind of world. Outwardly so prim and proper, and in company behaving as though they were all the Virgin Mary, no less, in the privacy of the solar they let themselves go, with sly hints, a special tone of voice, even a peculiar kind of smile.

Puzzling to a country-bred girl whose knowledge of sex was as simple and straightforward as the act itself, as performed by animals. Bull mounted cow, boar mounted sow; the female swelled with her burden and delivered it. With people something more was involved, fondness, loyalty—all that Joanna felt for Henry, and now hoped that Henry felt for her—but none of it funny. So why should the prospect of poor Maude's endless virginity make her great-aunt cackle in that special way? Never mind. Amusement however ill justified made for good humour; and this morning good humour was needed, for the insufficiently earthed venison had had the predicted effect.

"I'd like my box again. I have decided to give Maude my pearls. With the wedding so hasty, she will have few gifts. Few guests who are not already here. I am a member of the family and must make the best show I can."

Joanna opened the chest within the chest, brought the box

and laid it on the bed. Fumbling amongst her treasure, Lady Agnes muttered on,

"Too good really; it is a sacrifice. If they are quick enough and haste seems to be the order of the day, Maude will wear the Shefton diamonds. But no better pearls. And of course these will be hers, when the wife of his eldest son wears the diamonds and . . ."

Abruptly she became aware that she had lost her audience. The girl stood there, looking exactly—curious the tricks one's memory played—exactly like a knight who, in the mêlée with which a formal tournament often ended, had been transfixed by a lance; held upright for a moment in the saddle by the weapon that had killed him. Just for a moment, there, and yet not there. Before he toppled.

She said, "What is the matter?" and knew the answer to the question even as she asked it. It was pain; that terrible griping in the bowels which resulted from the eating of green venison, inadequately earthed. The girl had eaten less of it, so her attack had come later.

When she said, in a dazed way, "I must go," Lady Agnes knew why and where.

But it had happened again. That inside eye which Joanna had thought outgrown. Seeing again.

There, far more real than the room, the bed, the old woman handling her treasures, was the Knight's Acre kitchen, all cluttered and muddled and Henry, thinner, older, and in some way hurt, trying not to limp. No time to lose.

Joanna ran swiftly down the stairs and across the hall. The men guests had had a table set up near the fire and were playing some game with dice. The women, she guessed, were in the solar, busy with dresses and head-dresses. She slipped through the hall like a shadow, unseen, and into the vast courtyard with its many stables. The wind struck its first blow, but she did not notice. She needed a horse and, above all, she needed to be unobserved. And she needed to be quick; no time for argument, explanation, even to stableboys, so she avoided any building from which came sounds of activity and ran on until she found a stable holding horses only. The one nearest the entry was a big black animal and his harness, freshly oiled and polished, hung on the wall behind him.

The gentle ambling palfreys which she and the Grey girls had ridden were always brought, ready to be mounted, to the door; it was two years since she had slipped in a bit or buckled a girth, but she was too anxious to consider that she might have difficulty, that this was a different animal from Henry's old farm horse, or Mistress Captoft's mule. Her confidence served her, communicating itself to the animal, who was of tricky temper and capable of taking advantage of the slightest hesitancy or nervousness. As it was, he submitted docilely.

She had come to Stordford escorted by a man who knew the way and she had been too wretched, already suffering the first pangs of homesickness, to take any interest in her surroundings. All she knew was that the road she must take lay roughly towards the East. Straight into the wind. How rash, how foolish, how like a hen running round without its head, she had been to rush out dressed as she was for indoors: her velvet dress, provided just before she fell into disgrace; little kid slippers on her feet and on her head nothing but a head-dress, which the wind snatched away, and sent soaring—like the butterfly it was intended to resemble—into the hedge. But she excused herself; if she had tarried to dress for the ride, she could have been caught, prevented. And at least she had, by accident, hit upon just the horse for this venture. She steeled herself against the cold. Henry needed her and she was going to him as fast as she could, on a horse that could gallop, the kind of animal she had never ridden before. And he had never carried so light a rider . . .

She was out in the world, without a farthing, not certain of her way, depending upon the light for her direction on one of the shortest days of the year, but fear—that sense of ill to come, defeat inevitable—had no part in her nature. Sir Godfrey—her father, though nobody knew that—had never gone into a joust, or a serious battle expecting more than a trivial hurt; and Tana, her mother, had faced incalculable risks in her plan to get them both across the mountains, out of Moorish Escalona and into Christian Spain. The child of their union had been born as nearly without fear as a human being could be; and also without fear's concomitant, self-concern; that she was cut to the bone by the wind mattered nothing.

At Intake Father Matthew was a bit fearful—of the weather . . . of the numbers who might come to his feast; of the possibility that no child would come. Still he had done his best and chosen the day when Master Tallboys' gift of an old sheep and a bag of flour could be used to the best advantage. He had announced that on the Tenth Day of Christmas there would be a dinner for every child of Intake, under eleven years old. Nothing careless about the date chosen or the age limit. A peasant himself, Father Matthew knew how the rules ran. So far as they could in their crippled state, the people of Intake would keep Christmas. Two, in some places, three, days of full plates. Then would come the lean time, with what food there was being hoarded for Twelfth Night, and given mainly to the men, who must be strong on Plough Monday, when work would be resumed. But even then, Father Matthew knew from his own experience, there would be something for the children: the greasy salty liquor in which pork had been boiled, a bone to gnaw, the tough outer hide of ham or bacon to chew on. . . . Knowing it all, he planned his time and his age limit with care. Any child over eleven was a potential worker, worth feeding.

Tim, whom everybody except Father Matthew had despised and rejected, again proved his worth; sound common sense; he could not, he said, in his thick-tongued way, make enough bread on the oven floor for so many, but he could make pad loaves, one above the other, towers of bread, each layer separated from the next by a liberal sprinkling of flour. "And, sir, it'll save cutting; they'll just pull apart."

The sheep, Tim said, was too old to be roasted. It must be boiled, very gently.

Only the church itself was large enough to be used for this feast, and in the morning Father Matthew made ready, placing upon the altar a bowl of flowers, sprung from some roots which Mistress Captoft had planted and left behind when she moved. They had never flowered before, but this year unaccountably they did; braving the wind, elegant, delicate. A drift of white alongside the onion bed. A strange flower and unknown to him but he hit by accident on the name by which it was eventually to be called. Arranging them in a silver bowl—one of the gifts which Sir Godfrey had made to the church in memory of his wife—Father Matthew remarked that the drooping white petals looked like snow drops. And as he spoke he cast a weather-wise eye at the sky. Real snow threatened.

Just across the track, in the sheep-fold, Joseph was making preparations for the bad weather he knew was coming. Ordinarily only ewes about to drop lambs were sheltered from the weather, but this year the old shepherd built an enclosure capable of holding the whole flock, and his constant demands for more straw bales kept Henry and the waggon busy.

Once, as he unloaded, Henry caught a whiff of baking

bread and savoury stew coming from the priest's house and realised that he was quite hungry himself. His attempts at cooking had not been successful. He had not realised that pork taken straight from the brine cask needed a good soaking before it was boiled, and he was ignorant of timing; the pork had been difficult to carve, and was hard to chew, the bag of dried peas boiled with it, like little stones. He'd tried cooking a fowl on the spit, but he was ignorant of the need for basting, and of the fact that even a wind-up spit needed some attention. He left it, turning as it should, and then went out to feed his animals; the un-wound spit became stationary, half the fowl was charred almost to a cinder, the other side almost raw.

The best of the spoiled stuff must go to Godfrey, who was growing; next to Jem, an inveterate grumbler, next to Joseph, who never grumbled—that seemed unjust, but it was the way things went. Henry ate the worst, stuff which even his hearty appetite could not make palatable. Jem had not suggested, as he had done on a former occasion, that he should go home for his dinner, for food was not plentiful there, now; he had stayed at home on Christmas Day and the day following; he intended to stay home on Twelfth Night. That was all.

Now, as Henry smelt the proof that somebody in the priest's house could cook, Joseph spoke of food, too.

"I'll not come down to my dinner, Master. If I work straight through they'll lay snug tonight. Another thing, too. If the weather take the turn my nose tell me, maybe I shan't be able to come down for a day or two, so I'd obliged if you'd bring me a store of bread and cheese, a bit of frying bacon if you can spare it. Then I'll manage. Oh, and a little flour, in case things get really bad."

He had managed on his own in the past and could do so again. His diet was not quite so dreary as it might sound. The hard Suffolk cheese toasted well, and a spade made a good frying pan. Given flour he could make dough cakes to cook on the stones that made his hearth in the centre of his now snug and waterproof hut. Over the willow branches which shaped and sustained it, he had, working at odd times, plastered clay, inside and out; then he had turfed it on the outside—choosing a time when pasture was plentiful, so that the removal of some turf from the edge of the fold had not robbed them, his charges. In the turves there had been living roots, grass, weeds, wildflowers; they had reached out towards each other, woven themselves together in a tough outer hide, wind-and weather-proof. Joseph as well as his flock would lie snug whatever happened.

Henry said, "Have you enough for today, Joseph?"

"Yes, I was thinking forrard."

"So must I," Henry said. For even bread was running out now. Flour too. Tomorrow he must take action about such things.

The children came trooping in, rather shyly, for this was something new and their Intake blood made them distrustful of innovation. The little girl, Emma Edgar, whose thin shoulder had put this whole project into motion came in, carrying a child, rather over a year old, on her out-thrust hip, the traditional carrying way for females who must carry a child unable or reluctant to walk, and yet have one hand free for some other task. To her free hand another child clung.

After the briefest Benediction, asking God's blessing on the food, that Father Matthew could remember from his seminary days, the meal began. Tim went around—important for once—distributing the circles of bread, crusty on the outside, spongy in the centre, so that they made natural receptacles into which Father Matthew, following, could drop—from a ladle which Mistress Captoft had not thought it worthwhile to remove—cubes of meat, some lean, some fat. He had spent an hour carving and chopping and removing bones. It must all be as fair as he could make it. The meat was dished up in a luscious gravy into which onions, long and gently cooked, had disintegrated; there were shreds of finely chopped mint, too, the whole thickened, almost glutinous with flour.

Moving about amongst his young guests, Father Matthew reflected that his fears that after the humble feast he and Tim would have clearing up to do, were completely unfounded. A crumb of bread dropped was instantly retrieved; if a drip of gravy fell a finger dabbled in it, was licked, applied again, licked again until no smear remained. He thought: Well, in one thing I was right; they are hungry.

Feed my sheep. Christ had said that. And in his seminary somebody had explained the symbolism of it. Father Matthew had never understood what symbolism meant; but he understood hunger and determined that during this bad time, and in any other bad time, children must be fed. He'd defraud the Peter's Pence collector, sell his warm cloak and his beautifully embroidered satchel. He'd beg, cajole, threaten.

The candles on the altar took on a brighter glow as the day darkened, prematurely. Snow, looming in the offing for two days, was now about to fall.

He dismissed them with the briefest possible blessing and told them to hurry home. He expected no thanks—his own manners were poor—and was not surprised when they ran off. All except the little girl, Emma Edgar. The baby on her hip had gone to sleep, still sucking a gravy-soaked crust. The other child, crammed and half somnolent, dragged on her hand. Another man would have seen in her, perhaps, the symbolism of womanhood, burdened almost from the first by the claims of the helpless young. But Father Matthew's mind did not work that way. He said,

"Run along, Emma. You will be left behind."

She said, "Father. Did you see? She was there, too."

"Who?"

"Our Lady. Just there." Having no hand free the child jerked her head towards the slab of black marble, so distinct from the grey stone of the church floor. "All blue, with lilies."

He saw that snowflakes were already falling, big ones drifting down with the apparent idleness that concealed real purpose, so he hurried her along, saying, "Yes, yes, my dear child. Now hurry along and catch up with the others. Ask one of the boys to give your little brother a pig-a-back ride."

Then he turned back and looked at the black marble slab which, he had been given to understand, covered the last resting place of the Lady Sybilla, Master Tallboys' mother, dead and buried in old Father Ambrose's time; her death, if recorded at all, recorded on a page in the Parish Book, so over-scribbled as to be illegible. For a grown woman, even a very small woman, the black slab was, Father Matthew thought, quite inadequate. More like a child's grave covering. No mark identified it. Sir Godfrey, ravaged by grief—and remorse—had complained about his sweet Sybilla lying under cold stone; Tana had taken this literally and believed that his grief, all that now stood between him and her, might be eased if Sybilla lay under marble. So Henry had been commissioned to buy marble and the only piece in Baildon was this, left over from a job the stone-mason had just completed. The lack of inscription was due to the fact that, guided by old Father Ambrose, Sir Godfrey's memorial to Sybilla had taken a more practical shape—the restoration of the church, the proper furnishing of the altar.

Father Matthew did not know that Sybilla had always

brought what flowers she had to the church—a custom kept up by Griselda, faithful imitator—but he did know that lilies were the flowers most closely associated with Our Lady, even called by her name, Madonna lilies. And blue was her colour. He did not doubt that Emma Edgar had seen a vision. And what about those white flowers, springing up over-night at the edge of the onion bed? A sign of approval of what he was doing and intended to go on doing.

The thought flitted through his mind that the vision might be used to advantage; people would come to see the place, and hope to see what Emma Edgar had seen; they would leave gifts on the black slab. Many places of pilgrimage had grown from such humble beginnings.

But the first person who must be informed was his Bishop and Father Matthew shrank from another interview with that unfriendly man: he would not believe; he would mock; he would say: Last time it was a witch in your parish, now it is a child who sees visions! There was a further consideration. Suppose the Bishop believed and the word spread and people came with their presents; in no time at all, Father Matthew would find himself pushed aside. He could not actually be displaced; only an act of gross immorality could rob him of his living, but a man—or more than one man—with smoother manners and more learning would be appointed as custodians of the shrine. What little power he now had would be lessened and his plans would come to nothing.

He had his share of peasant shrewdness as well as the credulity, stubbornness, conservatism of his breed; better not start anything of which the outcome was uncertain, better not say anything not absolutely necessary.

The black horse, his first exuberance expended, settled down to a steady trot which ate up the miles. But now the short day was ending and Joanna realised that she had not—as she had hoped—covered the distance in one swift ride. She was still in unknown country and at every crossroads was obliged to rein in and ask direction, worthless, because so far she had not encountered anyone who had ever heard of Baildon. On such a bitter day only people who were compelled to venture out were abroad; a woman feeding some cooped hens, a man milking a goat, a boy scattering scanty wisps of hay to some sheep in a bare pasture. She did not ask at houses, because that meant dismounting and that she had done only once, for a most necessary purpose, and she was so stiff with cold that getting out of the saddle, and then back again was painful, even perilous. So much so that at a place where a stream crossed the road, much like the water-splash in the lane to Intake, she let the horse drink, but did not get down to drink herself.

At each divergence of the road she was obliged to rely upon her own judgement, holding to East as well as she could.

She remembered that on that miserable journey to Stordford she and the Bishop's man had stayed for a night at a religious house which had a hostel for travellers; but either she had not reached it yet, or, taking the wrong road, had missed it.

She knew from her experience of Stordford that large establishments kept open house for *bona fide* travellers, but although she saw several big houses, windows already lighted from within, she dared not ask hospitality; people in such places formed a close-knit network and she still feared pursuit, though she thought that thanks to the black horse, she had, so far, outdistanced it. She knew that she was a conspicuous figure, dressed for indoors on such a day, a girl riding what was plainly a man's horse.

And, in the fading light, the horse was becoming troublesome. Under-exercised since his arrival at Stordford, he had accepted her, as someone knowledgeable, smelling right and prepared to let him gallop. Now something inside his shapely head informed him that he was not being taken either towards his own stable or the one which was his temporary home. He expressed his disapproval of this procedure by tossing his head and occasionally jibbing, trying to turn.

Another crossroads. There'd been no sun all day, yet cloud-blotted as the sky was, there had been just that difference in the quality of the light to distinguish East from West, North from South. That shadowy guidance was now lost. A choice of ways and nobody to ask. Wrong! Out of the greyness more solid shapes took form: a well-head, a man with a bucket.

She asked the question she had already asked so many times: Which road for Baildon? And this time instead of the Dunno; never heard of it, she received, in turn a question.

"Would it be Bury St. Edmund's way?"

"Yes," she said eagerly. "They lie in the same direction."

"Then I can tell you. I been there. Bury, not Baildon. Carried my boy there; years ago when he was a bit of a cripple . . ."

Joanna had no time or inclination to listen to the marvellous story of how a crippled boy, carried to St. Edmund's shrine, had been miraculously cured and able to walk home.

"Which way?"

The man moved his free arm and then said, "No. You and me's facing different ways. Let's see." He turned himself about. "To your right," he said. "Then sharp left. It's a lonely road."

It was also, mercifully, sheltered; great thickets of trees on either side acted as screens from the wind. Though she was now so cold as to be almost numb; the only part of her body that had any feeling left was where, between saddle and stirrup, her legs were warmed by the horse. She thought what a fool she'd been to rush out so ill equipped, yet had she lingered to clothe herself properly, she might have been intercepted, prevented from setting out at all.

Could horses see in the dark? One might think so from the way in which Henry's old horse jogged home in the winter afternoons, but then he might know his way. How long could a horse go without food? She was reasonably certain that she had snatched this one from his stable before the dilatory, Christmas-season service had reached him. Was his slowing down of pace due to his becoming weak from hunger, or to his carefully picking his way? She bent stiffly and made encouraging noises, promising him everything, everything, if only he'd keep going and get her home.

Presently she began to worry about that turn to the left. Would she miss it?

At Stordford she had not been missed immediately. Lady Agnes knew what green venison could do. Then as time went on she suspected that Joanna had been dragged in to help with the wedding preparations. They'd need fresh garlands and even a girl in disgrace could be allowed to prick her fingers on holly. The fire burned low, and presently her bladder needed relief. She began to shout, and was either unheard or ignored. Weeping with rage and self-pity, she reached for her stick. It was no longer of use to her, but she cherished a half hope that one day she might hobble again, and it always stood propped within easy reach. She seized it and beat upon the floor, upon the frame of her bed.

It was some time before the noise she made was noticed, and then only by a servant, half tipsy, as was the usual state at this season.

"Where is the demoiselle Joanna?" Lady Agnes demanded.

The woman stared stupidly. How could she be expected to know? She rendered the essential service and went away.

In due course one of the pages brought up the dinner—prepared for two, the old woman noticed. She put the question to him, and he said, "With the others, I suppose."

"Ask your mistress to come to see me. At once!"

In the hall, dinner was already served, at the high table, and at his place, below the squires, his own awaited. Despite the *at once*, he saw nothing very urgent about the message and decided to eat before delivering it. Then for a time he could not find Lady Grey, who, in her own words, was obliged to be everywhere at once, just now. A wedding at such short notice took a great deal of organising. When the message reached her she went at once, and found the old woman alone, shedding tears of self-pity, rage, and frustration. The fire was almost dead, now, and although the tray had been placed in its usual place, on a table near the bed, much of its contents was out of reach of Lady Agnes' restricted motion.

Curiously, the urgent question was not immediately asked. Lady Agnes had never liked her niece-by-marriage, and now, in her disturbed state, embarked upon a virulent, if slightly incoherent denunciation. It was deliberate neglect; to place the girl here so that servants thought they need do nothing, and then to withdraw her, leaving a poor bedridden woman to die of cold and hunger. Just because she had had a visit from the Chaplain, they thought, no doubt that she had made her will, and the sooner she died the better. Well, they were wrong; she had made no will, and when she did, this piece of ill-treatment would be remembered.

Aunt Agnes must be soothed. With her own hands Lady Grey mended the fire, promised food, freshly cooked to be brought up at once; denied all blame for what had happened, accusing Joanna as fiercely as she had herself been accused. Another trick, typical of that false little jade, to pretend to accept banishment from the hall so cheerfully, pretend to be so dutiful, and then to do *this*. She was skulking somewhere. She would be found, severely reprimanded.

Only half-pacified, still unwilling to believe that Joanna, whom she liked, of whom she had become as fond as the limited emotion of old age would allow, had deserted her, Lady Agnes calmed herself enough to say, "She may have taken a fit and fallen somewhere. She looked—just before she left me—very strange."

"In all her time here, she has never had a fit to my knowledge. She is capable of pretending *that*, too." Horrible, hateful girl. And too leniently dealt with, Lady Grey now realised. She should have been cuffed and shaken, stood with her hands on her head, facing the wall until she dropped, as Maude and Beatrice had been. But I was in a difficult position, Lady Grey thought, excusing her weak handling—she was neither my child, nor my legal ward. She chose, at this moment, to ignore the fact that from the very first there'd been something which had warned her that Joanna was not Maude, or Beatrice . . .

Even now she was not, however, sufficiently aware of the difference to consider the possibility that the hateful girl had, in mid-winter, left Stordford, alone. She was hiding, sulking somewhere, doing her clever best—and even Lady Grey could not deny that in certain ways the wretch was clever—to make a confusion.

Outside the window the fading light changed; not a brightening exactly, a lightening. The first snowfall of the year. How wise to have settled upon Twelfth Night!

Downstairs again, giving orders, arranging everything, Lady Grey said, "Beatrice, go up to Aunt Agnes. She needs help; all her jewels are scattered on the counterpane; help her to sort them and put them away."

Then followed the resolute, but discreetly conducted hunt for Joanna. Discreet because Lady Grey did not wish the name to be mentioned in Lord Shefton's hearing; once it had been erased from that marriage settlement, and Maude's substituted, it would have been in the worst of taste to remind him. So she shut him away, with Maude, her father, and a waiting woman named Mabel to play with the Tarot cards while the rest of the household played another game. Not hunt the slipper . . . not simple hide-and-seek, but, under Lady Grey's expert handling, just a game. *Find Joanna.*

Joanna was not found. What was presently discovered was that Sir Gervase Orford's best, big black horse was missing.

Sir Gervase cuffed his squire about the head, but otherwise took his loss lightly, saying, "Whoever snatched Blackbird will have his hands full and by tomorrow will be only too glad to turn him loose. The best example of biting the feeding hand I ever met with."

Only Lady Grey made any connection between the disappearance of the girl and the horse. And, seeing further than Sir Barnabas, she broke down, once the privacy of the connubial chamber was achieved. Since her marriage she had never been the victim of self-pity; she regarded herself as a most fortunate woman, but now she was sorry for herself.

"Just when we were all so happy, this must happen. And you know what will be said—unless she is found and brought back immediately. That we so resented her behaviour—as regards Lord Shefton—that we bore on her too hard. Or even . . . even that for the sake of that half dowry lodged with you, we did away with her. Such stories are not unknown. Years," she said weeping, "years upon years, I have done my best. And now this! More than any mortal should be asked to bear, having done her best."

Sir Barnabas said, "My love; you are over-wrought. Too much excitement in a short time. Too much to do. Such fancies, indeed." He patted her and made soothing noises, behaving towards her much as he would have done to a startled horse. It did not occur to him to feel any compunction about having left everything to her, even the breaking of unwelcome news to Lord Shefton. Gertrude had always handled such things, leaving him to be merry and carefree. When she continued to fret, weeping in the graceless way of one to whom tears did not come easily, he began to think about age; that process so rightly known as the change, when amiable women turned shrew, and shrewish ones torpid, when slender figures thickened and sturdy ones shrivelled. Being fond of her, he thought: Poor dear. And made up his mind to be patient with her. "Come, come," he said, "calm yourself. At first light tomorrow, mounted men shall go in search of the little hussy. She cannot have got far. In this weather."

The snow which had begun in the afternoon, had thickened as night fell and the wind veered to the North and by morning Stordford and all the surrounding country lay deep under snow. Two feet deep, more where it had drifted. Any kind of search or pursuit was impossible now.

At Intake, though the clouds still threatened, the East wind still triumphed; as the knowledgeable said, it was too cold for snow. But it would fall, as soon as the wind changed. Henry knew that he must make the best of his time. Take a sack of wheat to the Nettleton mill and while it was being ground, drive on into Baildon, where surely the bakers would be back at work.

Knight's Acre had known its ups and downs but Henry could not remember a shortage of bread. Let this Christmas season get over and the first thing he would do would be to hunt for a good sensible woman.

Heaving the sack of wheat into the waggon caused a pang

which exacerbated his general feeling that something was wrong with the world. With him? So when Godfrey asked,

"Can Guard come?" the answer was sharp.

"No, he cannot. He stays here and does his duty. If you can't bear an hour's separation, you stay, too."

The dog was already ruined; actually sleeping on the boy's bed.

"Guard, you guard," Godfrey said, climbing into the waggon. He wanted to go with his father, out of temper as he seemed this morning. And he cherished a secret hope that during their absence something might happen to prove that Guard was not ruined. A wolf perhaps . . . Unlikely; he'd never seen one himself.

Like most other people who did business with Henry, the Nettleton miller respected him without liking him much. A just man, a civil man, but cold and aloof.

"I'll call back," Henry said. "I have to go to Baildon to buy bread."

"Buy bread!" What an astonishing thing, for a man who grew his own wheat.

"The woman who had charge of my house left—and took the maid-servant with her," Henry said, giving an explanation, not a bit of gossip, or a complaint.

The miller cast a glance at the lowering sky and said,

"There's no need for that, Master Tallboys. My missus is baking this very minute. She'd be glad to let you have a loaf or two."

"I wonder if she'd tell me how to make it."

Again astonished, the miller said, "I'm sure she would. Glad to. Though I say it, she's a dab hand at a loaf."

"Then I'll go in, if I may."

The miller looked at Godfrey and said, rather diffidently, "Would the young master like to come with me and see the mill at work?"

"Oh, yes, please," Godfrey said, answering for himself.

Moving a bit stiffly, Henry went towards the kitchen door, cursing Bert Edgar. Whatever the injury was, it would seem to heal itself, he'd forget about it until he lifted something heavy. Then it seemed to re-open and pain him again for a day or two. There was no outward sign of injury, and several applications of Walter's horse liniment had no effect at all. When the pain was there it was there until it chose to go. Most jobs, thank God, did not provoke it, he could lift a forkful of hay, a shovelful of manure without strain.

The miller's wife welcomed him warmly. She knew him—

as she knew all the mill's customers—by sight and by name and cherished a kind of romantic feeling for him. She thought him extremely handsome and his expression, which her husband thought surly, she thought was merely grave and rather sad. Not unlike—God forgive her if it was blasphemous—the picture of Christ on the wall of Nettleton church. (Griselda, years earlier, had felt precisely the same about Henry's father, and the feeling had saved his life by prompting her to do what she could for him when he was thrown out into an innyard barn to die.)

This morning she thought he looked not less handsome, but less well than usual. Certainly thinner. More lined. The man she saw most of—her husband—weighed on his own scales, just over fourteen stones and had a broad rosy face. You couldn't actually say that Master Tallboys looked pale, his face was too weathered for that, but she thought, in a slightly muddled way, that if he could look pale he would look pale. Maybe the cold.

"Sit here, by the fire, Master Tallboys," she said, and thought of mulled ale and ginger cakes, luxuries that a prosperous, childless couple could well afford.

Henry explained what he wanted of her—and his voice, which she had never heard, close-to, before, was just what she expected—beautiful.

"My bread's in the oven now," she said, almost as though in getting it in so soon she had been at fault, "but of course, I could *tell* you."

"I should be deeply obliged."

"We'll have something to warm us as we talk," she said. Not that she needed warming, but he certainly did.

As he accepted her hospitality and listened to her talk, Henry looked about him and saw how comfortable everything was. It was a kitchen, cooking hearth and wall oven side by side along one wall, shelves of mugs and other crocks and kitchen tools along another. But because it was living room too, the settles on either side of the hearth were cushioned and the table—now that the bread-making was over—wore a gay scarlet cloth.

He realised that in his own home two ways of life had always run alongside: the life of the kitchen, the life in the hall. Usefulness on one side of the wall, comfort on the other. Never really united, as they were here. Vaguely he meditated the possibility of bringing his own cushioned settle into his kitchen, but the thought of lifting made his pain worse. The sense of failure—never too far away—clamped down. He'd made a mess of everything he undertook. And, remembering the reproachful glance that his son had shot at him, as he climbed into the waggon, after hugging the dog, he was in a fair way towards making a mess of parenthood, too.

"They should be about done, now," the miller's wife said. "I'll show you how to test a loaf." She did so and was satisfied. Then with an air of modest achievement, she withdrew all the loaves and ranged them, even and golden and sweet-smelling, on the table. "There's another thing to remember, Master Tallboys. They must be quite cold before they're stored away."

She'd told him all he needed to know, but all the time she had been conscious of the incongruity of it: this handsome, dignified man, with his beautiful voice, turning baker!

"Can't you get somebody to do for you?"

"Oh, I shall in time. Once Christmas is over." He did not again explain about Katharine's unexpected departure; but he did give his rare and singularly sweet smile, as he added, "Until I find somebody, the boy and I must eat."

Godfrey and the miller came in; both aglow. It had pleased the man to show, the boy to see, how the mill worked, how the flour was sieved.

"I helped, Father. Didn't I?" He turned his sweet, confident smile upon his new friend.

"You did that. Good as a 'prentice."

Then the boy's eye fell upon the bread. "Please, can I have a piece?" Except for those infrequent occasions when Griselda's rage with life in general had touched him for a moment, and lately Father's criticism of the handling of Guard, Godfrey had never known anything but indulgence, so he made his request with assurance.

"You've earned it, by all accounts," the woman said, cutting him a great crust of bread unlike any that had come his way before; for who should have the best, most finely sieved flour, if not the miller's wife?

He ate it with zest, and was then aware that something had happened. What? A moment before, the miller and his wife had both looked at him smiling. Now their faces had changed, though they were both looking at him still. Was it wrong to have *asked?* Apart from Mistress Captoft's little offering he had never eaten a bite of food outside his own home. So how could he know? He must ask Father.

"That boy was *hungry*," the miller's wife said, with surprise in her voice.

"Never knew a boy that wasn't," said her husband.

Don't talk about, don't think about, boys. Married ten years and nothing to show for it; though they were both healthy and hearty and fitted together as hand to glove.

She'd done what was to be done. Prayed, of course. Gone to Bury St. Edmund's and taken a long look at the famous white bull, one glance at which was supposed to bring fertility. Consulted a wise woman, drunk her potions and crawled three times under a low crooked branch; borrowed a petticoat from a woman who had borne eight and reared four. Finally she had made a pilgrimage to the Shrine of Our Lady of Walsingham—a long journey for people of her kind, and the last lap of it walked barefoot.

All useless. They'd put the thought away; never spoke of it; pretended not to care. But it was such a pity, with the mill, and some savings to leave.

What Godfrey had sensed was a momentary dropping of this pretense. Watching the boy gnaw hungrily into bread of her making affected the woman exactly as showing how the mill worked had affected the man.

She said, suddenly, "I'm going to Canterbury!"

It was a name known, like Bethlehem, where Our Lord was born, or Calvary, where He died. Or like London. Far off the mind's map.

"Thass the wrong time of year," the miller said. He'd hoped, been disappointed, hoped again, been disappointed again so often that now he would *not* lend himself to it any more. "Spring is for pilgrimages."

"All the better," the intrepid woman said. "The fewer asking favours the more notice Blessed St. Thomas can give." She looked out of the window and saw that it had begun to snow, and she thought, undeterred—The harder the conditions, the more I show my faith. I'll walk knee-deep if that is what is asked of me.

For Joanna the snow had begun earlier, at a point where the wind from the East had finally failed in its battle against the wind from the North. As always the snowfall, bringing its own potential disasters and difficulties, released a slight, spurious warmth; she was soon wetted through to the skin, but not so rigidly cold, and the big black horse gave no trouble now.

Here was Baildon, the church by whose buttresses she and Henry had stood, enjoying their pies; the marketplace, all veiled by the snow; the way out of the town, known as the

Saltgate; then the road, partially sheltered by the trees of Layer Wood. Turn into the lane, down into the water-splash. . . . The horse showed an inclination to stop there and drink, but she forced him on. Not far now and he could have everything, buckets of water, a mangerful of oats.

Turn on to the track; the church, the priest's house and then, now plainly seen, now obscured by the whirling snow, was Knight's Acre. Exactly as she had in her nostalgic hours remembered it.

The place where I was born!

And of all the women who had approached in various circumstances and with wildly different feelings, Joanna, though she had no way of knowing it, was the only one who could feel just that link with the stark, slightly forbidding house. Sybilla, for whom it had been built, had thought it overlarge; Tana had thought it small; Griselda at first approach had known a faint feeling of homecoming, having very vague, childish memories of such a house. Mistress Captoft had approached it in a business-like manner, a place in which to live, a place to manage, and eventually to leave; Katharine Dowley knew it to be a horrid, haunted place. Of all the people in the world—now that Robert was dead—only Joanna and Godfrey could claim Knight's Acre as their birthplace.

Tears which Lady Grey's cutting remarks and other evidences of disfavour had failed to provoke, now ran scaldingly down Joanna's cold face; but they were tears of joy. She was home! In a minute she would see Henry. And nothing, nothing would ever get her away again.

She had still one obstacle to overcome. Guard was on guard. As his breeder had admitted, he was not yet fully trained, and he had been subjected to the petting which was held to be ruinous, but he knew that the house and yard had been left in his charge and that it was his duty to challenge and, if necessary, defend. He stood, alert, in the yard, and from time to time went on patrol, doing so in a curious manner. He never went through the usual opening of the yard, between the end of the outjutting house and a kind of mound. For him it was the worst of the three bad places, and he could only face it with Godfrey's hand on his collar. So when he left the yard he went around the other outjutting end of the house, through the garden, to the front, along the track on the far side of the house until he came, from a different direction, to the bad place again; then he turned and re-traced his steps.

The other bad places were in the hall, and on the stairs, but he was never alone there, though once or twice, he'd been worse than alone. He'd been with a woman, herself so frightened that he could smell the fear on her. She wasn't here now.

He stood in the yard, having just finished one of his patrols, when he heard sounds; not the ones he was awaiting. Different. Strange. He moved as near the yard opening as he could go without stepping into the bad place and waited. A horse and a rider, both unknown. Had he not, as his breeder had said, been a bit slow to learn, or had he fully completed his training, the dog would have known that people bent on mischief did not approach in this fashion, open and confident, coming by right, coming home. So from the yard side of the entry he stood and challenged, but the intruder came on; Guard braced himself to defend.

Sir Gervase's best horse, though considerably reduced in spirit by twenty-six hours on the road without food or water, had enough strength left to resist the urging forward towards an unfriendly dog. He jibbed and tried to turn, repeating almost exactly the action of another horse, in the same place, action which had led to a fatal accident. Joanna's mother had been taken unawares. Her daughter was not. Nor was she in a mood to tolerate a second's delay, for she had seen, between the swirls of snow, that the chimney was emitting no smoke, which meant no fire, which meant no meal. Something badly wrong, and she had been right to come.

Guard, muzzle wrinkled back to show sharp fangs, eyes gleaming green, found himself face to face with himself as Joanna, brought almost broadside on, by the horse's attempt to turn, leaned low, her face a mask of hatred, too, green-eyed, sharp-fanged . . . Wolfish, as Lady Agnes had remarked.

She said, "Get out of my way," and thought what to do if the brute disobeyed. He wore a spiked collar; one twist and he'd choke! Menace from the intruder and the proximity of the hated place were together too much for the half-trained dog; he backed away. Joanna pulled the horse round and they entered the yard. Anxious as she was to get into the house and find out what was wrong, she was obliged to dismount slowly and clumsily, almost immobilised by stiffness and cold. She entered the kitchen with the stumbling, uncertain gait of a very old woman.

She spared only a glance—and that a glance of recognition. The kitchen was exactly as she had seen it. She stumbled across the hall and heaved herself upstairs, fearful of finding Henry in bed. His room was empty, and his working clothes lay tumbled on the floor. For a moment relief was as sharp as pain; then apprehension struck again. This was not a market day in Baildon. So where had Henry gone in his tidy market-going, church-going clothes?

Not—oh, God!—not to his grave. Her mind rebutted the hideous thought. No! I should have known! I should have seen that, too. She had seen him injured in some mysterious way and the next thought that came into her head was that Henry had gone to consult the physician in Baildon. And the next immediate thought was about her own state. Unless she changed immediately from these wet clothes, she would need a physician herself! Wet clothes, as she knew, and believed, for it was a belief shared by all classes, could lead to anything, from stiff joints to the lung-rot.

She found, not what she wanted, but what was needed, in the room that had been Katharine's. Two summer frocks, clean, and the old working one. Hastily, she stripped and snatching a blanket from the bed, towelled herself dry and almost warm. Then she put on all that Katharine had left.

Shoes. No good, far too big. But she remembered the rule, instituted long ago by Sybilla, and adhered to by Griselda: dirty footwear left by the kitchen door and indoor shoes donned. Moving more briskly now—the friction of the blanket had restored her circulation—she padded barefoot into the kitchen and found that the rule still held. A pair of small slippers—Godfrey's? Yes, of course—fitted her well. Re-clad, re-shod, she thought first of the fire, which—as was the way with fires—was less dead than it looked. A core remained, and fed, poked into activity, it began to blaze, with every flicker showing more of the desolation which had overtaken this once so orderly place. There was the big black pot, swung aside on its hook and in it under a shroud of congealing fat, a lump of meat and some peas like pebbles. In the larder the carcase of a fowl which only people in sheer desperation would have tried to eat. No bread. No flour. And what could one do without flour to make even a pancake, or a hasty pudding?

One could pull the black pot over the fire and hope that further cooking would soften the hard meat and the peas. And one could begin to restore the kitchen to some kind of order.

Henry halted by the sheep-fold and left two of the four

loaves which the miller's wife had given him, refusing his offer to pay, some flour from the new sackful, and the cheese and frying bacon which Joseph had requested and which he had not bothered to stop and deliver on his way to Nettleton.

The bacon looked so meagre that he felt he must apologise for it.

"Just to tide you over," he said. "I've got another side in the smoke-hole. I'll bring it up tomorrow."

"If this lay—and it will—don't you fret about me, Master. Worst come to the worst, I'll kill the other old tup." He looked at the snow, now falling heavily, and at the sky. "This'll be bad, but we've lived through worse."

Back in the waggon, Henry thought about the sack of flour which the miller had heaved in so easily. The thought of hauling it down, carrying it to the larder and after that climbing up to take the fresh side of bacon from the smoke-hole, sent a pang through him.

That is sheer fancy, he told himself sternly. You are making altogether too much of a trivial hurt. How do other people with a real disability manage? Think how active David was, with his lame leg!

The curtain of snow was irregular, sometimes indeed the flakes appeared to drift upwards. In one such interval he saw his home plainly, smoke issuing from the chimney. All it conveyed to him was the idea that the fire, left very low, had flared up during his absence. There was nothing to warn him of anything unusual as he drove into the yard. A more experienced dog than Guard might have indicated the presence in some fashion, but Guard was overwhelmed with delight at the sight of Godfrey and had no other thought.

Thinking of the sack, and at the same time despising himself for his weakness of will, Henry took the waggon as near the kitchen door as possible, which was not very close, for at some time in the past Walter had occupied some of his scanty leisure in laying a kind of platform of flint stone, so that Sybilla could feed her hens and even reach the well without stepping into the mud.

"May I put the horse and waggon away?" Godfrey asked. "You may."

"Then you can have just a little ride, Guard. Up, boy, up!"

"Bring the bread when you come," Henry said, and dragged the sack onto his shoulders. The pain knifed him.

There was now enough snow on the cobbles to muffle his footsteps, and Joanna was scrubbing the kitchen table. A number of things, each small, had combined to re-assure her.

The ease with which the fire was revived was proof that it had been lighted that morning. Then she had thought: That poor horse! After all I promised him! There was an empty place in the stable; one horse, the old one she remembered, and which seemed to remember her, stood there, half asleep, but there was evidence in the manger, and in the freshly dropped dung, that there had been two there earlier on in the day. The waggon was gone. Put this alongside the fact that there was no flour in the house, and no bread, and it was more than likely that Henry had gone to the miller's, wearing, as he always did when he stepped off his own land, his decent clothes. Godfrey's absence was not significant; Henry had this fixed idea that the way of life which he had deliberately chosen for himself was not suited to other people, and might well have sent his son elsewhere, as he had sent Robert, and herself.

When the door opened they took one another by surprise. His surprise greater than hers because she had been prepared for the haggard, pain-stricken look just as she had been prepared for the state of the kitchen. He had had no warning at all.

His face was scored by the marks of pain, and others, more grim, his determination to ignore it; a stern set mask of endurance which changed as he dropped the sack just inside the door, not reflecting the relief he felt at shedding the load, not to welcome, but to blank dismay. Total, absolute.

She'd come—or so she had imagined—to help, to rescue him from whatever troublesome situation he was in. She had intended to say: It is all right, Henry. I am here; I'll see to it all. The words were still-born.

Henry said, "Joanna!" No gladness; no welcome.

They had sent her home. By that impulsive, thoughtless acknowledgement of a completely nonsensical betrothal he'd ruined her prospects, he thought, and here she was in a filthy old frock scrubbing a table: the very fate he had tried to save her from.

Joanna was thinking too. Better not mention that inner eye, about which he always been so sceptical. Better not mention the betrothal; nobody, not even Henry, could have greeted the woman to whom he considered himself betrothed in quite that way.

"They sent you home?" he said.

Quick, quick, a plausible tale.

"Nobody sent me. I came of my own accord. I incurred Lady Grey's displeasure and was given a punishment that was intolerable. I will tell you all, later. That is flour? Good! We can have dumplings."

Godfrey came bursting in, "Father, there's a strange horse . . . *Janna!*" He flung himself at her, just as Guard had flung himself at him. Between Godfrey and Joanna a curious relationship had existed; for a long time Griselda, his Mumma, had stood between them, and as he grew the boy had seen the girl doing all the things he longed to do, working in the yard and the fields, going with Father to market. Then, for a short time, with Mumma dead, he had been allowed to work—as well as he could—and to play with her. She knew a lot of games. He sensed, with a child's sure instinct, that she had no great feeling for him, and that he had no hold on her. She'd play if she wanted to, otherwise not. He was not important to her, as he had been to Mumma, and soon after, to Mamma-Captoft.

Nevertheless, he had missed her and was glad to see her; eager to see the connection between her and that horrible horse.

"He tried to bite me when I took our horse in. Janna, did you really ride home on him?"

"How else?"

They talked about Guard, too.

"How did you get past my dog?" In some indefinable way Godfrey felt that Guard had not quite lived up to his name and had proved Father right about spoiling by petting.

"Oh, he had sense enough to know that I belonged here. How long have you had him?"

That led smoothly on to the story of the rough men, his own heroic behaviour on that memorable day; how Mamma-Captoft had gone away and taken Katharine with her.

The child's eager chatter, his complete ignorance of all undercurrents eased the awkward situation. There was no need for Henry or Joanna to say much over the poor meal; even supplemented by the dumplings and re-cooked, the ill-prepared pork and peas were something to satisfy hunger and no more.

Covertly, now and again they glanced at one another and quickly glanced away.

Two years! He'd aged by far more. Even now, with lines of pain and the lines of determined effort easing away a little, and the look of absolute dismay gone. Just above his ears the fawn-coloured hair had a few silvery streaks in it, and cheekbones, jawbones and the bridge of his nose were sharper. None of this made him less desirable.

In her he saw almost no change at all. A mite taller perhaps, maybe two inches. He'd always thought that she was pretty and too fragile-looking for the life she had been obliged to lead, out of doors while Griselda lived and then here in this kitchen—the life he had always thought so unsuitable and done his best to alter. So far as he could see, Stordford had left no stamp on her at all.

Outside the snow, now determined, fell heavily. Every flake was welcome to Joanna, if to nobody else. It would hinder the pursuit and give her time to convince Henry of two things. That she was indispensable here; and would never, never go back.

"Milking time," Henry said. He stood up, walked into the dairy, came back with a bucket, walking in the ordinary way, no limp, no concealed limp.

But not to be ignored was the sack of flour dropped just inside the door, not taken into the larder and emptied into the bin. That routine act she performed herself, quite easily because although she had that delicate look she was actually as strong as steel.

What about bacon? Had Mistress Captoft, so busy and pernickety only two years ago, actually gone off leaving Knight's Acre with no bacon; no ham in the smoke-hole?

She had not. Joanna climbed up and fumbling about in the dark cavity, found a half side of bacon and a ham. The ham could stay there for a time, she thought, but she unhooked and hauled out the side of bacon, rubbed it clean and with a knife sharpened on the hearthstone cut rashers so thin that at the touch of a hot pan they would contract and crisp.

When Henry came in he brought a spade with him.

"If this goes on through the night it'll mean digging our way out in the morning." He noticed that the sack had gone and the bacon had been brought down. He protested that he had intended to see to both these things, presently; yet he was glad to be spared the effort and was ashamed of himself again. He remembered how, working with him and Jem Watson in the fields, she had always strained herself to the utmost, making up for lack of size and strength by sheer determination. He decided that over his mysterious injury he had been weak-willed. And that called up a very ancient memory indeed: Sir Godfrey coming home here to Knight's Acre—his first return—wounded in the knee. He'd been glum, full of self-pity, irritable. And he had limped. Limped right up to the time when he was invited to go to a tournament in Spain, and then the limp had vanished overnight and his usual sunny, optimistic temper had been restored.

Contrast that behaviour with that of his mother, Sybilla, who had taken a fall which had lamed her for life, never coddled herself, never complained. He really must, he decided, make an effort to follow his mother's example, rather than that of his father, and to begin *now* by being more resolutely cheerful.

It was not difficult, for Joanna had set herself out to be entertaining. She had always had, even as a child, an eye and an ear for anything ridiculous, and a gift for mimicry; she'd lightened his mood many a time.

Godfrey offered her an opening. He'd exhausted his account of what had taken place here during her absence, and now, happily stuffed with fresh fried bacon and more of the excellent bread, asked,

"What have you been doing, Joanna?"

"Learning tricks. I'll show you one." She stood up, selected a wooden bowl, placed it on her head, walked the length of the kitchen, made a curtsey, turned, came back and sat down again on the bench.

"That looks easy," Godfrey said.

"You try!"

He poised the bowl on top of his head, took two careful steps, and dropped it.

In Lady Grey's voice, Joanna said, "How can you ever acquire graceful deportment? Come here." She gave him two purely playful cuffs about the head. "Now try again, and remember, no supper until you have managed it." He recognised the smacks for what they were; and in all his life he had received only two or three smacks from Griselda—quickly compensated for by some small treat. He'd never encountered what he still thought of as roughness until the rough man had jabbed the poker at him. But he had the ordinary child's appetite for drama—and no Tom Robinson to satisfy it with stories.

"Did she hit you, Janna?"

"No. I could do most of those tricks—even when it came to carrying the bowl with water in it, and not a drop to be spilled. Poor Maude was clumsy from nervousness. Now and then I pretended, to shield her. Lady Grey couldn't well hit one and not the other for the same fault. There were other punishments."

"What?"

"Missed meals; poor meals; no riding; no tennis. That sort of thing."

Henry had taken no part in this conversation, but he had been listening. And thinking of all the beautiful, butterfly ladies at Beauclaire. Had they all been similarly trained by a process not unlike the harsh breaking-in of young colts? It was something which he, eager to get Joanna into a different, easier way of life had certainly not visualised.

Speaking after a long silence, he asked, "Joanna, what did you do to incur a punishment that was intolerable?"

She was prepared for that question, knowing that sooner or later it must arise. And she was cautious. Lady Grey might not wish to reclaim her, but the big black horse had an owner; somebody from Stordford would track her down and arriving at Knight's Acre, have a story to tell. Her story must not conflict. And since Henry, in the moment of meeting, had seemed to wish to ignore their betrothal—more sophisticated now, she knew that unwitnessed it was meaningless—she had ready a story in which Lord Shefton and anything to do with betrothals played no part at all.

"I offended her ladyship. How? Why? Who knows? I did it constantly. But this time the punishment was extreme."

Ruthlessly she sacrificed Lady Agnes. No mention of the relatively happy hours of reminiscences exchanged; no mention of the proffered gift of the garnet ring.

"Imagine," she said, "being set to wait upon a cross, demanding old woman, completely confined to her bed. In one small, malodorous room. I slept on a servant's truckle bed. What food was carried up to us, she had the best of. With Christmas being celebrated to the hall. No servants to do anything."

That was another trick she had learned at Stordford— how by leaving something out here, and emphasising something there one could tell a story actual enough to be uncontradictable, and yet not much like the truth. The ladies did it all the time. It was not difficult for her to make life at Stordford, where she had been genuinely miserable, sound a great deal more horrible than it had been. Henry, listening, thought that this was not all what he had intended. He also decided—as Joanna hoped he would—not to send her back there.

"Did you learn nothing of use?"

"Oh yes. To read and write and keep accounts without the aid of tally sticks. I failed with the lute. Her ladyship said I was all thumbs. As to embroidery, she was not prepared to waste good silk on me. I patched linen and darned. Hours and hours." She sounded very plaintive and withheld the information that the length of time spent was due to her dilatoriness and that usually Maude, so devoted, furtively finished the task set.

She did not mention Lord Shefton; that was too close to the betrothal which Henry, from a distance, had acknowledged and thus saved her, and yet at the moment of their meeting, seemed to put away. She needed time.

Henry did not mention Lord Shefton either. It was just possible, he thought, that Joanna had been less than fully informed; Lady Grey sounded quite capable of making such an arrangement, merely asking the girl, belatedly, whether she was betrothed. Getting a displeasing answer and venting her spite.

It was a subject better avoided.

And it was avoided while the snow fell, for about twelve days. Such a snowfall as even Joseph the shepherd or Old Hodgson could not remember. It was the most hampering kind of all, dry and fluffy, no mid-day sun came to melt it a little, no midnight frost hardened it so that it could be walked upon. In the low houses at Intake it was up to the eaves and at Knight's Acre level with the high-set windows.

Morning after morning Henry, aided by Godfrey, who used one of the small spades which Walter had made twenty years earlier, dug a path to the well, the byre, the pig-stye and the stable. Father Matthew and his ugly boy kept a path clear between the house door and the church, and at the rear, to their pig-stye. In the village men dug paths to their beasts, to their neighbours and to the river. It was possible to scoop up snow and melt it but the water thus produced had a curious flat taste and was considered to be unhealthy.

It was a time out of time and at Knight's Acre there was no hardship. They had food enough; apart from tending the animals there was no work to do. Joanna spoke of games played at Stordford and Henry said, "My mother had such toys. They may still be in her chest."

And Henry vaguely remembered similar games, played at Beauclaire, never at Knight's Acre; everybody too busy. Pretty things; painted cards, cubes of ivory with black spots; a chequered board upon which small carved figures moved this way and that. His mother might have kept them at the bottom of her clothes chest.

Father Matthew and Tim had little in reserve. At best their

housekeeping had been haphazard. Before disaster fell upon Intake, and before the priest had been forced to regard all the grown people there as enemies the village had supplied his small needs. Apart from what he'd been offered in friendly fashion, he had always paid for what he had, a little coarse flour, a bit of belly pork.

Now, cut off, he had the remainder of the sack of flour, given by Master Tallboys, and the bones of the old sheep. Tim, whom the whole world had despised and rejected, did wonders with those bones, cracking them to get to the marrow, boiling and boiling them into a kind of glue, onion-flavoured while the onions lasted.

Down at Bywater, Mistress Captoft's ideal arrangement for opening The Sailors' Rest on Twelfth Night had miscarried: not because her workmen were dilatory or she and David lacking in foresight. The weather was to blame; the East wind bringing battered ships in and preventing any sea-worthy vessel from leaving. And word of her enterprise had spread about. As soon as her furniture was seen to arrive, and smoke issue from the chimney, she was besieged.

Inevitably there were applicants who had never been to sea in their lives. Mistress Captoft, cautious of beggars, knowing many to be fraudulent, yet saw them as pitiable with that keen wind fluttering their rags.

She was grateful to David when he said, "Madam, best leave this to me. Once open it to all comers and half the beggars in England'll be on the doorstep. People like that"—in a word he dismissed all who were not seamen—"can go anywhere. The religious houses give them alms. I was thinking of sea-faring men who've got to be here, waiting for a ship or chucked out, sick or injured. Best leave this to me. I can tell a sailor a mile off."

Very willingly she left the business of selection to David. She had enough to do.

For one thing she was obliged to make a penny do the work of two; a new experience for her. Paying the five years' rent in advance, buying the absolute necessities for the house and paying for the repairs had practically exhausted her savings. It was in no way an alarming situation, for her rents were due at Christmas and her reliable agent in Dunwich would send the money to her promptly. There would also be, as David had said, men straight from the sea and able and willing to pay a little. No such had yet appeared; her household so far consisted of men much in the state in which she had found David, or men off battered ships, driven into Bywater by the East wind. They would not be paid until they were back in the port from which they had embarked and although some ships' masters did their best for their men, some vessels were unsafe and many stores were ruined.

Mistress Captoft found herself shopping for food at the worst time of the year and for the most expensive commodity of all—*fresh* food.

David did not know what caused scurvy, the sailors' scourge though it was known on land too in winter, especially among the poor; he did know what cured it. Any fresh food, anything that had not been salted. In his time he'd seen chance-come-stuff, fresh fish, fresh meat, a basket of cabbages, a few onions—and down in Spain, oranges or lemons, work miracles on men apparently dying, their sight failing, their teeth dropping out of spongy gums, their legs too weak to support them.

To the rear of the old house there was what had once been a garden. The various transient tenants had not tended it and weeds had overrun whatever had once been planted there. Nettles and a small plant which, broken, had an onion smell, but no fat, swollen root. Next year this garden would be cultivated, there would be rows of cabbages, onions, carrots. Plots of herbs. Next year the apple crop would not fall into the grass and nettles; whole, unblemished fruit would be gathered tenderly and stored; bruised or wasp-bitten ones sliced into rings—all the injured part cut away—and strung on strings, dried in a cooling oven and then hung up.

But this was this year and Mistress Captoft must do the best she could for what was in reality a large family which grew as the weather worsened and the East wind flung battered ships into Bywater, and then the North wind held up any ship not southward bound.

Leaving, as David had suggested, the sorting of seamen from others, she had said, "Try, David, to find at least two men who can cook, men who will stay."

He had found two, both like himself, beached through an infirmity more obvious than real. One had an empty eye-socket—unsightly, but did that matter in a cook? The other had only half a hand, but like many maimed men, given a chance, he could do as much with one hand and a half as any other man could do with two. Both evinced the gratitude upon which Mistress Captoft had counted, both were prepared to make the most out of little.

In fact, the men in general were splendid; well worth

helping, Mistress Captoft decided as she literally tightened her girdle, losing flesh as she shared not the privation, exactly, but the limited food.

The snow did not pile up in Bywater as it did further inland. It fell, lay for a while, and then with each coming in of the tide, cold as the water was, seemed to melt away. What was happening only a mile or two from the coast was made clear by a brisk, active young man who had a home to go to. He stayed overnight, paid his fee, expressed his thanks, and set out for Stratton Strawless, where his home was. At dusk he was back talking of snow ankle-deep, thigh-deep, and worse with every step. Soft fluffy stuff, ready to gulp down even the most determined man.

Then Mistress Captoft understood why her rents had not arrived from Dunwich.

Even in this terrible weather now and then a bold or desperate fisherman would venture out in search of herring. The hauls were small, so near to the shore, but brought in, silvery blue and often still half alive, were the subject of sharp competitive demand. When the price rose to the incredible height of a penny for six, Mistress Captoft decided that she could no longer afford herring. David then remembered a time when a whole crew of scurvy-stricken men had been saved by some edible seaweed. He could not remember its name but he would know it again, he said. So he and some able-bodied men searched the beach but failed to find the kind they were looking for. David realised later this was not the same kind of coast as the rocky shore where the life-saving weed abounded. This flat sandy shore did, however, at low tide, yield food of another kind, and even in blizzards men would go out to dig cockles. Others walked miles in search of nettles, for though the garden had seemed to have an inexhaustible supply, with so many men, some in desperate need of green stuff, and all craving it, even nettles were scarce.

The men, as Mistress Captoft never tired of saying, were wonderful during this time when storm-battered ships kept putting into harbour and none went out. They would rather eat half, they said, than that some poor fellow should be turned away; as for lying two or even three to a narrow bed, "Don't you fret, Madam. We lay closer than this aboard." Mistress Captoft shared in their resolute good humour, was in a way enjoying the shifts and contrivances. She had abandoned her little parlour, which now had three makeshift beds wedged in amongst the ordinary furniture. And a man sleeping on the settle. Just occasionally, however, she would wake in the night and think uneasily about the debts she was incurring—no household could survive without flour. She would wonder, too, how long this extraordinary weather could continue; and how long her credit would last. She was not yet well-known here—or known only as what Bywater people called half-cracked, a woman who had bitten off a lot more than she could chew. She had heard of a man who had killed a pig and when she went immediately and offered to buy half of it, to be paid for later, her best ring as a pledge of good faith, he'd looked at her very oddly indeed. More, perhaps, than other people, those who lived in a seaport were suspicious; for there was a pattern of thought, the sea offered a quick escape to cheats and debtors. All outsiders were suspect, and anybody you hadn't known from childhood upwards was an outsider.

Such night thoughts she put resolutely away and thumped her straw-stuffed pillow—her down-filled ones had gone to contribute to the comfort of sick men. God had brought her here, every step guided; He would provide.

The men made things; apparently aboard every ship there were slack times when a man must occupy himself as best he could, with whatever skill he had, on what material was available. Sitting in The Sailors' Rest, by the good fire of driftwood, they still made things. Trinkets. Useful things. Spoons with handles, beautifully carved, combs of bone indistinguishable from those of horn or ivory, crucifixes as realistic as Father Matthew's, necklaces of shells, little salt boxes with hinges of cloth or leather—salt must not come into contact with metal, instant corrosion was the result of that. Many of these things, lovingly worked over, were presented, with a kind of gratitude that approached love, to Madam. She had always craved gratitude. Now she could wallow in it; they were all grateful; they all called her Madam; they were her children, they must be fed. But Bywater was now like a town under siege. Everybody within the narrow area that was not snow-covered had either marketed what they had to spare, or was hoarding it, for fear that this terrible winter would never end. The market on the quay was deserted.

The cooks at The Sailors' Rest had stopped making bread and reverted to what they called hard-tack. "Take longer to chew, madam, and stay by you better," the one-eyed man said. "But of course I'll make you a proper loaf."

"Oh no, William," Mistress Captoft said bravely. "Bread must be for the sick only. But it was a kind thought . . ."

She was worried about her ailing guests, some of whom had made such good progress on a diet of fresh herring, the occasional cabbage, and the nettles, and now appeared to be slipping back. They needed more than bread; things like sops-in-wine and good chicken broth.

There were two places in Bywater from which help might be obtained—the Bishop's Palace and the inn. Gossip had already informed Mistress Captoft that the Bishop was not an open-handed man; he had withdrawn his support from the two charitable institutions which good old Bishop William had founded. Also, Mistress Captoft had a personal grudge against him—he'd never once paid a visit to Benedict, even when a hunting expedition took him past the church at Intake. The idea of appealing to him for help was repugnant to her. So it must be the inn, where at least she was known.

She was in her bedroom, dressing for out-of-doors, when her gaze fell upon the collection of little trinkets which the men had made and presented to her. An idea sparked. She remembered that her husband had often said that she had a good head for business. It was worth trying, anyway. She filled her basket with the representative selection of the articles, and set off, not to beg humbly for credit, but to make a business proposition.

The landlady of The Welcome To Mariners had a similar good head. In normal times men straight from the sea, with money to spend, were the best of the inn's customers; but there were others: dealers, carters, pedlars. Pedlars! What pedlar would not be glad to acquire a few such unusual, easily portable things?

"How much are you asking, Mistress Captoft?"

"Not money," Mistress Captoft said in the easy take-it-or-leave-it manner of a first-class bargainer. "Once the roads clear I shall have all the money I need. It is just that due to the weather, and the number of men temporarily stranded, and also the fact that I underestimated what I needed, my supplies are running low. I am compelled to barter. For this lot I am asking only a cask of good red wine, a fowl—a boiler would do—this week, and next . . ." Greed shone in the landlady's eyes. Wine was not expensive in itself, it was the duty on it which made it costly and she had a very workable arrangement with the collector of dues; her wine cost her next to nothing. As for fowls, except when cooped for fattening, they cost nothing either; many horses and donkeys in the yard had nose-bags and many grains were dropped.

A flurry of doves passed the window and Mistress Captoft went on, her sentence apparently uninterrupted, "and four doves each week for the next month."

"You drive a hard bargain, Mistress Captoft."

"If I am asking too much," Mistress Captoft said, and made as though to collect what she had displayed.

"But I sympathise with your situation. I agree."

They looked into one another's eyes and understood, just as Dame Isabel and Mistress Captoft had looked and recognised.

"Will there be more?" the landlady asked, thinking of how, after this lapse, custom would increase.

"Oh yes, I can guarantee a continuous supply. I have, alas, a number of men who will never go to sea again. And they like to be occupied. The poor fellow who made this"—she touched a necklace of cockle-shells—"has only one foot. Far worse than losing a whole leg, for which a wooden stump can be substituted. . . . I will send two men along for the wine; but I would like to take the fowl with me."

The landlady rose and shouted an order; then she came back and suggested that she and Mistress Captoft should take a drink together—the usual way of sealing a bargain. Mistress Captoft refused, pleading lack of time. Some sense of honour was left to her and forbad her to drink to a bargain which she was prepared to break at the first possible moment, for even as she sat there, making it, another thought had occurred. If these things were saleable in one place, why not in another, only a short distance along the quay? When the time came—as it must, surely it must, when money would buy things—the articles would be sold where they were made. Walking home, light-footed, light-hearted, she planned a kind of shelf, sloping, in the window of her little parlour; it would be covered in velvet—she was prepared to sacrifice a poppy-coloured gown which had not the happiest of associations for her. Against such a glowing background the things would look well.

Knight's Acre, cut off from the world, was enjoying a period of happiness and ease from work. Both cows were in calf, so there was no dairy work to bother with. They had casked meat and smoked meat, they had flour. Joanna knew how to make salted meat edible, and she could bake. Henry worried a little about Joseph and made one attempt to reach him, but the snow was still soft then and he was, like the man making for Stratton Strawless, obliged to turn back. Then the snow froze and upon the surface of it a man could walk. He set off with fresh bread, a whole cheese and more bacon, to find that all his anxiety had been wasted. Joseph had killed the other old tup and so far eaten only the best of it—the kidneys, the liver and a cut or two from the loin. The mangled carcase hung outside his hut, on the side farthest from the sheep-fold, from which a palpable warmth arose; so many woolly bodies in such proximity.

"All in good heart, Master," Joseph said proudly. "And I give this"—he looked around at the snow—"about another four days."

"How can you know?"

"There's a new moon, about due. Fickle as women the moon is. Yes, another four-five days'll see this out. And I shan't eat half that. Take what you like, Master."

"All right. If you're sure, Joseph, I'll take a leg."

As the shepherd hacked away, promising that the frost would have softened the tough meat, Henry looked across at the priest's house and was aware of—not a responsibility exactly, but a neighbourly obligation.

"What about Father Matthew and his boy?"

"Alive so far as I know," Joseph said, with far less interest than he would have shown in a couple of sheep.

"I'll take them a bit, too. If you can spare it."

Joseph used his knife again, hacking away this time at what was known as the scrag. Not that he had anything against either the priest or the boy. He was just being sensible.

By this time hunger had shown its ugly face in the priest's house. The flour and the stripped carcase that remained from the children's feast had been eked out to the utmost. Lately they had lived on a gruel made from the pig food, a coarse meal known, rightly, as sharps, sharp in the mouth, sharp in the belly. The husks which the swine did eat, Father Matthew thought, remembering the parable of the Prodigal Son. They still had onions, but they, though flavourful and healthy, added to the wreck the gruel made of one's inside. As a result both he and the boy were weak as kittens and for the last few days it had taken their combined efforts to keep a path to the church open. That morning, after a night of frost it had been more difficult than ever. Feebly, on the verge of collapse, the priest had performed his office, going through the motions, saying the words, but all the time appealing to God in an unusual, personal way, just as he had appealed when faced with the ordeal of the hot iron; but with less strength, less confidence.

And now here was Master Tallboys, with a hunk of fresh meat in his hand. A gift from God. Very welcome, too, was the news that Joseph, who considered himself to be weather-wise, predicted a thaw within four or five days.

To Joanna the news was less pleasing. The thaw would put an end to this enjoyable timeless time, the feeling of being a close family unit, apart from the world. Henry was already talking of finding a woman who could cook, starting the search as soon as he could get to Baildon. When he mentioned this, or indeed anything concerned with the future, Joanna remained silent. Time enough to protest when the moment came. She knew she would never go back to Stord-ford; she was almost certain that after the way she had behaved, Lady Grey would not wish to have her back, unless there was some nonsense about that dowry. But somebody from Stordford was bound to come sooner or later, if only to recover the big black horse, and then there would be talk and the word *betrothal* was sure to crop up, and that would put an end to the happy state in which she and Henry had lived for almost a month. She had been determined not to mention the word until he did, and he seemed equally deter-mined not to refer to it. It was a terrible thought but she faced it unflinchingly—Henry did not love her as she loved him. She'd known that in the instant of their meeting. That look of dismay, the question: Did they send you home? She knew perfectly well that had Henry suddenly appeared—say at Stordford—even if he had done a murder and been fleeing from justice with a price on his head, she would have wel-comed him very differently. And since that moment, when the joyous welcome had been withheld and only Godfrey had been entirely natural, she had watched Henry carefully. She was more sophisticated now and knew that special look which did not necessarily imply friendship, or any serious intention; just the hungry, *wanting* look. (That had also been a matter of preening and giggling amongst Lady Grey's la-dies.)

Tana, her mother, had believed that love on one side *must* compel love upon the other, and had be-devilled Henry's father; so sure of herself, so sure that nothing stood between them except his wife that she'd poisoned Sybilla and thus cleared her own way to nothing, except a man half crazed by grief, glad to go off to the wars and die. Joanna knew nothing of that old sad story, but she knew her own mind. She was prepared—now—to keep their relationship on a friendly basis. She'd made a mistake once; two years ago in the wood; and perhaps another, later, in making a makeshift betrothal a condition of her going to Stordford. Makeshift as it was, it had saved her from becoming the Countess of Shefton. That was enough for the moment. Let the future take care of itself.

They played various games. Henry said, quite eagerly,

"I believe my mother had such toys," and went up to look in the bottom of the chest in which Sybilla had kept her clothes—all long ago used by Griselda.

A box containing a board and all the little mommets for a game called chess; a pack of cards, soiled by much handling and with broken corners; six dice. None used since Knight's Acre was occupied.

After supper they had merry games, and with better feeding, and the pain not provoked, the lines in Henry's face faded out. Now and then he laughed, as in the old days, coming gloomily from a bad market day, he had laughed when she had set herself deliberately to cheer him. Brotherly, not loverly.

The snow had also isolated Stordford and Lord Shefton was restive; longing to get back to his house in the Strand and the lively company of London. He was bored and always uneasily aware that here at least were two people—Sir Barnabas and his wife—who knew that he had been fobbed off with second best. Being so pleased with the match they were unlikely to say indiscreet things, but he was always conscious of their knowledge.

Maude was young—attempts to deflower her had given him a certain amount of pleasure, not least because it proved his virility—almost. Not that she would ever know the difference! Out of bed she was a bore; too anxious to please; her every remark predictable, her every action intended to please, and therefore unpleasing. Even now she occasionally shot anxious glances at that old termagant, her mother, anxious for approval, fearing its opposite. It was impossible not to think, as snowbound day followed snowbound day, how different that other girl was, with her spark of wit, her ready tongue and her curious air of caring for nobody. To have captured *her* would have been—despite his wealth and position—flattering to his vanity. One had only to look at poor Maude to know that any husband would have done. In fact, Lord Shefton realised, he had committed the juvenile error of marrying on the rebound. In addition, one of his precious new teeth, shallowly rooted or worked too hard, fell out. At the dinner table! Rationally His Grace of Bywater could not be blamed for *that;* but for every other aspect of this dismal affair he was to blame; and would be punished. Once the snow melted and Lord Shefton was back in London.

The thaw came suddenly and floods followed. The drains under the sheep-fold at Knight's Acre could not deal with the water, so Joseph dug ditches, all slanted towards the river, and pushed the straw walls of the pen inwards to give his dear ones something to stand upon while the water drained away. At Intake some houses, nearest the river, were flooded, and some animals died. The only human casualty was Old Ethel, who, dipping water at the Steps, now invisible under the brown gush, missed her footing and fell.

Knight's Acre, standing a little higher, for Sybilla, seeing Sir Godfrey off to choose a site and order a house, had made only one request, "Let it not be damp, my love," did not suffer. It stood high and dry and bathed in a sunset glow for the exceptional winter was being followed by an exceptionally early and mild spring, when Lady Grey's emissary approached it and thought: What a mean house.

Chosen for his light weight—a consideration with roads so deep in mire, and because he was young, eager, hoping to be knighted at Easter, Peter Wingfield had been sent to track Joanna down. It had not, except for the mud, been difficult. Lady Grey, dispatching him, had not sounded hopeful; the silly girl had set out on a difficult horse, in terrible weather. "It is unlikely that she survived, Peter, but it is necessary for me to *know*. And naturally Sir Gervase is anxious about his horse."

During his time at Stordford Lady Grey had done little to endear herself to the young squire and now he thought, with disgust: What a typical speech! It was a wonder she hadn't mentioned the horse first.

Joanna's trail was not difficult to follow; many people remembered catching a glimpse of her, so unsuitably clad, so strangely mounted. "Went by in a flash. Riding like the Devil was on her heels." To some she had spoken, asking direction to a place they'd never heard of. Baildon. At each point where his questions received satisfactory answers, the young man thought: Alive so far! and ploughed on through the mud with rising hope. Because of the heavy going and the need to halt frequently in order to ask for information, his progress was slow and he was obliged to spend two nights on the way: one at the kind of big house which Joanna had avoided, one at a miserable inn. Where, he wondered, had *she* spent the night? The nights? In no likely place. Nobody at any great house, or any inn, or the religious house, knew anything of a bare-headed girl on a big black horse. It looked as though she had feared pursuit. And it would have been difficult to decide even which road she had taken on leaving Stordford, but for Lady Agnes' certainty that she would have made for home. Joanna's tales had been so vivid and the old woman's interest had been so keen that she could practically describe the road from Baildon to Intake.

After a lifetime of fairly decisive action, the poor old woman was now suffering the pains of a mind divided within itself. The way she had been abandoned on that dreadful day, was disgraceful: it made her angry to think about it, and when she was angry she had every intention of changing her will. Then she would remember those few happy days, the services rendered so cheerfully, so different from that of hirelings, and her mood would change. The girl must have had some *reason* for acting as she had done, and Lady Agnes was eager to know what it was. When Lady Grey said, "It is not that I want her back. I never wish to set eyes on her again. It is simply that inquiries must be made, for appearances' sake," Lady Agnes said, "I should be very glad to see her again; if only to know why she deserted me as she did. After being so kind and looking after me better than I have been looked after since I was forced to take to my bed."

It was a back-handed slap and Lady Grey was bound to admit that the girls—as she called them—were far less dutiful than they might have been. There was no need for Maude . . . and of course the Countess of Shefton could not be commanded; but Beatrice's future was still not assured. To the watchful mother it often looked as though Sir Gervase were less interested in Beatrice than in ingratiating himself with Lord Shefton. Naturally he gave Beatrice—the daughter of the house—the ordinary, courteous attentions to which the silly girl responded a trifle too eagerly. You could, Lady Grey reflected, train a girl into almost everything except dignity; and that for some obscure reason—she never blamed her own handling—both her daughters lacked. Maude was behaving like a stray dog to whom some kind person had given a bone and a casual pat on the head. Mortifying indeed.

Doggedly making his inquiries, Peter Wingfield came to

the point where a man remembered directing a girl on a big black horse towards Bury St. Edmund's. Apparently at this point she had no longer been riding as though pursued by the Devil.

"They both looked a bit weary like," the man said. "But she perked up when I pointed the road to Bury. She smiled. She said, 'Thank you. That'll do,' and set off like a shot. Pretty girl."

Baildon. She wouldn't need to ask direction here, and he, thanks to Lady Agnes' good memory, need only shout, "Which way to Intake?"

And now here he was, thinking what a mean house, for he had been born in a castle, served as a page in another, become a squire at Stordford. He, like so many of his kind, was a younger son, must make his own way in the world, make an advantageous marriage, hope that some legacies might come his way. He was at home in his world, and in his world a plain house like Knight's Acre, stark against the background of leafless woods, was something new. Even the approach raised a question. It had a main door, not un-imposing, and a way leading to it, between evenly planted rose trees. But that path looked unused, and there was no light in any window, though the afternoon was darkening now. He decided to take the more worn trail around the side of the house. At the entry of the yard he was challenged by a large dog, and from nowhere a boy—about the size Peter had been when he had left home to become a page—ran out and took the dog by the collar, pulling him aside and at the same time offering his own challenge. "Who are you? What do you want?" Then a man appeared.

"You are from Stordford? Come in. You are expected. Godfrey, run in and tell Joanna that we have a guest. We'll be there as soon as we have looked to the horse. My name is Henry Tallboys. I bid you welcome to my house."

"I am Peter Wingfield, sir."

"You have had a dirty ride. I'll throw down some extra straw. Given enough dry litter, horses clean their own legs. The rest we can deal with tomorrow."

"The demoiselle Serriff . . . ?"

"She arrived safely, and is well," Henry said, leading the way into the stable. "And so, you see, is the horse. I shan't be sorry to be rid of him." While the young squire unsaddled and unbridled his horse Henry forked down the extra straw, brought a bucket of water, put oats and hay in the manger. "Now for you," he said. "Come this way."

". . . covered in mud," Godfrey was saying. "And I'm sure Guard would not have let him in if I hadn't been there."

So the bad moment had come. She faced it calmly. She would never leave Knight's Acre again.

Calm, Peter Wingfield reflected presently, was the keynote of this most peculiar household, which could have been part of a tale. Eating at a bare, scrubbed table, in a kitchen, eating food cooked by the demoiselle Serriff, with whom he had never before been within speaking distance. Lady Grey believed in order. Each to his place. Sitting at the table with the family and favoured guests Joanna had seemed as remote as the moon, but it was in order, in fact it was traditional that young men, mere squires, or just attained to knighthood, should worship from a distance. It was good for them; it gave them something to aim at. It did not prevent them—human nature being what it was—from consorting with and making occasional use of milkmaids, goosegirls and such, but it did, in most cases, forefend incautious marriages.

In every way, Peter Wingfield had been a strict conformist, observing all the rules; he had therefore cherished an unrequited, unspoken devotion to the demoiselle Serriff. Now he was at the same table with her, eating food she had cooked. She wore a hideous black dress (Joanna had washed it on the day after her homecoming), and when he had entered the kitchen it had been protected by an apron. Any other wellborn lady he could think of would have been embarrassed. She had been calm, smiled at him, said, "Good evening. You're . . . Peter."

"Peter Wingfield, at your service, demoiselle," he said, and made his most formal bow.

"I have water already heated. And I hope you are not superstitious about eating hare."

Then Henry had lighted a candle and led Peter up to the barest sleeping chamber he had seen and gone away, to return with hose and jerkin of homespun.

"A bit big for you, I fear," he said. "But they'll serve while your own dry out."

There was that curious calm about him, too.

On the bare scrubbed table there was not a thing that would have been out of place in a clod cottage—except the wine, which was a surprise. But Joanna—her apron removed —presided with gracious dignity. Even the little boy, at an age where boys had usually to be cuffed into good manners, had that same peculiar quality, handing the salt in its plain wooden bowl, without being asked.

Talk seemed easy. Of all those she had left behind at Stordford, Joanna inquired only of two.

"Lady Agnes? I was sorry to leave her so hastily. But I had reached the end of my endurance."

"Understandable," Peter said, relaxed by the calm, and the wine, and something within him, moving from an empty, distant, purely formal devotion to something far more real. "All of us in the lower part of the hall, when we heard, thought her ladyship had been over severe."

So far, so good! Joanna had expected a more formidable messenger. More informed. More vocal about betrothals.

"Severe," Godfrey said, exploring a word not entirely unfamiliar, for now and then Mistress Captoft had used it. If he didn't try harder, pay more attention, she would be forced to be severe to him. "Cruel? Did Lady Grey ever box *your* ears?"

"No. By the time I went to Stordford, I was a bit too big for that. And at Jerningham, where I served as a page, the lady our mistress held that to give us a cuff on the ear would soil her hands. She would say: This boy spilt the gravy, or let the dish wobble . . . Then we were beaten, by the steward. Or his deputy. It did us no harm."

"And the wedding?" Joanna said, stepping out on to ground that could not be avoided forever. "How did it go?"

"Well," Peter Wingfield said, remembering the extra, rather wild festivities which had marked the double occasion, a wedding *and* Twelfth Night. Remembering, too, the malicious talk that had run around. For what those at the lower end of the hall did not know, they were ready to invent; and as the story went, that decrepit old man had set his lecherous eye on Joanna Serriff, and been fobbed off with Maude Grey. Common talk, but it could explain why, just at Christmas, Joanna had been banished. Feeling for once free of all rules, Peter Wingfield said, "It was unfortunate that one of his lordship's new teeth should fall out, only three days after."

Godfrey said, "Mine fall out, too. But better ones, bigger ones grow. Look!"

He smiled, showing the new tooth which was taking the place of the one Mamma-Captoft had said had been ready to fall anyway.

It was then that Peter Wingfield realised that in addition to the calm, the unruffled manner, the three people with him at the table shared another thing—a marked physical resemblance. Difficult to define, but unmistakable . . . They were of three generations. Like most people who came into contact with Henry Tallboys, Peter Wingfield overestimated his age; wind and weather, and worry, and responsibility—and tragedy—had given Henry the appearance of being well on into his fourth decade. Their colouring varied too. Henry had inherited his father's fawn-coloured hair, and there was grey just above his ears; Sir Godfrey's fawn colour, mingled with Tana's crow black had produced the dark copper, the dead-leaf colour of Joanna's hair; and Godfrey was almost golden, Henry's fawn colour muted by Griselda's—which until the child's birth, had been the bright pale colour of fresh straw. Their eyes varied, too, Peter Wingfield saw, looking from one to the other in the light of the four candles which Joanna had set on the table, an extravagance to honour the guest. All blue, but different blues. Master Tallboys' almost sapphire, or cornflower; the demoiselle's—well, who could describe, even to himself, eyes which were so changeable?—grey-blue, blue-grey, greenish; and the boy had a limpid almost a periwinkle-blue look. It was not so much colouring as shape, Peter Wingfield decided, the way the hair grew, in the same way from foreheads identical, except that the man's was grooved; and that smile.

The conversation at table was light; nothing of any importance being touched upon. Afterwards Godfrey said eagerly, "There are four of us now. Janna, we could play that game you said needed four, couldn't we?"

They played a lively game of Naib, using beans as counters, and Godfrey won outright. He was the only one whose mind was wholly concentrated on the game. Then Henry said he must take a last look round and lit his lantern. "I'd better take Guard out, too," Godfrey said, adding with that enchanting smile, "I enjoyed that. Thank you, Peter."

As soon as they were alone, Joanna, her manner changed, said, "Were you sent to take me back?"

"No. . . . At least . . . No. My orders were to find out, if possible, what had become of you."

"I am glad of that. Because nothing, nobody would get me away. And I should not wish to make you fail in a set task."

It was the custom to test young men aspiring to knighthood not only in feats of arms, but in other ways: persistence; diplomacy; self-control; behaviour when drunk.

"Her ladyship was naturally anxious about you, demoiselle. There was a difference of opinion. If you had gone afoot, the snow would have . . . hampered you, and forced you to seek shelter. Then there was the horse. Sir Gervase held that you could *not* have taken him; and held with equal assurance that *had* you done so you would have been thrown."

Youth spoke to youth across the card-scattered table and they both laughed.

"No," Peter said. "I was told to seek, if possible to find, but of retrieving there was no mention. Although the word goes round that Lady Agnes feels her loss."

"And with good cause." She must, she knew, be ruthless where Lady Agnes was concerned, make her appear to be the scapegoat. If she had a chance, once this innocent, young, terribly young young man was about to mount, she'd send a little message to the poor old woman. Until then let Henry accept, undisturbed, the tale she had told him. Let the word betrothal, with all that it would bring to the surface, remain unspoken.

"If," the young man said with great diffidence, "the thought of returning to Stordford is repugnant to you, my mother, I know, would welcome you. My father is dead, but my mother is able to maintain a substantial household. And she is . . . kindly."

"Like you," Joanna said, and smiled. And Peter Wingfield understood what it was about the family smile which made it distinctive. It flashed, swift, sudden and brief across faces not ordinarily set in cheerful lines. Serious faces, even the boy's.

"A kind offer," Joanna said. "But one I cannot accept. My place is here. And here I intend to stay. It is my home."

And the young, terribly young young man had a thought, sudden and brief as the Tallboys' smile: I wish it were mine, too! A mean house, he had thought it at first sight, and about that he had not changed his mind; it *was* mean, ill furnished, but there was something, the quiet, the calm and the dignity. He had the fanciful, but none the less positive feeling that if the King of England suddenly arrived here, Master Tallboys would greet him courteously, see to his horse, bring him in and offer what he had. It was a fanciful thought, for the King was growing old now and made only short Progresses and even in his best days could never have dreamed of visiting a mere farmhouse, miles from anywhere. But Peter Wingfield entertained the thought, comparing, favourably, in his mind, Knight's Acre with all the other places he knew; the crush and bustle, the jostling for place, the eagerness to be noted, the craving for promotion, the constant chase, even amongst those already rich, for money; money and more money. For a moment he viewed his own future—knighthood at Easter, attachment to the household of some great lord, an advantageous marriage, and perhaps with good luck, a manor of his own, or the castellanship of a castle—with distaste.

He was shrewd enough, however, to recognise that this sudden desire for the simple life, the abandonment of ambition, was only a passing thing and directly connected with the girl seated opposite to him at the table. In the course of an evening his distant conventional devotion, no more than an attitude, had changed into something warm and genuine. He thought: I am in love! And he knew that young men in love often did rash things. But even as he warned himself to be careful, he began to wonder whether it would not be possible to have the best of both worlds. Joanna *and* his career, if she had only a small dowry.

Henry came back, extinguished the lantern and said to Godfrey, "Off to bed with you, son. Joanna, you too, please. I wish to have a private word . . ."

She was not much perturbed. Peter was too young, too low in the hierarchy of Stordford to know much. He was unlikely to bring up the mention of betrothal and thus force Henry into the open before he was ready. That was the thing she dreaded.

"Remember, Peter, to turn your clothes again before you go to bed. They'll be ready to brush in the morning." The mud-spattered garments had been hung well to the side of the hearth, within range of the warmth, out of reach of any direct spark.

Into the coarse mugs Henry poured some more of the wine which he had, in a moment of exuberance, bought to share with Mistress Captoft.

"Whether you can help me or not, I don't know," he said with the directness that was characteristic of him, "but there are things I need to know before I decide upon *her* future. As a child, she was singularly frank and open. Now she is reticent. I do not even know why Lady Grey imposed a punishment which even you considered over-severe. Do you know?"

"By hearsay only," Peter said cautiously. "*Not* kitchen gossip, Master Tallboys." And how odd, that here, in a kitchen, such emphasis upon rank should seem necessary. "Squires' talk," he said, "but we are trained to keep eyes and ears open, to make rational judgements by deduction, even by elimination. It was considered that Lord Shefton was enamoured of the demoiselle and wished to marry her, came armed, for Christmas, with a marriage contract and a betrothal ring. Which she refused, and was therefore banished."

"Tell me something of him—what you *know*, that is."

"He is immensely old. Past seventy. Extremely rich, but said to be close-fisted." Nowhere else would Peter Wingfield have spoken so frankly of a man of the kind to whom young knights looked for preferment. Nowhere else would he have added, "There was an alternative story, sir. That Lady Grey coveted such a match for her daughter. . . . There may be truth in that, since it came about, betrothal and wedding so hard on each other's heels."

"I was badly advised," Henry said. He got up, laid a log of the kind unlikely to spark on the fire and turned Peter's clothes about. Some of the mud, dried to dust, fell on the floor. "I wanted the best for her. I said a *suitable* marriage. This I did not regard as suitable. But I have her future to think of. And now, what with one thing and another, I cannot feel, in good conscience, that I can send her back to Stordford."

"I agree, sir. But there are other places."

"None known to me. That was the trouble," Henry said. "I always wanted the best for her. I chose my way of life, and its suits me. I wanted something easier for her. And when I discovered that she had means of her own, I wanted them used to her advantage. But the only suitable place I knew was my aunt Astallon's, Beauclaire—totally destroyed in the civil war. So I sought advice, which was bad. This situation is the result."

Peter Wingfield was young enough, and at the moment infatuated enough to regret, very mildly, that two things in that speech pleased his ear. But he knew his world. Young knights, with no prospects, took service with a great lord, were housed, fed, equipped: there were prizes to be won at tournaments, loot and ransom money to be gained in any real fighting; but such sources of income were uncertain. A wife with means of her own was very desirable; equally desirable was that she should be of good family; and although Beauclaire was a ruin now it had been famous in its day, for splendour and hospitality. Even its end had been dramatic. Lord Astallon, the most neutral of men, had suddenly and inexplicably opted for the side of Lancaster, a lost cause.

People still talked of the long siege which had been necessary to reduce it.

He began to speak of his mother, in her comfortable dower house near Winchester; not a large establishment, but lively and gay, ruled by a gentle and accomplished woman. He had reason to speak well of his mother, who, out of her necessarily limited means, sent him money from time to time. Such gifts would cease with her death, when everything would revert to his eldest brother, but by that time . . .

"I am sure my mother would welcome the demoiselle. I am equally sure that she would be happy there."

"It is a kind offer," Henry said; but he looked dubious. It would be, like Stordford, another shot in the dark. His ignorance of the world which he himself had avoided, and yet wished Joanna to inhabit, clamped down like fog. Such different standards! Even this pleasant, likeable boy had seemed to see nothing fundamentally wrong in the mis-mating which Lady Grey had proposed between a very old man and Joanna, and had achieved between the very old man and her own daughter.

At the same time he could not help thinking that he himself had made a marriage of convenience, if ever man did. Not that he and Griselda had been so ill matched until Godfrey was born. There'd been no ecstasy, that rare thing, but they'd got along together well enough, until she had centred everything on the child, and begun to go a little queer.

"A kind offer," he said again. But how could he *know* that this unknown Lady Wingfield might not turn out to be another Lady Grey? Stordford Castle, to his ignorant ears, had *sounded* perfect.

He thought too of how happy Joanna had been since her return. How well she and he and Godfrey had fitted together. No echo, no sign of the thing that had so disturbed him. At least, he thought, I was right *there;* Stordford cured her of that fancy!

"It needs thinking about," he said. "And perhaps the person most concerned should have some say in the matter."

It was the only time in his life when he had deliberately tried to shuffle off responsibility.

The young man smiled; fairly sure of his ground now. In his world girls did what they were told. Joanna *could* have broken that rule by refusing to marry Lord Shefton—but the other story was far more likely. Lady Grey had wanted him for Maude.

"Surely, sir, as her nearest male relative . . ." He had worked it out; the family resemblance, the differing names; uncle, or cousin. He was totally unprepared for the effect of those few innocent words. The man stared blankly, rather wildly, and then said,

"Good my God!"

The realisation of how very blind he had been seemed to affect his physical sight and he put a hand across his eyes. Seeing it all, now.

Peter Wingfield, so worldly wise, thought of illegitimacy. He had plainly touched a very sensitive spot and hastened to make amends.

"I am indeed very sorry, sir, if I have said anything untowards. But . . . But the family resemblance is unmistakable. But if I have mentioned anything I should not . . . I assure you, sir, you may rely upon my discretion."

Henry was furious with himself for letting loose that exclamation. A second's thought and he could have said something casual about a resemblance between cousins. Too late for that now!

He said, gruffly, "No discretion is called for." More than that in his present shattered state of mind he could not find words for. And yet he must, because who knew what the boy was thinking?

He thought: All along, I have been blind as a bat and as stupid as an owl, and I've let my mind sink to peasant level. Dumb.

He divided the wine between the two mugs, making a bid for time. Reaching for the right thing to say.

"No," he said, in a more ordinary voice. "It is nothing needing discretion. No bar sinister or anything of that sort. It was simply that by reminding me that I am now her nearest male relative, you brought to mind an obligation which I had forgotten."

Even in his own ears it sounded a feeble explanation and he was aware that the boy was regarding him with curiosity, almost concealed by good manners, but not quite.

Anger with himself, with the world, with this innocent cub, seized him again. He reached for a candle and held it out.

"You'd better get to bed. You've had a long day," he said.

The remaining candle, its over-long wick in a puddle of tallow, flared and faded, flared again. The fire died down. And still Henry sat with his head in his hands, mulling over the past, thinking of the future. Need she ever know? Would she mind? Did it matter? No. If, as he hoped, she had forgotten that scene in the wood, and the makeshift betrothal made across this very table. Forgotten—except in time of need, as when faced with a distasteful marriage. And about *that* she had been reticent. Why not about all else? And all because he had been blind and stupid. Walter said knaves and fools were punished—fools first.

Once back in London, Lord Shefton did not waste a moment. Even before Maude made her first public appearance as his Countess, he had made his opening move against the Bishop of Bywater.

His teeth had failed him, and he had allowed rage and vanity to hurry him into an unsatisfactory marriage, but his memory was good for matters of this kind, his mind still subtle. He could remember a summer, two years ago, when His Grace of Bywater had been in London, trying to arrange the futures of two young people. The girl had not been brought to London, the boy had: a big boy, handsome in a loutish way and surly; apparently quite ungrateful to His Grace for bringing him to London and making efforts to get him into Eton College. Introduced as Richard Tallboys, the boy always added, "of Moyidan." This apparently trivial business had impressed itself upon Lord Shefton's mind, partly because he yearned to correct so unmannerly a boy; partly because he had suggested that Sir Barnabas, who owed him money, should take the girl who, on his first visit to Stordford, had attracted him so much.

A very short visit to the appropriate offices, gave Lord Shefton all he needed to know about Moyidan in the County of Suffolk. Later in the day he had a conversation, not with any great official or favoured courtier, but with one of the virtually faceless, nameless men, one of several, known to have the King's ear. The word Moyidan was not spoken. Even the crucial remark was made in a most casual manner. "I have sometimes wondered," Lord Shefton said, "if the law regarding young heirs is not often broken, to the detriment of our Lord the King." That was all; but enough.

Edward of York, Edward IV, was the richest man in England, just as he was reputed to be the tallest, and in youth the most handsome. After the victory which set him firmly on the throne, Edward had confiscated all Lancastrian property. But he was a man who loved splendour; his wars were costly; he had faithful adherents to reward and mistresses to please; he also liked to be independent of Parliament, which meant managing without the grants which it could give. When the faceless, nameless advisor murmured something about an untapped source of wealth, he had the King's ear indeed. In theory all heirs under age were the King's wards. He might never see them, or know their names, but a wardship, like many other things, was a property, to be bestowed as a favour, or sold. There was a lively trade in such things.

Wheels were set in motion. A Commission appointed.

Maude must be made to seem the chosen one. In cloth of gold, and with all the Shefton diamonds on display, she made three dazzling appearances, all on occasions when little more than appearance mattered. Her mother's training had fitted her, to some extent, for this puppet role; anybody who, after many failures—sharply punished—could carry a brimming bowl of water on her head, could wear a coronet. And before anyone could get beyond this glittering facade and discover that Maude had nothing to say for herself, no spirit, nothing to compensate for her lack of beauty—or even prettiness—she was whisked away to Shefton Castle in the wilds of Shropshire, where she enjoyed the first real freedom of her life and in a humble, quiet way, enjoyed herself very much indeed.

In London the rumour ran that she was pregnant, and men some fifteen years younger than Lord Shefton looked at him with awe and envy. Life in the old dog, yet.

Official wheels could grind slowly, but where the King's express order and a possible source of revenue were concerned they could be speedy. Moyidan and its history were soon under review. It was in the hands of the Church now; but prior to that it had been managed by another cleric—Sir Richard Tallboys, properly ordained, and an M.A. of Cambridge University, presently engaged in one of those pleasant, undemanding jobs at the Chancellory. It might be as well to consult him.

Sir Richard showed no shadow of loyalty to his old friend the Bishop of Bywater, who had saved him from scandal and procured him his present post. All Richard's actions, since his boyhood, had been dictated by selfishness, and ambition. Ambition never satisfied; even his present post, pleasant enough, almost a sinecure, was in fact a cul-de-sac. But it did enable him to keep an ear to the ground, and he had qualified as a lawyer as well as a priest. He could tell, by the framing, the tilt of a question what answer was desired. He also had charm.

Quite disarmingly he admitted that while in charge of Moyidan, he had mismanaged it to some extent. "But, my lords, with good intention. I may have been mistaken in thinking that in spending money immediately available upon improving the property, I was actually investing for the boy's future."

"His Grace of Bywater knew what you were doing?"

"Oh yes. And he approved. He visited me often, and when the place was comfortable, stayed."

All the commissioners had a vision of a young man being given enough rope, while he spent money, not his own, and the Bishop watched, gloating over what he would, at the right moment, take over for himself.

"The boy was your ward?'

"Not officially. His grandmother, my aunt . . ." He made quite a piteous story of how poor old Lady Emma had appealed to him to take charge and hold the estate together until young Richard attained his majority. It was one of those shuffling arrangements which, over the years, had leached away revenue that should have gone into the King's coffers. Not quite typical because in this case the unofficial guardianship had changed hands.

"The boy, the direct heir, is now at Eton."

"That I did not know. I left him at Moyidan with as good a tutor as I could find. I assumed that in taking over the castle and the manor, His Grace of Bywater took charge of him too. If I may *stress,* my lords. I was never his guardian. I am not even the head of the family. I have an elder brother."

Some commissioners were old and liked to sit in comfort, drawing up charts, comparing figures, while younger, more vigorous men did the riding and the digging for facts. All were busy; for the investigation proved that more young heirs had slipped through the King's net than anyone would have believed possible. There were some heiresses, too, and would have been more had not self-appointed guardians tended to marry off wealthy girls at an early age, on the principle of the highest bidder being the buyer.

The Bishop of Bywater did not defend his action as regards Moyidan and its heir: to have done so would have been to admit that defence was needed; he simply described the shocking state of affairs which had existed before he took control and explained that only by prompt, firm, remedial action had he avoided a scandal which would have damaged the Church. He mentioned a lawyer, of anti-clerical views, who had been poised to attack Sir Richard Tallboys for gross mismanagement. On the whole he was rather fairer to Richard than Richard had been to him; that was largely because he was more aware of the need for solidarity within the Church. He did not mention the ugly word *embezzlement;* he spoke of inexperience, of muddle due to lack of experience. He said that so far from profiting from Moyidan, he had incurred expenses. He rang a bell and asked that every paper dealing, in however remote a way, should be brought and displayed; and since he had a passion for detail, it was a formidable pile. The Commissioner, a man better with figures than with written words, flinched a little.

"Your Grace regarded the boy, Richard Tallboys, as a ward?"

"A ward? No; of course not. Why should I? I—well, one might almost say that I inherited him, together with other encumbrances. But I did the best I could for him. I secured him a place at Eton College. In fact," His Grace said, made irritable and therefore incautious, "I did my best for them both."

"Both? Two? Co-heirs?" Such cases had been discovered. A few early, and rather sudden deaths had been revealed, too. In the place where such statistics were reckoned the sinister words, "died of the small-pox," were gradually revealing the fact that unofficial wards were particularly prone to such ailments. Well above average, possibly as much as 30 per cent higher than the death rate even amongst cottagers' children; 50 per cent higher than the deaths in similar age groups in a class which could afford red flannel as wrappings, bed hangings, and curtains, sops-in-wine, and the attention of a physician.

"No," His Grace said, the ground firm underfoot again. "The girl was in no way concerned with Moyidan. She was . . ."

He told what he knew of Joanna's story; of the tumbling out of the jewels; of Henry Tallboys, "a most ignorant fellow," asking advice as to how such wealth could best be employed to the girl's advantage. And how Joanna's dowry had been deployed. Roughly two thirds of the money in Sir Barnabas Grey's keeping. A third, by the girl's own wish, invested at Knight's Acre, all running about on four legs.

The Commissioner believed that he had inadvertently stumbled across an heiress of whom there was no record; a find indeed! Leaving the pile of papers unstudied, he asked direction to Knight's Acre and set out at once. He took a list of the live-stock entrusted to Master Tallboys.

It was now April, and the mild weather had encouraged grass to grow, all the animals were at pasture; lambs were skipping in the fold, the herd of cattle in the meadow included five young calves. Knowledgeable about such matters the Commissioner noted the healthy look of all these beasts—they had been well cared for during the lean months.

Master Tallboys had no records to show, but everything was clear in his head; he could distinguish the animals entrusted to him on Joanna's behalf from his own, and a man apt at counting soon saw that both flock and herd had increased considerably.

"I have always regarded the girl's beasts as separate from my own," he said. "The fleece money from her flock I have put aside intact. I've sold animals from time to time; from what they fetch I take what I think compensates for their food and my labour. I put that aside too. Master Turnbull, the lawyer at Baildon, keeps the accounts and invests the money for her." Henry gave the Commissioner his straight blue stare. "My better horse is hers, too. As soon as I am able I shall add its worth to the money accumulating."

"That, sir, is correct," Master Turnbull said. "Master Tallboys is the most meticulous man I know. He is honest to his own detriment." The lawyer's trade brought him into contact with many men with varying standards of honesty. His own was high, for he wished to leave to his beloved son not only a comfortable fortune but an unsullied name. But even he felt that Henry, still putting away certain, much smaller sums, to be kept for a boy of whom nothing had been seen or heard for almost eight years, was carrying honesty to the point of folly. "You wish to see what has been done with the money?"

For anyone to whom written records mattered, fire, particularly in the night, was a threat. However careful one might be oneself, damping down, or raking out fires, a neighbour might be negligent. Master Turnbull had faced this hazard by having chests made, so much bound about by iron that they would not ignite easily. They were small enough to be lifted, if not with ease, with sufficient determination, by one man, and four slept under his roof every night: himself—still able-bodied—two clerks and a man-servant.

From one of these chests, which he did not lift, but stooped over, he produced every parchment and paper relevant to the business in hand. He was as dedicated a record-keeper as the Bishop. Here, in black and white—the black his own home-made ink made of rotting walnut husks steeped in vinegar—was evidence not only of Master Tallboys' exceptional honesty but of Master Turnbull's financial acumen. Money received; invested; withdrawn; re-invested; mortgages; foreclosures; loans; interest on loans. It was, in fact, a record of ruthlessness as well as of honesty, but the Commissioner was not concerned with that. He merely thought that if Sir Barnabas Grey had been only half as clever in handling the major part of the girl's fortune, this obscure Joanna Serriff would be a considerable heiress. And *he* had discovered her!

Presently another Commissioner, willing to ride, and less averse to wading through closely written pages, had discovered a fact which might exonerate the Bishop of Bywater's over-hasty action in regard to Moyidan. Apparently he had not simply taken the place as a summer residence, or a hunting lodge. The Abbey at Baildon was involved. And this was tricky ground. Between the secular Church, as represented by Archbishops and Bishops, and the heads of the great monastic establishments, like the Abbey of Baildon, there had always been a gulf, now widening, just as cracks in a wall, almost ready to tumble would widen. The monastic establishments—many of them founded by Orders vowed to holy poverty—had become enormously rich, and over the years, increasingly independent. The great breach was yet to come, but the climate for it was already building up.

The Abbot of Baildon did not feel that solidarity—or the need for it which the Bishop of Bywater had felt. He belonged to a wider community—the Benedictines. Part of an old Order, so old that Charlemagne himself had been their patron, and there were Benedictine houses as far away as Poland.

The Abbot of Baildon was sufficiently self-assured that he dared to keep even the King's Commissioner waiting for a while. And then, when the confrontation came, he, very gently, but inexorably threw His Grace of Bywater to the wolves.

"Yes," he said, "some suggestion was made, and I welcomed it. Purely on account of Moyidan's situation; Moyidan being nearer the sea. And it is fact that for some people —particularly those born within reach of the sea—the air from it has a recuperative effect. I considered that. Also the fact that it was rusticated and that any member of this community who had transgressed might there, in isolation, meditate and repent. But I soon saw that it was not a workable idea. To put it very bluntly: when His Grace was in residence ill-doers ate too well; and when he was not, convalescents were too meagrely fed. The place was not organised well, and I decided to ignore it."

As one little prop to the Bishop's well-planned scheme, the Abbot of Baildon had failed absolutely.

Down in Bywater, the better weather had eased things for Mistress Captoft. Her money arrived. Shipping began to move; able-bodied men went away—some of them thanking her with genuine tears. "Never, never shall I forget you, madam." "Madam, I'll remember you and your kindness, in my prayers, till the day I die."

She paid her debts, but was otherwise careful with money. This harsh winter had taught her a lesson. She supervised the reclamation of the garden. It was hardly likely that two winters in succession could be so savage, but she would be prepared. She'd have her own fowls next year.

Articles made by those who had gone, and by those who could never go, looked well, as she had thought, displayed against the red velvet with which David had covered the sloping board; and now that Bywater was busy again and the market in full swing, trade was brisk. Her little parlour was once again her own, but it was also a shop and she derived some amusement from the thought that by all known standards, she had fallen. Trade, as pursued by her husband, was one thing; petty shop-keeping another. But she did not care. She was enjoying everything; even a face-to-face row with the landlady of The Welcome To Mariners, who one afternoon, in the dead hour, dinner done with, supper hours away, walked down to The Sailors' Rest and accused Mistress Captoft of reneging on a bargain.

"You promised me a continuous supply," she said. "And now I have four pedlars clamouring and nothing to sell them."

"The supply is there," Mistress Captoft said, indicating the display in the window. "Buy what you wish."

"Buy?"

"Buy," Mistress Captoft said. "I certainly did not promise a continuous supply in return for such things as I was, in a desperate moment, forced to accept. The wine was the worst I ever tasted; the two fowls hardly needed their necks wrung—they were dying of old age. The doves, mere skeletons with feathers."

Allowing for a marginal exaggeration, these were true statements. Mistress Captoft had said to David that she could understand why the system of barter was dying out; it allowed of too much lop-sidedness. The truth did not make the accusation more palatable and the landlady lost her temper. She used terms which questioned not only Mistress Captoft's integrity, but her legitimacy and her standard of morals. Mistress Captoft, who with one word had so shocked Father Matthew, contrived to maintain a look of incomprehension, and almost had the last word.

She said, "I am sorry. I understand only English."

The landlady drew breath and said, "Bawd!" Then realising that it was inept in the circumstances, simply repeated the uncivil word as she retreated. She said it loud enough and often enough for David, hurrying to see who was shouting, and why, heard it twice, and limped in, expecting—hoping?—to find Madam in need of comfort.

"It was the landlady from the inn," Mistress Captoft said. "She objects to our board. Our shelf, David. She wanted a monopoly; but this way we cut out the middle man—or woman in this case."

He thanked God that he had been mistaken; or that she had not understood. Which? He did not know; never would know. The weeks of hardship had made him feel very guilty and once or twice he had tried to apologise: "Madam, this is not what I meant. *You* eating hard-tack!" But she had always smiled and said she had never been happier. And she *did* look happy.

Then she did something which annoyed him. One of the scurvy-sufferers, instead of making a saleable trinket, carved out of a log of driftwood, another sign for The Sailors' Rest. A huge thing, big enough almost to be a ship's figure-head. And it was coloured, as ships' figure-heads were, with crude colours, so well mixed with oil and cow-heel glue as to be resistant to salt water, rain and wind. David's own painted sign, hanging, creaking in the wind, showed a sailor, recognisable by his head wear and clothes, lying at ease on a mattress. A sailor at rest. The figure-head thing was different, just a head, with the recognisable sailor's woollen cap which could be pulled down over the ears, homespun, buffish in colour—as most were—the drab colour set off the face, reddish brown, and the eyes, blue, as sailors' eyes mostly were. The mouth of this crude and yet powerful image wore a carved smile, the red of the lips darker than the face.

"I like it," Mistress Captoft said after she had thanked the man who had made it and seen him off to whatever fate awaited him; scurvy again with no cure handy; or shipwreck, or accident. Actually, anxious as she was to restore and heal, every parting with a man restored and healed, hurt her. While they were under her roof, for a long time or short, they were her children and she felt towards them the helpless protectiveness, the defeated possessiveness of mothers the world over.

"It must be nailed up," she said, "above the shop window. It will attract attention."

It would also make David's swinging sign, already bleached, look like a shadow.

"It will give the wrong idea, madam. In no time at all this will be called The Jolly Sailor."

"And would that matter, David? Were we not, even during the worst times, jolly together? Sharing what little we had? Making merry over the hard-tack, and three to a bed? I think the sign apt. And being so conspicuous, a further annoyance to that woman."

The next inmate to arrive, however, was not attracted by the implied jollity. He came because he was in very poor shape, and, as David had foreseen, news of The Sailors' Rest had spread.

He was a big man, both tall and broad; he was in good health and his ship had been only just out from Hull, when he'd ducked his head, below deck, a thing he'd done many times before; but this time was different; he couldn't straighten his neck again. Worse than that, every movement, even the effort to walk, caused agony. No ship bound for Lisbon could afford a useless hand, so he'd been put ashore at Bywater; not utterly destitute, for the captain was a humane man. Somebody had said, "Make for The Sailors' Rest, mate. Madam there'll cure you if anybody can." So here he was, having been obliged to ask direction because it was impossible for him to lift his head to an angle from which either sign would have been visible.

For once Mistress Captoft was at a loss, never having met with this condition before. Flesh wounds, even broken bones she was prepared to deal with; but there was no wound; and had his neck been broken, the man would have been dead. As usual when she was in a difficulty, she called for David, and he, having so recently suffered defeat over the matter of the sign, was delighted to be able to say that he had seen a man or two in this state before; and he knew the cure.

It sounded very drastic.

"Hanging by the neck!" she exclaimed. "But, David, surely, that would kill him."

"Not properly done, madam. Hung people die one of two ways. They hang till they choke and that's a long business; or the jolt'll break their necks. We shan't let him hang long, and we won't jolt him. I'll make a kind of collar."

Cautious, in case of accident, Mistress Captoft asked the man if he were willing to submit to being half hanged; and he said anything, even a real hanging, would be better than this.

The operation took place in the kitchen, supervised by David, watched by Mistress Captoft and two or three reasonably able-bodied fellows who had orders to act immediately if anything seemed to go wrong.

The leather collar, well padded with straw, was fixed to the man's neck, and to a rope, slack, at the moment, tied to a beam from which, next year, hams and strings of onions and bunches of dried herbs would hang. The man—he gave his name as Dan Rush—stood on the kitchen table, David beside him. David moved the rope a little way along the beam and said, "Step on to the stool." Dan did so and the rope lost its slack. "Now on to the cask," David said. And then, "Cask away!" Mistress Captoft held her breath as the big man hung suspended. She heard, or imagined she heard a slight click, no more than the turning of a key in a lock.

"Hold him," David said, and two men ran forward to take Dan's weight while David unfastened the collar.

Dan stood on the kitchen floor, straight and tall, dumbstruck. He turned his head from right to left, bent it towards one shoulder, then the other.

"By God!" he said, in an awed voice. "A bloody miracle. I'm cured! I'm cured!"

He rushed over to Mistress Captoft, flung his great arms round her, kissed her on both cheeks; thumped David and the other men on the shoulders. He was beside himself with joy. He danced.

He was a newcomer, David reminded himself; not yet

aware of the rules of the house—many of them drawn up by David himself. One concerned the language unsuitable for use in Madam's presence, a rule that rendered many men practically dumb for the first forty-eight hours at least, since profanity was their natural tongue.

Another rule concerned drinking. David knew how easily men of quite mild disposition, quiet fellows, could become aggressive and noisy after that drop too much; and not only that, men of ordinarily clean habit became filthy, vomiting, the least of their offences.

Ale was served at The Sailors' Rest—even during that bad time when food ran short. Mistress Captoft had laid in stores and each morning each man broke his fast with a mug of very weak ale and a hunk of bread. Ale of a slightly stronger kind was served at supper.

Anybody who wanted more than this was free to go out and buy it. Mistress Captoft said she did not wish men to feel constricted as in the ordinary charitable institution. And on the whole the matter was—at this stage—largely academic, since most of those seeking shelter were destitute. Of the paying clients there had as yet been few. But David was prepared for the future. Like many people he associated drunkenness and immorality generally with the keeping of late hours, so supper was early, soon after the Vespers bell, and at the first sound of the Compline bell the door of The Sailors' Rest was barred for the night. This gave David a chance to judge the state of any latecomer.

On the first night after his miraculous cure, Dan was slightly late and slightly tipsy. He had spent a lot of time hunting about Bywater for a present for Madam, something pretty and not too expensive, for what money he had must last until he found a ship again. Also he had plans for the next evening, when he would, as he expressed it, feel more like himself. The days of agony when even to eat or drink was an effort, and the drastic, sudden cure had somewhat unmanned him. Tomorrow!

He found his trinket at last, a piece of amber, small, but genuine—he knew by the light weight and the warm feel of it that it was not a bit of the coloured glass so often sold as amber—slung on a thin silver chain. He then went to an alehouse and drank just enough to make him, in his exuberant state of mind, a little more exuberant. Not, David realised, being a just man, quite drunk enough to warrant the slammed door and the inexorable sentence: Get into the gutter and sleep it off, which in the past four months three bad characters had earned; but tipsy enough, and late enough to be admonished; tipsy enough to resent admonishment. He said, "Get outa my way, you little runt. It ain't your house anyway. It's hers. And I've got a present for her. Where is she?"

"I am here," Mistress Captoft said from the top of the stairs. There was, as she had planned, only one *she* in this house.

"Brought you something," the big man said, exhibiting the frail trinket on his huge horny palm.

She took it with exactly the unself-conscious, innocent assurance that she had accepted the home-made gifts of other grateful men—things which had formed a nucleus, given a start to, quite a flourishing little business.

"How very pretty," she said. "But there was no need. To see you better is reward enough. Now; you are late, supper is over. But there is bread and cheese in the kitchen."

"And if you must be sick, do it out of the window," David said.

The big man went off in search of the food and David followed Mistress Captoft into the little parlour, now, save for the counter, her own place again.

"Madam, you heard what he said?"

"In part. His voice was somewhat slurred."

"He called me a runt!"

"David, you are not so small as to resent that, surely. To a man of that size, I suppose we all look small." She moved to the court cupboard and poured wine into two silver cups. She could afford decent wine now, if she spared on dresses. "Sit down, David; drink and forget *runt*. I have been called worse things in my time. There is an old song that children sing: *Sticks and stones may break my bones; but names can never hurt me.* Shrug it off, David; he will soon be gone. And as soon as he goes I shall put this"—she indicated the bit of amber and the slender silver chain—"into the window, for sale with the other things."

All right; all right; but she had not said what she should have said. *Out he must go,* to quote from another children's game.

She did not say that; she said instead, "David, we must remember that the poor man was only this very day released from a crippling disability."

Yes—and to whom were thanks due for that? David Fuller. Pushed aside, called *runt* and reminded—as though he needed reminding—that he was not the master of this house.

Nursing his wine and his grievances, too painful to be put

into words, David sat and brooded, his mind like balanced scales tipping this way, that way. Mistress Captoft had saved him from starvation, given him a chance to rehabilitate himself, ventured out on this whole enterprise, at his suggestion, and when the thing looked like being a failure, he had apologised. And with things at their worst, she had said that she was happy. Had indeed looked happy. As he had been. Until now, when gratitude, devotion, a desire to serve, protect, had suddenly changed; just as a bowl of sweet milk could be changed by the addition of wine into syllabub, by a little rennet, into cheese. It was not his house, but he took a large part in the running of it, upheld, both by warnings and by his own example, that respectful awe with which the men regarded her. It was to him that she turned for help and advice in any material difficulty; and for comfort and cheer in those rare moments when her spirits were low. When men were bedridden, it was he who had undertaken the tasks which he considered unsuitable for a lady to do; when men were delirious he'd taken care always to be there. Now she had stood by and heard him insulted, and gone out of her way to be pleasant to the tipsy fellow, accepted his gift, bothered lest he should go supperless to bed. Just because he was a huge, handsome brute.

Mistress Captoft observed that the glass of good wine was doing little to lift David's gloom. Being a woman she did not understand the offence in the word *runt;* she had stated a fact when she said that to a man of that size everybody else must look small. The remark about who owned the house was also a fact. To mention it was not perhaps in the best of taste, but then the man was not completely sober, and had not been under her roof long enough to have learned that mannerliness was the rule here.

Then her gaze fell upon the bowl of cowslips which stood on the table between the two chairs.

"Oh, David," she said quickly, "it has been such a busy day, I neglected to thank you for the flowers. They gave me great pleasure. I love the scent." She leaned forward and put her face to the posy.

"There was just the one bunch. It looked a bit lonely alongside the cabbages."

The gloom did not lighten. She thought about how he had exerted himself over the hanging cure; scrambling up on to the table, reaching up to move the rope so that it was exactly above each decreasing level, table, stool, cask. His badly mended leg, she knew, served him well enough, with the properly built up shoe, but it was susceptible to changes in the weather, and to fatigue.

"Is your leg paining you, David?"

"No more than usual, thank you, madam."

A perfectly ordinary, civil reply, but cold, but off-hand, as his remark about the cowslips had been. Best to take no notice.

"I'd advise an early night for you. For myself, too."

In the morning Dan woke; stretched, turned, reached both arms above his head. No pain! Cured! He could remember the cure with perfect clarity; also the hunt for the right gift; after that his memory was hazy though he had not, by his own standard, been drunk. The way the man who had organised the miracle looked at him, however, indicated that something was wrong; and now he came to look at it, the man who had helped with the miracle, and the man who had tried to bar his way later on, were one and the same.

He made his graceless attempt at apology.

"No offence meant, mate."

"You're no mate of mine."

"You helped to cure me."

Something of last night's business, or something looming in the future, threw a shadow.

"Worst day's work I ever did," David said.

One of Mistress Captoft's projects—based now on experience—was the reclamation of the stables where the knights' horses had stood, in that brief, lordly interlude between times when humbler animals had been there. She thought it unlikely that next winter—or any in the foreseeable future—would be quite like the one they had just survived, but just in case, she wanted the stables put into such a state of repair that men could sleep there and not three to each narrow cell, and some in her private parlour as well as in the big communal room. The work on the stables was being done, not by hired labour—altogether too expensive—but by those of her guests fit for work. And of those, Dan Rush, yesterday a cripple, was by far the strongest and most able. He could carry a plank with which two ordinary men must struggle, sweating, as though it weighed no more than a stool; he could hold a supporting post steady and upright, dead true, while the hole into which it was planted was filled in and resolutely stamped down. Merely exerting his size and strength was, after the helplessness, a pleasure. And there was the evening still to come.

The evening held promise for David as well as for Dan. The big man was not present at the supper table, and tonight if he came back one second late, drunk or sober, the door would remain barred. And the mild wind which had brought the cowslips into bloom had shifted; sudden and keen, it now blew from the East. A night on the beach would not be pleasant—but no worse than the dog watch aboard ship. It might, however, teach the big brute a salutary lesson; David might not own the house; he did govern the door. And what could have been a weak place in the defensive action— Madam interfering and being sentimental—was, most fortuitously, forestalled. Madam had one of her headaches. Her headache, but part of the tiresome process all women suffered if they lived long enough. It took various forms, hysteria inexplicable pains; some completely honest woman took to stealing; some, married, became pregnant and bore children known as tails' ends.

Madam merely had headaches, for which, naturally, she had a palliative.

While the headache raged she lay in a darkened room took some drops of the stuff which dulled but did not remove the pain, and waited, subsisting on water since the very thought of food nauseated her. She had had three attacks since coming to Bywater and David knew that there was nothing he could do except tip-toe in, see that there was water in the jug and ask, solicitously, "How is it now, madam?" If she had taken the drops recently she would give a mere drowsy murmur; fully awake she would say with resolute cheerfulness, "Getting better, thank you." Which was true, for her headache never lasted more than twenty-four hours.

"Mind how you move about, mates," David reminded the men as bed-time came round. "Madam can't bear noise when her head is bad." Down in the big communal room noise didn't matter, for Madam's bedroom was immediately over her little parlour and the old house had thick walls and floors. Following the example of those who had been here on an earlier, similar occasion, the men shed their footwear and crept upstairs, stealthy as thieves. David made his final visit to Mistress Captoft's room. She was asleep, not merely drowsy. She would be perfectly well in the morning, he thought, as he stole away to his own bed.

Mistress Captoft woke in the dark, and, like Dan some hours earlier, was delighted to find herself free of pain.

When there were sick men likely to need her in the night she kept a candle burning, but there was no such man now, so she reached for the tinder box and not too steadily, made a light. She was slightly confused, as always after the headache and the doses of lovage-and-opium. She was unsure whether it was night or day until she listened. No sound from the quay. Night then! A conclusion confirmed when she moved, a little shakily, to the window and opened the shutter and looked out into the night; a clear night, with a lop-sided moon and many stars. Yes, it was night. And she was, as always after a spell of headache, ravenously hungry; not the natural hunger quite explained by the fact that she, a woman of good appetite, had fasted through a day and part of a night. The hunger—she had observed this before—was in some curious way connected with the headache, as though it had stolen something from her, something which must be replaced before recovery was complete. And it must be either cheese, or ham. Nothing else would do. She pulled on her loose robe and pushed her feet into her slippers, just as she had done many times before, called up suddenly to tend the sick, and then, taking her candle, went down to administer to herself as she had so often administered to others. But not for her, sops-in-wine, or chicken broth, or egg custard. Such items of good invalid diet still roused faint echoes of nausea. She wanted cheese, or ham. She padded her way, silently, down the stairs, into the kitchen. A walk she made twice a day in the ordinary way, tripping lightly, but tonight, in the silence, and the loneliness, a dragging effort which to her momentarily disturbed mind, held the creeping threat of old age. When I am old, crippled, dead, what will become of them all? What will become of The Sailors' Rest? And my property? I must make a will—but to whom shall I leave it all? David? But he is only younger by a few years. That would be no solution. . . . She carried this wretched problem into the larder and immediately shrugged it aside, for there on the shelf was a ham.

She had no knife, but she needed none. At the narrow end of the well-cooked ham the meat had come away from the bone, and just lay there, ready to be plucked away, not in slices, in hunks. Mistress Captoft pulled, crammed the meat into her mouth, ate as though she had starved for a month and immediately felt better. Strong, restored, good for another twenty years! It was a recognised fact that any woman who got over this particular hurdle lived on and on.

And why should she worry about the future? God had brought her here; He would take care of everything.

Carrying the candle in one hand and a piece of ham in the other, she retraced her steps and was at the foot of the stairs when the door knocker banged. Without hesitation, she set the candle on a little shelf and slid back the heavy bar, greased by David to make it run smoothly.

Destiny blundered over the threshold.

Dan's much anticipated evening had been a disaster. He'd begun moderately and sensibly, with a couple of mugs of good ale at a house in one of the Lanes, a recognised drinking place which sold liquor only. There a mere hint of his other need brought simple instructions and he found himself in the house by the tanyard; the house belonging to Katharine Dowley's cousin. Here he was supplied with a drink for which he had not asked, and was not required to pay. "It's on the house, mate," John Dowley said; "it'll set you up like nothing you've ever had before." He enlarged, in a gross fashion, upon the manner of the setting up.

For John Dowley it had been a hard winter. His eldest daughter—the mainstay of the establishment—had got herself a husband; his second had run away. His third was quite old enough in the eyes of everybody but her mother. That downtrodden woman had suddenly rebelled in a shocking way. "Over my dead body, till she's twelve," she said, and was prepared to back her defiant words with force, armed by anything that was to hand. Then that fool Katharine had arrived. She brought a little money with her, but then the snow began, traffic with the inland ceased, shipping—except for a few battered ships seeking shelter—was at a standstill; and food prices doubled. When the land roads and sea roads were open again, he had only Katharine to work with and in the end he had talked her round: for, with nobody to say a good word for her, she had failed to find a job. She had finally seen the necessity, but she was doing the business no good. One dissatisfied customer had expressed his complaint in plain language. "Any time I want to bed with a sack of chaff, I can do it in my own barn. Free."

Resourceful, John Dowley had found a way to get round this situation.

Dan Rush was sipping it now. It looked like water, had no particular taste or smell, just a faint oiliness on the tongue. Dan had moved about quite a bit; he knew ale, weak, medium, strong; he had from time to time drunk wine, red and white and yellowish and on even rarer occasions, some stuff called brandywine.

He sipped this unknown stuff, waiting for it to take effect—not that he needed it. John Dowley knew the effect. It made men unaware of whether the bulk in the bed behaved like a woman, or a sack of chaff.

Dan was aware that this was not what he had promised himself. And after that there was a gap, even in what he remembered. He came to full consciousness, lying in the gutter. Being sick. After that he felt better, though angry because the body bought and paid for had been such a bad bargain, so unresponsive. It was night, but a moonlit night, and in the quietude he could hear the sea, the waves coming in, breaking, and then the outward, dragging sound. He set off towards it.

At one corner there was a stone drinking trough, meant for cattle or pack animals. He stopped by it and drank, splashed water on his face. He was sober enough to realise that he had been drunk. Had he been robbed, too? Yes. Not a farthing left. It was common practice. Brothels and thievery went together. Few men complained. Ordinary decent citizens didn't wish it to be known that they frequented such places, and men just passing through had no time to bring a charge. Sailors least of all.

But just wait till morning, Dan thought, and that man by the tanyard would have something to think about.

The water had the curious effect of making him drunk again and lustful again. But it was dead night now; everything must wait.

And here, opening the door to him was a woman. Lightly clad, smiling, saying, "You are *very* late."

He fell upon her like a tiger.

Apart from that horrible affair at Intake which Mistress Captoft had pushed to the back of her mind, and had almost forgotten, there was nothing in her life to prepare her for such an assault. She'd had loving parents, a kind if ineffectual old husband; a gentle lover. She should have been helpless, managing at most a scream; but as her loose robe fell open and her night-shift tore, the real Mattie Captoft took command. She even remembered to which side the big man's head had lolled. She went limp, deceptively, put up a soft hand in what might have been a caress and then *pushed* with all her might. If his neck clicked again she did not hear it because he yelled as pain shafted through him. His hands lost their grip and he stood there, huge and helpless as he had been when he arrived. She skirted past him and opened the door again and pushed him out and down. No effort at all. A child could have done it.

She closed and bolted the door quietly, hoping to keep all secret, hoping that David and all the other men were too sound asleep, would perhaps only half wake, attribute the cry to a couple of mating cats who did sometimes make such human noises that two or three times Mistress Captoft had been almost sure that the function of The Sailors' Rest had been mistaken and that an unwanted infant had been left on her doorstep.

In this hope that the noise might be ignored, she picked up her candle and turned towards the stairs, and there was David. Very lame without a shoe. Wearing nothing under the snatched-up quilt.

She was very conscious of the torn shift, and the marks on her neck and bosom—not kisses, bites. She tried to pull the edges of her robe together and was surprised and dismayed to find that *now* she was more tremulous than she had been when she first rose from her bed. Her mind was shaking too, wavering between a desire to laugh, and a wish to cry.

David seemed to take the stairs in three hops, put his arm around her, and said, "Did he hurt you?"

"I hurt *him!*" she said, and laughed, but too unsteadily to deceive. Her guided her into the little parlour and sat her in a chair; then he went back for the candle, carefully knotting the quilt around him. Back in the parlour he poured wine and held it for her to sip. She would have been incapable of holding it herself. He did not ask *what* had happened, he seemed to know without being told. He said, "Why did you open the door? So late."

"I didn't know. I didn't know *he* was still out. People do come at night. Sometimes."

"And I've told you and told you; not to go to the door alone, after dark. Why didn't you call me?"

"I was there. I'd been to get something to eat. There was the knock. I answered it. I didn't think, David. I didn't know how late it was. I was still confused. You know how I am when my headache lifts."

"You should have called me for that, too. Something like this was bound to happen, sooner or later. You so pretty and kind, and a rogue in every dozen. And what a rogue'll see— in us—is a woman with no man to protect her, and a man with no authority."

Some rancour, older than that inspired by yesterday's little affair, sounded bitterly in his voice. It was just the damned money, he thought, just the damned money, which she had, and he had not. All the wrong way round. Not, he realised sensibly, that money was responsible, except indirectly, for this state of affairs. He was to blame. He'd suggested this refuge for sailors; partly because he felt strongly about sea-men's plight, but, in even greater part because he didn't want her to go burying herself in a convent. The last place suitable for her. But he had not visualised her here, the one woman amongst so many men. That dangerous situation he had done his best to make harmless by his own behaviour, by his insistence upon the behaviour of others, by making every-body think that Madam was practically as holy as the Virgin Mary. And he had been very vigilant. But the landlady of The Welcome To Mariners had a carrying voice and though, thank God, Madam had misunderstood, David had understood only too well.

He'd given her an opening; it was for her—because she had the damned money—to make the next move.

Mistress Captoft, able now to manage her wine-cup with one hand while clutching the edges of her robe together with the other, took one of her impulsive decisions. Why not? He is completely devoted to me; honest, industrious, clean. And apart from that lame leg, not a deformity, the result of an accident, a fine figure of a man.

She did not think, and if the thought had ever occurred to her she would have repudiated it with scorn, that the near rape had fired old hungers which she had thought never to feel again.

She said, "That could be easily remedied, David. If you would ask me to marry you."

That decision at least she was never to regret. Happy ever after. For once it was true. David absolutely the head of this house, a stern, but genial autocrat; and Mistress Fuller no longer craving for vicarious motherhood. Just in time, on such a narrow edge of time that she herself found it, for a while, difficult to decide whether it was pregnancy or the end of all that, presently she knew and presently bore a good strong boy. They named him Benedict, for as Mistress Fuller ex-plained, two Davids in one family would be a bit confusing. "And the name will commemorate a relative of mine of whom I was once very fond."

At Intake, life drifted on, busy and for a time uneventfully.

Peter Wingfield's visit had left no trace; the word betrothal was never mentioned. Occasionally Joanna thought that perhaps Henry was waiting for her birthday in June. She would be fourteen then. Now and then she had the darker thought—that it would never be mentioned. Henry looked at her often, sometimes broodingly, often fondly, but never in *that* particular way. However, as day followed happy day, she became resigned and told herself that it did not matter; that she would be content if things could just continue as they were; to be with him, here at Knight's Acre, would be enough. She rejoiced in being free again; in every change which the lengthening days brought to the fields and to the woods. She resisted all his suggestions for hiring what he called kitchen-help. "Why? Don't I manage to your liking?"

"You manage splendidly. But I don't like to see you doing such rough work."

"When I complain it will be time enough to change. After all, your mother managed single-handed for years."

"And I didn't like that either. It aged her. And how do you know about my mother and the hard times? You were not even born."

"Tom Robinson told me. All about the plague, how the one good old servant died and your mother had the nursing to do, as well as the work.

Henry looked at her curiously, wondering whether Tom, resident here in the house when Sir Godfrey came back after that long absence, bringing Tana with him, had ever noticed anything which he himself—younger than Tom—had missed, blinded as he was by such conflicting emotions, infatuation at first sight with the beautiful lady from Spain, and disgruntlement at losing his place as head and mainstay of the family.

Not that he needed proof in words or reminiscences, of the thing which the young squire from Stordford had seen and spoken of, in all innocence. It was there, and he could see it now as he looked at Joanna and Godfrey—and at himself, in Sybilla's small looking glass. Allowing for differences in sex and in age . . . the family likeness was strong.

And it had been just as strongly marked, Henry now realised, belatedly, between Joanna and Robert. Now and then people had said that they might be twins—the girl bigger and more lusty, as girls often were. They *were* born on the same day, but different mothers: Joanna a full-term baby, Robert premature, hardly expected to live; Tana had suckled them both, and for some people that had explained the exceptionally close bond between them. Wet nurses were supposed to leave a mark on their nurslings. That was why they were carefully chosen.

What Peter Wingfield had in innocence and ignorance said, explained everything—even that scene in the wood, Joanna flinging herself into his arms and declaring a love which, in *her* innocence and ignorance, she had misinterpreted. It explained, too, the shame he had felt because for a moment his body responded. He had thought it was shameful because she was so young. Now he knew differently.

Apart from this burden of knowledge and how it would affect the future, Henry enjoyed that spring, too. Joanna's housekeeping was on the happy-go-lucky side; there was always something to eat, but no trouble made of it. Even the inevitable mending she tackled with goodwill.

"Somebody once complained that my stitches were like hedge stakes," she said, snipping off the thread after making a patch. "And so they are. But they hold."

The casual, happy, drifting time was disturbed by something that neither Joanna or Henry had foreseen. It was the first Wednesday in June and with Godfrey, they had gone to market; the last market day before sheep shearing and the hay-making ended such outings.

On the way home—at the end of a financially satisfactory day—Joanna had referred to that other day, when that horrible boy Richard Tallboys of Moyidan, had had such a well-deserved thrashing. And at the end of the journey, turning into the track alongside the house, she said,

"Well. Speak of the Devil!" For there Moyidan Richard was, being held at bay by the dog, which had found that with *this* intruder, there was no need to venture on to the hated strip of ground. A snarl and show of teeth were effective.

Leaning across Godfrey, Joanna grabbed Henry's arm.

"Don't keep him, Henry. He'll spoil everything. Send him back where he came from. Remember how he behaved last time."

"We must just hear what he has to say for himself," Henry said. "He may have nowhere else to go." He did not feel particularly welcoming. Even at a time when he felt sorry for the boy he had been unable to like him much; there was something surly, uncouth about him. Inclined to whine, too. And of course he had stolen in Baildon and told lies about his treatment at Henry's hands. And there was truth in Joanna's words about spoiling everything. Henry thought in a flash about what would be spoiled—the easy, friendly, happy atmosphere that had prevailed here for hard on six months. Joanna loathed the boy and would not hesitate to show it. There would be rancour again. However, Dick was family and there was no choice. And maybe school had improved him.

They were now level with the entry, where Dick stood, leaning against a rather poor horse which showed signs of having been hard ridden. Forcing some heartiness into his voice, Henry said,

"Hullo, Dick; this is a surprise. Hop down, Godfrey and tell your dog it's all right."

Consciously showing off, Godfrey did so. His own recollections of this cousin were very vague for Dick's stay had been in Griselda's time and she had disapproved of him almost as much as Joanna did—but for different reasons—and had kept her son apart from that pauper as she had insisted upon calling the heir to Moyidan. Godfrey had heard about him—even this very afternoon—and was somewhat surprised to see that a bad *boy* could be so big, so almost a *man*. And rather handsome, too.

Poor old Lady Emma had thought her grandson the most beautiful, wonderful thing on earth. He was the child of first cousins—a thing forbidden except with a dispensation—but she got her way around that, because her son, Richard, had fallen in love with Sybilla's dim-witted daughter and wouldn't eat until he was told that he could marry her. Since the boy himself was little better than half-witted, Lady Emma had lived in dread of what such a marriage might produce. She knew nothing of the drover's encounter with one of the Little People on a warm, wild-strawberry-scented afternoon. That Little Richard, as she called him, was strong and sound and in full possession of his wits had been such a surprise, such a relief that she had doted upon him slavishly.

She would still have thought him handsome if she could have seen him. In height and precocity of maturing, he was typically a Tallboys, and there were black-haired, dark-eyed men in her family. And she would have attributed his surly look to the treatment he had suffered since her death. Possibly she would have been right. The boy himself thought that nothing had gone right with him since his grandmother died.

And nothing was right with him now. Joanna was as unfriendly as ever, and when he offered to carry something that she was unloading from the waggon, she spoke to him for the first time; four words. "Look to your horse!"

Uncle Henry was more civil, but he asked too many questions.

"Now tell us, why were you sent home?"

"I don't know. Honestly, Uncle Henry, I don't know."

"Had you given trouble?"

"No more than usual. No more than any other boy. Just a prank. We were starved, you see."

"You don't look starved," Henry said.

"It was not the food at school that kept me going. There was an old woman who came in from Windsor with loaves and pies. And she was a cheat; sometimes there was no meat in her pies. She tried that trick last week, and one of the boys said that if she had sold meat pies, with no meat, on the open market, she'd have been in the stocks but because she was in the school yard, we had no redress. So we punched a hole in her basket and put her head through it."

Godfrey thought the picture thus evoked amusing and laughed. A mistake, for Janna gave him a cold look and said, "I see nothing funny in that!"

"What was unfair was that I was the only one to be punished. Three of us did it. Only I was dismissed."

To a degree he had again been a victim of circumstance. The Provost of Eton had a wide circle of acquaintances and had heard two rumours. One concerned the possible closure of the College because, somewhat belatedly, Edward of York saw it as a Lancastrian foundation, a possible centre of Lancastrian sympathy. The other concerned the inquiry into the wardship business. The presence in the College of one of what were beginning to be called illegal wards might be detrimental.

Of minor, but still relevant consideration, was that Richard Tallboys, though greatly improved, showed no promise as a scholar and was regarded as a trouble-maker. The latest prank formed the perfect excuse.

The Provost, a man of scruples, first made certain that the boy had somewhere to go; for he was one of those who had spent vacations at school. Assured that Richard had an uncle, he provided a mount, money for boy and horse for the journey and dismissed him.

At roughly the same time, earnest discussions about the fate of young heirs and heiresses were under way. One of the nameless, faceless men suggested to the King that the usual method of disposal of wardships, as rewards for service, as a sign of favour, or in return for a "gift" was not the most profitable way of taking advantage of what this net of inquiry had dragged up. Guardianship was earnestly sought after because for some years—dependent upon the age of the ward—the guardian had the use of the estates, and short of actual peculation, was free to benefit himself. Why should not these benefits accrue to the King? If the lands, the businesses, the stored wealth received the same treatment as most of the confiscated Lancastrian land had done, there would be an immediate, and welcome increase in the King's revenue.

Edward saw the point in this argument; but he saw something further, a chance to endear himself and the Yorkist cause to a certain section—small but potentially important—of the growing generation. This was important, for though the struggle between York and Lancaster had apparently ended at the Battle of Tewkesbury, it had not yet ended in the minds of men. Just across the Channel, in Normandy there was a young man with the very unroyal name of Henry Tydder, or Tudor, who called himself Earl of Pembroke and claimed the throne of England through his descent from John of Gaunt. This descent was somewhat devious, but enough to make a rallying point for discontented Lancastrians.

A man skilled in the craft made a map of England, colouring the lands already belonging to the King and looked after by his agents, in pale blue; and the lands of the recently discovered wards in pale yellow. Where a yellow patch was within easy distance of a blue one there was no problem; the already-tested-and-proved-to-be-honest agent could simply assume more responsibility, duly rewarded. Where the yellow patch was isolated, a new agent must be sought.

Moyidan was such a patch. In that remote corner of Suffolk, while the war was on, people had been neutral, or, during a French invasion to support the Lancastrian cause, Yorkist. An agent must be found for Moyidan, honest and competent and capable of putting into action the King's policy of so treating all his young wards that they would grow up grateful to him and devoted to the Yorkist cause.

The King was so enamoured of his policy that his new wards' idiosyncrasies were taken into account. Some were studious and must be provided with books and tutors, a spell at one of the Universities if they so wished. Boys of differing nature could train as knights. All were to be well fed and well clad, be treated as the heirs that they were, so that years after he was dead and his son ruled England, they would remember their kindly guardian. Some of them would remember him as their saviour; Richard of Moyidan was far from being the only young heir in England whose patrimony had been mismanaged.

There were young heiresses, too. Their personal wishes were less regarded, for apart from a few exceptional cases, their hold on what they had inherited was only a temporary thing. When they married everything they possessed would pass into the control of their husbands. Foresighted as he was, the King did not regard females of political importance. In such matters a woman was what her husband was. He chose to forget that the toughest and most indomitable Lancastrian of them all, his most resolute enemy, had been a woman, Henry VI's wife. He also overlooked the fact that women were the mothers of men and that the first seven years of a boy's life, spent in his mother's company, could be formative. So he disposed of the heiresses rather casually. Some marriages, based on the usual bargain basis, roughly the equivalent of a cattle sale; how much for this girl *and* her property? A far more profitable way, in the long run, was to put the girl into a convent, handing over some part of her dowry; cash on the nail. Most religious houses were already feeling the effects of inflation and realised that a pound today was worth two at some unspecified date. Some were so rich in land that they did not desire more acres and would take only money—usually only a fourth of what was due to the girl—others were so poor that anything was welcome. Dame Isabel, who had so summarily rejected Mistress Captoft, saw no threat to her own position in the admission of a young girl who would bring with her not a large fortune but a steady income.

It was in connection with this steady income that Henry Tallboys' name was mentioned in the wider world. One third of Joanna Serriff's dower was being discussed and the question came up—Would it be better to sell the stock, or leave it where it was, to be dealt with as it had been in the past? The Commissioner who had visited Knight's Acre said, "Leave it. Master Tallboys is a splendid manager; and a strictly honest man." He told—rather amusingly—the story of how, in the course of a few hours, he had met *two* men of complete probity.

It was a virtue rare enough to be remarkable; and one which few men could afford in their official capacity, however honest they might be in their private lives. All the Commissioners understood that this whole project had been mounted in order to enrich, this way or that, the King. The rest of this particular girl's dowry was lodged with Sir Nicholas Grey of Stordford Castle. It would be taken away from him and the girl, or the convent would never see more than a token sum. By manipulations at which these men were adept most of that money would find its way into the King's purse.

Simply one, not very important case. As one Commissioner with a fanciful turn of language put it: Heirs with land were like sheep that could be sheared once a year; heiresses were like sheep killed off; the most possible profit must be made on the carcase. All in a day's work . . .

Somebody, however, remembered that mention of an honest man, and when it became a question of finding a steward for Moyidan, Henry's name came up again.

Before any move was made, the man's antecedents, and particularly his political affiliations must be scrutinised. Henry could not have had a better record. Son of Sir Godfrey Tallboys, who had died alongside his liege lord, that passionate Yorkist Lord Thorsdale, in that memorable year when the tide had turned. In fact, upon the face of it, it rather looked as though this man, son of a knight—and a famous knight in his day—now a working farmer, might be regarded as one who had *suffered* for the Yorkist cause, one of those who had borne his decline of fortune bravely and not come begging, as so many had done. He deserved an appointment; he should have it. Two hundred pounds a year? Surely ample, a dazzling sum to such a man. It was by such judicious cutting of corners that the King's men served the King.

Henry was not dazzled. He was, to start with, annoyed by being visited, again, and just at the busiest time. Up in the fold the shearers were busy and he was needed there because shearers were so hasty, not bothering to keep the marked fleeces apart, which was important because this flock had three owners. Joanna, Robert and himself.

At the same time the hay-making was in progress; this year a splendid crop; there had been rain at the right time, sun at the right time. Henry was needed in the hayfield, too. Jem always slacked off unless supervised, and Dick—who now preferred to be called Richard—was a lazy young devil. He did not seem to understand that he must earn his keep.

And now on one of the busiest days of the year, when Henry had decided that running to and fro between fold and field was in itself a waste of time and had allowed Joanna to take charge; to see that the sheep regarded as Robert's and those regarded as his were marked—hers, far more numerous, were left unmarked—and Henry was swinging his scythe, there was this man—not the one who had come to count animals earlier in the year. Another one.

They sat in the hall, relatively cool even on this warm day, and drank buttermilk, all that Henry had to offer at the moment. And when the man had said what he had come to say, Henry was not dazzled.

He said, moodily, "My aunt, the Lady Emma, put much the same proposition to me and I refused. I felt I had enough to do, here."

Lady Emma had offered no salary; she had simply promised to will to Henry, as reward for his stewardship, what was indisputably her own—a bit of land, of small value, even as a sheep run, because it was remote, with no means of access except through Moyidan.

"Two hundred pounds a year, Master Tallboys, is a considerable sum. And added to it there would be a percentage on the increase. That is the rule. Any steward-in-charge of an estate belonging to one of the King's wards, is entitled to five per cent on the overall productivity."

And still the man was not dazzled or cajoled. He said, "It needs thinking over. One thing I should make clear from the start. If I did take on the job, I should not live at Moyidan."

Why not? the Commissioner wondered, looking round the stark, comfortless hall; the walls bare except in two places; one narrow hanging and one wide one. The narrow one had been old Bishop William's house-offering to Sybilla all those years ago; the large one Mistress Captoft had left because at The Sailors' Rest the only place where it could have found a place was in the big communal room, and she thought—correctly—that it would put ideas into the heads of lonely men.

There was the one settle with cushions, sadly frayed; an imposing court cupboard, completely bare. A stark room. And the Commissioner had a shrewd idea of what the beds were like in this house. He had lodged, the night before, at Moyidan, from which the Church, in the person of the Bishop of Bywater, had withdrawn without protest, but taking with him, as indeed Sir Richard Tallboys had done, some few things which he could rightly claim as his own and which would not be missed. Even so, compared with this, Moyidan was still palatial. However, if this curious fellow preferred to live here . . .

"That, of course would be for you to decide, Master Tallboys. The distance is small. You could ride over once or twice a week."

"If I undertook it, I should go every day."

"That would be very good. And of course the upkeep of the horse, or horses, would be an allowable charge against the estate. When may I hope for your decision?"

"Give me two days. This is my busiest time, shearing and haymaking. Two days from now . . . You are at Moyidan? I will come there, in the evening."

"I could wait upon you, Master Tallboys."

That sudden, flashing blue smile appeared and Henry said, "No. I must come to you. I must see what, if I decide to take over, I am taking over. So I will wait upon you. The day after tomorrow. In the cool of the evening."

The Commissioner rode back to Moyidan carrying with him the thought that this Henry Tallboys was not only honest, but cautious and hard-headed; a suitable man for the post.

Next day was Joanna's birthday. Nothing was said of the betrothal, but Henry had remembered the day and had a present for her. One which represented both thoughtfulness and ingenuity. A new gown of blue linen, of the very finest weave—almost like silk, and with bands of real silk around the skirt, the bodice and the sleeves.

"It is the prettiest I ever had, Henry."

"Try it on."

She went into the hall and there shed the dress she was wearing—one that Katharine had left behind—and donned the new one. It fitted perfectly. Sounding, and looking, rather well pleased with himself, Henry explained how such fit had been achieved.

"I bought the stuff in the market; then I accosted a woman who looked likely to know and asked if she knew a good sewing woman. She did. After that I kept watch for a girl of your size and shape." That girl had not been easy to find; those tall enough were either too thick or too thin, but he'd found one at last. "Glad enough to earn fourpence," he said. "Twopence for being measured, twopence for being fitted. I'm glad you like it."

She was deeply touched by the gift, and the trouble he had taken, but when she tried to express her thanks, looking at him with glowing eyes, his face seemed to cloud over and he said, "Work won't wait; even for birthdays."

She changed back into her working dress and went to the fold, where the shearing should finish today. Henry began scything, thinking as he worked. Turning over and over in his mind the proposition made to him by the Commissioner. It was impossible for him to ignore the fact that the farm's easiest times had coincided with his father's two brief periods of steady, paid employment. In fact he had resented Sir Godfrey's earning more, just by riding about and supervising Lord Thorsdale's property at Bywater, than he could wrest out of the land, however hard he worked. Equally plain was the thought that the land remained after the well-paid, easy jobs had vanished.

Knight's Acre was bigger now, and stock needed constant attention.

Two hundred pounds a year was not to be sniffed at.

One of his reasons for refusing to look after Moyidan when Lady Emma appealed to him, was that he had not enough learning: that no longer held good, for Richard was, or should be, capable of looking after that kind of thing. He'd work, once he saw that it was to his own advantage.

If I don't take the job, who will?

Last time he had been able to suggest his own brother, Richard. And what a calamity that had been.

Five miles, twice a day, even on a good horse—a permissible expense—would consume valuable time.

On and on, round and round, as the scythe sang through the sweet-smelling hay.

Godfrey ran up.

"Can I leave off for a little? I want to look for wild strawberries, for Janna's birthday supper. I'm well ahead of Dick anyway."

"Off you go. The best place is on the bank of the water-splash."

In his mulling over the future he had deliberately avoided the inclusion of Joanna in his plans, either way. Any kind of looking ahead so far as she was concerned brought the inevitable, dreaded confrontation to mind.

He honed his scythe, and imagined *that* bad moment over and looked ahead again, fitting Joanna in.

In charge of Moyidan, and with a salary, he could change his way of life; entertain; give her chance to meet people, find some man to her liking—and to his!

But I can do that without splitting myself in two, half at

Moyidan, half here: the divided loyalty which he feared. In two years' time—and that would be time enough, she was only fourteen—with reasonable luck, this would be a prosperous place, too. Luck, he knew, no farmer could count upon, always at the mercy of the weather. Good this year. Heavy hay, enough to keep a lot of sheep, a lot of store cattle through the winter. Other crops thick and promising, too; the oats thick and silvery, ready for cutting next week; the barley and wheat standing tall and just about to change from green to pale buff, to golden. He *knew* that two weeks' steady rain could ruin everything; no, not everything; rain could ruin a harvest, but it made the grass grow, and animals could find their own food, perhaps as far as Michaelmas. It was not unknown, in a wet season, for a second hay-crop to be gathered in.

He reached his decision. Stay here. Be his own man.

Up in the fold, Joanna was supervising, and when able to, doing a bit of cheating. Like Griselda, like Master Turnbull, she regretted Henry's stubborn determination to go on saving for Robert. She knew that Robert was dead. She'd gone to Moyidan to save him from the misery he was enduring; they'd lost their way in the wood and he had died. He'd never been strong and a night in the blizzard had killed him. She had told no one.

Now she was doing a little bit to put matters right by shuffling a few fleeces, with Robert's mark, and a few unmarked ones—her own—into Henry's pile. Nobody noticed. The shearers were rather more hasty than usual, and less sure of hand and eye; for by custom shearers were provided with ale as well as food, and towards the end of a job were inclined to indulge. No good leaving ale behind. Joseph was busily applying new markings to the closely shorn sheep. Nobody noticed for a while that Joanna had ceased to supervise; stood rigid, a marked fleece in her hands, staring straight ahead of her.

It had happened again. This time an almost exact repetition of what she had seen once before—a mounted man bringing bad news.

Blinking her way back into the ordinary world, she saw the shearers pushing their shears into canvas or leather sheaths and Joseph putting the ochre mark on a sheep, the last to be shorn. And beyond, just turning from the lane into the track, a man on a horse.

She said aloud, "Too late!" She could not possibly reach the house first, and even if she did warn Henry he would take no notice. He would ignore her, just as he had done before. With a shrug she resumed the sorting of fleeces which had piled up around her. What was going on in the house?

Henry, working bare to the waist as men did in hot weather, saw the horseman approach and turn towards the door in the house-front. By his clothes and the quality of his horse, someone of importance.

Hell and damnation! More waste of time. He laid his scythe down and jumped across the bank which formed the edge of this field, rounded a rose tree and stood between the visitor and the door.

"I wish to speak to your master." A natural enough mistake, faced by a field worker, bare-chested, sweaty and with hayseeds in his hair. The mistake did not ruffle Henry: the man's manner did. Damn it all, he thought, even to a servant he should have said Good morning. Some of Sybilla's teaching had taken root.

With an edge to his voice, Henry said, "Good morning. My name is Henry Tallboys." He opened the door and holding it, allowed his visitor to enter; indicated a seat on the shabby-cushioned settle.

The Commissioner found himself at a disadvantage. He was not a man to whom an apology came easily. He took refuge in an extra pomposity.

The search for, the disposition of all these submerged heirs and heiresses, had fallen into departments. Heirs to estates large, moderate, small; boys who bore titles, those who did not. And heiresses, sub-divided according to fortune and rank.

This Commissioner dealt with girls consigned to convents.

Henry listened, incredulous, to the arrangements that had been made, in a distant place, for Joanna. Clevely! And he to keep her stock and pay what he had formerly done to Master Turnbull to the nunnery.

Boiling rage must be mastered. He mastered his and said, simply,

"I shall never agree to such an iniquitous arrangement."

The Commissioner, hostile, and in a strong position, said, "Master Tallboys, you cannot contest a decision made by the King's Commissioners. It is in perfect order. Perhaps you would like to look . . ." He produced from his pouch some papers.

God damn me, Henry thought; I can't read!

"I have no need to look. I know the facts. The girl was left without parent or guardian. So now she falls into the

King's hands. And he deputes people like you! Did *you* ever take a look at Clevely?"

"I have not yet had the opportunity. I think one of my fellow colleagues inspected it and other places deemed suitable."

Suitable! Years ago his father had considered it unsuitable for dim-witted Margaret; more recently Mistress Captoft had considered it unsuitable for herself. Henry had never seen it. But quite apart from Clevely's suitability, what about Joanna? Less suited to life in a nunnery than even Mistress Captoft had been. Young, lovable, loving: so active, so eager for life and for freedom.

"I will not allow it."

"It is not for you to allow or to prevent."

"Oh! They want the dowry, don't they? Sooner than have this happen I'll slit the throat of every beast she owns and leave the carcases to rot!"

Plainly a violent, unreasonable and ignorant fellow.

"To do that would be to incur severe penalties, Master Tallboys. This demoiselle is now officially a ward of the King and her property is tantamount to Crown property. To damage or destroy it would be perilously near an act of treason."

That shot went home. The big man emitted a sound curiously like a groan, and on his unpadded bench, slumped a little.

In summer, especially in a hot summer, most of those able to do so left London, where the plague-threat increased, and retired to their country properties. The King himself went on Progress, sometimes visiting his own outlying manors, more often staying with favoured subjects who paid dearly for the honour, enormous feasts and costly entertainments being essential. The Bishop of Bywater did not expect to meet Lord Shefton in London during a hot June. Ordinary he would not have been there himself, he would have been at Moyidan, cool and shady. From this pleasant place he had not been expelled. No such forthright term as confiscation or sequestration had been used; no admonition administered. He was a cleric, and so were most of the Commissioners. Dog did not eat dog; and amongst men of education a mere hint was enough. The Bishop had simply withdrawn.

He knew that unless he absented himself from London entirely he must, inevitably, encounter Lord Shefton, sooner or later. He hoped later, when that bit of what looked like negligence on his part—but was actually quite understandable ignorance—might be forgotten. Yet here, on a June evening, in the garden of a mutual friend, a pleasant place running down from the Strand to the river, they met.

His Grace of Bywater had always liked to speak of the Earl of Shefton as his friend, but between them the links had been tenuous, and that letter of congratulation had been sycophantic in intent, the watering of a tender, but frail plant. In effect, it must have seemed a blunder, too. Or a bit of the perfidy so common in sophisticated circles.

Had Lord Shefton ignored him completely, or merely recognized his existence with a distant nod, the Bishop would not have been surprised, would indeed have been slightly relieved. But Lord Shefton came and greeted him with the utmost affability; far more friendly than he had ever been.

The Bishop had no inkling—and neither had anyone else—that this re-organisation, this search for illegal wards, this readjustment of property rights, had been instigated by one man, with one trivial, spiteful aim.

Lord Shefton was far too cunning a man to have shown any interest in the operation which his casual words had launched. He saw the machine lurch into action and knew that sooner or later the last tiny grain would be ground. The mill of officialdom, like the mills of God, ground slowly, but they ground exceeding small. In this case they had ground more swiftly than usual; otherwise His Grace of Bywater would not be here; he'd be at Moyidan. Moyidan was a word which had never once crossed Lord Shefton's lips.

The lime trees were in flower, and the roses breathed out their evening fragrance; it was one of those rare evenings when supper could be served out of doors. An evening for confidences. Their host had provided excellent food and wine and presently the mood was mellow enough to embolden His Grace to speak of and to explain the awkward little incident, and his own mistimed letter. He mentioned the name Henry Tallboys, the man who had so grossly deceived him.

It was the first time that Lord Shefton had heard of Henry. His pride and vanity, as well as his well-bred desire to put Lady Grey at ease had forbade his asking: Who is the man? His identity did not matter; a betrothal was a betrothal and must be accepted; the whole affair made to seem of no importance whatsoever. His Lordship's rage had centred upon the Bishop of Bywater, whose negligence had brought the embarrassment about.

"I assure you, Your Grace has no need to apologise. A mere tentative approach on my part. Taken perhaps a trifle too seriously by Lady Grey."

To this amiable, understanding friend—yes, friend, now!— the Bishop could say things which convention prevented his saying to a fellow cleric. He told the whole story of Moyidan, how he had saved it from wreck, cherished it, enjoyed it, and then been edged out. By this time dusk had fallen and servants were bringing candles which burned steady in the still, sultry air. They did not, however, give enough light for the Bishop to see that Lord Shefton's intent expression was tinged with gloating. His lordship had made light of his loss, so in the end His Grace felt obliged to make light of his, saying, with just the right touch of irony,

"Imagine my delight when I learned from a friend, one of the original Commissioners, that this same Henry Tallboys had been chosen as custodian of Moyidan and guardian by delegation to its heir. With a salary of two hundred pounds a year—and of course, whatever he can squeeze."

The realisation that all the steps taken to punish the apparent culprit had simply resulted in the enrichment of the real one was too much. The red rage ran up, reddening the scrawny throat, swelling the shrivelled face; it could only go so far; stopped short by the bony skull it checked and exploded.

Heat-stroke, they said. Old men—and although nobody knew Lord Shefton's exact age, he was certainly old—were unduly susceptible to extremes of heat and cold. Somebody sped off to the West to inform Maude; somebody rode in another direction to inform his heir. Maude had been trained not to reveal her real feelings, but to cry for almost nothing, so nobody, even those nearest to her, knew how joyful she was behind the tears. Free, not just for a short time, for life; free, rich and independent, about to embark upon the youth which had been stolen from her.

When the latest Commissioner left, Henry did not sit down with his head in his hands as he had when facing up to Peter Wingfield's revelation. That had been a shock, a thing to be accepted or rejected, a thing about which he could do nothing. This was also a shock but it concerned, as the other did not, the outer world, and demanded not deferred, but immediate action. Meantime the hay must be cut. Swinging his scythe, in the easy, seemingly effortless rhythm which Walter had brought to all such work, Henry asked himself: What sort of a world is it where a girl like Joanna could be married off to an old, old man with no teeth? Or shoved away into Clevely, which years ago Sir Godfrey had declared unfit to house pigs. The answer rang loud and clear: *it was a damned rotten world.* One that could only be fought by somebody armed with its own damned rotten weapons—the chief of which was money, which he had never had, but could have now. And not only money, but some kind of prestige.

Slashing away at the last hay, as though felling enemies, Henry indulged in self-pity, an ignoble, despicable emotion as he well knew. Both the people who had influenced his youth, his mother and Walter the ex-archer, had decried it, in differing words, but with the same meaning. Sybilla had said apropos of some crisis he had now forgotten: "If I allowed myself to be sorry for myself it would be merely to admit myself mistaken. What I chose, I must bear."

Walter had said: "Once you put on that *Pity me* look, somebody'll kick you in the teeth. Try again, say to yourself and the rest, *Catch me.*" Both right, both wrong, because their lives were so limited; and both were speaking of material things. Sybilla would not pity herself, because the hardships which came her way were the result of her choosing to marry a poor knight. Walter really meant that it was no good blaming the wind or the weather or bad luck, you must be resolute and try again.

But now Henry was sorry for himself because he had had no choice in bringing about the frightful situation in which he found himself, and no amount of being resolute and trying again would help him out of it. He'd done nothing except blunder on, doing his best from day to day. And here he was, faced with a most hideous decision; at least, not a decision, since there was only one way out. And what a way!

Joanna came and stood on the bank. As he worked towards it she said, "Dinner is ready when you are, Henry."

"I'm ready." He looked at her and then away, quickly. He'd heard men in the market laughing about the way their womenfolk had carried on about sending an animal, practically a pet—to market. He knew how those women felt.

Joanna had no need to ask had the man brought bad news; she knew he had; and Henry's face showed it. He could not look pale because he was so sun-tanned, but the lack of colour under the tan gave him a dirty, sallow hue; and all the lines of worry and pain were back in his face, deeper than ever. She was surprised and relieved when he said, eating hastily and without enjoyment,

"I have to go to Moyidan this afternoon."

Richard—he now objected to Dick as much as he had once objected to Little Richard—gave his uncle an alert look. Through all the vicissitudes of the years since his grandmother's death, he had clung, as to a tenet of faith, to the belief that Moyidan was his, and to the hope that despite everything, he would one day come into his own.

"Is it about me?"

"In the main," Henry said curtly. He got up, tipped the pot of hot water which always stood by the verge of a well-managed hearth into a jug and went up to wash and change into his church-going, market-going clothes. The sight of them always reminded him of the young squire on whom they had hung so loosely that evening. And some of the self-pity drained away as he realised that he was partially to blame. For putting things off; for being blind.

One of Sybilla's stories which he had always thought so inferior to Walter's, skimmed back into his mind. . . .

Once upon a time, long ago and in a place far away, there was a Prince who, before he could inherit his dead father's throne, must fight a lion, single-handed. He'd shirked the contest and gone out into the world to seek his fortune. And at every turn, whenever an opportunity offered, there was the same obstacle; first he must face a lion, single-handed. In the end he had thought to himself that he might as well go home and face his own lion, which in the end proved to be a tame, toothless old beast who'd licked his hand!

It was a story with a moral, as most of Sybilla's were, which was why Henry had so much preferred Walter's, which never began with Once upon a time, but with One time when I was in France, or the Low Countries . . . Stories which made far more appeal to a boy who had never seen a lion. Or a prince. Now, donning his decent homespun, Henry saw the point of what he had dismissed as a fairy tale. Sooner or later the lion must be faced and he should have done it, back in the winter, when an innocent young man had pointed out where and what the lion was. If he'd faced up to it then, perhaps consulted Master Turnbull, this particular situation could possibly have been avoided.

The Commissioner who dealt with heirs was taking his ease in the great hall of Moyidan Castle, which with its high roof, thick walls and small windows, was by far the coolest place on a hot afternoon. He sat in a cushioned chair, with his feet on a stool, and beside him on the table stood a great bowl of strawberries and a small one of powdered sugar. Sugar, at fifteen pounds a pound, was a luxury, but a Government official was entitled to *some* comfort. On account of the heat he wore a loose robe and slippers.

"Why, Master Tallboys," he said as Henry was shown in, "I did not expect you. Until tomorrow, in the cool of the evening. You did say that, did you not?"

"Yes. But something else cropped up and I thought it better to get this over and done with. I am prepared to take the post—but not for two hundred pounds a year. Three. Is that agreeable to you?"

The Commissioner was empowered to offer more than that, particularly when an estate was difficult, encumbered by old women with inalienable rights, some of a highly complicated nature.

He said, quietly, but with incision, "It is not what is agreeable to me; it is what is acceptable to the Commission. Three hundred pounds would raise no quibble."

"That is settled, then. I have another condition. I want everything checked, every quarter, by a man I know to be honest. Master Turnbull, the lawyer in Baildon."

"A wise precaution," the Commissioner said. And most unusual! So far—and however regarded, by value and size, or alphabetically, Moyidan was low on his list—he had not met with this suggestion before: An independent accountant.

"And now," Henry said, "I would like to look around and take a reckoning. Two copies."

Safely back in London this Commissioner said wryly: "Dealing with an honest man bears hard on the feet!"

In the down-bearing heat of the scorching afternoon, Henry, the Commissioner and two copying clerks, tramped miles, peering into stinking styes, byres, stables. Sheep on the open runs were less odorous, but they took longer to count and in places where the grass had been eaten away their sharp little hooves kicked up dust. A very trying afternoon.

There was, Henry noticed, a singular dearth of young stock; but that was because since his Aunt Emma's death, this place had not been in the hands of a practical person. First his brother Richard, intent upon grandeur; then the Bishop of Bywater, using it more or less as a pantry; eating, no doubt, suckling pigs, calf meat, lamb; things no *real* farmer would ever look upon as food. Only the rich, the careless, the idiots, gobbled down what represented the future.

"Given ordinary seasons and ordinary luck, I can improve on this," Henry said grimly. "And not for the sake of my share. In fact, in view of the scarcity of young stuff my share had better be limited for the first year."

They were approaching the castle again and on the permanent bridge that had replaced the drawbridge, Henry paused for a moment, remembering the day, in another life, when he had ridden here with Tana, obeying a very human wish to impress. That was the kind of memory which he had ruthlessly suppressed all these years.

Only half-humorously, the Commissioner said, "Do you propose to count the ducks on the moat?"

As though against his will, Henry half smiled.

"No. They can wait. I was wondering if you could tell me something. Nothing to do with Moyidan."

"Whatever I can. But sitting down. And over a glass of cool wine."

Sitting down, and with a glass of wine so cool that it misted in his hot hand, Henry told, with his usual brevity, of the other Commissioner's visit and what it concerned, ending with the question: "Is it true that the girl can be forced into Clevely? Against her wish? Against mine?"

"I am not involved in the disposition of heiresses, Master Tallboys. But I know the general principles. Any female with property, and lacking a natural guardian—that is, a father or husband—becomes a ward of the King. Things have been lax of late and the King has been robbed of his rights; but things are tightening up. That is why I am here now. And why my colleague called upon you. Yes, it is true, the King has absolute power in such matters. He could give the girl— and her dower—to any man he selected as a husband for her; either as a present or in return for a . . . a consideration. He can choose her dwelling place, the style in which she lives. Not, of course, personally; through deputies."

"Nobody else has any say in the matter? No other relative?"

"I think not. No. Brothers, cousins, uncles would merely confuse the issue."

"Betrothed?"

"That *is* somewhat different. In the eyes of the Church, and indeed in the eyes of the law, a betrothal—properly witnessed of course—amounts to a marriage. No man in his right senses would make a bid . . . hum, hum . . . offer his hand in such a case. And I very much doubt whether any convent would accept such a young person, except on a very temporary basis, as a parlour lodger as the word goes. And reputable houses are becoming wary of such; with their pet dogs and their lovers, they have done much to bring calumny upon the genuinely religious."

"Thank you, sir," Henry said. It was just as he had thought, as he had worked it out in his own ignorant mind. Only the one way.

He was a practical, not an imaginative man, but as the formalities were concluded—the signing of the agreement between Our Sovereign Lord the King and Henry Tallboys of Knight's Acre in the County of Suffolk, his mind did run forward and shrank from what it saw.

"Now I have a favour to ask. Could you lend me a little wine?"

"Fortunately, yes. Uncertain of how or where we shall lodge, we carry our own supplies. And here a small cask had been overlooked." Inadvertently, of course, the Commissioner thought to himself: not much that was portable had been left when the Bishop withdrew. "Would you prefer red or white?"

"Whichever is most heartening," Henry said.

What he had not foreseen was that Joanna was celebrating her birthday in a humble way. She had decided Henry's glum look at dinner was concerned with business at Moyidan; bad news perhaps. And bad news for Dick—she always used the name since he had expressed a preference for Richard—would be good news for her. It might worry Henry for a while, he was such a family man, but he'd get over it and a cheerful meal might help.

The rose trees, for so long neglected, no longer bore the kind of flower of which Lady Randle, who had sent them to Sybilla, would have approved; but the inferior flowers were plentiful and Joanna had set a great bunch, some upright, some trailing, in the centre of the table of the hall. There was every excuse, this evening, for not eating in the kitchen—she had baked new bread there this afternoon. The hall was cooler.

Sybilla's herb garden—which included the vegetable patch —was as neglected as the rose trees, but amongst the weeds there were a few hardy self-sown plants which, eked out by young dandelion leaves, which were plentiful, made a cool-looking salad. There was ham, properly soaked, properly cooked; new bread; a great bowl of wild strawberries, fresh cream.

She wore her new blue gown. (This had evoked a remark more wistful than reproachful, from Dick. "If you'd taken those blue beads I offered you, they would have gone well together." She had answered him with her usual acerbity. "How could I? The receiver is as bad as the thief!" For once a rebuff from her failed to depress him, because he was sure that any business at Moyidan must be concerned with his restoration to it. The fact that Uncle Henry looked sour and spoke shortly, did not affect him. In fact it boded favourably. He sensed that Henry had no real fondness for him and would not rejoice if his fortunes took a turn for the better.)

Godfrey decided to change into his better clothes, and Dick did the same. All was ready.

However the business at Moyidan had gone, Henry looked no better. The dingy look behind the sunburn, the lines of strain were still there.

Joanna ventured to remark upon it. "You look tired, Henry."

"Who wouldn't? I've tramped all over Moyidan this afternoon. And some things I saw did not please me."

"Never mind. Look, I set supper here. It is cooler. And, Henry, I even have ale. Joseph held some back. He said the shearers had quite enough last night and it would do them no good to arrive at their next job drunk."

"They hadn't lacked," Henry said. "They sounded merry enough when I passed them in the lane."

The food, good as it was, tasted of nothing, but he choked it down, conscious of Joanna's eye upon him. Let her enjoy this pitiable little feast!

Presently Richard, unable to bear uncertainty any longer, said, "Am I to have Moyidan back?"

"Yes."

"I knew it! I always knew it!"

"Not quite as you think," Henry said, giving way to the sourness within him; taking out his spite against the whole bloody world on the boy, who was in no way to blame for *this*. "Not quite as you think, my boy. There's a lot of hard work to be done there, and you'll do most of it. You'll go first thing tomorrow morning and start cutting hay."

"Cutting hay?"

"Yes. It should have been started a week ago."

"Moyidan is *my* manor," Dick said, for perhaps the thousandth time. "Who can *make* me cut hay?"

"I can."

"Because you are . . . my uncle?"

"No. Because the King has appointed me to take charge of you, and your manor, until you are twenty-one."

There were many stories about uncles who had usurped their nephews' rights. Richard Tallboys had, in fact, contributed one, having learned in a painful way that it was unwise to go about Eton grumbling that the Bishop of Bywater had taken Moyidan away from him. Eton was a clerical establishment and such talk was not to be encouraged. He was beaten for three serious faults: untruthfulness, lack of respect, ingratitude. Not being stupid, he changed his story and said that his Uncle Richard had robbed him.

Now he suspected that Henry, in some mysterious way, had usurped the Bishop, as the Bishop had usurped Uncle Richard.

Richard's rule had been careless, but not harsh; there'd always been enough to eat, new clothes when they were needed. There'd been Master Jankyn, the tutor, too, but he'd soon learned not to be strict with the boy, who was on such good terms with the servants that a blow struck at him rebounded in the form of bad service. And for a time there'd been Robert to act as whipping boy. Life had not been too bad then. After the Bishop had taken over, the heir had been ill fed, and in the end practically without shoes; but at least nobody even then had suggested that he should work! At last he had appealed to Uncle Henry, who had taken him in, provided him with clothes, fed him after a fashion—but made him work. Then came Eton, sounding promising, but quite horrible. Then Uncle Henry again. And now Uncle Henry for the next almost eight years. It was intolerable.

Inside this Richard Tallboys there still lived, and would always live the pampered little boy whose grandmother had doted upon him; who had so often assured him that he would be rich, that Moyidan was his.

Sullen, defiant, he said, "Another dirty trick! As though the King would lend himself . . ."

"See for yourself," Henry said, jerking a thumb towards the cupboard, on whose open shelf lay the two parchments, the agreement, the list of Moyidan's resources at the moment—and standing alongside, the stout leather bottle of heartening red wine. The sight of it reminded Henry of what he had still to face, and once again he groaned, inwardly.

Now the moment had come. The table, cleared of everything but the roses, two candles just lighted, the wine bottle and two cups. The boys dismissed, summarily to their beds; Godfrey still young enough to be almost drunk on such a meal and a mug of ale, Richard reduced by one glance at that so official, so final a document.

Outside one lonely belated cuckoo gave her last cry, and the wild doves took up the mournful sound.

"Joanna, I have to tell you something."

She thought she knew what it was. Everything, since her return, had been nudging towards this moment; the day when she was fourteen, and no longer too young. When that hasty, unwitnessed betrothal must be either acknowledged or repudiated. In her mind she was prepared. Six months, and the word never mentioned, glances fond, brooding, amused, but never right. Never *wanting*.

She sat, straight and still, her hands, undamaged by six weeks' rough work, folded in her lap.

"Spare yourself, Henry. I know. That was a makeshift betrothal. I forced you. . . . But, my dear, I did not keep my side of the bargain. I should have spent another year at Stordford. You are absolved."

"It isn't that. Far less simple. Joanna . . . I think no two people were ever placed as we are. That makeshift betrothal must be made anew, and witnessed. Unless you are to be sent to Clevely."

"Clevely. The nunnery. Who could *send* me there?"

"The King . . . But that is not the nub of the matter. Honey, by claiming to be betrothed to you, I saved you from marriage to an old, toothless man. It was all I could think of at the time. And *now* all I can think of, to save you from Clevely, is to claim it again, but on sounder ground, with the priest as witness. But, my dear, my sweet . . . It would be only a stop-gap, a time-saver . . . Marriage between us is impossible. We are blood kin. Your father was mine."

There, it was said. He drew a gasping breath of relief which co-incided with one of hers, let out as though she had been punched. Her lips whitened, her eyes turned black as the pupils widened. Time for the wine.

"Drink this," he said. "Good for shock." His hand, holding the cup to her, was not quite steady; hers, pushing it gently away, was firm as rock, but so cold that it sent a shiver through him.

"Later," she said. "Have you . . . known all along?"

He shook his head. "Not the faintest suspicion. It was that young man, Peter Wingfield . . ."

"How could he know? Who told *him*?"

"The family resemblance, he said. Then I saw how blind I had been."

"In what way?" Her colour had come back and she sounded interested, as though discussing something which concerned neither of them intimately.

"In not putting two and two together. You and Robert were born on the same day; he was premature, you were full time. That was frequently mentioned—to account for the difference in size. Your mother and mine, and the father of us both, kept the secret well. But, Joanna, once he let something slip. In all, from the land of the Moors to England, the journey had taken *four* months. So they set out in September!"

"I see. Well, apart from the betrothal—and we can get around that—it isn't such a calamity, is it? I mean . . . I don't mind having you as a half brother. In fact, I'm rather proud."

"I have always been very proud, and very fond, of you."

He was proud of her now. None of the fuss which he had dreaded.

"As for the betrothal," he said, reverting to practicality, "it must be made, first thing tomorrow morning. And last until . . . until this threat of Clevely has died down. The King may change his policy. Or die. A new king often alters laws."

"Quite apart from everything else, my dear, you can't spare me to Clevely now. With Moyidan on your hands, you need me to take charge here."

"That is true. Knight's Acre must not be neglected."

Nothing would be neglected. Nor need be, for suddenly life and vigour and tireless energy came flowing back. There was nothing he would not tackle, nothing he could not achieve.

Joanna looked to the future, too. One aspect of it bleak, empty of hope, dead. But then that hope had been dying, little by little, ever since her return from Stordford. For the rest . . . She'd have Knight's Acre, which she loved; that horrible boy would be gone, the happy family life resumed. Family!

Something remained to be done. She braced herself to tell a gallant lie.

"Henry. That day by the pool. I said a lot of things that

I didn't mean. At least, not how they sounded. I was too young to tell one sort of love from another." Then she added in her own special, light way, "*And* I was half drowned!" She smiled, and Henry smiled back.

"So I noticed at the time!"

They laughed, as they had done, years ago, jogging home from market. Two against the world.

Dorothy Eden

Ms. Eden's novels have enthralled millions of readers for many years. Here is your chance to order any or all of her bestselling titles direct by mail.

☐ AN AFTERNOON WALK	23072-4	1.75
☐ DARKWATER	23153-4	1.75
☐ THE HOUSE ON HAY HILL	X2839	1.75
☐ LADY OF MALLOW	23167-4	1.75
☐ THE MARRIAGE CHEST	23032-5	1.50
☐ MELBURY SQUARE	22973-4	1.75
☐ THE MILLIONAIRE'S DAUGHTER	23186-0	1.95
☐ NEVER CALL IT LOVING	23143-7	1.95
☐ RAVENSCROFT	22998-X	1.50
☐ THE SHADOW WIFE	22802-9	1.50
☐ SIEGE IN THE SUN	Q2736	1.50
☐ SLEEP IN THE WOODS	23075-9	1.75
☐ SPEAK TO ME OF LOVE	22735-9	1.75
☐ THE TIME OF THE DRAGON	23059-7	1.95
☐ THE VINES OF YARRABEE	23184-4	1.95
☐ WAITING FOR WILLA	23187-5	1.50
☐ WINTERWOOD	23185-2	1.75

Buy them at your local bookstores or use this handy coupon for ordering:

FAWCETT BOOKS GROUP, 1 Fawcett Place, P.O. Box 1014, Greenwich, Ct.06830

Please send me the books I have checked above. Orders for less than 5 books must include 60¢ for the first book and 25¢ for each additional book to cover mailing and handling. Postage is FREE for orders of 5 books or more. Check or money order only. Please include sales tax.

Name_____ Books $_____
Address_____ Postage _____
City_____State/Zip_____ Sales Tax _____
                                  Total $_____

Please allow 4 to 5 weeks for delivery. This offer expires 12/78.

Mary Stewart

In 1960, Mary Stewart won the British Crime Writers Association Award, and in 1964 she won the Mystery Writers of America "Edgar" Award. Her bestselling novels continue to captivate her many readers.

☐ AIRS ABOVE THE GROUND	23077-5	1.75
☐ THE CRYSTAL CAVE	23315-4	1.95
☐ THE GABRIEL HOUNDS	22971-8	1.75
☐ THE HOLLOW HILLS	23316-2	1.95
☐ THE IVY TREE	23251-4	1.75
☐ MADAM, WILL YOU TALK?	23250-6	1.75
☐ THE MOON-SPINNERS	23073-2	1.75
☐ MY BROTHER MICHAEL	22974-2	1.75
☐ NINE COACHES WAITING	23121-6	1.75
☐ THIS ROUGH MAGIC	22846-0	1.75
☐ THUNDER ON THE RIGHT	23100-3	1.75
☐ WILDFIRE AT MIDNIGHT	23317-0	1.75

Buy them at your local bookstores or use this handy coupon for ordering:

A-11